MOBBED UP III

ENDGAME

A Novel by Stephanie Baldi

DANCING CROWS
PRESS

Text Copyright©2025 by Stephanie Baldi

This novel is a work of fiction. Names, characters, businesses, organizations, places, events, and incidents are the product of the author's imagination or are used fictionally. Any resemblance to actual persons, living or dead, events, or locales is entirely coincidental.

ISBN: 978-1-951543-42-6 —Print

ISBN: 978-1-951543-43-3 —eBook

Library of Congress Control Number:

Front Cover Art by Mary Rogers
Cover Design and Layout by Colin Wheeler, PhD, MFA

Printed in
The United States of America

Dedication

Dr. Margaret Elyse Wheeler, whose hard work, friendship, and guidance has never have wavered.

Dr. Colin Wheeler, for his time and expertise in completing the cover.

To all my fans who enjoy reading my stories. You inspire me to keep writing and creating the characters who have forever become a part of my life.

Acknowledgments

To all my dear friends at Fairfield, whose continued love and support enable me to write down the stories in my head.

My Brooklyn gals, as always, Doreen, Marianne & Pat.

To the talented Mary Rogers, who designed and painted a canvas for the cover. Your talent never ceases to amaze me.

The Carrollton Writers Guild, whose members continue to encourage me.

Prologue

Eddie Marconi trained his eyes on the body slipping below the surface of the Atlantic Ocean. A full moon cast just enough light over the water to illuminate the top of its head before it vanished without a trace. With a good amount of weight attached, they could never emerge to tell the tale of their demise. How many more lay asleep in the murky depths only to become bait for the sharks? The briny tang of the salty sea air filled Eddie's nostrils. His stomach burned. He tasted bile in his throat, and for a moment, he thought he might be sick.

He pulled out a pack of cigarettes from inside his heavy wool coat and lit one. Dragging deep, he steadied himself against the rail of the rocking boat. Looking up toward the helm, he gave the signal to head back to shore.

The engine caught, then roared. The boat lurched forward and sped away. Eddie sank onto a bench and took another drag of his cigarette. Whoever thought things would end this way? This hit had not been easy but definitely necessary. He studied his swollen hands—the knuckles bruised and red from pounding flesh.

What he remembered most was the wide eyes staring back at him in disbelief. They spoke of betrayal. The most heinous kind that made one want to rethink the decision they had made. When loyalty was everything, how could he justify what he had done? There was no coming back from this.

Eddie rose from the bench and watched the shoreline lights twinkle in the distance. He stubbed out his cigarette and tossed it over the side. The engine slowed as they docked in Sheepshead Bay, Brooklyn. Both of them jumped down onto the wooden planks. Grasping the heavy rope, they secured the boat. There were no words between them, no reason to speak. Trudging along the dock, they stepped off onto the sidewalk and disappeared into the night

Chapter 1 — Monica
Several Months Before
A New Day

With spring fast approaching, New York City clung to the slight chill in the air. The cloudless sky held a soft blue tint. The Staten Island Ferry docked, and Monica made her way to the Federal Building with Andrew in tow.

One year had passed since the arrest and conviction of Alexei Volkov. Everyone on the task force felt relieved when he pleaded guilty and received a sentence of twenty-five years to life without the possibility of parole. The bodies unearthed in the Catskills had cemented his fate. Rurik Bortnik received a lighter sentence of ten years for cooperating with the authorities. Frank Uzelli seemed to have vanished into thin air. More than likely, the victim of a mob hit.

Monica tugged Andrew's hand. "Gotta hurry. We're running a little late."

"Okay, Mommy," he said, his tiny feet doing double time.

He grew to resemble Eddie more each day. The same nautical blue eyes looked up at her, and a captivating smile produced two tiny dimples on his cheeks.

With an agreed-upon schedule between her and Eddie, Andrew spent every other weekend and one day during the week with his father. Neither spoke about her work at the Bureau nor his status as a Capo in the Mafia. She insisted on leaving things of that nature out of their co-parenting. As for sex, it was off the table for her. It would only complicate things between them. Not to say there weren't days when she almost gave in to his charms.

Things worked even more easily between them since her parents had moved back from Florida. They wanted to spend as much time as possible with her and their only grandchild. On Eddie's days, she would drop Andrew off at their house. Although they weren't thrilled with the arrangement, they understood Andrew needed to have a relationship with his father.

She reached the Federal Building, and after leaving Andrew at daycare, she took the elevator to her office. With Bob Acosta's departure to the Los Angeles office, the new Assistant Director In Charge was due to start today.

Monica's guilt surfaced when Bob told her of his decision to transfer. Although she didn't see their former relationship leading to something permanent, she still admired and respected him. But Bob, unable to come to grips with their break-up, thought it best to leave. His absence would be felt throughout the office here in New York.

Monica settled herself at the desk. Her phone dinged, alerting her to a text message. It was from Chase. *Can't wait to see you tonight. Pick you up at 7:30.*

Dr. Chase Hunter had entered her life courtesy of her best friend, Cookie Asante, now Mrs. Damien Volkov. She insisted that Monica start dating again. He worked at the same hospital as Damien, who also thought they would make a good match.

Well established as a cardiac thoracic surgeon, he understood Monica's dedication to her job. They had gone out on several dates, and Monica found herself somewhat attracted to him. Realizing the need to move forward after Eddie and her short relationship with Bob Acosta, she decided it was time to let someone else into her life again.

On their last date, Chase mentioned a fundraiser for a new clinic at the hospital, and she agreed to go with him. Luckily, her parents would be watching Andrew.

She texted back, *See you then.* About to lay her cell phone down, it buzzed with an incoming call. It was Austin Faulkner. Still a member of her task force, she found him to be invaluable in securing much-needed intel. His work on the Volkov case proved his dedication to the Bureau.

"Morning, Monica. The new ADIC is here, and she would like to see you."

"Good morning, Austin. Why didn't she call me directly?"

"I bumped into her. She introduced herself and asked if I would—"

"Okay, no worries," Monica cut in. "Thanks, Austin. I'm on my way." Her nerves a bit rattled, she headed for Bob's old office. Taking a deep breath, she steadied herself. She needed to make a good impression. The new director had arrived from the Dallas, Texas office. Monica had asked around, but no one here seemed to know anything about her.

Alice Monroe, Bob's former secretary, not wanting to relocate, had stayed on. "Good morning, Alice. I understand I've been summoned."

Alice removed her reading glasses and chuckled. "Yup. You certainly have." She punched a button on her desk phone. "Special Agent Monica Cappelino is here … Yes, ma'am, I'll send her right in." Alice hung up and gestured toward the door.

Monica held back a moment. "How is … she? I mean, well…"

Alice leaned forward and lowered her voice. "I think you'll find her quite interesting. I'll let you form your own opinion."

Monica approached the heavy wooden door. She focused on the lettering inscribed on the frosted glass. Assistant Director In Charge, Brooke Adams. She tapped, turned the knob, and stepped inside.

Monica glanced around, surprised at the changes. She had entered an entirely different office from the one belonging to Bob. Pale yellow paint covered the walls, and greenery filled every available space. Tall potted plants stood beside each floor-to-ceiling window. On the far wall were two oak bookcases with glass fronts and intricate carvings. A small loveseat, covered in a pastel-printed damask, sat next to the doorway, and the worn grey carpet had been replaced by a soft beige one. Only Bob's large wooden desk hinted at his former presence.

Brooke Adams looked away from her computer and pointed to one of the two chairs stationed in front of her desk. She tucked strands of honey-colored hair cut into a bob behind one ear. Her blue eyes held steady on Monica as she tapped a polished red fingernail on the desktop.

Monica remained standing. She leaned over and stretched out her arm. "Monica Cappelino. It's nice to meet you."

After a slight hesitation, Brooke shook her hand. "Please sit, Special Agent Cappelino."

A real ice princess, Monica observed as she eased down onto a chair.

"I've been going over the files of your task force members. I must say that I am very impressed with their work." She leaned back, the oversized, maroon-colored leather chair swallowing up her petite frame.

"Yes," Monica said. "They are all very accomplished at their jobs."

"I also studied your file and was a bit disturbed by what I found."

"Disturbed?"

"Of course, your career has been exemplary thus far. Several commendations and high-profile cases you managed to close stand out to me, but…"

Monica waited. Refusing to address Brook's demeanor, she forced herself to remain stoic.

"I'm a bit rattled by your association with a known criminal. I think you understand what I'm getting at," Brooke continued.

"If you mean Eddie Marconi, then yes, I do," Monica said.

Brooke leaned forward again and clasped her hands. "I realize he was a big help to the Bureau in the past … as an asset. But why did he leave witness protection and end up right back in Organized Crime?"

"Look," Monica said. "I can tell you the main reason he came out of witness protection. We have a child together. It wasn't planned. But he needed to forge a relationship with his son. I can assure you, he and I do not discuss his Mafia dealings, nor do we discuss my work at the Bureau. It is a part of our co-parenting agreement. Eddie knows I won't let him see Andrew otherwise."

"That may be so, but what if he gets caught breaking the law?"

"Then I would treat him no differently than any other criminal."

Brooke let out a slow breath. "Really? You expect me to believe you could be impartial even though he's the father of your child?"

Monica seethed inside. Her hands gripped the side of the chair. This woman asked valid questions while attempting to get a rise out of her. "You say you looked at my record."

"That's correct."

"When we went after Alexei Volkov, Eddie and other members of the Mob were involved with him. If Eddie had been at the seaport the day we raided it, I would have arrested and charged him with the others."

Brooke's body visibly stiffened. "Don't you see how that looks, Special Agent Cappelino? Maybe the reason he wasn't there is because you tipped him off."

That last statement was enough for Monica. This woman hardly knew her, and what she had sacrificed for the sake of the Bureau. "No disrespect intended, Assistant Director Adams. You can think whatever you want, but my record speaks for itself. I will never compromise the Bureau. Eddie knows that, and my former boss knew it, too. But if you feel I can't be impartial or perform my duties as charged, then I respectfully ask for a transfer to another regional office away from New York City."

Brooke's posture relaxed, and she sank back into the oversized chair again. "That won't be necessary. I needed to hear certain things directly from you. Right now, I believe you."

"But you need to understand," Monica said. "I will not stop Eddie from seeing his son. He doesn't take him around any criminal element. That is part of the rules I set down. If he does, he will not see Andrew anymore."

"Good," Brooke said, a smile threatening to form on her lips before she pulled it back. "Let's put this aside. I wanted to ask if you're happy with your current team."

"Absolutely. They are all exceptional agents."

"Since you lost Wanda Simmons, and she is exactly where she belongs, I'm assigning another agent to your task force to replace her. His name is Special Agent Nico Vasilios. He has already infiltrated the Greek Mob here in New York City and has also made connections with the Italian Mafia.

"The Greeks and Italians have been operating together. This connection is the focus of our next operation. We needed Nico on the inside. Our objectives will be on drug smuggling, offshore gaming, as well as back-room gambling and racketeering."

"How long has he been undercover?" Monica asked.

"Going on two years. It is essential that we do not blow his cover. I'm appointing you as his new handler. You've been under before, and I believe you have the experience and knowledge to perform the job." Brooke reached inside her bottom desk drawer and handed Monica a folder.

"Take a thorough look at this file. It's crucial you establish a strong, trusting relationship with him. You'll need to develop secure and discreet communication channels.

"Yes, ma'am," Monica said. "I understand."

"I'll meet with you and the rest of your task force tomorrow at 9:00 a.m. sharp in the conference room and bring everybody up to speed."

"Can I ask who his handler was before?"

Brooke rose, indicating the meeting was over. "No. There is no point in discussing that. We are moving forward, not backward. Sorry if I upset you earlier. But it was necessary. I need to feel comfortable with my agents."

Monica got up. "I'll inform my team about the meeting tomorrow."

Monica returned to her office. It had proved to be an interesting meeting with her new boss. For now, she decided to reserve any further opinion of Brooke Adams. She would work hard, as always, and ensure that everyone on the task force maintained their usual pace.

With a member deep undercover, everything needed to be done to ensure his safety while he gathered intel. But almost two years was a long time for Nico Vasilios, and Brooke had not answered her question regarding his previous handler.

Every agent who goes under has a safety net. Whoever was Nico's must have screwed up somehow. Undercover agents were not typically assigned a new handler during the middle of an operation.

Feeling like she could breathe again after her meeting, she gazed out the window and down to the street below. Traffic crawled by while pedestrians navigated the sidewalks.

For a split second, she saw herself as one of them. No Bureau, no Task Force, just living a simpler life than the one she had dedicated herself to.

Monica went to her desk and opened Nico's file. If Brooke continued to refuse to answer her question, she'd find someone who would.

Chapter 2 — Kai
Secrets

Kai Nez propped herself up against the pillows and pulled the sheet over her breasts. She glanced around the hotel suite. A sleeping Tony Morello lay on his side, facing away from her. His temporary home here in the Beekman Hotel included living in a grand suite, even though they spent most of their time in the bedroom. The posh hotel room featured soaring ceilings, vintage furnishings, aged oak floors, a minibar, designer toiletries, rainfall showers, and plush robes. Beautifully appointed artwork adorned the walls. Kai had no complaints when it came to the luxury bedding with Sferra linens.

She swept her hand along Tony's dark hair, the soft strands slipping through her fingers.

He stirred and turned to face her, a smile creeping across his lips. "Good morning. Did you sleep okay?"

"What little of it I got," Kai said. "You, Tony Morello, are insatiable. I wasn't sure I could keep up."

He burst out laughing. "I think you did a pretty good job." He rolled onto his side and lifted the telephone receiver on the nightstand. Kai waited while he ordered room service. He never asked what she wanted. But she was used to it. Whenever they were together, Tony always took charge.

"I can't stay too much longer today," Kai said. "I need to get to work."

Tony rose and stretched. Stark naked, he made his way to the bathroom. "That's what you always say," he called over his shoulder before closing the door. Minutes later, she heard the shower.

They had been meeting at least twice a month. No matter how often she told Tony that being with him could cost her everything, it didn't seem to sink in. Their secret trysts had been going on for the past six months. Her heart just couldn't let him go. The constant phone calls and texts, along with the 'I love you more than anything in this world,' had broken her resolve to move on with her life.

Emerging from the bathroom in a hotel robe, he plopped down next to her. He fingered her juniper bead necklace. "Still wearing this?"

"Always. It's the last gift my grandmother gave me."

"Does it really protect you?" he asked.

"I'm here with you, aren't I?" she said, giving him a sly wink.

"For now," he said. "We can't keep going on like this, Kai. I want to make a life with you. I want it all. The house, the kids, everything."

"What about my career?" she asked. "You have no idea how hard I've worked to get where I am."

Tony hung his head. "I understand that's important to you, but what else do you want, Kai? Just your career?"

"Please look at me," Kai said. She waited as he slowly lifted his head and met her eyes. "We have been through this before. I'm not ready to leave the Bureau, just like you're not ready to leave the Mafia."

He flinched. A painful expression marred his handsome face. "You know where I stand with that. I'm a Capo now, but I intend to be an Under Boss one day. That's real power. Besides, it's not something I can walk away from. When you're in, you're in for life."

"Not if you enter into witness protection."

"You mean become a rat? Are you kidding me? Besides, where will you be if I go? I saw the toll it took on Eddie, losing Monica, and never getting to see his son. Being miserable is not a life, Kai."

She leaned close and wrapped her arms around him. Inhaling the crisp scent of hotel soap, she whispered, "I know, babe. We're on a speeding train and neither of us wants to get off. I don't have the answer right now. Let's enjoy the days we do get to spend together."

"Enjoy? You mean not being able to go out anywhere or do anything together other than stay in this hotel and—"

She pressed her finger over his lips. "Don't spoil what we do have. You're well aware of the risk I'm taking."

He pushed her finger away. "Correction. We're both taking. Consorting with an FBI agent could get me whacked. My boss would never believe I'm not informing you about our operation."

The door buzzed. Tony got up and returned a few minutes later. "Breakfast is here." He reached for her hands, pulling her up from the bed. He untied his robe and wrapped his arms around her, their naked bodies pressed against each other.

"I think breakfast can wait a while," Kai said softly as she melted into him.

***

Later that evening, in her apartment, Kai lay awake, contemplating her conversation with Tony. How would they ever make this work? After the Volkov case finished, she tried to dismiss her feelings. But her love for him had ingrained itself deep inside, and keeping her visits with him secret racked her with guilt.

Not even Monica knew what she was doing. It made her wonder if Monica was being honest with her when she insisted she wasn't sleeping with Eddie Marconi. Surely, their little arrangement regarding Andrew stirred up old feelings.

If only she could confide in someone. She wanted to tell Monica. Somehow, the words never found their way out. As head of the task force, Monica could report everything to the new Assistant Director. Then, a transfer or dismissal would be her fate.

Leaving the Bureau for Tony could never be a reality. Not with him being a Capo with soldiers underneath him and a boss who, like Tony said, could have him whacked.

Would there ever be a world where they could exist out in the open without repercussions on either side? She sighed and fluffed her pillow for what felt like the one hundredth time. Her cell phone buzzed. She picked it up and read the screen. The number was unfamiliar.

"Hello."

"Kai?"

"Yes. Who is this?"

"It's Eddie. Eddie Marconi."

She sat up and switched on the light. "How did you get this number?" She knew Monica would never give it to him.

"That's not important. We need to meet and have a talk."

"What about?"

"Do you take the Manhattan Ferry from Pier 6 by the Brooklyn Bridge to get to work?"

"Yes, but—"

"When will you be at the Pier in the morning?"

"I usually catch the eight o'clock."

"I'll see you there at seven-thirty."

Before she could say anything else, the line went dead. She tried calling the number back. A message came on saying the number was no longer in service. Eddie was probably using a burner phone. Something Tony also did when calling her.

FBI agents' phones could be tapped or confiscated at any time, and their numbers could be traced. Restless, she got up and paced. An unsettled feeling hit the pit of her stomach. Did something happen to Tony? Why did Eddie Marconi call, and what, if anything, did he want from her?

Chapter 3 — Nico
All In a Day's Work

Nico Vasilios settled his muscular six-foot frame into the silver Corvette Z51 convertible. The Bureau sure did the right thing, car-wise. He needed an image, and this car spoke volumes.

Fingers brushing through his curly, dark hair, he flipped the visor down. He glanced in the mirror. A tanned, angular face with green eyes stared back at him before he slipped on his sunglasses. Scheduled to meet with Tony Morello in Little Italy later in the afternoon, he headed for his apartment in Astoria, Queens.

Having met Tony several times before, he initially seemed easy enough. However, Nico soon learned Tony was all business when it came to making money. He exhibited a dangerous edge to his personality, something Nico sensed every time they met.

Raised in New York with boyhood summers spent in Kavala, Greece, Nico Vasilios became the FBI's link between the Greek and Italian Organized Crime in New York City.

Excelling at Quantico, he made a name for himself. Intrigued by undercover work, he endured extra training at the academy, hoping to one day utilize his skills. Fluent in Greek, his qualifications gave him an edge when the opportunity to go undercover presented itself.

Deep undercover, just shy of two years, the road to gaining the confidence of both sides proved to be a challenging one. Plus, neither was easy to work for. The Italians were very protective of their turf and loyal to one another. Meanwhile, the Greeks were plagued by the curse of trying to outdo one another. Power and control were everything to them individually.

However, the Greeks mainly operated under the umbrella of the Italians, who approved everything before it went into operation. Then there were the Russians to consider. Even after the FBI's New

York Task Force put Alexei Volkov out of commission, there were rumblings someone else had taken his place. Nico quickly learned fighting Organized Crime would always be an uphill battle.

When he reached his apartment, he showered and changed before making his way to La Vito Vino on Mulberry Street in Little Italy. He parked around back and tapped on the door. It opened slowly, and one of the servers appeared. He led Nico through the kitchen, where pots boiled on stoves, meat sizzled in pans, and the aroma of rich red Italian Gravy wafted throughout the room. Several sous chefs, their hands expertly slicing and dicing vegetables on cutting boards, prepped for the dinner crowd.

Nico found Tony Morello in the private dining room at the rear of the restaurant, just off the kitchen. Another man he'd never seen before sat at the table. He glanced up at Nico, his deep blue eyes raking over him. His posture appeared to stiffen a little. Glasses of red wine and plates of pasta sat before the two.

Tony rose as Nico approached. "Hey, Nico. How's everything going?" He held out his hand, and the two shook.

"Everything is good, Tony."

Tony gestured to the man seated at the table. "I want you to meet Eddie Marconi."

The man rose, and Nico extended his hand. "Good to meet you, Mr. Marconi."

"Call me Eddie, please, Nico." He pointed to a chair across from him. "Come, sit."

Almost out of thin air, a waiter appeared and stood erect by the table.

"Hungry?" Tony asked.

Nico eased into the chair. "I could eat. Maybe a glass of that wine you're drinking and some pasta."

The waiter nodded and hurried off to the kitchen without a word. Nico watched Tony grab a piece of Italian bread and dip it into the thick red sauce on his plate, wiping it clean. After tossing his napkin onto the table, he leaned back in his chair.

The waiter reappeared with the wine and pasta and set them down in front of Nico.

"Thanks," Nico said. One of the things he loved about this undercover job was the food. New York surpassed everywhere else. It couldn't be beaten.

"So," Tony began. "Let's talk about this game you Greeks play. This bar thing."

"You mean *barbouti?*" Nico asked.

"Yeah, the dice game. It makes a lot of money in the backrooms in Astoria, Queens. I want to expand it even further. You Greeks are also holding the games in secret rooms at your restaurants." He motioned toward Eddie. "We would like to front nightclubs in New Jersey and Staten Island. People would come to play the game and do some other gambling."

Nico slipped pasta into his mouth. He swallowed and then studied Tony for a minute. In his circle, the Greeks and even Arabs loved to play *barbouti*. "I'm a bit surprised," he said, taking a sip of wine.

Tony eyed him. "Why?"

"Well, all this time, we've reserved the game for our people and the Arabs. You always get your cut. Why the sudden interest?"

"Look, you know as well as I do that game makes good money. You're pulling in at least $200,000 a week. Besides, since Frank Uzelli disappeared, I control the seaport in New Jersey. You have no worries bringing in contraband. And yes, we get our cut, but I'm thinking we can go bigger."

"We?" Nico said. He was treading on dangerous ground. "My people might get upset at the idea."

Tony raised an eyebrow. He grabbed his fork, tossing it onto his empty plate where it landed with a loud clatter. "This is our territory, Nico. Do I have to remind you here in New York and New Jersey, we run things?"

Nico caught the anger behind Tony's dark eyes. His meaning was clear. *Do as I say, or there will be trouble.*

"We can all make more money," Eddie said, speaking for the first time. "I can bring the game to Staten Island. Tottenville, Caselton Corners, and New Springville all have Greek populations."

"Okay," Nico said. "Let me take it to my boss. You do understand I don't have the final word."

"Oh, I understand, alright," Tony said. "You tell your boss if he wants to keep things neutral and the money flowing, he needs to agree. Besides, this will be a win for all of us."

Uneasiness filtered through Nico's body. His boss, Konstantin Zervas, could be difficult at times. He often mentioned how having to bow down to the Italians frustrated him. He believed things would turn around one day, and the Greeks would be on top. Plus, *barbouti* was the one thing the Greeks always held dominion over—no way he'd spread it out and let the Italians take control.

The three men sat in silence for a moment until Eddie spoke. "Look, Nico. I'm sure your boss likes making money just as we do. This doesn't have to be such a hard decision. We're open if he wants to meet and discuss it further."

"I appreciate that," Nico said. It appeared Eddie wasn't cut from the same cloth as Tony. He detected no veiled threats in his voice or mannerisms. Maybe he was more of a negotiator.

Tony pointed his finger at Eddie and chuckled. "Always the diplomat."

Eddie eyed him. "It's better to talk things out than to stir up hard feelings."

"I agree," Nico said. He nodded at Tony and got up. "Like I said. I'll run it by my boss. Thanks for the meal." He turned away. Feeling like a target was on his back, he slipped out the rear door.

***

In his apartment the following day, Nico retrieved a burner phone from a dresser drawer and dialed a number. The Bureau had assigned a new handler. He needed to reach out and bring them up to speed.

"We need to meet," Nico said.

"Just say where and when."

He sucked in a quick breath. A female for a handler. "Water taxi from Astoria, 7:00 a.m. tomorrow. Meet me at Pier 11 by Wall Street."

"Got it. See you then."

Nico hung up, his nerves a bit on edge. His hand shook as he placed the burner down. He needed to click with his new handler. Nothing could go wrong this time. His last one almost blew his cover. He could have gotten killed. If either side ever found out he was an FBI agent, he would lose his life for sure.

It had happened to others in the past, but Nico was determined not to be counted among them. The entire operation, along with nearly two years' worth of undercover work, would be compromised. Trust meant everything in a case such as this.

His hands clenched. Nico forced them to relax as he debated if he had been under too long and in too deep.

Tomorrow, he would find out whether or not he would be satisfied his safety came first.

Chapter 4 — Cookie
The Stranger

Carlotta 'Cookie' Assante switched on the Brides & Blooms lights. The heady floral scent hanging in the air immediately put her at ease. Monica's decision to make her a partner in the flower shop had fulfilled a lifelong dream. Although she missed Monica working here on a day-to-day basis, she understood her desire to keep her job with the FBI.

Cookie proceeded to the office at the rear of the store, her black stilettos tapping on the tiled floor. She removed her light jacket and hung it on a hook by the door along with her purse.

She stopped and held up her left hand, still astonished by the six-carat princess-cut diamond ring resting next to her wedding band. It caught the light and displayed a kaleidoscope of colors.

Damien and their life together meant everything to her. Although he made it clear he would give her the world, Cookie wanted nothing more than to be with him. But still, she would have been crazy to turn down a ring like this.

Since Cookie's mother abandoned her and her father when she was only four, her mother-in-law, Darya, delighted in wedding dress shopping and hosting an engagement party for her and Damien. As a result of her pleading, they had planned an elaborate affair. Having lost her youngest son, Roman, to murder and her husband, Alexei, to the penal system, planning a wedding helped take Darya's mind off her grief. Plus, raising Roman's illegitimate child, Alexander, or Alex as they called him, also aided in her healing.

After their honeymoon in Italy, Cookie agreed to move into Damien's apartment. The complex, known as Urban Farms, featured outdoor gardens growing fresh produce and terraced pools. On-site dining gave way to waterfront views of the Verrazano Narrows

Bridge. Cookie made it her mission to turn Damien's sparse apartment into a cozy home.

Smoothing her pale pink silk blouse, she stepped before the full-length mirror on the opposite wall. Her black skirt hit several inches above the knee. If she had her way, it would be a lot shorter. Things had changed when she married Damien. He preferred she not 'show so much leg' as he put it.

Initially, she resisted his desire to alter her appearance. However, as the wife of a prominent orthopedic trauma surgeon at Staten Island Hospital, she had agreed to compromise.

But her long false eyelashes and the many pairs of stiletto heels remained. Occasionally, her dress or top would dip just a bit too low in the front. The strait-laced doctors' wives' disapproving stares only egged her on. Cookie could tell their husbands didn't mind her appearance at all.

Turning sideways, she slid her hand across her stomach. Just this morning, after Damien left for the hospital, she had taken a pregnancy test. They had been trying for the past six months, and now, she would have some wonderful news to tell him. But it wouldn't be tonight. They had another dinner to attend, raising money for a new clinic at the hospital.

With Damien running his practice and agreeing to be on-call at the hospital several days a week, there was little time left for them to be together. Additionally, the numerous charity engagements and dinners with other doctors and their spouses bored her to death.

"Why can't we just donate money and call it a day?" she asked Damien.

"Because appearances matter, Carlotta," he admonished before pulling her into his arms. That was when they made a pact. After every event they attended, upon leaving, they would go home and make love like two out-of-control teenagers. When Cookie counted back, it was on one of those very nights she had conceived.

She headed up to the front and checked the glass cases holding numerous arrangements. Today would prove to be a busy one. There were orders to prepare for a wedding shower this afternoon, plus two appointments for future brides to pick out their bouquets.

Cookie plucked yellow daisies and baby's breath from one of the cases, the bride-to-be's favorite. She spread them out on the counter and searched for the right vase.

Ducking behind the counter, her eyes searched the shelves. The bell on the door jingled. She rose as a man in a long, dark overcoat and tweed newsboy cap closed the door behind him. Cookie thought it odd for him to be wearing such a heavy coat on a warm spring day. He lumbered toward the counter, head down, his slight frame seeming unsteady as his left foot dragged a bit.

"How can I help you?" Cookie asked, the finger of her right hand resting just above the red alarm button below the counter.

He lifted his head. His mouth edged up into a lopsided grin. She took in his sallow skin, the dark eyebrows above deep-set light brown eyes. He leaned forward, the front of his body pushing up against the counter.

Cookie's finger edged closer to the red button. Dread hit the pit of her stomach. The air in the shop thinned. Even the lights appeared to dim. She tried to smile and asked again.

"How can I help you?"

"I would like to purchase some flowers," he said, his voice raspy and just a notch above a whisper.

Cookie recognized the Russian accent. She had heard it enough around Darya. "For delivery?" she asked.

"No, I will take them with me."

"Is it a special occasion?"

The man cocked his head to the side. "Maybe," he said. "Yes … I think it is."

All Cookie wanted to do was prepare this man's order so he would leave as soon as possible. She pointed to the round wooden table. "If you like, you can look at the catalog over there and pick out what you want. It will only take a few minutes for me to assemble a nice arrangement for you."

He hesitated, his face passive and his eyes vacant. "Could you put something together? No yellow, please, and odd numbers only."

Cookie nodded. She pointed at the table again. "Please have a seat."

He sat while she prepared the flowers.

His directives were all too familiar. They brought up memories of the first time she had dinner at Damien's parents' home. He instructed her on Russian culture, how yellow was a solid no when bringing flowers, and that arrangements must consist of odd numbers.

Unsure which ones to choose, as he had given her half answers, she removed pink cremons, green hydrangea, and blue delphiniums, all a mix of textured petals in soothing pastels, from the refrigerated case. Fluffy lavender scabiosa and baby green hydrangeas naturally offset the slim stems of the blue delphiniums and white stock spray. She made sure all were odd in number.

Finished, she said, "Shall I place them in a vase with a card?"

He got up and lumbered over to her again. "Yes, that will be fine."

She rang up the purchase, and he handed her the appropriate bills. He lifted the vase of flowers and studied her for a moment. "I was surprised you did not question my particulars regarding the arrangement."

"My husband is Russian," Cookie blurted out without meaning to. Having any further conversation with this man was the last thing she wanted.

"Oh, I see," he said, the dullness in his eyes vanishing momentarily. "So you know all about these things."

"Yes. I hope the person who receives the arrangement will be happy with it," she said.

"Happy, perhaps. But for sure, surprised," he said. Bowing slightly, he tipped his hat before exiting the shop.

Cookie hurried to the door, flipped the open sign to closed, and turned the lock. She let out a long breath, the knot in her stomach loosening.

Watching as he crossed the street, she saw him climb into the rear of a black sedan. A heavyset man with a dark mustache sat behind the wheel. They pulled away and sped up the block. "Such a weird guy," she said.

His Russian accent bothered her more than his odd demeanor. When Darya and any of her Russian friends spoke, Cookie found it endearing. With this man, it struck a different chord, making her jittery inside. At least he was gone now.

She would probably never see him again. But as soon as the thought filtered through her mind, somehow, she knew it wasn't true.

Chapter 5 — Eddie
Kai

Wind skimmed across the East River, whipping up foamy white caps. Pulling up the collar on his black leather jacket, Eddie scanned the area for Kai. Morning commuters milled about waiting for the eight o'clock ferry to Manhattan. He moved away from them and leaned against the railing. After a few minutes, he noticed Kai threading through the crowd, her raven hair billowing out behind her. She approached him, a displeased look on her face.

"Why am I here, Eddie?"

"I think you know why," Eddie said. "This thing with you and Tony has got to end."

Her face flushed while her dark eyes lit with indignation. "What's going on with us is none of your business."

"I'm afraid you're wrong, Kai. When it puts Tony and even you in danger, then it is my business."

"Look, we are well aware of our situation," Kai said.

"Situation? Is that what you think this is? Your being together is much more than that." If anyone inside the Mob figures out you're in the FBI, both of you, especially Tony, will become a target."

Kai turned away. She looked out over the East River. Her hands gripped the railing, her body swaying slightly.

"Listen to me," Eddie pleaded. "What you're doing goes against everything Tony's involved in."

She released her hands and faced him. "But we're careful. We make sure no one sees us together."

Eddie shook his head. "All it takes is one mistake, Kai. If you love Tony, then you'll let him go. He's like a brother to me, and if anything should happen to him—"

"What about you and Monica?" Kai cut in.

"There is no me and Monica. I spend time with Andrew. We never discuss her job at the FBI or my dealings with the Mob. That's the pact we made. Monica knows I'm as good as dead if we have anything else between us. I don't even go to her place. She drops Andrew off at her parents' house, and I pick him up there."

"Do you mean to tell me your boss is aware of your little agreement and he accepts it?"

"I have a son. I made it clear there is no relationship between Monica and me. He understands that. Family means everything in the Mob. They would look down on me if I didn't make an effort to see Andrew."

Kai crossed her arms. "Is he aware Monica is an FBI agent?"

"There is no reason for me to tell him. My loyalty to them is what counts. But there is no justification for what you and Tony are doing. Nothing is out in the open. So, when they find out, they'll assume information is being passed back and forth." Eddie stepped closer. With both hands resting on her shoulders, he said, "Be smart about this, Kai. I understand you love Tony. But you wouldn't want anything to happen to him."

She met his eyes. "Did you tell Tony you were meeting me?"

"Of course not. You have no idea how much it bothers me to say these things to you. I see how over the moon he is about you. But his love has blinded him to the danger that exists if you continue to be together." Eddie dropped his hands.

"He wants me to quit the Bureau," Kai said, looking forlorn. "As much as I love him, I can't see myself doing that."

"That means you're well aware there is no future for the two of you." Eddie saw the turmoil on her face and knew exactly how she felt. Letting go of Monica was one of the hardest things he had ever done. Even today, if somehow he could go back and change things between them, he would.

People scurried along the pier as the ferry pulled into the dock. With Eddie walking beside her, Kai joined the last of the group. "Give me time to digest everything," she said. "I can't make any promises right now."

"Sure. But don't take too long. Every day you spend together puts Tony at risk."

Eddie watched as she disappeared among the throngs boarding the ferry. Heaviness engulfed him. He understood all too well how Kai felt. Losing Monica made his life hell at times. There were days when he could only think about her and what might have been.

How did everything end up being so complicated between them? Her decision not to follow him into witness protection ruined any possible future between them. He acknowledged that blaming Monica for his decision to return to a life in the Mob was wrong. He chose this path and needed to accept his actions. These days, the time he spent with Andrew was the only thing that brought him happiness.

Eddie headed to where he had parked his car, his thoughts returning to Kai. If only she would listen to him and make the right decision. He held back the part of the rumblings already happening about Tony. Paulie 'The Shiv' Martello had summoned him one afternoon. They sat alone in Paulie's restaurant, La Vita Vino. He assumed Paulie wanted to go over his earnings, but small talk soon turned to Tony instead.

"What's the deal with Tony?" Paulie had asked. "He keeps his private life close to the vest, no?"

Even though Eddie knew what he was getting at, he didn't let on. "It's nothing new. He's always been that way," he answered.

"You've got your son keeping you busy on days off, and I know you date around. But I never hear anything about Tony."

Every word Paulie said was true. He dated occasionally but tried hard not to get entangled in a relationship. It was all a ruse to make things look normal. Deep inside, his heart still belonged to Monica.

"Oh, he gets around," Eddie lied. "He just likes keeping things private."

Paulie had eyed him. "Private is okay in some things, but not all things. *Capito?*"

"Yes, understood," Eddie said, his nerves on edge. With Paulie's suspicions, he needed to warn Tony his relationship with Kai needed to end. Knowing Tony's temper, he decided to try her first, hoping she would listen. But she didn't seem to understand the full force of his words.

A feeling of dread washed over him. If neither one of them took his advice and ended things, someone was going to die. More likely than not, that someone would be Tony.

With little faith he had tried to convince Kai to end things, he needed to get Tony to listen before Paulie dug his nose in further.

Chapter 6 — Damien
The Note

Damien removed his surgical gloves and tossed them into the bin. Unable to catch a break after his second surgery of the morning, he headed for the ER. A construction worker had fallen off a scaffolding, and Damien still had hours of on-call duty to finish.

Arriving at the double wooden metal-framed doors, he tapped his key card, causing them to swing open. A cacophony of coughing, hacking, and wheezing greeted him as he passed a line of curtained hospital beds. Ignoring the familiar smells of antiseptic, body odor, and vomit, he hurried over to triage, where a man lay on a gurney. An IV line trailed from one arm while heart monitors beeped behind him. He wore a cervical collar around his neck. Two nurses and Dr. Robert Norman, an ER physician, were in attendance.

"Glad to see you," Dr. Norman said, nodding at Damien.

"What do we have, Bob?" Damien asked.

"Name's Mark Coleman. Thirty-year-old male. Fell from a height of two stories. Respiration is under 30, and pulse is normal. The patient is alert. On the initial examination, there appears to be a fracture of the tibia and fibula on the right leg, along with multiple contusions across the upper body. I've given him minimal sedation. Right now, he's stable. The family has been notified, and the wife is on her way. Two of his co-workers are in the waiting room."

"Thanks," Damien said before addressing the patient. "Mr. Coleman, I'm Dr. Volkov. Seems you took a nasty fall."

A moan escaped the man's lips. He blinked several times and shook his head. "Yeah, Doc. I tried to catch myself and ended up with my leg twisted underneath me. Pain is pretty awful right now. Can you give me some more meds?"

"Try to hang in there," Damien said. "With possible multiple fractures on your right leg, you're going to need surgery. Unfortunately, we need to minimize the amount of pain medication before operating. I'll order some scans so I can see just how bad the breaks are and ensure there aren't any other internal injuries."

"Can you fix me up, Doc?"

"As long as we don't encounter anything unforeseen, I'm sure you'll be okay. But your recovery will be a long one. Now, let's get you upstairs before those pain meds wear completely off."

Viewing scans and repairing Mr. Coleman's fractures took up the rest of Damien's day. Although surgeries could sometimes be grueling, he wouldn't trade his chosen career for anything else. At home in the O.R., he enjoyed the adrenaline rush he experienced right before an operation.

He made his way to the waiting room to update Mr. Coleman's wife on her husband's condition, then headed for the hospital parking lot, greeting colleagues along the way.

Exhausted, he looked forward to seeing Cookie at the end of the day. Remembering how she finally convinced him to stop calling her Carlotta made him smile inside. Damien only used her first name when he felt she was being unreasonable. Of course, she never balked when his mother called her Carlotta. The bond between the two grew stronger every day. Cookie had become the daughter Darya never had.

Damien climbed into his white BMW740i and prepared to drive home when he noticed a piece of paper stuck under one wiper blade. He got out and removed it. Settling into the leather seat again, he unfolded the sheet and read.

As an acquaintance of your father, Alexei, I hope we can meet soon to discuss some important matters. The last line contained a phone number.

His stomach sank. Damien stared at the note and read it again. No way did he want anything to do with someone who claimed to know his father. Locked away in a federal prison in Allenwood,

Pennsylvania, he had not seen Alexei since his sentencing a year ago. Damien would have skipped the whole ugly mess if not for his mother insisting they attend court.

To think the man who adopted and raised him could be capable of such heinous crimes, including torture and murder, made him sick inside. Plus, he would never forgive him for his brother Roman's death. Had Roman not tried to emulate Alexei, he might be alive today.

Damien folded the note, stuck it in his jacket pocket, and pulled out of the parking lot. He would not tell Cookie about it. At least not for now. Despite his tiredness, they were scheduled to attend another fundraiser for the hospital later tonight.

Dusk descended while he sat stuck in traffic on the Staten Island Expressway. Damien sighed and glanced in the rearview mirror. A black sedan edged up close to his bumper. He hated tailgaters.

The traffic crawled along until it finally eased. Damien crossed into the next lane and sped up. When he rechecked the rearview, the sedan was nowhere in sight. He reached home, parked, and rode the elevator upstairs.

Inside, Cookie greeted him at the door. A tight red gown with lace sleeves clung to her body in all the right places. The front dipped low enough to show the swell of her breasts. Her long auburn hair hung in waves down her back, while a few loose strands framed her face. Diamond stud earrings, a Christmas gift from him, sparkled in the light. An emerald tennis bracelet encircled her wrist. Black stilettos with gold embossed tips peeked out from underneath the hem of her gown.

Damien removed his jacket and tossed it on a hook by the door. He stepped forward and pulled her into his arms. "You look beautiful," he said, kissing her lightly on the lips. He avoided mentioning the amount of exposed cleavage. He quickly learned it was one battle he would never win. On the other hand, he didn't dare tell her how much he enjoyed the envious stares from some of his colleagues when they looked at her.

"I do try," she said. "Now, you need to get out of those scrubs and shower. I laid your tux out on the bed. We need to be to the banquet hall in thirty minutes."

He released her and moaned. "If only we could skip tonight."

Cookie's eyes swept over him. "You're talking my language, Dr. Volkov. I can be undressed and in our bed in a few minutes."

"I wish," Damien said. "If it weren't for all the big donors attending, I would gladly remove that dress of yours in under thirty seconds."

Cookie gave him a little shove. "Go on. Hurry up and get ready. Maybe we can leave the fundraiser early," she said and winked.

***

Forty-five minutes later, they pulled up to Pavilion on the Terrace. The exquisitely restored 1835 Greek Revival building in the St. George/New Brighton Historic District lay nestled on Staten Island's North Shore. Damien got out and handed the keys to a valet while another opened the door for Cookie. With one hand tucked around Damien's arm and her small clutch in the other, they walked past the lit fountain and up the ruby carpet runner covering the front steps. Massive columns graced the entrance. White-gloved staff manned the large, ornate doors.

They entered the main ballroom, where a vaulted ceiling embellished with scalloped edging, plaster medallions, and custom moldings graced the room. Velvet drapes in a deep forest green hung from the large French windows. Massive, tiered crystal chandeliers glittered in the soft light above a glossy marble floor. Dining tables arranged for intimate parties of four displayed perfectly polished silverware and gold-edged china place settings. Napkin puffs stood erect in wine glasses, and large multi-colored floral centerpieces filled the air with a heady fragrance.

A small orchestra played soft music. Wait staff filtered through the crowd offering smoked salmon bites, spicy crab tapas, bacon and sundried tomato phyllo tarts, and parmesan mushroom tartlets. Others balanced trays carrying flutes of champagne. Guests wearing tuxedos and gowns conversed, the women with updos, sequins, and expensive jewelry discreetly taking stock of one another.

Damien and Cookie circulated around the room offering obligatory greetings before going to their assigned seats.

"I can't stand that woman," Cookie said.

"Who are you talking about?" Damien asked.

"Beverly. Dr. Cosgrove's wife. She always has something snotty to say to me."

Damien gave her a look. "I didn't notice anything."

"Of course not. You were too busy talking to her husband."

Damien sighed. "What did she say?"

Cookie scrunched up her face. "Oh, I wouldn't have the nerve to wear red to an affair like this. It's just not proper," she mimicked in a voice several octaves higher.

"Don't pay any attention to her," Damien said. "You have to learn to ignore things like that."

"Are you serious right now?"

"Carlotta, please. Not tonight. Let's just enjoy the rest of the evening."

Cookie eyed him. "Oh, I see," she said. "So that's how it is. You never take my side."

Not wanting to argue, Damien excused himself and stepped out into a long hallway leading to the restrooms. He couldn't stop thinking about the note. Dare he call the number to find out who this person was and why he contacted him?

He was about to return to the table when Beverly Cosgrove passed him. She gave him a curt nod and proceeded to the ladies' room. Cookie rounded the doorway and made a beeline in the same direction. Before he could stop her, both women disappeared into the restroom. His evening was about to get worse.

Chapter 7 — Tony
Not Giving In

While a light rain drizzled outside, Tony and Eddie sat inside a booth in Shanghai 21 and dug into an array of dishes spread before them. The Chinese restaurant on Mott Street in Manhattan's Chinatown was one of their favorites. They were surrounded by bright lime green walls covered with illuminated glamour shots of menu items. Pots clanged in the kitchen. Chinese-speaking voices rose above the din. The aroma of pork, pan-fried noodles, and spices filled the room. An extensive line of people waited for orders at the take-out counter. Every seat remained filled in the small establishment.

Chopsticks in hand, Tony plucked a steamed pork dumpling from a plate and inserted it into his mouth. Savoring the taste of the soft, chewy wrapper and juicy, flavorful filling, he couldn't help but smile. "Man, this is so good," he said, taking another one.

Eddie nodded. "Foods always great here." He filled an empty plate with jumbo shrimp bathed in ginger and scallion sauce.

Tony pointed his chopsticks. "Hand over the Braised Noodles with Chicken." The two continued to eat until Tony broke the silence. "So, what's your take on this thing with Nico?"

Eddie devoured another shrimp. "We'll just have to wait and see what his boss thinks."

"There is nothing for him to think about," Tony said. "This deal is going through no matter what. You play things too soft sometimes."

Eddie stopped eating and looked up from his plate. "How so?"

"You're too easy when it comes to straightening somebody out. People come around only when you make things clear, let them know right up front how it's going to be."

"Maybe," Eddie said. "But your way isn't always my way. I've managed to cut quite a few lucrative deals on Staten Island without threats. You don't want to stir things up and draw attention. Because then, somebody gets pinched, and they start talking. My crew works hard. Each one of them is a good earner. They score their action with very little trouble."

"Yeah, but I still think being upfront is the way to go. Either the deal is going to happen or someone is going to pay … produces quicker results."

"How are things at the Jersey Seaport?" Eddie asked.

Tony smiled. "Better than when Frank Uzelli was handling it." He glanced around before adding, "The bum is exactly where he belongs."

"Has Paulie ever asked you what happened out there in the desert?"

Tony shook his head. "Naw. I don't think he wants to know. He agreed with me on sending money to Frank's widow. She gets an envelope every month. Enough for her and the kids."

"That's as it should be," Eddie said.

"By the way, you would do well getting more involved at the Jersey Port."

"No thanks. The gambling operations bring in enough."

"You could make a lot more," Tony said, giving him a quick wink.

"No. Paulie knows exactly how I feel about the drugs and whatever else comes in from overseas."

They finished off most of the food. Tony leaned back against the booth, his eyes focused on Eddie. "So, I'm guessing there's a reason for the sudden insistence we go out for food." He caught the change in Eddie's demeanor, the sudden serious expression on his face.

Eddie sipped some water before saying, "We need to have a talk."

"About what?"

"You and Kai," Eddie said. "You need to break things off with her."

Heat flushed through Tony's body. This was the last thing he expected Eddie to say. "Are you for real right now?"

"Paulie is asking questions, Tony."

"What kind of questions?"

"Like, how come you never bring any women around? Or talk about anyone special. It doesn't look right and you know it."

Tony placed his chopsticks on his plate and leaned against the leather booth. "I don't care what Paulie thinks. Just because he shows off his *goomar* while his wife sits at home doesn't mean I have to bring a girl around. My private life is none of his business."

"Now you're talking a load of crap, Tony," Eddie said. "Most of the married guys have a side piece, and you can bet their wives are well aware. They put up with it in order to keep their lavish lifestyle." He glanced around the room and lowered his voice. "A boss has the right to know everything about his Capos. Everything we do out there in the street can have consequences."

Tony shook his head. "You're one to talk. What about Monica?"

"First of all, we have a kid together," Eddie said through tight lips. "That is all there is between us. I haven't even seen her face-to-face in a long while. I pick Andrew up at her parents' house and drop him off after. I date around. There is no one special right now, but who knows what might happen. At least, Paulie has met a woman or two."

Tony's pulse spiked. He rubbed the back of his neck as the beginning of a headache surfaced. "I love Kai, and she feels the same. We need time."

"Time for what?" Eddie asked.

"For me to convince her to leave the FBI so we can have a real relationship."

Eddie let out a long sigh. "I don't think that's ever going to happen. She's all in, just like Monica."

"You can't be sure of that." He picked up his chopsticks and pushed a shrimp around on his plate. "Did you say something to her?"

"We spoke," Eddie said. "She wasn't too receptive. But she made it pretty clear that leaving the FBI wasn't an option for her."

"Wow, of all the people I trust the most, you had to go behind my back."

"I was only trying to help. I don't want anything to happen to either one of you. Look me in the eye and tell me I'm wrong, Tony," Eddie pleaded. "If Paulie starts digging, and he will, sooner or later, things won't end well."

Tony got up. He pulled out his wallet and tossed money onto the table. "Enjoy the rest of your meal."

"Come on, don't be like that," Eddie said, rising. "I care what happens to you. If I were in danger, wouldn't you do the same for me?"

Tony took note of the curious stares from the other people in the restaurant. "Later, Eddie. In the future, mind your own business. I can take care of myself and Kai, too." He wheeled around and headed for the door.

* * *

Outside, he stepped to the curb, searching for a cab. Streetlights cast a glow across the rain-slicked streets. Trying to settle his nerves, he inhaled the cool night air. With no taxi in sight, he made his way farther up the street and rounded the corner.

Continuing up the block, his hands curled into fists at his side when he thought of Eddie meeting with Kai. It didn't sit well with him. Best friends don't go behind one another's backs for any reason.

Besides, Kai would come around. Her willingness to take chances all these months proved how much she loved him.

Halfway up the block, a cab crawled up the street. Tony waved the driver down and climbed in. The tightness in his body eased as the headache became a distant throb. He and Kai belonged together. After tonight, Tony became even more determined to convince her to leave the FBI and be with him forever.

As for Paulie, he'd throw him a bone. It would be easy for him to arrange to be seen with some woman. His good looks were like a magnet for the opposite sex. Before long, he'd satisfy Paulie's curiosity and get the situation under control. No one, not even Paulie, had the power to break Kai and him apart.

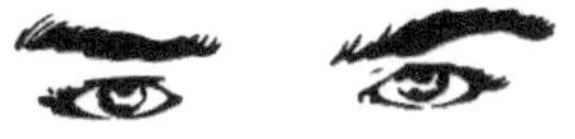

Chapter 8 — Monica
Rumble in the Ballroom

Monica checked her lipstick in the visor mirror as Chase pulled his silver Lexus LS up to the valet. They walked up the carpeted steps hand in hand. Chase stopped at the entrance and turned toward her.

"Have I told you how gorgeous you look in that dress?"

Monica gazed up at him. She focused on his deep-set brown eyes and long, thick lashes. His blond hair held hints of russet. She traced her finger down his handsome face. "Only about ten times," she said. Sweeping her hand down the sapphire blue gown, she added, "Take a long look, because after tonight you will probably never see me in a gown again. I'm only doing this for you."

"And later, I hope you'll let me show you how much I appreciate it," he said and winked.

He draped an arm around her as they went ahead into the ballroom. Warmth spread through her body. Her feelings for Chase were growing. For the first time, she found herself letting go of her past with Eddie and all he once meant to her.

She searched the room for Cookie as Damien rushed toward them.

"Thank God, you're here," he said.

"What's wrong?" Monica asked, alarmed at the anxious look on his face.

"Chase, I'm sorry. I need to borrow Monica," Damien said, grabbing her arm. "Hurry, come with me." Damien led her out into the hallway and toward the women's restroom.

"Cookie's inside. One of the wives made an offhand remark about her dress. She followed her, and I'm afraid—"

"Say no more," Monica cut in. She hurried up the hallway and pushed the door open. It swung shut behind her. Inside, she found Cookie standing before a heavyset, middle-aged woman dressed in a black gown and a short curly blonde wig. Neither one noticed her. She checked the stalls, making sure they were empty then turned the lock on the door.

Well aware of her friend's temper, Monica approached slowly. "Cookie, come on. She's not worth it."

Cookie spun around. "Stay out of this, Monica."

"Do you have something against me, Beverly?" Cookie asked, inching closer to her.

"You don't fit in, Mrs. Volkov," she snapped, backing up against the long marble vanity, a look of disgust on her face. "You're an embarrassment to the other wives. Half the time, you look like a tramp."

Cookie placed her hands on her hips. "Some embarrassment," she mocked. "Your husband can hardly keep his tongue in his mouth when he sees me."

"You're obnoxious!" Beverly screeched, her round cheeks flushing a bright red.

Cookie nodded at Monica. "This bitch has had something nasty to say every time she sees me."

"Who do you think you are calling me a bitch!" She lunged at Cookie, almost knocking her to the tile floor.

Cookie caught herself and launched her body at Beverly. She snatched the wig off her head and flung it across the room. It hit the wall and toppled into the trash can.

Beverly's face turned from anger to horror. She covered her nylon wig cap with both hands.

Cookie came at her again, shoving her backwards. Beverly's legs flew out from underneath her. She let out a yelp before landing hard on her backside. Huffing, she struggled to her feet. Pointing her finger at Cookie, she yelled, "You're going to regret this. I'll have you banned from every charity event."

Cookie let out a shrill laugh. "You think I care? I can't stand half the people here. You're all a bunch of sanctimonious assholes!"

Scowling at Cookie, Beverly advanced again. This time, Monica stepped in between the two.

"I think you need to leave," Monica said. "Because if you don't, I can assure you, losing your wig will be nothing compared to what comes next."

Beverly hesitated. Her eyes swept over Monica. She turned and marched over to the trash bin, grabbed her wig, and set it back on her head. "You just wait, Mrs. Volkov. We'll see what my husband thinks of your behavior. He's good friends with the Hospital Administrator. That husband of yours just might lose his privileges."

Cookie lunged towards her again, but this time, Monica was able to grab her arm. Beverly slunk across the far wall until she reached the door. Fumbling with the lock, she pulled it open and left.

Monica let go of Cookie. "I don't think you should have done that."

"Screw it," Cookie snapped. "I've taken enough from her."

Monica reached and smoothed one of Cookie's curls away from her face. They stared at each other for a moment before bursting into fits of laughter.

"Did you see her face when I ripped that cheap wig off her head?" Cookie said, between gasps.

"Feels like old times, doesn't it?" Monica said, wiping her eyes.

Cookie stopped laughing. "Sure does. And I'll never forget how you were always there for me."

"What else could I do?" Monica said. "Watch you get beat up every day."

"Well, it wasn't every day," Cookie chided.

Monica surveyed her friend. How cruel the kids back in High School were. A group of girls had chosen Cookie to be their punching bag. First, they taunted her. The name-calling and bullying almost non-stop. Later, they pushed, shoved, and hit until Monica stepped in.

Becoming Cookie's friend and teaching her how to fight back until, one day, those girls got a big surprise. It cost her and Cookie a week's suspension, but giving out black eyes and split lips made it well worth it.

Monica shook her head. "I think I created a monster."

"No, you gave me courage when I needed it most. I'll always love you for that, Monica." A sly look in her eyes, she said. "Can I tell you a secret?"

"Sure," Monica said.

Cookie swept her palm across her stomach. "I'm pregnant."

"Oh, Cookie, I'm so happy for you. Does Damien know?"

She shook her head. "Not yet. I'm waiting for the right moment."

"Well, I don't think this is it." Monica wrapped her arms around Cookie. "You're going to be a great mom."

"You think so?"

"Absolutely. But if I had known when I first walked into this fiasco, I would have dragged you away. Promise me you'll be more careful."

"I will."

"Time to go and face those sanctimonious assholes," Monica said. "And you do realize Damien is beside himself."

"He'll get over it. Nobody died," Cookie said flatly. Grinning, she added. "And now I don't have to attend any more of these events. I will be banned!" she shouted.

"Come on, silly," Monica said, pushing her towards the door. "Time to go and make nice with your husband."

Back in the ballroom, everyone was seated for dinner. All eyes swept over Cookie. With the orchestra taking a break, the sound of hushed whispers reverberated throughout as Monica and Cookie took their seats.

Dr. Cosgrove, his wife at his side, came toward the table. He nodded at Damien. "I think we need to talk. See you at the hospital tomorrow."

"You need to control that wife of yours," Beverly added as they continued through the ballroom and out the door.

Damien's fingertips drummed on the tablecloth. He gave Cookie a sideways glance. "Are you happy, Carlotta?"

"I'm starving," Cookie said, eyeing the table and ignoring Damien.

Small bowls of pear and gorgonzola salad with mixed greens and walnuts sat beside plates of filet mignon with Zinfandel reduction and truffle potatoes.

"Everything okay?" Chase asked.

"Fine," Monica said, giving his hand a gentle squeeze. "This looks delicious."

The three of them continued to eat and make small talk while Damien sat with a sour expression. Every once in a while, his eyes shot daggers at Cookie.

After devouring her meal, Cookie pushed her plate away. She turned toward Damien. "Is this how you're going to act for the rest of the night?"

"I don't think you realize the seriousness of what you have done. Most of the people here are my colleagues. I'll have to face them tomorrow at the hospital."

Cookies' cheeks flushed a deep red. "I don't care, Damien. I'm tired of these women looking down on me and saying hurtful things. Maybe, after tonight, they'll think twice about insulting me."

"This isn't only about you, Carlotta. Your behavior affects me, too."

Damien calling her Carlotta made Monica aware of how serious the situation was getting. Wanting to diffuse some of the tension, Monica said, "Listen, you two, I think you both need to take a step back. Each of you has a valid point, but you're not going to accomplish anything here. Talk it out when you get home."

Monica watched Damien swallow the last of his wine and wondered if he noticed Cookie's untouched glass. They were about to become parents, and this bickering could spoil everything. She understood Damien's position, but she also wanted him to defend his wife.

At that moment, Eddie came to her mind. If she had done what Cookie did to one of the wives, Eddie would have cheered her on. No one was going to disrespect her on his watch.

Waiters cleared the dinner plates while others set down petite éclairs and mini tiramisu. Another brought a silver coffee pot, cups, milk, and sugar.

Chase leaned over and whispered, "Awkward" into her ear.

"I think it's time for us to go," Monica said, rising with Chase beside her.

"Not staying for dessert?" Cookie asked, plucking an éclair from the tray.

"No," Monica said. "You two need to work things out. Nothing good ever comes from tearing each other apart." She bent and kissed Damien's cheek and then Cookies. "I'll call you tomorrow."

Once inside Chase's car, Monica relaxed. "Boy, what a night."

"You can say that again." Chase glanced over at her. "What the hell happened in there? Dr. Cosgrove's wife tore into the ballroom. She grabbed her husband's arm and shouted, 'We are leaving. I will not stay in the same room with Mrs. Volkov.'

A smile crept across Monica's face. "You have to understand, Cookie. She never planned on living a life like this. Having to pretend to be somebody she's not just to impress people."

"I get it," Chase said. "I wouldn't want you to be anyone except yourself."

"And who am I, Dr. Hunter?"

"A stunningly beautiful FBI agent and an awesome mother to her son."

She studied Chase's profile. Something surged up inside her. How long had it been since she let someone in? Not even Bob Acosta could break through the barrier she had built since losing Eddie. Determined never to feel such deep hurt again, she kept men at bay. So far, she and Chase hadn't slept together.

But tonight for the first time, she wanted a man. Wanted to be intimate and let him peel back the layers, even if it meant exposing herself once again. They pulled up in front of her house, and she reached for Chase's hand.

"Coming inside?" she said softly.

Desire written all over his face, he asked, "Are you sure?"

"Absolutely sure," she said.

They went inside, and Monica led him to the bedroom. Pale moonlight seeped in through the window. She removed her jewelry and set it on the dresser. Without speaking, she turned for him to unzip her gown. She let it slide down her body, where it landed in a heap on the carpeted floor. Stepping out of the gown, she then took off her bra and panties.

Sweeping back her long, dark curls, Monica led him over to the bed. Chase removed his tux. Her arms came around his neck. She pulled him closer. Their lips met, the kiss edging deeper and deeper. For the first time, Monica let passion drive her forward as they tumbled onto the bed. Hot kisses trailed along her neck and down her breasts.

Her fingers traced the sculpted muscles along his chest. He hovered over her, his dark eyes assessing her face. He kissed her again. Heart racing, she pulled him down on top of her. Monica's arms traveled along his muscular body and then wrapped around him. She felt smooth skin beneath her fingertips and then the sharp edges of his shoulder blades.

Passion overtook her. She reached and guided him inside her. Moaning when he entered her, their rhythm natural and easy at first, became more urgent, as he drove faster and harder. Her breath caught while her mind exploded. She cried out his name, urging him on until they climaxed together.

There, in the dark, they clung to each other. Neither speaking a word nor wanting to break the tender thread between them. Within minutes, Monica drifted off to sleep. For the first time, she left memories of Eddie far behind.

Chapter 9 — Nico
The Handler

Nico disembarked from the water taxi. Commuters hurried toward the subway station entrance to catch nearby trains. He strode away from the crowd, surveying his surroundings as he waited for his handler. Even though he had no idea what she looked like, he knew she'd recognize him from his file. He checked his watch. Two more minutes, otherwise she would be late.

Nico studied the foamy brine of the East River. A seagull swooped and then screeched before flying off. Something made him turn. A woman with long, dark curly hair approached. The word beautiful was far too simple to describe her. Dressed in a black pantsuit with a white blouse open at the collar, her steps were steady and sure, her self-confidence evident in the way she moved. It threw him off balance a bit.

"Special Agent Monica Cappelino," she said, extending her hand.

Nico smiled and reciprocated. "Good to meet you." He surveyed her green eyes and flawless skin. "No formalities, please," he said. "Just call me Nico."

"In that case, Monica will do." She pointed down the pier. "Walk?"

Nico glanced over his shoulder. "Sure, but I'm not comfortable staying too long."

"I understand," Monica said. "Your safety is of the utmost importance." As they moved farther along the pier, she asked, "Can you give me an update as to where things stand?"

Nico nodded. "The gambling operations are hot and heavy—some local, some offshore. The Italian and Greek drug operations are aided by the Greeks' shipping connections and the Italians' control of the seaports. Of course, there is loan sharking on both sides. I've got locations on the local gambling but nothing concrete yet on the offshore side. They keep that pretty close to the vest. As for the drugs, I've kept records of how they come into the country and are distributed."

Nico reached into his jacket pocket and pulled out a thumb drive. He casually reached for Monica's hand as they continued to stroll and slipped it into her palm.

"Principal players?" Monica asked, depositing it into her pants pocket.

"Right now, I'm dealing mostly with Tony Morello, who's a Capo under Paul Martello. He's pushing me to convince my boss, Konstantin Zervas, to let them in on a Greek-operated gambling game." Nico stopped walking.

"What is it?" Monica asked.

"Them wanting in on this game could blow up into a big thing. I know for a fact when I bring it to Konstantin, he's not going to like it one bit."

"If things start to go sideways," Monica said. "You need to reach out immediately."

"Yeah," Nico said. "It's just that …"

"Look," Monica said. "I have no clue as to what happened between you and your last handler. But I need to ensure your safety here. You've been under for a long time. Maybe, too long."

He eyed Monica a moment, refusing to address her last statement. "I'm guessing no one at the Bureau told you anything."

Monica shook her head. "No. And that concerns me."

"Well, what happened before is a story for another time. I can't stay any longer. But because I don't have any other choice, I'm going to trust you, Monica."

"You can, Nico. But trust goes both ways. Reach out when you can," Monica said.

He gave her one last look and hurried away.

***

Later that afternoon, Nico sat in a booth at the Acropolis Diner in Queens. In between the lunch and dinner crowd, the place was nearly empty—the smell of meat sizzling on a grill mixed with the aroma of fresh-brewed coffee. Clinking sounds of cutlery and voices speaking in Greek emanated from behind the swinging doors leading to the kitchen. He brushed away some loose sugar granules from the tabletop as a waitress approached.

Tall in stature, blonde hair tied in a ponytail, her smile widened when she saw him. "Hey, Nico. How are you?"

"Good, Dina," he said. "You're looking pretty as always."

Pale pink rose across her cheeks. "Thanks. What can I get you?"

"Coffee will be fine," he said. "No cream, just black."

"No need to remind me," she said before giving him a wink. "I'll be right back."

Nico's eyes followed her every movement, the exaggerated sway of her hips, and the way she glanced over her shoulder seductively at him. They had been playing this little game off and on for the past year. But Nico held the line on dating anyone who worked for his boss. Entanglements like that could be dangerous. Unless Dina was privy to some critical intel, which, knowing Konstantin was highly unlikely, he'd continue to keep her at bay.

Dina set his coffee down. "If you need anything else, I'll be around."

Konstantin Zervas approached. He smiled and squeezed his heavy frame into the seat across from Nico. He nodded at Dina, who quickly scurried away. His thick silver hair glinted under the pendulum light hanging over the booth. His dark eyes focused on Nico, and he asked, "So, how did your meeting go?"

"That depends," Nico said.

Konstantin let out a long breath. He leaned forward, hands clasped together. "What do they want now?" he asked.

"Barbouti." With that one word, Nico observed the man's smile fading, a frown swiftly taking its place. A vein pulsed on the side of his skull.

"Never," he growled. "That is the one thing they cannot have. I pay them enough money as it is."

Nico sipped his coffee, taking time to measure his words. "I agree, but unfortunately, the Italians control most of the territory. They want to set up games in New Jersey and Staten Island. I understand how you feel, but what's the alternative?"

Konstantin slapped his palm on the table. "The alternative is, I stand up to them and refuse. Do you think they want to lose the money they're getting now? I will shut down all the games if I have to."

Nico's stomach coiled at his words. "You do realize that's not smart. It will only bring bad blood between us and them. You have the goods coming into the seaport to consider. Without their protection, you stand to lose much more than giving them some games of *Barbouti.*"

Silence fell between them. Used to Konstantin's outburst, Nico drank his coffee and waited. If he wouldn't agree, there would be trouble ahead for sure.

"Who did you meet with?" Konstantin asked.

"Tony Morello and another man named Eddie Marconi, who seems to be connected to Staten Island. But it's Tony that worries me. There are stories about him. Things he has done to get what he wants … none of them pretty."

"Before I agree to anything, I want to meet with Morello. You set it up." Konstantin inched his way out of the booth and stood. He glared at Nico. "Make it quick. I need to settle this before I do something I might regret later." He turned and stalked off. Slamming one of the swinging doors back against the wall, he disappeared into the kitchen.

Nico tossed a twenty-dollar bill onto the table and left. Outside, the glaring sunlight and blue sky contradicted the storm that had just taken place inside the diner. Getting Tony and Konstantin together in the same room would only introduce more animosity into an already volatile situation.

At this point, Nico understood he needed to broker a deal between the two to satisfy each side. The intel he had provided to Monica was good, but much more would be necessary to build a solid case against all parties involved in illegal activities.

He could only hope this meeting didn't end with someone losing their life.

Chapter 10 — Brooke
The Task Force

Brooke took stock of the agents seated at the conference table. Based on what she had read in their files, Monica's task force appeared to be an elite group. Intelligent, well-trained, and eager, she couldn't have asked for more.

Brooke nodded at Monica. "Special Agent Cappelino, would you bring everyone up to speed on the new intel you received?"

"Of course," Monica said. "I met with our undercover operative who gathered some very interesting information. He gave me a thumb drive with names, dates, and places of drug and gambling operations overseen by the Italian Mob and the Greek Gangs."

"Is all of it local?" Austin Faulkner asked.

"Some, yes, but of course the drugs coming in can be traced to the overseas cartels, the Albanians, Serbians, and even the Liverpudlian in the U.K."

Austin swept his hand through his dark brown hair, irritation plastered on his angular face. "Let me guess. Most of it is coming in through the New Jersey Seaport."

Monica eyed Kai a moment before answering. "Well, yes. And some through Mexico and Canada. That means they have protection again, probably from the Italian Mob, just like before."

Austin frowned. "We cut off one head and another one grows back. I had hoped with Frank Uzelli gone, things would die down a bit."

"We all thought it would make a difference," Brooke said. "But the reality is, unless we can put every single one of them away, it will never stop."

"Then what's the point?" Kai said, speaking for the first time. "I mean, it seems they're one step ahead of us all the time. Maybe we need to look at what we're doing wrong."

The room fell silent.

Finally, Brooke spoke. "Look, as FBI agents, we have one of the most frustrating jobs. But we all know, it can be gratifying. Every criminal we take off the streets is still one less breaking the law. That must be our focus. We don't question or second-guess ourselves, and we don't stop moving ahead." She looked at Kai. "Of course, mistakes can and will probably be made on our part. We go off the intelligence we have and use it to the best of our ability." She nodded at Monica. "Please continue."

"There is a Greek dice game called *Barbouti,* which the Greeks and Arabs love to play. It can rake in upwards of two hundred thousand or more a week."

Austin let out a slow whistle. "For a dice game?"

"Yes," Monica said. "Now, according to our UCA, the Italians want more control. They're not satisfied with just getting their cut. If this isn't ironed out, there could be an all-out war between them."

"Do we know the principal players in this?" Brooke asked.

Monica avoided looking at Kai. "Tony Morello is one, but I'm sure there are others involved. As a Capo, he needs to keep his boss happy. I believe he'll make a strong push to get this deal done."

"Okay," Brooke said, getting up. "Let's all continue digging. Austin, I understand you have a C.I. in the loop. Reach out if you can. See what else he can give us."

"He's been a bit skittish lately, but I'll try," Austin said.

"That's all for now," Brooke said. "Keep up the good work. We'll get ahead of their game sooner or later."

***

Back in her office, Brooke collapsed into the leather chair behind her desk. It was hard to see her agents so disheartened. But it came with the territory. Sometimes, days turned out to be so good you wanted to celebrate for a week. Other times, it felt as if you were trying to stop an incoming ocean tide. An impossible task. All you could do was push back against it, not let it drown all the good you're accomplishing.

There was a soft tap at her door. *Where was Alice?* She shifted in the chair, sat straight up, and said, "Come in."

Austin Faulkner eased through the door. "May I speak to you for a minute, Assistant Director Adams?"

"Please, not so formal," she said, gesturing for him to sit down across from her. She studied his self-assured stride, along with his handsome face. "What's on your mind?"

"I just wanted to apologize for earlier."

"Not needed. The work we do can get underneath our skin at times."

Austin smiled. "Comes with the territory, as they say. But I want you to know it won't affect my performance in any way."

"I've seen your file, and I have every confidence in your abilities. You don't have to worry about my perception of you."

"Thank you. I appreciate that." He got up and went to the door. "I'll contact my C.I. right away."

Brooke nodded as he left and closed the door behind him. A funny rumbling hit the pit of her stomach. He sure was an attractive man. Even so, she couldn't go there again, not after what happened in Texas. It wasn't easy getting herself untangled from that mess before her transfer here to New York.

Her cell phone buzzed, and the call was from an unknown number. "Not again," she mumbled. When would it stop? There was no longer room for him in her life. She had made things clear before she left. Even after blocking his number, the calls kept coming in from burner phones.

Her hand shook slightly as she picked up her cell phone. "Why are you calling me, Charlie?"

A low chuckle came through the line. "I miss you. I miss us."

"There is no us. You have to accept that and move on."

"I can't. You know we belong together. Running away doesn't change that, Brookie."

"Stop calling me that," she hissed.

"You used to like it when I called you Brookie."

A slow chill crawled down her spine. "I'm telling you for the last time. Don't call me again, Charlie." She ended the call and tossed her cell phone onto the desk.

This had to stop. Changing her number twice still hadn't kept him from calling. Leaving the Bureau in Texas had done nothing to shake him loose. Elbows on the desk, she dropped her head into her hands and rubbed her eyes. One way or the other, she'd rid herself of him. She'd make sure he would never put his hands on her again.

Chapter 11 — Cookie
Flowers

Cookie rode the elevator to her mother-in-law's penthouse apartment. Darya insisted on staying there after Roman's death and Alexei's imprisonment. Raising Roman's son after his girlfriend agreed to give him up had breathed new life into the home.

Cookie stepped off the elevator and rang the bell. The door swung open, and a smiling Darya answered with little Alex on her hip. She still couldn't get over how much at 12 months old, he resembled Roman with his blond curls and impish smile.

Cookie said hello, kissed both her cheeks, and, as was the custom, removed her shoes. She put on a pair of slippers sitting inside by the door.

"Come, come, Carlotta," Darya said. "I have something to show you."

She followed her down the hall. Alex occupied Roman's old room, which Darya completely redecorated for the baby. Pale blue walls held a mural painted by one of Darya's friends' daughter. A green forest with smiling bears, wide-eyed tigers, and laughing hyenas peeking out from behind trees and shrubs gave the room a whimsical feel.

The room held a lavish Karisma Convertible Crib in dark walnut, along with a matching dressing table and chest of drawers. A deep tufted Vera Glider in pale grey resided on the opposite wall.

Taking it all in, Cookie imagined how she might decorate the guest bedroom in her and Damien's apartment in anticipation of their little one's arrival. But she couldn't see spending a fortune on a baby who would quickly outgrow it. Her stomach cinched a bit, remembering she still hadn't told Damien. Since the incident at the charity event, they had hardly spoken.

Darya gave her a quick wink. "Now, watch," she said, setting Alex down on the beige-patterned Aubusson Rug. She slipped down beside him and motioned for her to do the same across from him.

Alex made a gurgling sound and smiled at Cookie. Leaning forward into a crawling position, he moved toward the crib. Grabbing onto one of the wooden legs, he pushed himself up. He pivoted, let go, and then rocked back and forth trying to steady himself. Taking wobbly steps, he walked to Darya, crying, *"Baba!"*

Cookie knew this was short for babushka, which meant grandmother in Russian. Darya held out her arms, and a squealing Alex fell forward into them.

"When did he start walking?" Cookie asked, a small lump rising in her throat. What would Alexi think if he could see his grandson now?

"Only a few days," Darya said, hugging him close. "He had me so worried this little *pupsik.* Roman walked at nine months! Nine months. Can you imagine that?"

"That is early," Cookie said.

Darya rose. "Let me put him down for his nap. This way we can have tea and talk."

***

After Alex settled in his crib with a bottle, she followed Darya into the living room. Two custom-made sofas covered in a patterned damask flanked the fireplace. Darya insisted on preparing the tea herself, so Cookie eased down onto one of the sofas and waited. Her slippers brushed across the Persian hand-knotted Isfahan Carpet with its vivid pattern of burgundy and beige. She swept her palm along her middle, wondering whether or not to tell her mother-in-law the news. But then again, it wouldn't be fair to Damien. As close as she and Monica were, she almost regretted telling her about the baby, but the events of the other night let it slip out of her mouth easily.

Darya arrived carrying a silver tray with a pot, two white porcelain cups situated on saucers trimmed in gold, and a sugar bowl laden with cubes. She set the tray down on the coffee table and sat next to Cookie.

Darya poured the tea, and when the two had fixed their cups, she said, "So, I have been thinking about something, and I want your opinion."

Cookie was flattered Darya valued her advice on various matters. The closeness between them had grown tighter since the wedding. After her father sold his restaurant and made a well-deserved move to a retirement community in Florida, her mother-in-law became her closest living relative.

"What is it?" Cookie asked, setting her cup down.

"I want to take Alex to see his grandfather, and it would make me feel better if you came with me."

Knowing how Damien felt about his adoptive father, Cookie weighed her words. "Do you think that's a good idea? I mean, the last time you went to see him, things didn't go so well."

Darya waved a hand. "It was nothing really. Just a little argument between us."

"How can you say it was nothing?" Cookie asked. "You called me in tears and said that was the last time you would ever go to see him again." She watched Darya's cheeks flush a bright pink.

"Yes, you are right. I said those very words, but…"

"Why are you having second thoughts? Especially since you're aware of how Damien feels about Alexei."

"I love my son, but he doesn't understand everything. If it were not for Alexei, I would have stayed in Russia and raised Damien as a single mother."

"But you can't be sure of that. You might have met someone else, someone who—"

"Was not a criminal," Darya cut in. "Maybe, but Alexei saved me when I was alone, shunned by my family, and almost penniless.

Besides, I made vows, Carlotta, and I intend to keep them. Although Alexei may never be free again, I will always remain his wife."

Cookie took in the love in Darya's eyes when she spoke of her husband. A love that would endure no matter what. If the situation were reversed and Damien had saved her, could she turn her back on him?

"Okay," she said. "If that's what you need me to do, I'll go with you under one condition."

"What is this condition?" Darya asked, an apprehensive look on her face.

"I'll have to tell Damien. I can't keep something like this from him. He won't like it, but I'm not going to let you go alone with Alex."

Darya set her cup aside and hugged her. "Thank you, Carlotta. I knew you would understand how I feel." She released Cookie and smiled, her face bright once again. "Now, tell me, what is new with you?"

"Oh, nothing," Cookie lied. "Just working at the shop. With Damien's long hours, I'm glad I can do something I love to keep me busy."

"I hope he is not overdoing it," Darya said. "Such dedication he has."

"Yes. But I don't fault him. Everyone should be happy with whatever it is they choose to do."

"Oh, I almost forgot," Darya said, rising. "Come with me to the dining room. I need to show you something."

Cookie trailed behind Darya, stopping dead when she reached the doorway of the dining room. There, in the center of the long mahogany table, stood a bouquet of flowers. The very ones she had prepared several days ago for the Russian man at her shop.

"Aren't they beautiful?" Darya asked. "I have no idea who sent them, but I have my suspicions. They were delivered without a card—left downstairs with the concierge. She turned toward Cookie, still in the doorway.

"Are you sure?" Cookie asked, still stunned by the bouquet.

Maybe, somehow, Alexei arranged the delivery." Darya studied her for a moment. "Is something wrong, Carlotta? Do you have information about these flowers?"

"Yes … I … I do," Cookie stuttered. "Those are from my shop."

"Who sent them?" Darya asked. "Tell me then, who was it?"

Cookie told her everything about the man who came in to purchase them. When she described him, Darya's face paled.

"Do you know him?" Cookie asked.

"It might be someone I was acquainted with a long time ago." With that, she hurried Cookie out of the room. "I'm quite tired, Carlotta. Little Alex keeps me very busy. I think I might nap before he wakes up. You don't mind, do you?"

"No, not at all," Cookie said, going to the door and exchanging her slippers for shoes. Something was terribly wrong. Her thoughts about the Russian man were right. If only Darya could tell her why she became visibly upset at the description of the man.

"It's obvious this whole thing has upset you," Cookie said, slipping on her jacket. "You can share anything with me. I don't like seeing you this way."

Darya shook her head, an obvious false smile on her face. "Don't be silly. Of course, I would tell you if there were something wrong. I'm just surprised by such a nice gesture from an old friend. Now, really, Carlotta, I must lie down."

"Okay." Cookie sensed she wasn't going to make any headway. She kissed Darya on both cheeks and left.

***

Arriving home, she was surprised to find Damien sitting in the living room. His new habit of keeping longer hours began after the charity event incident.

Cookie hung her jacket on a hook adjacent to the door. "You're home early," she said.

"Seems so." He angled his head toward her and then quickly looked away.

"I saw your mother today." She sat beside him on the sofa.

Damien inched away. He folded his arms and gave her an icy stare. "That's nice."

"Really," Cookie said. "You can't even stand to sit next to me. I think you're taking things a bit too far, Damien."

"Did you say I'm taking things too far? How about you assaulting my colleague's wife?"

"She came at me first. What else was I supposed to do?"

"You shouldn't have followed her into the restroom in the first place. Why can't you learn to let things go, Carlotta? It doesn't help to turn a bad situation into a worse one."

The bathroom scene crossed Cookie's mind again, and the image of her and Monica bursting into laughter made her smile.

Damien threw up his hands. "Unbelievable! How can you find any of this funny?"

Cookie giggled. "Because it was. If you could have seen Beverly's face when her wig came off, you'd be laughing now, too."

"And you wouldn't be so amused if you were called into the Hospital Administrator's office and told your spouse is banned from any further charity events," Damien snapped.

"I hated going anyway. So, now you won't have to worry about what devious thing I'll do at the next one." She inched closer and leaned her head against his shoulder. "I mean we." Letting out a deep sigh, she added, "I guess it would be setting a bad example for our son or daughter."

Damien's body jerked. He reared up, almost knocking her back against the cushions.

"What did you just say?"

"You heard me, Dr. Volkov. You're going to be a father."

The anger vanished from his face. He reached and pulled her closer. "But, when, how?"

"Oh, I think we both know how," Cookie said. She cupped his face in her hands and kissed him lightly on the lips. "As for the when, if my calculations are right, I believe it was the night we left the previous charity event early."

"So, you've known for a while."

"Yes. I was trying to wait for the right moment to tell you. But then, the wig thing happened, and we were hardly speaking. I didn't want our anger to spoil it. But I just couldn't hold it in anymore. Imagine if you stayed mad at me for the next several months. Then you would probably think to yourself, gee, why is my wife gaining so much weight and—"

Damien pressed his finger to her lips. "Hush," he whispered. "You don't have to explain. I get it." His eyes captured hers and held them. "I'm sorry," he said. "I've been acting like a fool."

Cookie took both his hands in hers. "I don't want you to be sorry just because I'm pregnant. You have to mean it, Damien. It hurt me when you didn't stick up for me against that awful woman."

"And if I had, would you still have followed her?"

Cookie looked away for a split second and then gave him an impish smile. "Well, I always said there shouldn't be any lies between us. So, yes, I probably would have."

"That's my Carlotta," he said softly. "And yes, I'm truly sorry. From now on, as your husband, I will always have your back."

Later that evening, after making love and as he lay fast asleep, her mother-in-law came to her mind. She hadn't told him about her wanting to take Alex to see his father or about the flowers. That could wait until tomorrow. But Darya's reaction to the description of the man kept playing on her mind. What had upset her so? Just what was his connection to Darya?

Chapter 12 — Monica
Old Feelings

Saturday started out fine—until she saw Eddie for the first time in over a month. Dropping Andrew off at her parents' house, which was situated several blocks away from hers, became routine. Both she and Eddie agreed it made things easier if they avoided seeing one another.

Throwing on jeans and a sweatshirt, she got Andrew ready, grabbed her purse, and left a few minutes early. They strolled past the row of townhomes with views of Clove Lake Park across the street. Yellow daffodils and various hues of tulips lined front walks and rose high inside the many flower boxes. An intense sun had burned off the last of the mid-morning chill.

Turning the corner with Andrew in tow, she found Eddie sitting on the front steps. Before she had the chance to decide what to do, Andrew decided for her.

Breaking away from her, he cried out, "Daddy," making a beeline for Eddie, who rose from the steps, his arms outstretched.

"Here's my little man," he said, scooping Andrew up. Hugging him tight, he looked over the boy's shoulder, and their eyes met. "Hey, babe," he said softly.

A tingling swept through her at the very sound of his voice. Every muscle in her body went weak. He sauntered toward her, sending a tremor of excitement down her spine. It was happening all over again, the deep ache sleeping inside her woke. Trying not to let him see her reaction, she took a breath.

Andrew tugged at his hand. "Can I say hello to Grandma and Grandpa?"

"Sure," Eddie said. "I'll wait right here. Don't be too long. We're going to do some fun things today." Andrew scampered up the steps. Still too small to reach the doorbell, he tapped on the door. Within seconds, it opened, and Monica's mother appeared. Taking one look at Monica and Eddie, she ushered her grandson inside.

"You're fifteen minutes early," Monica said, a slight edge to her voice.

"I had a little extra time. Didn't feel like sitting in my car watching the house like someone casing the joint."

"Really, Eddie? Am I supposed to believe that? You knew I would be dropping him off."

"Why are you making such a big deal out of this?"

"It's just that we have an agreement and I—"

"You what?" He stepped closer until they were only inches apart. "Admit it, Monica. You still have feelings for me. It's written all over you."

"Don't flatter yourself," she huffed. "I want us to stick to the agreement we made. It's better for Andrew."

Eddie let out a chuckle. "No, I think it's better for you."

He reached for her hand. Her heartbeat sped up. Her tongue played tricks on her as she tried to form the words she wanted to say. Before she knew what was happening, his lips covered hers, and she fell into his arms. Both oblivious to the people passing by, someone let out a whistle, and Eddie broke the kiss. "I think we have an audience," he said.

Warmth spread up her cheeks. She pulled away. Sweeping back her long curls, she grumbled. "We need to stop."

"I was just getting started," Eddie said, reaching for her again.

Monica moved away. "I mean it. We can't do this. Not after all this time. I need to—"

"You need me," he cut in. "Why can't you admit it?"

"I have to go now," she said. "Please don't say anything else. Let's just leave things alone. I'll never accept the life you chose."

"Maybe, I wouldn't have if you had come with me when I went into witness protection."

She shook her head. "That's an old record, Eddie. You need to stop playing it."

His eyes, filled with hurt, bore into her. "Yeah, but it's true."

"I won't let you blame me anymore, Eddie. Nobody forced you." She backed away until they were a few feet apart. The ringing of a cell phone inside her purse broke through the conversation. Monica hesitated.

"Aren't you going to answer that?" Eddie asked.

As Nico's handler, it was crucial she have a burner phone with her at all times. It continued ringing until she said, "I've got to go. Make sure you have Andrew back on time."

"Oh, I get it. It's probably some guy you've been seeing," Eddie sneered. "Go on. Don't keep him waiting."

"Whoever it is, it's none of your business," she shot back as the ringing stopped. Monica turned and hurried up the street without looking back. Rounding the corner out of Eddie's sight, she pulled the burner out of her purse and listened to a voicemail from Nico. They needed to meet. He would text the time and place. She let out a long breath. At least he was okay.

Reaching her house, she went inside and collapsed onto the sofa. She lay there with thoughts of Eddie. The taste of his kiss still lingering, she ran her fingertips across her lips and almost burst into tears. No other man had ever kissed her the way he did.

"Stop," she admonished herself. There would be no more tears over Eddie Marconi. Going backwards could ruin everything she had worked so hard to get over.

Monica remembered the night with Chase. The first man she slept with since Eddie, and the only one who made her forget about him for a while. She needed to focus on him. Things could be really good between them if only she let it.

The burner phone rang. Retrieving it from her purse again, she read, *Meet me in an hour at Teardrop Park.*

Good, safe choice, Monica noted, rushing out the door. She got in her car and drove toward the Verrazano Narrows Bridge, where the Brooklyn Queens Expressway would take her to the Brooklyn Battery Tunnel and into Manhattan.

Thankful for a bit less traffic on a Saturday, she reached the park on the corners of Warren Street and River Terrace with five minutes to spare. The small 1.8-acre public park in lower Manhattan, near the site of the World Trade Center, made a perfect meeting place. Being less crowded than the other major parks and attractions, it would be easy to keep sight of anyone close enough to overhear or observe them. Tons of trees encircled by shrubs and plants filled the area. An abundance of spring flowers in a kaleidoscope of colors were everywhere.

Monica spied a small playground with a slide built into a rock formation. She continued on past, navigating the maze of paths until she found one of the many benches situated on the perimeter and sat. The squeals of children could be heard above distant traffic noise, and mothers paraded by with little ones in strollers. A few benches away, one person sat reading a book while another a newspaper. A young girl farther down held a cell phone to her ear.

Vigilant, Monica's eyes swept over the area for anyone or anything out of the ordinary. So far, everything appeared normal.

Farther up the path, she spotted Nico approaching who was casually dressed in a pair of jeans and a black turtleneck with a brown leather jacket slung over his shoulder. Dark glasses covered his eyes. He leaned down, kissed her cheek, and sat. She knew this display was all part of an act. They needed to look like any other ordinary couple.

"You picked a good place," Monica said. She caught what sounded like a sigh of relief.

"Yes. It's pretty quiet and easy to survey."

"The intel you gave me last time was invaluable. We're digging into it."

"I'm trying," Nico said. "But lately it seems things are being held back."

"What do you mean? Is anyone suspicious?"

"No. I don't think it's that. It feels like some of the big bosses are trying to tighten things up. They still talk about the FBI raid at the Jersey Port."

"Isn't Tony Morello the big fish in charge of that now?"

"Yeah. He got in good after Frank Uzelli disappeared." Nico removed his sunglasses and wrapped one arm around Monica's shoulders.

"Has there ever been any talk as to what happened to him?"

"Nothing. Not a peep. It almost seems like everyone is glad he's gone. I wouldn't be surprised if the contract they had out on him never really went away."

"That makes sense," Monica said.

"But I wanted you to be aware of a meeting coming up between my boss, Konstantin Zervas, and Tony Morello. I'm not sure who else will attend. Konstantin is unhappy about the Italians trying to join the *barbouti* games. Konstantin wants me to set things up so I'm sure I'll be present. He usually wants me with him at these meetings."

"Let me know the time and place. As your handler, I always want to make sure you're okay." She saw his body stiffen slightly.

"You do understand," Nico said. "No one from the Bureau can be anywhere nearby. These guys are not stupid. They hone in on surveillance as if they have radar."

Monica met his eyes. "Agreed. You don't have to worry about that. I'm not going to send anyone out. It just gives me peace of mind."

A couple with two small toddlers in tow came down the path toward them. Monica took Nico's hand and snuggled up against him. He smiled at her, leaned in, and kissed her lightly on the lips.

After they passed, Nico laughed. "We sure put on a good show."

A bit stunned by what happened, an uneasy feeling swept over her. Was all this really an act on his part? If he thought for one moment just because his handler was a woman, he could get away with certain things, he was dead wrong.

"I don't think that was necessary," she said, letting go of his hand and inching away.

Nico's calm demeanor swiftly changed. He leaned forward and hung his head. Rubbing his palms up and down his thighs, he let out a long breath. "You say you want to keep me safe, Monica. If that's true, then this is all a part of doing it." He glanced back up at her.

Were her suspicions correct? Had Nico been undercover too long? Now, for the first time, she noticed the slight tick beneath his right eye, which had suddenly appeared. She was also familiar with the trick of rubbing one's palms to prevent one's hands from shaking.

"Nico," she said gently. "I'm sorry. I know exactly what you're going through, having to play at being someone else."

"How would you?" he mumbled.

"Because I did it myself. Several years ago. Only I wasn't under even half as long as you."

Nico sat up straight, a look of disbelief on his face. "What was your cover?"

"I worked to turn someone close to me who was mob-connected into an asset. In the beginning, he had no idea I was FBI, nor did anyone associated with him. At least not until I was near the end of the case."

"So, then you understand what I'm going through?"

"Yes. But as your handler, I'm going to be very blunt with you. Anytime you feel you need to get out, there is no shame in making that decision. Going under affects your life, your health, and can determine whether or not you will survive. Even if this case is successful, you will never be the same."

"I'm sorry if I offended you in any way," Nico said. "I didn't mean to be disrespectful."

"No, I'm the one who's sorry." Monica tapped him lightly on the back of his hand. "If what you did with me made you feel safe, then it's okay. I will never doubt your intentions again."

They grew silent as a young man jogged by. After he was a distance away, Monica said, "Let me ask you something. Does Konstantin ever hold meetings at his diner?"

"Yeah. He has a separate room in the back."

"Does he ever include anyone from the mob?"

Nico laughed. "Are you kidding me? First of all, no one from the mob ever comes to the Acropolis Diner. It's not an option for them. They wouldn't feel safe. And second, Konstantin would never invite them. They always meet somewhere on neutral territory, so to speak. There is not one ounce of trust between them."

"I see. So it's safe to say I could insert a UA."

"What do you mean?" Nico asked, his expression leery.

"I've been thinking. There must be times when meetings are held without you present."

"Probably. Konstantin trusts me up to a point. But that's to be expected. I'm not related to him by blood."

"I have a female agent on the task force who's been under before. She's excellent at it. Does Konstantin have a weakness for beautiful women?"

Nico laughed. "What do you think? He's Greek after all. He's always hiring waitresses, and looks play a big part."

"Then what I'm thinking might work. Let me run it by Brooke."

"All I can say is, if you decide to move forward, she'd better be good. Konstantin can smell a rat a mile away. I've been lucky so far, but it took a long time for him to trust me." Nico got up. "I'll let you know the details of the meeting as soon as I have them."

"Good. I do have one question, though."

"What's that?"

"Are you ever going to tell me what happened with your last handler?"

Nico's face grew grim. "Yes. But like I said, it's a story for another time."

He turned to go and then stopped. "Oh, there is one other thing I wanted to tell you. When I met with Tony Morello, there was another man with him. A Capo I never met before but heard of.

"I believe he covers Staten Island. I haven't had any dealings with him up until now. He also wants in on the game, but I can tell you his attitude was far different from Tony Morello's. I think he's going to be easier to deal with."

Monica tried to calm her escalating heartbeat. A tight band slowly encircled her chest. Of course, she knew the answer already, but she forced the words out. "What's his name?"

"Eddie. Eddie Marconi. I'll be in touch." Nico turned and disappeared up the path leading out of the park.

Chapter 13 — Kai
Mother

Kai packed an overnight bag and then pulled on a pair of jeans. Searching through her dresser, she grabbed a tan turtleneck and paired it with a blue blazer. She gathered up her long ebony hair. Fashioning it into a *tsiiyéél*, she took a length of white yarn and wrapped it around her ponytail. Nearing the end, she tucked the rest of her hair into a bun and then proceeded to finish tying the yarn around it. Taught this sacred tradition as a child, and how it represented a woman's connection to spirit and earth always made her feel more connected to her people.

She picked up the folded red and black Navajo Chief's blanket that once belonged to her grandmother. Pressing it closely to her chest, she inhaled, the scent bringing her comfort. Clutching it tighter, she whispered, *"shimá sání, ayóó'áníínishní, I miss you, grandmother."*

Two hours later, she boarded a plane for Arizona at JFK. Memories of her last flight home to see her dying grandmother surged up. Images of her murdered uncle and her mother standing over him with a shotgun made her shudder.

She felt no remorse over his death. Years of his abusing her mother, her two aunts, and his assaults on her put to rest all the guilt from the past. Her visit home would be different this time.

Kai changed planes in Phoenix, where she boarded her final flight. Taking an aisle seat, she ignored all the other passengers until she felt a light tap on her shoulder from behind, confirming his presence.

After touching down at Gallup Airport, she rented a car. While waiting in the parking lot, she sent a text. Within a few minutes, Tony, handsome in jeans, a pale blue shirt, and a brown leather jacket, sauntered toward the car carrying a black leather overnight bag. Tossing the bag in the rear, he got into the passenger seat, a broad grin on his face.

"I feel like I'm in a covert operation," he teased.

Kai reached for his hand. "We are. I'm just glad to get away for the weekend."

He gestured toward her hair. "I like that. It's different."

"It's called a *tsiiyéél*. It exhibits my connection to spirit and the earth as a Navajo woman."

She pulled away, and they started the forty-five-mile drive to the Rez. Bringing Tony to meet her mother might be a mistake. But since the past incidents were settled, she didn't want any lies between them. Years of denial had torn them apart. Kai was determined not to let it happen again. She wanted to let her mother into her life and tell her about the choices she made, whether she would agree with them or not.

When she entered the Navajo Nation, she relaxed behind the wheel. Her eyes rested on the beauty of the land around her. Grasslands, forests, mesas, and canyons surrounded by red and orange rocks jutting up from the surface comforted her.

The monster who hunted her childhood playground was dead and buried, and with him, her fear of coming home to the place where she first entered the world. All the tension of the past few months drained away, reassuring her the decision to make this visit was right.

"Wow," Tony said, his vision focused on their surroundings. "So, this is where it all started."

Kai nodded. "Yes. Despite everything that happened to me, sometimes I miss it."

"I can see why," Tony said, squeezing her thigh. "I've been surrounded by concrete all my life." He let the window down and inhaled. "Earthy," he said. But mixed with…"

"The fragrance of the creosote bush and desert lavender, two distinctly different aromas," Kai said. "Those, and others like sagebrush and desert willow, will always remind me of my home, Tony."

She turned down a winding dirt road leading to her mother's house. For the first time in years, the sight of the simple one-story ranch with tan siding made her smile. Her mother's grey Ford pick-up truck sat in its usual spot out front.

Kai parked, and they got out. With a hint of surprise in his voice, Tony said, "Nice little place."

Kai laughed. "What were you expecting, a teepee?"

His face flushed. "No, I mean…" He placed an arm around her shoulder. "Honestly, I didn't know what to expect."

"Silly white man," Kai teased. "You've been watching too many westerns. Most tribes used teepees when they hunted bison on the plains. They were easy to transport."

She turned, and her heart jerked a bit when she spotted her grandmother's hogan a little over a hundred yards away. No words could convey how much she missed her. She fingered the ghost beads, a last parting gift from the woman who had taught her so much about life and herself.

"That was where my grandmother lived. It's called a hogan. The Navajo tribe once used them as their primary dwelling. Some, like my grandmother, still prefer them today. It's probably where we'll stay during our visit."

Grabbing their overnight bags, they climbed up the steps, and Kai knocked on the door. It swung open, and her mother, Secoya, surveyed them and then broke out into a smile. Shoulder-length hair, the same ebony color as Kai's, framed her face. Her denim shirt with embroidered cuffs was unbuttoned at the throat, exposing a silver and turquoise necklace.

"*Yááteeh*!" She exclaimed. "Come in. I've been waiting. I'm so excited to see you."

Inside, Kai set her bag down and kissed her mother on both cheeks. "*Nídin sélíí,* Mommy."

"I've missed you, too." Secoya's eyes swept over Kai, a look of adoration at the sight of her hair done up in a *tsiiyéél*. Taking a step toward Tony, she held out her hand and said, "I'm Secoya."

Tony extended his own. "Tony Morello. It's so nice to meet you."

"Please have a seat at the table. You two must be hungry."

"Smells delicious," Kai said. She took Tony by the hand and led him to the table already set with beige dinnerware trimmed in a Navajo pattern of pale blue and yellow.

Secoya hurried around the small kitchen. She placed a bowl by a pot on the stove, filled it with corn, beans, and squash, and then set it on the table.

Kai sat next to Tony. "This is called three sisters. It's one of our traditional dishes."

Tony stared at the bowl. "Pretty different than what I'm used to."

"Don't be rude," Kai said.

Tony gave her a sideways look. "I know how to act."

A second bowl held mutton stew consisting of vegetable broth, diced potatoes, celery, onion, and cabbage. Lastly, Secoya placed a platter of fry bread drizzled with honey on the table.

Kai stared at the platter. Her eyes grew moist. "Mommy," she said, her voice breaking. "You remembered."

"Of course. I know how much you loved your grandmother's fry bread."

"Thank you," Kai said. "This means so much to me."

"Kai, will you say the blessing?" Secoya asked.

Kai and Secoya bowed their heads, and Tony followed suit.

"We thank the Great Spirit for the food before us and the Earth for nourishing us. May we be filled with strength and joy," Kai said.

"That was beautiful," Tony said. "So, I guess the Great Spirit is the same as God?"

"No," Secoya said, as they filled their plates. "The Navajo Great Spirit is responsible for the existence of the universe. It dwells inside the animals and is part of both the land and the water. It consists of everything in the natural world. Some believe the Great Spirit is the same as the Christian concept of God, but we Navajo disagree."

"But didn't God create all these things?" Tony asked.

Secoya took a piece of the fry bread and dipped it into her stew. "You see God as a single entity, but the Great Spirit is an omnipresent force who lives in all things."

A confused look on his face, Tony said, "Then you're saying what I learned growing up and what is in the Bible is wrong?"

Catching Secoya's raised eyebrow and pinched expression, "No," Kai said quickly. "Not wrong. Just … different." She refilled her bowl with corn, beans, and squash. "Let's drop this for now and talk about something else." She eyed Tony. "How do you like the stew?"

"Everything tastes great." He smiled at Secoya. "Thank you for this wonderful meal."

"You're welcome." She studied Tony for a second. "So, how did you meet my daughter?"

"Well, I'm in finance," Tony said. "On one of my trips to Washington, we happened to meet at the restaurant in the hotel where I was staying."

Kai averted her eyes momentarily. *There's lie number one.* How could she have been so stupid? Of course, he couldn't reveal what he really did for a living.

Looking directly at Kai, she asked, "How long have you been seeing each other?"

"A little over a year," Kai said. "But things didn't become serious until recently. That's the reason why I haven't mentioned anything to you."

"Have you made any future plans?"

Tony swallowed the last of his stew and set his spoon inside the empty bowl. "I've been trying to convince your daughter we should make things permanent."

"Marriage, then?" Secoya asked, her eyes still on Kai.

"Absolutely," Tony said. "I love your daughter more than anything else in the world."

Kai rose and gathered up the dishes. "I'm not ready yet." She stepped to the sink and loaded the dishwasher.

"Not ready to leave your job is what you mean," Tony said.

"Why would she have to give up her job at the FBI? Are you that old-fashioned?" Secoya asked. "Kai has worked very hard at what she does for a living. There aren't many Native Americans in the FBI."

Kai looked over at Tony, saw the color rising in his face. Anger was brewing between him and her mother. Not wanting things to progress any further, she quickly finished and asked, "Would it be okay if we stayed in Grandmother's Hogan?" But their conversation continued. It appeared as if neither one heard her at all.

"No, it's not that, I make enough money that when we do marry, it would be nice if Kai were able to stay home and take care of the children. Not many women today can do that," Tony continued.

"Not many women today *want* to do that," Secoya shot back. "Most women today have careers while raising their children."

"Sure," Tony said. "But just take a look at what happens to some of these children. They get into all sorts of trouble."

"Excuse me," Secoya said. "I think I did a pretty damn good job raising Kai while I kept my job with the Tribal Police."

Tony's face flushed. He pulled at the collar of his shirt. "I didn't mean any disrespect. Of course, you deserve a lot of credit for the way Kai turned out. But—"

"Enough. Both of you," Kai said. She turned to Secoya. "Can we stay in the hogan or not?"

For the first time, her mother's face softened. "Sure. I knew you would prefer to sleep there. I put logs in the wood stove. It's still chilly, so you'll need to light a fire. I'll get fresh sheets, a blanket, and some pillows."

"*Ahéhee*, Mommy," Kai said.

"You're welcome," Secoya called over her shoulder as she disappeared into one of the bedrooms.

"Really, Tony?" Kai hissed. "Did you have to talk about marriage and kids?"

Tony got up and stretched. "I wanted your mother to know how serious I am about us, that I'm not just some bum screwing her daughter."

Before Kai could answer, her mother returned. She handed them the things they would need for the night. "Sleep well," she said. "See you two in the morning."

"Thanks again," Tony said, his voice much softer than a few minutes ago.

Kai caught the doubtful expression on her mother's face. It was more than apparent she had mixed feelings about him. They grabbed the overnight bags and headed for the hogan. When they reached the door, Kai explained the tradition of walking clockwise around the room before setting their things down.

Tony sighed. "I'm not going to dig into that one."

Kai immediately set about starting the fire while Tony prepared the bed. Within twenty minutes, the hogan warmed enough for them to strip down to their underwear and get in bed.

"Is there a bathroom in here?" Tony asked.

"Of course, silly." She pointed to a door at the rear of the hogan. "My mother had a toilet and sink put in when my grandmother insisted on living here instead of inside her house. "But we'll have to shower at my mothers in the morning."

"Fine," Tony said, reaching and pulling her close. "I don't think I made a good first impression."

Wood crackled in the stove, and shadows from the firelight danced along the walls. Kai pressed her body against him and inhaled the scent of the burning wood. "I can assure you, my mother isn't an easy person to impress. Besides, you stepped right into it when you mentioned marriage. She'll come around sooner or later."

Kai let out a long sigh, "I have many wonderful memories of this place," she said. "I just miss my grandmother so much."

"Did you ever tell her about me?"

"Yes. She asked me what path I wanted to take in life. Which one would make me the happiest … to stay with you or let you go?"

"What did you say?"

She caught the flames flickering in Tony's dark eyes, a mirror of the complexities inside him. Warm and inviting one moment, then burning hot and almost cruel the next.

To her, there wasn't a yes or no answer. How could she begin to explain the push and pull he caused inside her?

"I told her the truth," Kai said. "That I wanted to be with you, but I'm scared—afraid your past would collide with my present. My grandmother said I needed to be in *hozho*, which means to be in peace, balance, and harmony with the world around me. She said it was what I should seek in life. That only I knew whether or not you could bring me these things."

"And do I?" Tony asked.

The times she spent alone with him brought all of them to her. But then, afterward, when her mind cleared and reality set in, her *hozho* dissipated. Her world became upended once again by the choice she ultimately would face in the future.

"Yes, when we're together," she said softly. "We both know the truth, don't we? One of us will have to decide how our story will end."

Tony rolled onto his side, his back to her, he said, "I know how I want it to end, and that will never change. I want more than what we have now. To think you might choose your career over me is almost more than I can handle."

Kai reached and squeezed his shoulder. "Let's not do this here. All I want right now is for us to enjoy this place and for you to love it as much as I do."

Tony turned toward her again, his arms encircling her body. His lips left a trail of kisses down her neck. Kai shuddered, her longing for him renewed. There in the firelight, they found each other twice that night—all thoughts of what might be gone.

The following morning, with Tony still asleep, Kai stoked the fire in the wood stove, bringing it alive again. She threw on jeans and a sweater and headed up to the house, where she found Secoya, dressed in her uniform and preparing a pot of coffee.

"*Yááteeh,* Mommy," Kai said, coming up behind her and wrapping her arms around her waist.

"Did you sleep well?" Secoya asked, unraveling herself and turning to Kai.

"Yes. It felt good to feel Grandmother's spirit."

Secoya poured two cups of coffee and handed one to Kai, a sour expression on her face.

"I bet you felt more than that."

Kai shook her head. "Mommy, you're embarrassing me."

"Come sit. We need to talk." They seated themselves across from one another.

Kai busied herself by adding cream and sugar to her coffee while avoiding her mother's eyes. "I have an idea what you're going to say."

"I'm going to try very hard not to upset you," Secoya said. "But I just don't have a good feeling about Tony. He seems to be the controlling type. Just the fact he automatically expects you to quit your job after marriage and stay home and raise kids is a bad sign."

"If, and I mean if, I decide to marry him, it will be my choice whether or not I leave the FBI."

"So, nothing is set then … I mean, as far as marriage goes."

Kai shook her head. "No. I'm not ready, and even though he keeps trying to change my mind, Tony knows that." Kai sipped her coffee, awash with guilt for not telling her mother about Tony's real background and the danger their relationship posed.

"Mommy, we don't talk about my father often, but do you think you would have had your career if he hadn't died all those years ago?"

Her mother's face softened. A slight smile played across her lips. "Your father was kind and gentle, especially with me. As a matter of fact, after you were born, without me even discussing the Tribal Police job, he said whatever decision I made was okay with him."

Kai felt her eyes brim. "I wish I had known him."

"At least he got to hold you and love you those first six months. The cancer spread so fast, there was nothing anyone could do."

"Did you ever want to marry again?"

"No. I would only be comparing every man to him. It wouldn't be fair. I had my one great love. No use searching for something you will never find again."

Later, after her mother left for work, Tony and Kai showered together. She cooked a breakfast of bacon and eggs before the two set out to walk the land. Kai prided herself on showing him all the places she played as a child and teaching him more about the Navajo people and traditions. Kai didn't mind Tony seemed distracted at times. She relished being back home on the Rez. A man like Tony, having grown up in an entirely different world, would probably never understand her attachment to this land and her people.

Kai cherished their last night in the hogan. The next day, just as they had come, they each boarded the plane separately, with Tony ready to get back to his world and Kai afraid to leave hers behind.

Chapter 14 — Damien
The Call

After working an on-call Saturday shift, twilight descended as Damien sat inside his car in the hospital parking lot. He reread the note for the fourth time. *As an acquaintance of your father, Alexei, I hope we can meet soon to discuss some important matters.*

With the stunt Cookie pulled at the fundraiser and then her good news about the pregnancy, he had almost forgotten about it.

What kind of important matters could this person possibly have to discuss with him? Over the years, Damien had either met or heard of the people his father associated with. If this person knew Alexei, why all the secrecy? He took a breath, reached for his cell phone, and dialed the number. About to hang up after eight rings, someone answered.

"Hello." The man's voice had a rasp to it—almost whisper-like.

"I believe you left a note on my car window a while ago." Damien heard a sharp intake of breath and then silence. "Are you still there?" he asked.

"Yes. I did not think I would hear from you after all this time."

The Russian accent immediately recognizable, Damien said, "You claim you were a friend of my father's."

"If I recall correctly, I think I wrote an acquaintance."

"What do you want from me?" Damien said, ignoring the remark. "Are you aware my father is currently serving a life sentence?"

"Yes, yes. I am quite up to date on Alexei Volkov."

"Good," Damien said, his grip on the cell phone growing tighter. "Now that we're both on the same page, would you please answer my question?"

"It is not something I want … it is more about certain things I have to tell you."

"So, go on then," Damien said. "Tell me." Growing tired of the conversation, he tapped his free hand on the steering wheel.

"I think we should meet in person. It is the only way I can make things clear. There is much about Alexei and me you do not know. Your mother also has information."

"First of all," Damien huffed. "I have no idea who you are or even what your name is. Meeting you in person makes me very uncomfortable, especially since you say you know my father. I'm well aware of the type of people he had dealings with. He's in jail for a reason, and unless this is a matter of life and death, I think I'll pass."

Damien ended the call. His jaw clenched, and a wave of heat soared through his body. He started the car and raced out of the parking lot. Even though he was locked up for life, the things his father had done hovered over them like an invisible specter. He would never forgive him for Roman's death, and even though his mother delighted in Alex, she still grieved for Roman, as … he did as well. Alexei had torn the family apart, and, as far as he was concerned, the man was dead to him now.

By the time he arrived home, Damien's ugly mood had calmed. Since the news of the pregnancy, he looked forward even more to seeing Cookie. He discovered her in the kitchen, removing one of his favorite meals from the oven—a stuffed chicken breast filled with a creamy three-cheese blend consisting of spinach, herbs, and sun-dried tomatoes.

"Smells great," he said, coming up behind her and wrapping his arms gently around her waist. He kissed the back of her neck. "I missed you today."

"Just today? Or every day?" she teased and turned to face him. "Go get out of those nasty scrubs and get ready for dinner. I thought you were going to leave some extra clothes at the hospital."

"I'm working on it. Soon I'll have a couple sets to change into, so when I need to go to my practice after surgery, I can look like a normal human being," he said with a flourish.

After dinner, they snuggled on a terrace lounger overlooking the Verrazano Narrows Bridge. Ribbons of moonlight illuminated the surface of the water below. The sharp scent of sea salt permeated the night air.

"I need to talk to you about something," Cookie said, her head resting on his chest.

Damien kissed the top of her head. "Everything okay with the baby?"

"Yes, fine. Actually, it's about your mother. She wants to take Alex to see your father, and she asked me if I would go with her."

Damien let out a deep sigh. "After the last time, why does she want to go again?"

"She feels your father should get to see his grandson in person." Cookie lifted her head and smiled. "You do realize no matter what he's done, your mother still loves him."

"And that makes you smile? My mother still loving a man who committed so many heinous crimes."

"It's the love part … I mean, that's deep."

"Would you still love me if I committed murder?" he asked.

"I guess it would depend on the circumstances. Sometimes your love for someone doesn't just go away, no matter what. Take Monica, for example. She's still madly in love with Eddie Marconi even though she won't admit it."

"Wait a minute," Damien said. "If that's true, then why did you bug me to get her together with Chase?"

"Because Eddie is not the right person for Monica. She needs to move on. Someone like Chase can help her do that."

"I hope you're right. Otherwise, someone is going to get hurt. Chase is mad about her."

"I've been trying to push her in his direction," Cookie said.

Damien sighed. "Stay out of it, Carlotta. Let things happen as they should."

"Uh-oh. You must be serious. You called me the 'C' word." Cookie laughed and then pecked him on the lips.

Damien moved away and got up. He reached for her hand. "Come into the bedroom, and I'll show you just how serious I am."

Cookie rose. "I'm guessing this is doctor's orders?"

"Absolutely," Damien whispered in her ear and led her inside.

They quickly undressed and slid beneath the covers. He pulled Cookie close and kissed her long and deep. A moan escaped her throat. She trailed her hand down his back and pulled him against her naked breasts. With each movement of her body, his desire swelled. From the very first time they made love, Damien decided he never wanted to be without her. Cookie had upended his dull grey world and filled it with color and light.

There in the dark, he took complete possession of her. His heart overflowed with love.

With Cookie fast asleep, he pulled on a pair of pajama bottoms and padded into the kitchen. He grabbed a bottle of water from the refrigerator. Out on the terrace, he twisted the cap off and took several sips.

Sleep eluded him as thoughts of his earlier conversation with the unknown man buzzed inside his head. A bit of guilt resided there, too, since he didn't tell Cookie about the note or the phone call.

Had he done the right thing by refusing to meet him in person? He wondered if somehow Alexei might be involved in sending this man. Maybe to try to persuade him to visit his father in prison. And what did he mean by telling him his mother had information, too?

He didn't like the idea of Cookie going with his mother, but it was better she didn't go alone, in case there was another argument, sending her home in tears.

Staring out at the bridge, the realization hit him the man would never leave his mind until he found out who he was and what he wanted.

Chapter 15 — Brooke

Shaken

At 7:00 am on Sunday morning, Brooke grabbed her gym bag and left her apartment on the 15th floor of East 82nd Street and headed for the Equinox Gym. After a busy Saturday, arranging new furniture and unpacking more of her boxes, she needed a good workout to ease the stress of moving to a new state. Not knowing anyone in the city, she had purchased a day pass and invited Monica to meet her there.

Under a cloud-covered sky, she made the easy walk to the gym, located on East 85th Street. Brooke sniffed the air filled with the distinctive smell of ozone. Rain showers could not be far off. Most of the agents worked out at the gym in the Federal Building, but she preferred to use an outside facility. When she arrived, Monica was waiting by the door.

"Good morning," Brooke said. "I hope this isn't too early for you."

Monica grinned and shook her head. "I wasn't going to pass up this opportunity. I've heard about Equinox gyms, but with raising a child, their membership is a bit out of my reach. I appreciate your inviting me."

They signed in at the front desk, headed for the locker room, and quickly changed. Brooke put on sapphire blue leggings, with a matching T-shirt, and sneakers. Monica dressed in black leggings, with a white T-shirt and sneakers, her long curls pulled back into a ponytail. Then they grabbed their water bottles and cell phones before heading out onto the main floor.

Brooke loved the atmosphere of the high-end, state-of-the-art facility, which included a juice and snack bar, lounge area, and full-service spa.

"Wow, this place is awesome," Monica said, her eyes scanning the room.

"We need to warm up," Brooke said. "I signed us up for a cycling class."

"Thanks, I love those classes. They give you a total body workout," Monica said as they walked toward a refrigerated case.

Brooke opened the door and pulled out two cold eucalyptus-scented towels. She handed one to Monica. "We'll see how thankful you are when we're done."

Monica inhaled and smiled. "This is going to spoil me. How will I ever use the ratty gym at the Federal Building again?"

Brooke laughed and bumped her shoulder against Monica's. "Come on, let's get on the treadmill."

This early on a Sunday, the gym was much less crowded. A few men worked out on the weight machines, while a mixture of men and women used the ellipticals. Brooke and Monica each got on a treadmill. Brooke slipped on her earbuds and tuned her cell to her playlist. She rolled the cold towel and draped it around her neck.

Watching Brooke, Monica nodded and did the same. "Oh, this feels great," she said, inserting her earbuds and scrolling to her music.

Within thirty seconds, the two were off and running. Brooke's heart pumped faster while rock music blared in her ears. All the pressures of the move from Texas and the job, receded.

Forty minutes later, they finished. Both slowed their machines, letting their heart rates return to normal. After tossing the used towels into one of the bins, Brooke led Monica over to one of the Filtrine Dispensers, where they filled their empty water bottles with purified drinking water. With only five minutes until the cycle class, they chugged down their water and headed over.

Brooke loved taking the ARMY Cycle class. One of the most challenging cycling experiences in the world, it gave her an intense workout. Surrounded by about twelve others on bikes, while the female instructor readied herself, they hoisted themselves up on ones next to one another.

The lights dimmed, the music queued up, and the cycling began. They peddled slowly at first, but then much faster as they gained speed. Amid shouts of encouragement, within minutes, Brooke was ready to climb, sprint, lift, and ride to the beat.

"Trust your inner athlete!" the instructor yelled. "Keep going!"

Brooke pushed herself to the limit. Sweat streamed down her back, dripped off her forehead, and glistened on her arms. She thought of nothing else except making it to the end of the class. Immersed in the cycling, she hadn't even glanced over at Monica. She took a quick look and was surprised to find her, covered in a sheen of sweat, keeping up with the class.

The session came to an end, and the music stopped. Everyone applauded, and the room filled with light again. They got off their bikes and stepped out.

"That felt so good," Monica said. "I needed a good workout."

"Well, you surprised me," Brooke said, as they grabbed two more towels from the refrigerated case and wiped themselves down.

"Well, I've taken cycling before, but I will admit, this one was the most grueling."

"Let's shower and then grab something at the snack bar," Brooke said, pointing to the locker rooms.

Twenty minutes later, they sat across from one another at a small table with protein smoothies and salads.

"I have a spa appointment here in an hour—just a quick facial. I made one for you, too," Brooke said.

"That's so nice of you, but as much as I would love to, I need to get back to Staten Island. Andrew is with his father, so it gives me time to get things done around the house."

Brooke sipped her smoothie and stared at Monica. "Do you trust him with your son?"

Monica stopped eating her salad and set her fork down. "Look, under the circumstances, allowing Eddie to see Andrew is unusual. But let's face it. If he decided to go to court tomorrow to demand joint custody, without a criminal record, it would be granted. His past illegal activities were wiped clean when he entered witness protection."

"But he's back in," Brooke said. "It's only a matter of time before—"

"And if and when that happens," Monica cut in, "he will be prosecuted the same as anyone else who commits a crime."

Curious, Brooke leaned forward. She wanted more background on this past relationship so she could better understand her lead Case Agent. "Do you mind telling me the history between the two of you?"

Monica hesitated, then picked her fork up and speared another bite.

"Please don't think I only asked you here today to pry?" Brooke said.

"Didn't you?" Monica asked, a slight edge in her voice, her posture stiffening.

"Absolutely not. Monica, listen to me. I can only imagine how you once felt about him. Having a child together says a lot. I've been in love before, I know what it's like not being able to be with the person you thought was meant for you." Brooke looked away and slumped back into her chair.

"Then you can imagine the hell I've gone through just to get over him."

Brooke shook her head. "Sadly, I can." She observed Monica's posture relaxing again. "It's okay if you don't want to talk about it. I shouldn't have asked."

"Actually," Monica said, "Eddie and I have known each other since we were little kids. Our parents were good friends. We didn't start dating until well after high school. I was finishing up college then. When I pushed for marriage, he wasn't ready, and he ended up cheating. I couldn't live on Staten Island anymore … too many memories. Plus, I decided I wanted something more, so I applied for the Bureau and left without telling him. My parents were in Florida by then. They were the only ones I told."

Monica's eyes misted. "I guess you've read my file and everything that happened after I was let go from the Bureau and then reinstated."

"Yes," Brooke said. "Including all about slimy, Daniel Gage."

"Well, before being reinstated, I opened my Florist Shop. That's when Eddie and I reconnected. It felt wrong, but I did it anyway. Later, he became an asset. Finding out what really happened to his parents was a real shock. When he agreed to go into witness protection, I wasn't aware I was pregnant."

"Wait," Brooke said. "I'm a bit confused. When did he find out?"

"I had a friend in the U.S. Marshall Service who did me a favor. I put a picture of Andrew in the mail and sent it to him. Andrew was about two years old at the time."

"Monica, do you realize how wrong that was?"

"Of course, and I realize admitting it to you could be detrimental to my career. But I was trying to convince Eddie to become a better man. One Andrew could be proud of." She leaned forward and rested her chin in her hands. "Believe me when I say, it sure backfired on me. Eddie has never forgiven me for it."

"Sorry," Brooke said. "But I have to ask. Are you the cause of Eddie coming out of witness protection?"

"No. There was a contract on his life. The contract was cancelled after Eddie discovered valuable information and shared it with the mob. He wouldn't tell me what it was. But it must be true, otherwise, Eddie would be dead. But it also dragged him right back into the life of a mobster. I will never condone that."

"I see," Brooke said. "I admire you for having the fortitude to stick with the Bureau despite everything and for managing to handle a difficult situation. Since Eddie left of his own accord, I don't think taking action against you for what you did regarding the photograph is warranted."

"Thanks. But I meant what I said when I told you if Eddie is caught breaking the law, I won't hesitate to have him arrested and prosecuted."

Brooke smiled. "And I believe you."

"What about you?" Monica asked. "Who broke your heart?"

"Oh, it was a while back in Texas. Just someone who I thought was for me," Brooke said, wanting to evade the question. "Nothing as earth-shattering as your story."

"Before I go," Monica said. "There is one other thing I want to run by you. I'm thinking of putting a member of the task force undercover on the Greek side."

"Why?"

"Well, for two reasons. One, I think it will help Nico to have backup around. Second, I'd like someone inside at the Acropolis Diner. Greeks hold meetings there. You never know what intel we might be able to get."

"Let me think about it," Brooke said.

Monica drank the last of her smoothie, grabbed her gym bag, and got up. "Thanks again for inviting me. I enjoyed this."

"Anytime you feel like hiking up this way, just give me a ring. I liked having the company."

Brooke watched Monica leave, glad she had decided to invite her. She was one of the Bureau's best agents.

***

Later, exiting the gym after her spa treatment, Brooke hurried up the street under a light drizzling rain. She ducked into H & H Bagels on 2nd Avenue. Discovering New York sold the best bagels she had ever tasted, this was one of her favorite stops. The place was packed with customers standing at the counter shouting out their orders. A flurry of people ran back and forth, filling up paper bags with bagels. The aroma of fresh-baked bread, with a hint of yeast and a slight smokiness, hung in the air. It mingled with fresh-brewed coffee and sweet pastries.

Feeling like a true New Yorker, Brooke clutched her gym bag in one hand, slung her purse over her shoulder, and then waded through the crowd until she reached the counter. She ordered one cinnamon raisin, one poppy seed bagel, and a small container of strawberry cream cheese.

After paying for her purchase, she turned to go but stopped dead. Austin Faulkner, dressed in jeans, a grey polo shirt, and a black leather jacket, holding a closed umbrella in his hand, grinned down at her.

"Hey," Austin said. "I see you like bagels as much as I do."

Stunned for a moment, she tried to smile. "What brings you to my neighborhood?"

"Well, it happens to be my neighborhood, too. I live on East 86th Street, moved there two weeks ago. I used to live on the West Side of Manhattan."

"Hmm, I think you need to update your personnel file." Feeling awkward, she quickly added, "I was just coming from the gym. I enjoy an early morning workout."

"Me too," Austin said. "Gets the day going right."

"Well, I guess I'll see you at the office tomorrow."

"Are you on foot?" Austin asked.

"Yes. I'm not far, just over on East 82nd."

"Well, give me a minute to get my order, and I'll walk you to your building."

"Oh, that won't be necessary," Brooke said.

Austin pointed to the window where heavy sheets of rain beat against the glass. "I can give us some protection." He laughed and lifted his umbrella. "I think I'm a bit more prepared than you."

Brooke glanced out the window and then back at Austin. He was right. She'd get drenched in that downpour. Her scalp prickled. She shifted from one foot to the other and clutched the bag of bagels tighter.

"Sorry," Austin said. "Am I making you uncomfortable?"

Cursing herself inside for this ridiculous display of nerves, she shook her head and lied. "No, not at all."

"Okay, then. I'll get my bagels and walk you back to 82nd."

She waited for Austin near the exit, annoyed at herself for accepting his invitation. Once she left Texas, she had vowed never to get close to another man again, at least not for a long, long time. She needed to heal before even thinking about getting friendly with the opposite sex.

"Ready?" Austin asked, coming up behind her.

"Yes. Let's go." All she wanted now was to return to her apartment, shut the door, and calm herself down.

Austin stashed his bag under one arm while she put hers in the outside pocket of her gym bag. He pushed the door open, and they stood under a small awning while he opened his umbrella. He motioned for her to take his elbow, and they hurried up the street together, dodging several puddles along the way.

They reached her building, Brooke swiped her key card, and Austin ushered her through the sliding glass doors and into the lobby. He closed the umbrella, and she glanced up at the raindrops glistening in his wavy brown hair. Kind eyes stared back at her. A flush swept through her body. For a moment, neither spoke a word.

This is wrong, Brooke thought. This is all wrong. I shouldn't be acting this way. Especially not with a member of my task force.

"Well … I … I mean, thanks for trying to keep me dry," she said, moving away toward the elevator.

"Sure. It was my pleasure," Austin said. "See you in the morning."

He turned and headed out of the lobby. Her gaze followed him as he hoisted the umbrella, opened it again, and disappeared up the street. Why was this man having such an effect on her? Before making her way to the elevator, something made her take one last look outside the lobby doors.

The rain fell fast and furious now, coming down in blinding waves. People hurried past, some with umbrellas, and others dripping wet, defeated by the downpour. The barrage continued, making it almost impossible to see clearly. A figure approached the lobby doors. As best as she could tell, it appeared to be a man. He cupped his hands against the glass and peered inside. At first, she thought it might be Austin. Maybe he had come back hoping to get in out of the rain. Brooke strode to the door, key card in hand. She went to swipe the monitor and froze.

Those eyes staring at her were familiar. They were *his* eyes— ones she never wanted to see again. Brooke moved backward, inching her way to the bank of elevators. Her fingers tapped furiously at the buttons while her eyes scanned the numbers as an elevator descended to the lobby.

"Hurry, hurry," she whispered, glancing over her shoulder. "Please hurry." The elevator opened. Brooke stumbled inside, almost dropping her purse and gym bag to the floor. She hit fifteen and then peered out between the closing doors. The rain continued, but the figure was gone.

Minutes later, she stepped out of the elevator and ran toward her apartment at the end of the hall. A woman, her neighbor across the way, came out of her door just as Brooke flew past.

"Are you okay?" she called out.

Brooke fumbled with her keys. "Yes, I'm fine."

"Are you sure?"

Brooke turned and tried to smile. "Yes, just trying to get in and dry off."

"I hear ya," the woman said. "I think I'm gonna change my mind and stay home."

"That's a good idea," Brooke said, finally able to turn the lock. Her legs shook uncontrollably. Nervous knots twisted inside her body as she slid down onto the floor.

Had she really seen him? Or maybe it was someone else with the same eyes. Forcing herself to take a deep breath, she gathered her things and stood up on shaky legs. Tonight would be another one of those many nights filled with terror and dreams of him.

Chapter 16 — Eddie
Knowing

When Eddie dropped Andrew off on Sunday afternoon, he ignored the disapproving look on Lillian's face—one he was used to going all the way back to his high school days. Her furrowed brow and pursed lips sent out a warning signal. She bent and kissed the top of Andrew's head and ushered him inside.

"Mommy will be here soon to pick you up," she said. "You can go see Grandpa and tell him about your day."

Eddie jogged down the front steps, but before he reached his car parked at the curb, Lillian called out. "Eddie, can I speak to you for a moment?"

"Sure," he said, turning to go back up, but she had already reached the bottom. His body tensed up. This couldn't be good. The only words Monica's mother and father had spoken to him since his return were hello and goodbye.

"Listen," she said. "I haven't spoken to Monica as yet, but I don't think I like what's going on."

Eddie shrugged. "No disrespect, Mrs. Cappelino, but I have no idea what you're talking about."

Arms crossed, she took a step closer to him. "I saw the kiss," she said.

"Oh, that." He instantly relaxed. "What about it?"

"I know what you're trying to do, Eddie. And I don't like it one bit. Monica has made every effort to move on from her past relationship with you. I believe you're trying to confuse her."

Eddie sighed. "Whether you want to believe me or not, what we had was much more than a relationship. I think Andrew is proof enough of that. We loved each other very much. I won't stand here and lie to you because I still love your daughter, and she loves me. She may not want to admit it, but she does."

Lillian uncrossed her arms. Her hands clenched into fists. Eddie saw a flush creep up her face. For a moment, he thought she was going to punch him.

"Don't do this, Eddie. I'm warning you. Do not try to pull my daughter back into your life. I've known you ever since you were a little boy. I was good friends with your parents, for goodness' sake. If that uncle of yours hadn't …." She uncurled her hands and looked away for a moment.

"Go on, say it," Eddie said, his voice rising. "Killed them. Isn't that it?"

Her face suddenly softening, she said, "I'm sorry. Truly, I am. I never meant to bring that up. I loved your parents. They should never have died the way they did. I guess I'm just disappointed."

"Disappointed how?" Eddie asked.

"That you chose to follow in your Uncle Sal's footsteps. I thought once you knew the truth about him and your Uncle Lorenzo, you would turn away from the mob. Become a different person. Someone better than them."

A cold wave rushed through his body. She had no idea how hard it was for him to leave here and pretend to be happy in Arizona. All the while longing to see his son and facing the fact he would never get the chance if he stayed in witness protection.

"I tried that, Lillian," he said. "Unfortunately, it didn't work out." The conversation between them left him feeling suffocated. He needed to go.

Eddie turned away and walked to his car. When he reached the driver's side, she still stood there staring at him.

"By the way," he said. "That kiss should tell you everything you need to know about Monica and me. She didn't try to stop me, did she?"

Before she could say anything else, Eddie got in his car and drove away.

*****

Sitting with Tony in one of the many corner bars in Manhattan, Lillian's accusations kept Eddie in a sullen mood. The dark interior and moody jazz music emanating from the speakers only served to reinforce his feelings. Regardless of his circumstances, she would never accept him. He believed she only put up with him because he happened to be Andrew's father.

"What's up with you?" Tony asked.

The two had put aside their differences from the previous argument about Kai. Eddie accepted the fact that so far neither one of them would leave the relationship.

"Bad day," Eddie said. He gulped down his vodka tonic and signaled the bartender for another.

"I thought you were with Andrew today."

"I was. Everything was great until I dropped him off."

"Monica?" Tony asked.

Eddie shook his head and then related what had taken place earlier with Lillian. Tony slapped his palm loudly on the bar. A few patrons at the other end looked in their direction for a moment.

"I knew it. Here you go telling me to drop Kai, meanwhile you're trying to get Monica back."

"No. It was an impulse. She just looked so damn beautiful standing there. But we will never be together again. My leaving witness protection killed any possibility of that happening. But the things her mother said make me feel some kinda way, like I'm beneath her. When she brought up my parents, it shook me a bit. I haven't thought about their murder in a long time. I don't want to dwell on the past. I can't change any of it."

"It was wrong of her. You've gone through enough," Tony said.

"She tried to apologize. Right now, Andrew is too little to comprehend what I'm about. But later, when he's older, there will be no way he won't find out. The streets talk … and I'm known out there on those streets."

"Don't do this to yourself, Eddie. You're a great father to Andrew, and that's what he's always going to remember, no matter what anyone else says."

"Maybe," Eddie said. "But if I'm being honest, I would never want this kind of life for him. I want him to go to college and choose a career he'll love. I want him to be safe. Something you and I never really are. Not in this business."

"I understand," Tony said, looking down and swirling the scotch inside his glass. "When I have kids, I want those same things for them."

The vodka easing his trepidation, Eddie signaled for a third drink.

"Better slow down," Tony cautioned. "We meet with Nico and Konstantin Zervas tomorrow. If we can pull this thing off, we'll be golden with Paulie."

"No worries," Eddie said. "I'll be fine. You just make sure you keep that temper of yours in check. If we make things fair, we can convince the Greeks to expand."

Tony swallowed the rest of his scotch. Always on alert, the bartender was about to pour him another when he shook his head no. "By the way, I took your advice regarding Paulie. I picked up a woman the other night. I'll show her off a bit, throw him off my scent."

"Does Kai know?"

Tony raised an eyebrow. "Hell no. And there is no need for me to tell her. It won't turn into anything serious. She's just arm candy."

A grin lit Eddie's face. "Okay, if you say so."

"By the way," Tony said. "I met Kai's mom—actually visited the Navajo Reservation."

"Boy, you're really taking chances."

"We were careful. Kai covers the ins and outs."

"How did things go with her mom?"

"Let's just say, I didn't exactly endear myself to her. She's with the Tribal Police Force. I sure found out where Kai gets her tough streak."

"What was the Reservation like?"

Tony hesitated. "Different in every way. I couldn't imagine growing up there. There are some beautiful parts of the desert … I mean, the scenery was awesome. But there are so many traditions the Navajo practice. Plus, their belief system is so different from ours. If we ever did have kids, between my background and her culture, they would walk around confused all day."

"Come on," Eddie said. "Kai values her native traditions. That's something to be proud of. We hold true to ours. Besides, everyone knows how unfairly the Native Americans were treated and, to some degree, still are."

Tony waved his hand. "Okay, enough talk about that. Let's get out of here. No getting behind the wheel tonight. You're staying in Manhattan at my hotel."

"Geez," Eddie said. "Are you ever going to get your own place?"

Tony shrugged. "It's convenient. Less responsibility, and you can't beat the room service."

Eddie made sure his BMW was locked up tight while Tony hailed a cab. Later, when Eddie settled in his room at the hotel, sleep eluded him. Monica's face swam before him, the memory of her soft lips on his bringing an unbearable ache. His cheating on her all those years ago had left its mark. If she only knew how much he regretted what he had done—how ashamed he was of hurting her.

Didn't she understand the torture of leaving everything behind and trying to start a new life? He did it for her and Andrew—to prove he could be the kind of man she always wanted him to be.

Although Tony had played an integral part in convincing him to leave witness protection, he had always known one day he'd make the same decision on his own. Regardless of what Monica or Lillian thought of his life now, because of Andrew, he would do it all again. But on this night, as he tossed and turned, his mind refusing to shut down, an uneasiness crept over him he could neither make sense of nor shake.

Chapter 17 — Monica
Truth And Lies

Before Monica could ring the bell, the front door opened, and Lillian appeared. Her facial expression reminded Monica of when she was little, and her mother proceeded to discipline her for some infraction. She must have been peering out the window, waiting for her to arrive.

Trying to sound casual, Monica said, "Hey, Mom. Is Andrew ready?"

Lillian's hands gripped her waist. "We need to have a talk first."

"Is something wrong?"

"You tell me, Monica. I had a little confrontation with Eddie earlier. I hope you'll be honest with me."

Monica glanced up and down the street. "Am I allowed to come in, or do we have to stand out here on the steps?"

Lillian turned, and she followed her inside. Monica could hear Andrew in the living room with her father. She peeped in the doorway. Her son sat on her father's lap listening to him read a story. She managed to slip past without either of them noticing.

Lillian waited in the kitchen. She leaned back against the white quartz counter with the same sour expression. "Sit down, please."

Monica sighed. She tossed her purse onto the large center island and dropped down onto a stool. "Okay, enough of the dramatics, Mom. What's going on?"

"First, I want to make one thing clear. I wasn't spying. I happened to glance out the window when you dropped Andrew off."

A hard knot hit the bottom of Monica's stomach. "Before you say anything else, I need to make things clear. Eddie came at me so quick … I mean, I wasn't expecting him to kiss me."

Lillian raised an eyebrow. "Yes, but as he pointed out, you didn't push him away."

Monica wanted to explode. Why did Eddie have to pull a stunt like that right in front of her parents' house? Lying was never a part of who she was, but she couldn't tell her mother the truth either. That kiss was all she kept thinking about. Those familiar lips made her body go weak and stir something inside her heart.

"Like I said, it happened so fast. It didn't mean anything," Monica lied.

"That's not the impression Eddie gave me. You need to come clean with me. Are you still in love with him?"

Monica got up and grabbed her purse. She looked her mother in the eye. "Eddie is the father of my son. I will always feel something for him, but no, I'm not in love with him." She went over and kissed Lillian's cheek. "I need to get Andrew home."

***

With Andrew fed and bathed, she tucked him in. "Night, night," she said, kissing his forehead.

"Mommy, can Daddy come and live with us?"

"No, Andrew. I'm afraid not."

His eyes grew large, and a tiny wrinkle creased his brow. "But why not? I don't like him being alone. I want him here with us."

A hard lump formed inside Monica's throat. How could she explain this crazy situation to her three-year-old son? No, Andrew, your father is a criminal, and Mommy might have to arrest him one day. Monica sat on the edge of the bed. She swept her fingers through Andrew's curls, the sensation bringing back the memory of Eddie's dark strands beneath her hands.

"Listen, Andrew," Monica said softly. "Daddy can't come live with us. He has a job just like Mommy has a job. It takes up a lot of his time right now."

Andrew's lips formed a pout. "But I want him here."

"Maybe someday," Monica whispered. "Now, it's time for you to go to sleep." She kissed his forehead again, turned on the nightlight, and left his door cracked.

Trying to fall asleep that night became almost impossible. Spending time earlier with Brooke had been great, but she was a bit unnerved by revealing her past with Eddie. Convincing her boss her feelings for him were in the past was a must if she had any hope of staying in charge of the task force. There again, she kept the truth at bay. But she did find it odd when she asked Brooke about her past relationship, she wasn't forthcoming in the least bit. Monica got the feeling there was much more to learn about the lover Brooke claimed had broken her heart.

Tossing back and forth amid the covers, she punched her fist into the pillow and screamed, "Damn you, Eddie Marconi!" Why couldn't she let go? It was as though he had an invisible tether wrapped around her heart.

Hiding her true feelings was becoming a full-time job. Making sure to show no reaction when Nico mentioned Eddie's name also put her at odds with her job as a handler. Eventually, Nico was bound to discover their past connection. Would he still feel comfortable with her? Besides, anything Tony Morello was involved in couldn't be good for Eddie.

At the thought of Tony, Kai popped into her mind. She hadn't mentioned Tony in a very long time. At least there was no indication they were still involved with one another.

***

The next day, everyone on the task force gathered in the conference room. Monica brought them up to speed regarding the upcoming meeting between the Greeks and the Italians.

"This card game, this *barbouti,* appears to be at the core," Monica said. "Anything from your C.I., Austin?"

"Not yet. I'll be seeing him later this evening. It's become a real cloak-and-dagger situation between us. He's extremely nervous lately, and I need to find out why."

Monica focused on Kai, who sipped some coffee from a Styrofoam cup, a distant look in her eyes. "Kai, I've been thinking about you going undercover at the Acropolis Diner. The mob never goes there. According to Nico, they meet strictly on neutral territory. They deem the diner unsafe."

"That's not possible, Monica. I have a history with the mob." She looked at Brooke. "Are you in agreement with this?"

"Yes. I think it might bring some good intel. But only if you want to. No one is going to force you."

"How would I even get in?"

"Nico said they're always hiring waitresses. Apparently, Konstantin has an eye for the ladies."

"Can I have time to think about it?" Kai asked, her eyes fixed on Monica.

"Sure, take all the time you need. If you feel too uncomfortable, then it's a no-go for me. We'll find another way."

"I can't see any other way," Brooke added. "Nico wearing a wire is totally out of the question, and besides from what Monica learned, he isn't always invited to every meeting."

"Okay, everyone, I think this is enough for today," Brooke said. She turned to Austin. "Let's pick up again after you meet with your C.I."

Everyone got up except Kai. The others left while Monica held back and sat across from her.

"Sorry if you felt I ambushed you."

"You kinda did, Monica."

"Look, you're good at what you do. I just thought if I want someone else on the inside, it has to be you."

"Thanks for the compliment, I guess," Kai said. She tapped her polished fingernails nervously on the tabletop. "It's just that, if somehow anything gets back to Tony, it could mean big trouble for me."

"The chances of that happening are slim. Tony doesn't hang out in Queens. Mobsters stick to their territory where they're comfortable. Unless there's a war of some kind, they stay where it's safe."

"True," Kai said. "Give me a few days, and I'll have an answer for you."

"Have you heard from Tony at all?"

Kai avoided her eyes. "No. I let go of all that a long time ago, just like you did with Eddie."

"I'm sorry," Kai. I know you loved him. But being with him was not a good choice. I let Eddie go for the same reason. Their lifestyle choices go against everything we've been trained to do. I don't think either one of us was ready to give up the Bureau in exchange for a life of danger and uncertainty with them.

Kai jumped up. Without a word, she grabbed her empty coffee cup and stormed out of the conference room.

Monica felt a twinge in her gut. Something wasn't right with Kai. Did she tell the truth about Tony? Her body language contradicted her words. Of course, she sympathized with her. Why was it so hard to get these men out of their system?

Gathering up her laptop, Monica left and headed down the hall to her office. She couldn't let her suspicions about Kai interfere with the work of the task force. For now, she'd put those thoughts on hold. Until she had proof Kai lied, she had no choice but to trust her. She only hoped sending her undercover was the right choice.

Chapter 18 — Austin
The C.I.

At six o'clock in the evening, Austin drove across the Manhattan Bridge toward Vinegar Hill. The neighborhood in the borough of Brooklyn encompassed a six-block area along the East River Waterfront between Dumbo, an acronym for Down Under the Manhattan Bridge and the Brooklyn Navy Yard. Most of Vinegar Hill consisted of Federal and Greek Revival style homes with a mix of industrial buildings. It was behind one of these buildings that Austin agreed to meet with his C.I.

He pulled his car around to the back of an old, abandoned warehouse. The frosted glass inside the window frames on the upper floors were threaded with wire. Others at street level had been boarded up with plywood. Tuffs of weeds and grass shot up through the cracks of the black asphalt. Discarded sheets of newspaper clung to the chain link fence along the rear of the property while scraps of trash and countless cigarette butts littered the lot.

Fifteen minutes later, a small sedan pulled up next to his. A tall man with wavy auburn hair, deep-set eyes, and a slightly crooked nose climbed out. He wore jeans, a polo shirt, and a light tan jacket. Before slipping into the passenger seat of Austin's car, his eyes scouted the lot.

"You're late, Stan," Austin said. "I started to think you were going to bail on me."

Stan wiped his palms down the front of his jeans. The puffy skin under his left eye twitched. "Look, you know how dangerous this is for me. I gotta make sure there's no tail on my ass."

"Listen," Austin said. "It seems there's a meeting coming up between the Greeks and the Italians concerning a gambling game the mob wants in on. You got anything on that?"

Stan shook his head. "Yeah, if you're talking about *barbouti*, that game is like lifeblood to the Greeks. It pulls in a lot of money."

"Let me ask you this, Stan. What about the offshore gambling side of things? Isn't that much more lucrative?"

"Sure. The mob is into all of that, but their card and dice games make the fast money. They got those set up in every borough. If they expand with the Greek game, then you're talking a huge take every single week."

"So, why are the Greeks holding back?" Austin asked.

"Like I said that game is theirs. From the very beginning, they always kicked money up from *barbouti,* and everyone seemed satisfied with that."

"So, what changed?"

"Tony Morello is what changed," Stan said, the twitch under his eye growing more pronounced. "Me coming from Nevada and joining his crew might have been a mistake. That guy is hungry in a way I've never seen before. He runs all his action with an iron hand."

Austin studied Stan for a moment. "Meaning he's got something to prove. But to whom?"

"He reports to Paulie 'the Shiv' Martello. But I'm starting to get the impression Tony would like to move up. But that ain't an easy thing to do in the mob, unless …"

"Unless what?" Austin asked.

"There's a strict hierarchy." Stan clasped his hands together. Austin observed the tightness as his knuckles turned white. He had never seen his C.I. this anxious.

"Look," Stan said. "I'm just gonna give you my take on things. Tony controls the Jersey Seaport. That's a major deal. So much contraband comes in that way. I'm talking drugs, guns, stolen art. I even heard about gold bars once."

"Frank Uzelli used to have that in his back pocket," Austin said.

"Yeah, before he got whacked."

Austin sat straight up. "You're certain of that?"

"The rumbling is Paulie gave Tony permission to get rid of him. Supposedly, he's buried out west in the desert somewhere. It makes sense, since Frank cut Tony up bad with that razor of his."

"Are you sure Paulie sanctioned the hit?"

"There is no way it would have gone down unless Paulie gave the okay," Stan said. "As one of Tony's made men, I overheard one of the bosses say that's the way Frank went out."

Austin tried to digest what Stan had told him. "There is one thing bothering me," he said. "How does Tony plan on getting Paulie out of the way?"

Stan let out a long breath. "I'm not sure, but if Paulie ever disappears, you should be looking in Tony's direction." He paused and fidgeted with the door handle. "Remember what you promised me. I want out of this life, get myself back on track. I need to put my family first, and we need to be safe."

"I understand how hard this has been for you, Stan. The Bureau appreciates everything you've done so far. As soon as we make a solid case against Tony Morello and a few others, I'll make sure you and your family are in witness protection."

Stan reached for the door handle again and then glanced back at Austin. "There's one other thing. If this meeting doesn't go well, somebody's gonna die for sure." He exited Austin's car, jumped into his own, and drove away.

Austin sat still for several minutes before pulling out of the lot. If what Stan had told him was true, then Tony Morello had big plans. Eliminating Frank Uzelli gave him control of the Jersey Seaport and revenge all at the same time.

On the drive back to Manhattan, Austin's mind buzzed with the information he had heard from Stan Amato. He put a call in to Monica. This also put Nico in an even more dangerous position.

Apparently, this meeting meant much more than a simple card game. It was all about control.

Later, passing East 82nd Street on the way to his apartment, he thought about Brooke and their little trek through the pouring rain.

Had he imagined the longing in her eyes in the lobby of the building? In that moment, something passed between them. But he felt her suddenly pull away as if she was frightened. He could only deduce that someone in her past had hurt her.

But he needed to forget about that brief moment. After all, she was an Assistant Director. Fraternizing with a superior was frowned upon at the Bureau. Still, he couldn't get Brooke Adams out of his mind.

Chapter 19 — Kai
Going Under

Kai sat in front of her computer in the Federal Building, her eyes fixed on the screen, but her mind wasn't absorbing anything. Monica asking her to go undercover was the last thing she expected. Tony's face swam before her. How could she look him in the eye if she agreed to Monica's request?

She checked her watch. It was just shy of four thirty, almost time to leave.

A light tap on her shoulder made her jump. She swung around.

"Sorry," Monica said. "I didn't mean to startle you. Come to my office. We need to talk some more."

"Sure. Be there in a minute," Kai said. "Let me log out." What timing. Monica couldn't wait to try and talk her into going under. Sighing, she shut down her computer and went down the hall. Closing the door behind her, she sat down across from Monica.

"Look, Kai, I didn't mean to put you on the spot."

Kai narrowed her eyes. "Well, it sure felt like it. I mean … you should have waited, pulled me aside, or something without the entire task force there."

"I'm sorry. You're right. I didn't think it was such a big deal. You've been under before and even told me how much you liked pretending to be someone you're not. Hell, you said it gave you a rush."

"I know, I know, but …"

"But what? Tell me your reservations about the whole thing. Why is this so different from the other times?"

Kai leaned back into the chair. How could she explain her feelings to Monica? If she told the truth, she would either be transferred or lose her job. Monica could not have an agent on the task force who was in a relationship with someone the Bureau was actively investigating.

"I'm just not feeling comfortable with this one. There are too many what-ifs."

"You mean, the mob finding out you're working at the diner?"

"Yes. Of course," Kai said.

"But not one of them knew you were involved at Volkov's club when you and Austin were under together. And as far as the raid on the seaport, Enzo Carbone and Rocco Fischetti both died at the scene. Alexei Volkov and Rurik Bortnik are both locked away in prison. Is there something you're not telling me, Kai?"

Kai's heart raced. A tingling sensation swept over her body. She didn't want to lie. Especially, not to Monica. "I'm not sure what you mean." She managed a weak smile. "I'm just telling you what my fears are."

"You'll be well protected," Monica said. "I'll make sure of it. Nico can only do so much. It would help if he had someone else on the inside."

"Like I said before, I'll think about it. Can I go now?"

"Of course. I'm not holding you prisoner, silly."

***

Back at her desk, Kai mulled over her talk with Monica. It all made perfect sense, and she didn't doubt the Bureau would have her back if she decided to go under. But if Tony found out, it meant the end of everything—possibly the end of her.

Kai reached for her purse, the trembling in her hands surprising her. Did she believe Tony could kill her? If she did, that meant their love for each other wasn't on solid ground. His loyalty to the mob came before anything else. He had made that clear so many times. His desire for her to leave the Bureau and his refusal to distance himself from the mob cemented exactly where he stood.

Kai grabbed her purse and jacket. She hurried for the elevator. Outside, a cool breeze filtered through the air. Rush hour traffic filled the city streets. Cabs honked, while hordes of pedestrians crisscrossed the sidewalks. Walking several blocks before pulling out her burner phone to call Tony, she ducked into a doorway and dialed.

She needed to hear his voice, needed to be reassured about how much he loved her. The ringing continued. "Please pick up," Kai whispered. Voicemail came on, but she decided against leaving a message. Darting to the curb, she hailed a cab and gave the driver Tony's hotel address.

During the endless ride, Kai could hardly breathe. Traffic showed no mercy as the car moved at a snail's pace. A ride that should have taken twenty minutes took twice as long.

When she finally reached her destination, she paid the cabbie and rushed inside the hotel. Hardly able to control herself while standing in front of the bank of elevators, she repeatedly tapped the up button. Thankfully, she was the only one waiting. The doors opened, and Kai stepped inside. Her chest burned while her heartbeat quickened.

Exiting on the twenty-sixth floor, she ran to the end of the hallway and rang the buzzer several times. Expecting Tony to open the door and pull her into his arms, her anxiety grew as the minutes ticked by.

She pulled out the burner phone again and dialed. There was still no answer. Despondent, she rode the elevator back down to the lobby. Loads of plush seating filled several areas. Soft lighting accented the deep blue velvet sofas and club chairs stationed on Persian rugs. Artwork filled the dark walls trimmed in mahogany moldings. Except for a few people on cell phones, it was relatively empty. She found a quiet corner and sat down to wait.

Twenty minutes ticked by. With no sign of Tony and feeling somewhat foolish over her fears, she was about to leave when he walked through the lobby doors looking handsome, dressed in a navy suit. Only he wasn't alone. Her blonde hair trailed down past her shoulders. She wore a print dress cut low, showing her ample cleavage. Her shapely legs and black three-inch heels made her appear as tall as Tony.

They stopped for a moment, and the woman whispered something in his ear. They both laughed, and then she tucked her arm neatly around his, and they walked toward the elevators.

Unable to move, Kai stared after them as they disappeared behind the sliding doors. Her stomach burned. A sick feeling welled up inside her. This couldn't be happening. There must be a logical explanation for what she saw. All sorts of thoughts exploded inside of her. Is this why he would never give her a key to his hotel suite? Was he afraid to get caught cheating?

Hurt and anger boiled to the surface—one as raw and real as the other. She marched to the elevator bank. What a fool she had been to think she was the only one. How many others were there?

The doors opened, and by the time Kai reached the twenty-sixth floor, the only thing fueling her body was rage. Her heart was beating so fast she thought it might burst out of her ribcage. She reached his door. Heat flushed through her body, while her pulse sounded in her ears. Gritting her teeth, she jammed her finger against the bell.

"Hold on," Tony shouted through the door. As it flew open, she heard, "What the fu—"

"Yeah, what the fuck, Tony!" Kai shouted.

His face went pale while his eyes locked on hers. "Kai … I—"

"You what? Didn't expect to see me, did you?"

He stepped out into the hall, shut the door, and then reached for her. "It's not what you think."

Kai backed away. "Don't you touch me, you lying son of a bitch!" She didn't want to cry, not show any weakness. But the hurt and anger he caused pained her to the core. Tears flooded her eyes, blurring his image.

"Please," Tony pleaded. "You need to listen to me."

She moved farther away. "No. I don't have to listen to anything. Go back inside to your … your whatever she is. We are done, Tony. Do you hear me? We are done!"

She turned and ran for the elevator. Tony's footsteps sounded behind her. Her fist pounding on the button, she couldn't get away fast enough.

"Kai, wait. Don't go. If you love me, you'll let me explain."

"If I love you?" she said, her tears coming hard and fast. "Did you actually just say those words?"

"I didn't mean it that way," Tony said. "I know you love me."

The elevator opened, and Kai stepped inside. "I used to love you, Tony. But not anymore."

As the doors closed, Tony stood, arms outstretched, a tear running down his cheek. "Kai, please!"

She reached the lobby and tore out of the hotel. Breathless, confused, and hurt, she continued up the block. Night had fallen over the city. Skyscrapers twinkled with lights, and the cool breeze from earlier had settled.

She walked the city streets for hours. Her legs ached, and her muscles went slack, forcing her to collapse onto a bench overlooking the East River. She stared out at the waves rippling across the surface in the moonlight.

Was their whole relationship a lie? Could she have been that naive to think he really cared for her? All those times she told herself it would be impossible to let go of him. She had loved Tony with every ounce of her being. Now, here she was left with an ache so deep it seemed insurmountable.

She walked over to the railing and tossed the burner phone into the river. Taking her time, she gathered herself and slowly walked back up to the street and hailed a cab.

All she wanted was to be home in her apartment. She needed to push thoughts of Tony and what could never be away. But how? How to move on from the hurt?

She dug inside her purse and grabbed her cell phone. She dialed Monica's number. When she answered, Kai said, "I'll do it, Monica. I'll go under."

Chapter 20 — Tony
A Negotiation

Seated next to Eddie at the round table in Betty Alvarez's dining room in the Bronx, Tony jumped up and peered out of the white lace curtains. Stan Amato leaned against the far wall.

"Where the hell are they?"

"Calm down," Eddie said. "Maybe they hit traffic. It was your big fat idea to meet all the way up here."

"Yeah, well, we all agreed it had to be neutral territory. Betty's a good friend of Paulie's."

Eddie cleared his throat. "I think she's a bit more than a good friend. She comes around to his social club an awful lot."

"Still, it's nice she let us use her place while she's away in Florida," Tony said. "Although it's not my taste." He nodded toward the floral wallpaper and gold-framed pictures of green meadows and mountain tops, likely purchased at a bargain store. He sat down and drummed his fingers on the tabletop.

"Any word from Kai?" Eddie asked.

"Nada. Not a word. I guess you're happy. Your wish has come true."

"I only wanted what was best for both of you."

"So, I guess my broken heart is okay with you?" Tony shot back.

"Of course not. I feel for you. I know exactly what it's like to lose someone."

Tony got up again and went to the window. "Kai wasn't just someone. That woman meant everything to me. She's irreplaceable.

I've got to get her back somehow. If she had only given me a chance to explain."

Eddie let out a low chuckle. "You mean explain why you took a woman up to your room. I'm sure she didn't think the two of you were going to play Scrabble—"

They're here," Tony cut in. "Go wait in one of the bedrooms, Stan. But stay alert." All he wanted right now was to finalize the deal with the Greeks. Then he could take care of things with Kai. He opened the front door. Konstantin walked in, followed by Nico and another man Tony had never seen before.

"Whoa," he said, putting up his hand. "Who's this?"

"My bodyguard," Konstantin, said. "This is Stavros Papadakis. He goes everywhere I go."

"We agreed to no extras," Tony said through clenched teeth. "He stays outside."

Konstantin shook his head. "Then I go, too!"

"Look," Nico said. "Let's take a breath here." He gestured at Tony. "He can stay in another room while we talk. That is, unless … maybe you have someone here, too?"

Tony hesitated. He didn't like being called out. Nico was smarter than he first thought. He put on a false smile. "Okay, okay. The guy can stay. Go on in and sit down. But Stavros here can sit in the living room. Hey, Stan," Tony called. "Come on out." He gave Stan instructions to keep an eye on Konstantin's man and then sat down with the others.

"So," Tony began, leaning forward, his hands clasped together. "I guess Nico told you we want to expand the territory of your *barbouti* game. I want to add it to my territory, and Eddie here will handle the games on Staten Island. Of course, we'll need two of your guys to make sure the game is run right."

Konstantin's expression hardened. He stared at Tony and then at Eddie. "*Barbouti* is not for sale," he spat. "We already give you more than a decent cut. That game belongs to us."

Tony's hands clenched, and he pounded his fist on the table. "Do you think this is a negotiation? Like I told Nico, we run things, not you!"

"Let me ask you something, Konstantin," Eddie said with a sideways glance at Tony. "If we expand the games, that's more money for everybody. You'll keep your original cut, and we'll throw in ten percent of what we gross on top of it. Don't you agree that's more than fair?"

Tony couldn't believe what he was hearing. What the hell did Eddie think he was doing? He cut his eyes at him. "I think you're mistaken in what you just said. The cut stays as it is. No percentage on top."

"Come on, Tony," Nico said. "It's only fair you give a little. Especially, if you need manpower from us."

"If I agree to let you run the game in your territory," Konstantin said. "Then we need to be compensated."

Tony's pulse skipped. "See, there you go again, thinking this is a negotiation."

"What the hell is it then?" Nico asked, his face flushed red. "We didn't have to come here today."

"Well, I guess you must've considered the alternative then," Tony said.

Eddie rose. "This back and forth isn't getting us anywhere." He looked at Tony. "Let's just cut a deal. The main thing here is we're all gonna make more money."

Tony fumed inside. Even though he knew Eddie was right, he didn't like anyone forcing his hand. He jerked his head toward Konstantin. "So, do you agree to Eddie's deal?"

Konstantin eyed Nico, who nodded his agreement. "Okay, our cut and ten percent on top. I will have someone monitor the games in both territories."

"Just so you understand. There better not be any funny business," Tony said. "If anyone is caught skimming, he's gone. And I do mean gone. Understood?"

Konstantin and Nico got up. "Understood," Konstantin said. "We will work out the details. I will be in touch."

After they left, Tony turned his fury on Eddie. "What the hell was all that? We never talked about ten percent on top."

"You want the deal done or not?"

"Of course. But we can never appear weak, Eddie. You know that. If Paulie were here, he wouldn't be happy with the way things were handled."

"Don't lecture me about Paulie. He stands to make a lot more money. That's all he'll care about. Sometimes your pride gets in the way too much. It may get you killed one day."

Tony moved toward him until they were the two inches apart. "What are you trying to say?"

"You're a hot head at times. It prevents you from thinking clearly. Our job as Capos is to focus on generating revenue. We do that, and we're golden every time." Eddie backed away. He dug in his pocket for his car keys. "I love you like a brother, Tony. But I'm not gonna let you get me killed." He turned and walked out the door.

Stan came into the dining room. "You good, Boss?"

"No. I don't like to be disrespected. People need to follow orders. That Stavros guy, Konstantin's so-called bodyguard.

"Yeah, what about him?"

"He wasn't supposed to be here tonight. That makes me think I'm not being taken seriously. Choose a button man from the crew and make him disappear. Maybe then, Konstantin will show me some respect."

***

It was three in the afternoon when Stan dropped Tony off at his hotel. He headed straight for the bar. Relatively empty at this time of day, Tony seated himself on a stool at the far end. He ordered a scotch neat and then took out his cell phone.

Breaking their agreement and certain she would have ditched the burner phone, he tried calling and sending text messages to her cell phone number, which he pried out of Eddie. Scrolling through each unanswered text made his dark mood worse. Now that she had blocked him, there was no way to reach her.

The love he felt for her burned deep inside him—a fire he was unable to extinguish. He gulped down the scotch and ordered another.

Never could he have imagined himself crying over a woman. The image of her tear-filled face, as the elevator doors closed, refused to erase itself from his mind.

What was he thinking bringing a woman he hardly knew to the hotel? He had come from Paulie's social club with her. All of it a show to keep Paulie at bay. Several rounds of drinks later, and feeling somewhat attracted to her, they wound up here.

But once they got upstairs to his room, he found his initial attraction waning when thoughts of Kai crossed his mind. He was about to call for a cab and escort her out of the hotel when Kai appeared outside his door.

Never in all their time together had she come here unannounced. It made him continue to wonder what prompted her visit.

Without Kai, his life had become almost meaningless. He needed to find a way to explain everything. Surely, if given the chance, she would forgive him, and they could move on. He gulped down his second shot, the whiskey doing nothing to soothe his anguish.

Pulling up his photos, he stared at a picture of Kai. Taken while she was asleep, he had broken their agreement of no photographs. At least he could look at her during all those hours they were apart.

But if Kai wouldn't come to him, then he'd go to her. He charged the drinks to his room and left the bar.

Chapter 21 — Cookie
The Visit

Cookie, having never visited someone who was incarcerated before, tried to calm her nerves. It had taken over two weeks for Darya to get her and Alex on Alexei's approved visitor list.

After a grueling three-and-a-half-hour ride, with Darya unusually quiet, they finally arrived. Cookie's eyes swept over the imposing entrance of the red brick building topped with a green metal roof. Alexei was being held in the high-security section of the prison, consisting of four housing units surrounded by a double razor-wired perimeter fence with an intrusion detection system.

Cookie parked in the assigned spot sent to Darya earlier in the week. They got out, and Darya lifted Alex, who was fast asleep, from his car seat. They proceeded through a metal detector at the main doors, then on to the visitors' waiting area.

Cookie looked down at the clear plastic bag serving as her purse. No regular handbags were allowed inside the prison. The strict dress code only allowed for simple clothing, excluding brown, tan, and green as these were the colors the inmates wore. Both were dressed in simple black pants, a white button-down blouse, and sweaters. They sat and waited to be called.

The room was crowded with both male and female visitors alike. A good number of children of all ages completed the mix. The frigid air inside the room chilled Cookie to the bone. She adjusted her sweater securely around her shoulders.

Twenty minutes later, after completing visitor forms, they were standing in a small room. A guard checked the contents of their plastic bags. The only items allowed were a driver's license, necessary medication, female hygiene products, and car keys. A separate tote bag for Alex allowed Darya to bring three diapers, a baby bottle, a sealed container of baby food, a plastic spoon, a sippy cup, a second plastic bag with wipes, and a change of clothes. Darya had also brought photographs of herself and Alex, as well as one of Cookie and Damien's wedding day. When all their items passed scrutiny, Cookie held Alex while a female guard searched Darya, and then it was her turn. The whole process became exhausting.

Once they were finished, they were finally led into the visiting room. Sterile and devoid of any decoration except a few vending machines, Cookie found it to be even more depressing than she imagined. Other visitors were scattered about the room. Several children whined and cried. Cookie smiled at Alex clamped on her hip. His eyes wide, he silently scanned the room. One of several guards pointed to a small table and told them to sit.

Moments later, the main door opened, and the prisoners were led inside. There were brief hugs and pecks on the cheeks, the guards alert to any improper behavior. Alexei came toward them, a broad smile on his face. Cookie tried hard to hide her shock at her father-in-law's appearance. Deep lines furrowed his brow and creased his face. Thick strands of silver threaded through his dark hair, and his prison clothes hung from his diminished frame.

"Privet," Alexei said as Darya stood and kissed his cheek. They sat back down across from one another. His eyes swept over Cookie and Alex, tears brimming in them. "So, Carlotta, I am sorry to have missed your wedding."

Perplexed and unsure of what to say, Cookie focused on Alex. "This is your grandson. Roman's little boy, Alexander."

Alexei shook his head and smiled. *"Krasivyy malen'kiy mal'chik."* He reached and patted Alex's tiny hand.

"Yes," Darya said. "He's as handsome as Roman."

Darya held up the photographs to one of the guards. He nodded, and she passed them to Alexei.

He studied the photo of Cookie and Damien standing beneath an archway of flowers. Her white lace wedding gown trailed behind her as Damien, handsome in a navy tuxedo, smiled down at her. *"Moy syn, moy syn,"* he whispered. "My son." He looked up at

Cookie. "Such a beautiful bride I have never seen before, Carlotta. Except, of course, my Darya all those many years ago."

Darya tugged at the collar of her sweater. "They are very happy together." Her face turning serious, she asked. "So, how are you, Alexei?"

"As well as I can be, in here." He hung his head and stared down at his hands for a moment. "I am sorry about our last visit. I should never have pressed you about Damien."

Busy distracting Alex so they could talk, Cookie's ears perked up at the mention of Damien's name.

"Believe me, Alexei," Darya said. "I have tried to get him to come visit, but…"

He held up his hand. "I know my asking you to try harder was wrong." He turned toward Cookie. "So, Damien coming to see me is not an option?"

"I'm afraid not," Cookie said, experiencing a combination of sadness and anger. How could he expect his son to come after everything that had happened? Not when Damien blamed his father for Roman's death. Trying to emulate a man who was nothing but a gangster and a murderer contributed to his demise. "Maybe in time," Cookie said. "But I can't make him come." She debated telling him about her pregnancy but decided against it. They had not even told Darya yet. Besides, it was doubtful Damien would ever let a child of theirs near this place.

Darya swept a hand through her long blonde hair. Her continual fidgeting led Cookie to believe something was up. Ever since she inquired about the man who sent the flowers, things seemed strained.

"I need to tell you something, Alexei," Darya said almost in a whisper. "I believe Dimitri Orlov is here in America. Were you aware of this?"

Alexei rocked back in his seat. His face twisted into an ugly scowl. "He could not be here in this country. It would be too difficult for him to get out of Russia."

"But not impossible," Darya said. "There are ways of getting out."

"What makes you think he is here?"

She glanced at Cookie. "Carlotta has seen him. He came to her shop, and then there were the flowers."

"What flowers?" Alexei demanded through clenched teeth.

"He bought them at her shop and then had them delivered to me."

Alexei glared at Cookie. "Is this true?"

She brushed back a lock of Alex's hair. After falling asleep on her lap, her legs tingled from his weight pressing down on her. Now she was supposed to talk about the man who bought a bouquet for Darya, and she had no idea who he was or why he caused such an uproar.

"Look," Cookie said, "The man had a Russian Accent. He seemed kind of creepy to me. But I didn't know who he purchased them for."

Alexei let out what sounded almost like a low growl. "Listen, Darya. You must never speak to him. Promise me if he tries to make contact, you will not acknowledge him."

Darya sat up straight, her eyes focused on Alexei. "Why? Is there something else you are not telling me?"

"Promise me," he repeated.

"Okay, okay. If that is what you want."

"You will gain nothing by talking to him. All of it is in the past."

Confused and feeling left out, Cookie asked. "What is so awful about this man? He may come to the store again. Should I be afraid?"

Alexei's anger appeared to vanish right before her eyes. His face relaxed, and he produced a smile. "No, no. Just inform Darya if he comes around again. He will not harm you in any way."

Cookie didn't believe him. The exchange between these two about this Dimitri person didn't sound good. But she didn't want things to blow up into an argument, so she let it drop.

Visiting ended, and they prepared to leave. Darya kissed Alexei's cheek again, and he leaned over to kiss Alex's forehead. "Thank you for bringing our grandson, Darya." He stared at Cookie for a moment and then reached for her hand. "Take care of my son. I am glad he is happy. Please tell him for me."

On the long ride back to New York, Cookie couldn't help wondering what had gone on all those years ago that made this ghost of a man rattle the two of them.

Maybe Damien would be able to tell her something. With all the excitement of her pregnancy, she had failed to mention the man or the flowers. If he didn't know, then she needed to press Darya for more information. The fear on her mother-in-law's face definitely signaled danger.

Chapter 22 — Damien
Questions

Damien rode the elevator to his mother's apartment. Using his spare key, he let himself inside. Darya had gone with Alex and Cookie to visit his father in prison. Although he disagreed with it, he couldn't stop Cookie from going. Out of habit, he removed his shoes and then took off his jacket and tossed it on top of the credenza in the hallway.

He still hadn't told Cookie about the note and his brief discussion with the man who left it. His decision to come here and rifle through his mother's belongings filled him with guilt. But depending on what he found, maybe it might explain some things.

Starting in the bedroom, he went over to the dresser and pulled open several drawers. Checking beneath the neat piles of lingerie, slips, and underwear made him burn inside with embarrassment, but he found nothing. Next, he entered the walk-in closet. Boxes lined the upper shelves, and he searched through those, too. Some held hats, gloves, winter scarves, and pairs of heavy socks—another filled to the brim with old photographs. His eyes stung when they landed on one of Roman's baby pictures. What he wouldn't give to have his little brother back again. He wiped his eyes and slowly closed the lid.

Next, he tackled a small file cabinet in the corner of the closet. It held copies of the deed to the penthouse, which was in his name— copies of paid utility bills and envelopes filled with letters written from prison by Alexei to his mother. Deeming them too private, he returned them to the cabinet.

Pushing back a row of dresses, the familiar wall safe came into view. Damien always knew it was there. No longer in use since Alexei went to prison, it lay open and empty.

Damien checked the two nightstands. Still nothing unusual. Discouraged, he wandered into the living room and sat on the sofa. What had his mother hidden so well that he couldn't find it anywhere? Maybe this man was lying about her knowing something.

He stood and was about to leave when his eyes landed on the tall antique secretary across the room, its polished mahogany exterior almost beckoning to him. There were three drawers below with brass pulls. One by one, he searched through them, still finding nothing but more photographs, only these were more recent. Most of Alex and others from his and Cookie's wedding. He remembered his mother mentioning she needed more albums for all the pictures she had accumulated.

Turning his attention to the drop-down desk, he noticed a keyhole. He gave the brass pull a tug, but it wouldn't open. Out of everywhere he had searched, only this piece of furniture was locked.

Where could his mother have hidden the key? He rifled through the two end table drawers next to the sofa and came up empty. He walked over to the secretary again. Kneeling, he slipped his hand under the bottom and searched.

His fingers landed on something. The key had been taped to the bottom. Crouching low, he yanked it free. Intricately carved, it weighed heavily in his hand. He inserted it into the lock and pulled down the desktop. There inside lay a large, thick, expandable file folder. Its sides bulging, it appeared to be stuffed to its capacity.

Damien grabbed it and went into the dining room. His body trembled as he set it down on the table. Guilt washing over him, he paced back and forth. Afraid to find out what was hidden inside, he almost put it back.

"Maybe it's nothing important at all," he whispered. But why then was it locked away? Still, he had no right to open it. Easing into a chair, he took a deep breath and unbound the clasp.

The pockets held envelopes addressed to his mother from Russia. Damien studied the dates. They went back over twenty years, the latest being only two years old. The name on the return address was Dimitri Orlov.

Damien had never heard the name before. Picking up the oldest envelope, he opened it and read the letter inside. He continued to read each one in succession. His heart rattled against his chest. A choking sensation filled his throat. He found it harder and harder to breathe.

After he read the final letter, he dug inside the last pocket and pulled out a plain white envelope. An official document written in Russian and stamped with a gold seal at the bottom stared back at him. It was his original birth certificate. In that moment, Damien grasped the consequences of what his mother had done and knew he could never forgive her.

Chapter 23 — Nico

After

Nico sat across from Konstantin in the Acropolis Diner, shots of Ouzo liqueur in front of them. It was past midnight, and the twenty-four-hour diner stood empty except for Dina and one of the cooks in the kitchen. Konstantin's bad mood refused to lift since the meeting with Tony and Eddie several days ago. His giving in to their deal had left its mark.

"We need to move forward," Nico said. "Let's put everything in place so the games run smoothly."

"Ha!" Konstantin snapped. "I am sick and tired of having to do things their way."

"But that's reality. Besides, an extra ten percent doesn't hurt."

Konstantin finished his shot of ouzo and slammed the glass down. "Sure, we get an extra ten percent while they get most of the profits." He snapped his fingers at Dina. She quickly came over and refilled his glass.

"Another for you, Nico?" she asked.

"No thanks," Nico replied as she smiled and then disappeared into the kitchen. "Why is she here so late? Doesn't she usually work the day shift?"

"Minka called in sick, and Dina agreed to cover. I like having her around if you know what I mean," Konstantin said, giving him a wink.

Nico's long-held suspicions regarding Dina and Konstantin's relationship were cemented with that last statement. Now he understood the expensive bracelets and rings he had noticed her wearing lately came with a price.

"I'll let Stavros pick a couple of men to monitor the games," Konstantin said. "But I will tell you, Nico. No more bowing down to Tony Morello."

"Be careful, you still need him for the Jersey Seaport. Our goods won't get through customs without him."

"This is true," Konstantin said. He rubbed at the dark stubble under his chin. "I have no trouble dealing with the Albanians and Russians, but Morello gets under my skin."

"When does the next shipment come in?" Nico asked.

"Not for several more weeks. I am hoping to find another way to bring them in without using the Jersey Seaport."

Nico sighed. "I don't think you have any other choice. Besides, if Tony Morello finds out, there will be even more trouble ahead."

Konstantin waved his hand. "Let me worry about it. I cannot be a puppet on a string much longer." He picked up his cell phone. "I will call Stavros now. It is strange he did not show up today."

Nico's pulse ticked up a notch. "That's not like him."

"Voicemail again. I have already left three messages. Check the usual places tonight and then swing by his place in the morning, Nico. Make sure he is okay."

Nico nodded and left the diner. For the rest of the night, he checked the local clubs, restaurants, and bars Stavros sometimes hung out in. No one had seen him. His thoughts kept returning to the meeting with Tony Morello, particularly how angry he became when Konstantin brought Stavros with him.

Early the next morning, he drove to Stavros' house in Ozone Park, Queens. The simple two-story brick and frame structure sat sandwiched between a long line of similar-looking houses. He glanced around, looking for Stavros' black Ford Expedition, but didn't see it parked anywhere on the street. He climbed up the steps and rang the bell. There was a shuffle of feet, and the door opened. Stavros' wife, Amelia, her long auburn hair swept back in a twist, smiled up at him. Her brightly colored, floral print dress complemented her store-bought tanned skin.

"Nico. It's so good to see you."

"How are you, Amelia?" Nico asked, his intuition still telling him something was wrong.

"Fine. Come inside."

He followed her into the living room and sat across from her in a chair opposite a long beige sofa. "Is Stavros home?" he asked.

"No. He left yesterday morning. Something about important business he needed to take care of."

Fearing her answer, he asked. "When did he get back?"

"He hasn't come home yet." Her tanned face slowly evaporated into a pasty white. "Is he okay? I mean, he's stayed away before. His working for Konstantin isn't an easy job."

Nico got up. "I'm sure he's fine. Let me do some more checking, and you call me as soon as you hear from him."

Amelia nodded and accompanied him to the door. She bit her bottom lip, her eyes bore into his. "Please, Nico," she said. "Find him. Find my husband."

Nico got back into his car and called Konstantin. "I just spoke to Amelia. He left early yesterday. He hasn't been home since."

"You are certain you covered all the places you think he might be?"

"Yes."

"This is not good. I am starting to get suspicious. If anything has happened to him because of our meeting, there will be trouble, Nico. I will not stand for idle killing just because someone's feelings are hurt."

The line went dead. Nico drove to his apartment, panic rising inside him. He steadied his shaking hands and called Monica on one of his burner phones. "We need to meet. Tear Drop Park, same place … in an hour."

***

When he arrived at the park, she was already sitting on the same bench as before, dressed down in jeans and a grey turtleneck. He hurried over and sat beside her.

"What's going on, Nico? Why the urgent call?" she asked.

He relayed everything about the meeting. "Now, Stavros is missing. I think Tony Morello was involved in it. He's getting worse—more demanding and headstrong about what he wants. If Eddie Marconi hadn't been there to smooth things out, I'm not sure an agreement would have been made between Tony and Konstantin."

"Okay, unless his dead body turns up, you really can't be sure what happened to Stavros."

Nico gritted his teeth. "I don't need to see a body. I've been under long enough. I know how things work. I'm positive Konstantin will confront Tony Morello, and if that happens, we go into an all-out war."

"Let's say you're right," Monica said. "There hasn't been a war of any kind in years. Yes, people do disappear on occasion, but the last thing the big bosses want is to draw attention to themselves. Those days are over. This is why it makes everything harder for the Bureau. Nothing is out in the open anymore."

Nico sighed. "I don't think Tony's playing by those rules."

"As a Capo, he has to," Monica said. "If he puts out a hit on anyone outside his crew without permission, his life is on the line."

He rubbed the back of his neck and sighed. "Maybe he got permission."

"Right now, I'm more worried about you, Nico. I can tell you're stressed beyond normal limits. It might be time for you to come in. The intel you've managed to gather so far is good. We can seek prosecution with that."

"No!" Nico said through clenched teeth. "I need more time to make sure these people are put where they belong. There's a shipment of drugs arriving soon. A pretty big one. It's coming in on

Konstantin's dime. Between that and all their gambling operations, we should be golden."

"Okay. For now, I'm going to trust you're making the right decision. As a matter of fact, I'm putting someone else undercover with you. She is going to apply for a job at the Acropolis Diner. I need you to make certain she gets that job."

"How experienced is she?"

"Very," Monica said. "It's the reason I chose her, and our ADIC agrees. Her name is Kai Nez. Of course, we'll set up a false background for her."

"Brooke Adams agreed to this?"

"Yes. She'll be Kai's handler. Is that a problem?"

There were things he could tell her about Brooke, but he chose not to. When the time was right, he'd let Monica in on how his cover was almost blown because of Brooke Adams. How he nearly lost his life. But not yet. He'd hold back on that for a bit. Unfortunately, Brooke was his superior, and she could order him to end the operation and come in.

Nico shook his head. "No. Not a problem at all." He got up. "I'll be in touch. Call me when Kai Nez is ready. Konstantin trusts me. I'll make up a story, get her hired."

"Great," Monica said. "Can I ask you one other thing?"

"Sure."

"What did you mean when you said Eddie Marconi smoothed things over?"

"Seems he's determined to keep the peace. Nothing like Morello at all. He persuaded him to agree to a deal he knew nothing about. Apparently, the extra ten percent was never discussed prior to the meeting."

"I see," Monica said.

"I'll let you know if Stavros shows up. Maybe it's a false alarm." Nico moved down the path and out of the park.

Later, at home, he grabbed a cold bottle of beer from the fridge. The last twenty-four hours had nearly sucked up all his reserve. It worried him how astute Monica was. Her perception of him being under too long made the trembling in his body worse.

Nico popped the cap and took several swallows, the cool sensation of the beer making its way through his body. He needed to complete the entire operation. Once everything was behind him, he could relax again. That is, if he made it out alive.

Chapter 24 — Eddie
A Dilemma

Eddie sat in one of the empty gaming rooms and finished counting the money from his crew. The backroom gambling joints still made profits over and above what he kicked up to Paulie. His offshore gambling operations were also pulling their weight, and with the Greek game added, he would be flush.

He checked his watch and saw it was a little past eight in the evening. He tucked the money inside a hidden safe beneath the floorboards. With the two car wash businesses and the purchase of Romano's Restaurant, he would give Paulie his cut tomorrow and start laundering his earnings again to make them appear legitimate.

The restaurant opportunity had come as a surprise. When the owner, Joe Romano, told Eddie he was going to retire, he jumped at the chance to buy the place. Memories of his and Monica's many dinners there were always at the back of his mind every time he was there. Knowing little about the restaurant business, keeping the original staff on had been a godsend, and his degree in hospitality came in handy as well. Overall, it was a smart move.

Eddie's cell phone buzzed. He glanced at the unfamiliar number. "Hello, who's this?"

"It's Nico Vasilios. Konstantin gave me your number."

"Why the call?" Eddie asked.

"I think we need to meet. I'll come anywhere you say. It's important."

Tired and hungry, Eddie gave him the address for Romano's. "Be there in thirty minutes, otherwise, don't come." He was in no mood to talk about business, but the call from Nico rattled him a bit. Maybe they were thinking of backing out of their agreement.

Arriving at Romano's, he parked and made his way inside. The usual aroma of garlic, onions, and rich red gravy hung in the air. Every seat at the long, sleek mahogany bar was occupied. Soft Italian music played in the background.

After he purchased the place, he had the red checked tablecloths replaced with crisp white linen. Fancy tea lights sat in the center of each one. Most of the tables were filled except for a small table for two in the rear, usually reserved for him.

Federico, a long-time waiter at the restaurant, came toward him. "Good evening, Mr. Marconi. Will you be dining alone?"

"No," Eddie said. "I'm expecting someone. I'll sit at my usual table in the back. Just a vodka and tonic for now."

Federico nodded and headed for the bar, while Eddie took a seat. He checked the time. Nico had ten minutes left. He meant what he said.

With only two minutes to spare, Nico rushed through the door. Eddie signaled to him. They shook hands, and Nico sat. "I like a guy who's on time," Eddie said. "Drink?"

"Sure," Nico said. "I'll have a whiskey, neat."

After Federico set the drink down, Eddie studied Nico's body language. His former job in Arizona at the resort had taught him a lot about a person's demeanor. "I'm going to assume there is some sort of problem, otherwise, you wouldn't be here."

Nico nodded and sipped his whiskey. "I'm hoping you could tell me if there's one."

"Look, I've had a long day. I don't have the patience to sit and play guessing games."

"Okay, I'll get to the point. Stavros Papadakis is missing."

"Who?" Eddie asked.

"Konstantin's bodyguard. The one he brought to the meeting."

"Oh," Eddie said. "Sorry, I couldn't place the name. But what does this have to do with me?"

"It's not so much you," Nico said. "I think your friend Tony Morello had something to do with it."

Eddie drew back in his chair. "That's a helluva accusation, Nico."

"But it's the only thing that makes sense. You saw how upset Tony was."

Tony's behavior of late had worried him, too. True, he pulled no punches when someone needed what he called a behavior adjustment, but to kill someone from the Greek Mafia was out of the question unless Paulie sanctioned it.

"Before things go any further, let me talk to Tony, find out if he's involved," Eddie said.

"And if he is?"

"One step at a time, Nico. I'm not committing to something I'm not sure even happened. Your guy could be missing for a lot of reasons."

"Not likely, Eddie. Stavros is devoted to Konstantin. The reason I came to you first is my boss is already getting ideas in his head regarding Tony being responsible."

"Like I said, let me find out if Tony's involved."

Nico finished his drink and got up. "Fair enough. But don't take too long. Konstantin is not a patient man."

After Nico left, Eddie, his stomach rumbling, ordered chicken parmigiana and a side of pasta. When the food came, he practically inhaled it. After a solid day with his crew pulling in good money, he wasn't going to let Nico's suspicions spoil his appetite. Tony might be a hothead at times, but doing something that could start a war between them and the Greeks was out of the question. He finished his meal and left the restaurant. Without even realizing it, he found himself driving past Monica's place. He pulled in across the street, parked, and killed the engine. The lights were on in the front bedroom where Andrew slept. Behind the curtains, a shadow moved about the room. A few minutes later, the light went out. He assumed Monica must have had a hard time getting Andrew to sleep.

Tired, he started the engine and was about to drive away when the front door flew open and Monica came out carrying Andrew. She hurried down the steps, only a car fob in her hand.

Eddie got out and ran over to them. Monica's eyes widened when she saw him, and her bottom lip trembled. In all the time he knew her, he had never seen that look on her face before.

"Monica, what's going on?" he asked, glancing from her to Andrew.

"I'm not sure. He's burning up. I tried to bring the fever down, but nothing worked. I need to get him to the emergency room."

"Come on, get in my car. I'll take you."

Eddie's foot pressed hard against the gas pedal all the way to Staten Island Hospital. Andrew clung to Monica, his face flushed a deep red. Several moans escaped his lips. After careening around corners and running two red lights, they pulled up to the ER. Eddie got out and opened the door for Monica. She swept past him and ran inside.

The next several hours found them answering what felt like a million questions while the pediatrician on call, a Dr. Morgan, examined Andrew. At one point, Monica refused to let go of Andrew's hand.

"Please, Ms. Cappelino. I need to examine him more thoroughly."

Eddie gently led her away to the opposite side of the room. "Let him do what he needs to, Monica. Everything is going to be okay."

"You don't know that," she said, her voice filled with worry. "He's been sick before but never this bad. He started complaining after dinner, but I thought it was just his usual whining when he's over tired. I got him ready for bed, but then…" Tears streaked down her face. "I should have paid more attention. This is all my fault."

Eddie wrapped his arm around her. "It's no one's fault. Kids get sick. You're a good mother, Monica. Don't start blaming yourself."

Dr. Morgan turned toward them. "We need a blood sample, Ms. Cappelino. So, now's the time he's going to need handholding.

"Let me," Eddie said. "Please, I can keep him calm."

Monica nodded as Eddie approached Andrew. He sat and smoothed back his dark curls.

"Remember how I told you men need to be brave so they can take care of things."

Andrew nodded. "Yes. I remember, Daddy."

"Okay, so for you to get better, the doctor needs to do a test. He needs a tiny bit of your blood to find out why you got so sick. So, while they do the test, you hold my hand and look at me. This is the time to be brave, Andrew."

His feverish eyes on Eddie, he reached out his hand. Over the next few minutes, without Andrew saying a word, they drew a sample and rushed it to the lab. Eddie beamed with pride at his little boy. "You did well, Andrew. Mommy and Daddy are proud of you."

Medication was administered to bring Andrew's fever down, and since they were able to get him to take fluids, there was no need for an intravenous line, which made Eddie sigh with relief.

It felt like an eternity before the test results came back. "Bacterial Infection," Doctor Morgan announced. "I've prescribed antibiotics, and as soon as his fever breaks, you can take him home."

"Thanks," Eddie said. He vowed right then and there he would never tell Monica just how scared he had been when they first brought Andrew to the hospital. Seeing his son so sick made him weak in the knees. He couldn't even process the possibility of losing him.

It was dawn by the time they climbed the steps to Monica's house and put a sleeping Andrew to bed. Little talk had passed between them while they sat at Andrew's bedside earlier and then on the drive home.

"Coffee?" Monica asked, heading for the kitchen.

"Absolutely," Eddie said, following behind and tossing his jacket on the back of a chair.

Seated together at her kitchen table summoned memories of so many times they had sat here before. Eddie's chest swelled, a longing deep inside coming to the surface. He studied Monica's exhausted face, the puffiness beneath her heavy eyelids, and the tumble of curls in disarray.

"What?" she said, noticing his stare.

"You look more beautiful than ever. I think worrying becomes you."

"Very funny," she mocked. "I'm not so sure what to say about how you look."

Eddie chuckled. "I'm still the same handsome devil you fell in love with."

"Devil being the operative word," she shot back. Her face softened as she added, "I'm so glad you were with me tonight. Andrew scared the heck out of me. How did you happen to be right outside my door?"

Eddie sighed and sipped his coffee. "I honestly can't say. I left Romano's and, for whatever reason, ended up on your block. Do you believe in fate?"

"I'm not sure. All I know is sometimes people end up right where they're supposed to be."

"And us?" Eddie asked. "Where are we supposed to be?" Saddened by the way she averted her eyes, he pressed on. "You don't want to answer, do you?"

Monica got up and carried her cup to the sink, her back turned to him. "I think we are exactly where we should be right now." She swung around, the softness gone from her face. "Don't ruin things, Eddie. Tonight, we pulled together. It was important for Andrew to see that. I'm glad you were with me, but there is nothing more to it."

The ache inside him grew. He rose and handed her his empty cup. "Okay, Monica. We both felt something when we kissed. But it's alright if you wanna make believe you didn't because I know the truth." He grabbed his jacket and slipped it on.

"We're both tired, so I'm gonna go. Kiss Andrew for me when he wakes up. If you need anything, you know how to find me."

Outside in the brisk morning air, Eddie sucked in a deep breath and stretched. If only Monica weren't so stubborn. Why couldn't she just admit she still loved him?

Word on the street said she was dating some doctor. But it couldn't be serious. Not the way she returned that kiss. He dated on and off, mainly to keep Paulie at bay and out of his personal business. Besides, no one made him feel the way Monica did.

Thankfully, his little boy was okay. He whistled a soft tune as he crossed the street to his car. It had been a stressful night, and he was ready to go home and get some sleep.

This thing with the Greeks and Tony Morello could wait until later. He started his car and was about to pull away when his cell rang. It was Paulie.

"Come to the club, Eddie. Rumors are flying around, and I don't like what I'm hearing."

Eddie sighed. Apparently, he wouldn't be getting any sleep for quite some time.

***

Eddie went down the steps to the basement of Paulie's Social Club. The place was used strictly for in-house games and socializing among Paulie's men. He found Paulie, dressed in his usual business suit, sitting at the bar with a cup of coffee in his hand. The place was empty except for the two of them.

"Come, sit down," Paulie said. "Can I get you anything?"

Eddie shook his head. "No thanks. Long night with my kid in the emergency room."

"Everything okay?"

"Yeah, he's good now."

Paulie pointed to the long sectional sofa. "Let's get more comfortable."

Eddie sat down a few feet away from him. His heart thumped a bit, and he tensed. His boss calling him this early in the morning to meet couldn't be a good sign.

"I'll make this simple," Paulie said. "You met with the Greeks, a deal was cut, and now one of them is missing. How is that okay?"

"I just heard," Eddie said. "Nico came to see me."

"Yeah, and I got a call from Konstantin. A threatening call." He quirked an eyebrow. His silver hair gleamed under the recessed lights. "I don't like those kinds of calls, Eddie."

"I was as surprised as you when Nico showed up. We all ended on good terms. We would never go after someone inside or outside the family unless you sanctioned it."

"By we, I'm guessing that means you and Tony?"

Eddie shook his head. "Correct."

"Konstantin told me Tony was a bit of a hothead at the meeting. He said if it weren't for you, he wouldn't have done any deal."

"Maybe," Eddie said. "Tony got squirrely because I didn't run the percentage by him beforehand. But I knew it was the only way things were gonna move forward."

Paulie grew quiet and sipped some coffee. Minutes ticked by. Eddie's palms grew damp. He wanted to jump out of his skin. You could never tell which way Paulie was gonna lean.

"Look," Paulie finally said. "The two of you are my best earners. I've never had any trouble before with either one of you. So, tell me. Do I need to worry?"

"Not at all," Eddie lied. "Like I told Nico, Konstantin's man could have gone missing for a million reasons. Maybe he owed money, or perhaps he had a gambling habit his boss was unaware of. Of course, they looked at us first because—"

"Because," Paulie's eyes cut through Eddie like steel. "Tony didn't act the way he should have. You need to have a talk with him. Tell him if a body shows up that shouldn't, we're gonna have issues, me and him."

"Sure," Eddie said. "But you don't need to worry. Nothing's gonna show up because nothing happened."

Paulie nodded in his direction. "You can go."

Eddie got up. "I'll talk to Tony, make sure he controls himself better." Weariness overtaking him, he shuffled over to the stairs. Outside, he breathed in the morning air and let out a long breath.

Wanting to get things over with, he sent a text to Tony telling him they needed to meet tonight. He gave him an address and then drove home, his gut telling him Tony might be their undoing.

***

After dinner, and over too many drinks later that evening, Eddie sat with Tony in a private room at a popular Staten Island restaurant. Feeling refreshed after getting some sleep, he decided to dive right in.

"I got called on the carpet today."

Tony ignored him. His eyes scanned the room. "This is a really neat place. Can't believe I'm on Staten Island."

"Why? Don't you think we have nice restaurants?"

"Well, the only one I've been to is yours. But looking around here, I think Romano's needs to step up its game."

"Romano's is fine the way it is," Eddie said, bristling. "It's a local family place, been around a long time."

Tony shook his head. "Still, you could take some cues from this one."

Eddie drummed his fingers on the table top. "Did you hear what I said earlier?"

"Yeah, yeah, I heard you. The carpet." Tony smiled and swallowed his fourth drink.

"Did you have something done to Konstantin's man?"

"Of course not," Tony said. "I'm not stupid."

Eddie eyed him. "Somehow, I don't believe you. I'm being serious when I tell you that you better convince Paulie that guy is walking upright somewhere."

Tony threw up his hands. "Scout's honor. I never touched him."

"First of all, you were never a scout. Second, you wouldn't do it yourself."

Tony set his drink down and leaned in. "You're becoming annoying, Staten Island."

He hadn't heard Tony call him that in a long time, and it made him even more irritated. "I can promise you this," Eddie said. "I'm not taking the fall for a hit that was never sanctioned just because you got your feelings hurt."

"Calm down," Tony said, leaning away. "No one's taking a fall. I'll talk to Paulie."

"Good luck with that. He already heard how you blew up at the meeting from Konstantin."

Tony's face hardened. "I didn't blow up. I wanted them to remember who's in charge. Paulie would respect that."

"You haven't been the same since the break-up with Kai."

Tony dipped his head and stared down into his drink. "I'm working on getting her back. I need a chance to explain."

"Bad move," Eddie said. "You need to let go."

Tony got up. "Enough said. I think we're done here."

Eddie saw it was no use continuing the conversation. He didn't want anything to happen to Tony, but at the same time, he needed to consider the stakes. Andrew growing up without him wasn't an option.

Eddie eased up to his feet. The room suddenly grew too hot, and things looked a bit fuzzy. He hadn't drunk this much in a long time. They weaved their way down the long hallway leading out to the main dining room. Tony swayed and stopped short, making Eddie almost tumble into him.

"Now, what have we here?" Tony asked.

Eddie followed his line of vision. His heart gave a jolt. There, across the room, looking as sexy as ever, the love of his life was having dinner with another man.

Chapter 25 — Monica
Double Whammy

With the morning sunlight held at bay by the dark blinds in the conference room, Monica pointed to the large two-hundred-inch projector screen. A photograph of Stavros Papadakis stared back at the task force.

"Our latest intel from Nico Vasilios says this man went missing after a meeting between the Greeks and the Mob. He is Konstantin Zervas's bodyguard and right-hand man. It seems the apple cart was upset when he brought him to the meeting after he was told not to bring any extra men besides Nico."

"Now," Monica continued. "The attendees were Tony Morello, Eddie Marconi, and Stan Amato, who is Austin's C.I. and part of Morello's crew."

"Wait a minute," Kai said. "If Stan Amato was there, why would that upset things if Stavros Papadakis came, too. Both those men are on equal footing."

"You're right," Monica said. "From what Nico told me, Morello had Stan hidden in another room. I guess for protection, just in case anything went wrong."

"So, Morello wasn't playing fair," Austin said. "My C.I. alluded to the fact there might be trouble at the meeting."

Monica nodded. "It appears that way. Nico said Konstantin threatened to leave unless they allowed Stavros to stay. Fast forward, and now he's missing."

"Which is a pretty big deal," Brooke said. "If Morello made him disappear, it could mean an all-out war."

"My C.I. has told me he believes Tony is power hungry," Austin said. "He said if anything happens to Paulie 'the Shiv' Martello, we should be looking at him for it."

"That's huge," Austin." Monica said. "For something like that to happen, the heads of the five families would have to sanction it."

Austin nodded. "But that's not all. He claims Tony took out Frank 'The Razor' Uzelli. Says he's buried somewhere out west in the desert. He swore he got permission from Paulie to get rid of him."

Monica and Kai both looked at each other at the same time. "That could explain a lot," Kai said. "Could be the reason why Frank never showed up when we staked out the border last year after the seaport raid. The illegal weapons never made it there either."

"And yet," Monica added. "We learned later on they did land in the hands of the Mexican Cartel."

"Unless someone talks, the body will never be found," Austin said.

"There is a shipment of drugs coming in soon," Monica said. "This one is on Konstantin's dime."

"Keep on top of your C.I. for that one, Austin," Brooke said. "If he wants the deal we promised him, then he's got to keep feeding us."

Monica turned to Kai. "I spoke to Nico about you going under. He'll get you in with Konstantin Zervas. He says it's a sure bet. You'll be staying in the apartment the Bureau rented close to the diner.

"I'm ready," Kai said. "If I get the job, they can move my things on Friday."

"In the meantime, Austin, see if Stan has anything regarding Stavros."

"Will do."

"I think we're finished here," Brooke said. "Monica, please stay a minute."

After the conference room emptied, Monica sat across from Brooke, already aware of the reason she was asked to remain.

"Look," Brooke said. "Eddie Marconi attended that meeting. But I want to hear how you feel about it. Do you need to step away?"

"Absolutely not. I've told you before. Eddie goes away with the rest of them. But there is one other thing Nico told me."

"What's that?"

"That meeting turned out to be extremely tense. It was Eddie who managed to cool everyone down and get the deal done."

Brook eyed her for a moment. "So, what, you want to give him a pat on the back?"

"No, no. It just proves what Nico's been saying regarding Tony Morello being power hungry. Nico said the deal almost didn't happen because of him. I believe there's lots more trouble ahead, especially if Stavros isn't found alive. I can't imagine Paulie letting Tony get away with a hit without his knowledge, and at the same time, I can't imagine Tony bowing down to Paulie."

"So, you think there's going to be a major upheaval inside the five families?"

"Yes. Unless someone gets to Tony first."

***

Later that day, Monica sat in her office, thinking about the trip to the emergency room with Eddie. Witnessing how well he handled the crisis with Andrew only made her worry for him even more. The thought of having to arrest the father of her child one day made her feel sick inside. Would he still love her then? Even worse, how could she explain it to Andrew?

She was supposed to see Chase this evening for a double date with Cookie and Damien. But all she could think about was Eddie.

His face, those nautical blue eyes, his disarming smile, and, of course, the kiss. A kiss that had shaken her to the core.

A kiss she had willingly returned. But she could never admit to him or anyone else how much she still loved him.

Her feelings raged back and forth between anger at herself for being weak and her desire to be with him. But she couldn't live her life pining away for something that would never be. She needed to give this thing with Chase a chance, the first man to have made her forget about Eddie for one night—made her feel everything would be okay without him.

Monica pulled up Eddie's file on her computer. She followed any little bit of intel about him, including his purchase of Romano's, their favorite restaurant. How many nights had they sat at their special table by the window? Did he think of her every time he was there, the same way she did when she passed by?

Her eyes filled, blurring his picture. "I *will* move on without you, Eddie," she whispered.

***

Monica relaxed into the grey, tufted velvet chair at Violetta's Restaurant on Hyland Boulevard. Chase sat next to her, while Cookie and Damien sat opposite them. After dropping Andrew off at her parents' house, she took extra time to get ready for her date tonight. She slipped on a black cocktail dress with a sequined lace bodice, three cutouts at the neckline, ruching down the front, and cap sleeves. Gathering up her hair into a twist, she let just a few curls fall softly around her face. Black heels completed the look.

Her glass of Chardonnay lifted the heaviness she'd been feeling all day at work. The soft lighting and rich mahogany coffered ceilings put her at ease. The walls, which held 10,000 wine corks arranged between wooden slats of varying shades of wood, caught her eye. Past the plush banquettes, a gleaming black bar top glittered.

Delighted by Cookie's pregnancy, Monica studied her friend. After everything she had gone through, she deserved every happiness.

"How have you been feeling?" Monica asked.

"Lucky," Cookie said. "No morning sickness." She looked longingly at Monica's glass of wine. "Boy, the sacrifices you have to make just to push a kid out."

Monica giggled. "You think not having a glass of wine is a sacrifice? Wait until the baby comes and keeps you up half the night. Your days will revolve around catering to your child twenty-four-seven. Everything else becomes unimportant, just background noise."

"What about you?" Chase said, nodding toward Damien. "Ready to be a father?"

"Yeah, sure," Damien said.

It didn't escape Monica ever since they arrived at the restaurant, Damien appeared to be preoccupied. She hoped he and Cookie didn't have words earlier.

The waiter came to take their dinner orders, and Chase smiled at Monica. "What are you thinking of having?"

"I think the pan-seared salmon looks good."

"I'll have the same," Cookie piped in. Both men ordered steak, and after the waiter left, Cookie got up. "Restroom is calling once again. All I do is pee lately."

Monica laughed. "I'll join you. Excuse us, fellas."

Inside the restroom, Monica checked herself in the mirror while Cookie entered a stall.

"Is everything okay with you and Damien?"

Cookie finished and joined her at the sink. Soaping her hands, she said, "Something isn't right. We didn't fight, but he's been acting funny these past few days." She frowned and grabbed a paper towel. "I don't know if it's because I accompanied his mother to Allenwood—"

"You went to see Alexei Volkov?" Monica cut in.

Cookie folded her arms. "Excuse me, but he is my father-in-law after all."

"Sorry. I didn't think you would visit him."

"It's not like I felt like going. Darya asked me. She wanted him to see his grandson."

"Roman's boy?" Monica asked.

"Yes. How could I say no, especially after that fabulous engagement party she threw for us and all her help with the wedding? I thought Damien understood, but now I'm not sure what to think. I've asked him if anything is wrong, but he denies it."

"Well, it's obvious something is," Monica said.

Cookie sighed. "It will all come out sooner or later, that's the way Damien is." Her eyes swept over Monica. "You look mighty sexy. Expecting to get some tonight?"

"I'm trying very hard to move on," Monica said. She told Cookie about Andrew, Eddie, and the hospital. "He was so good with me, with Andrew, with everything."

"Did something happen after the hospital?" Cookie asked.

"No. He wanted it to, but no, nothing happened between us. I can't go back there again, even if I want to. My job at the Bureau comes before Eddie. Chase is a great guy. I want to give him a chance."

"You're right," Cookie said. "Okay, no more talk about Eddie. Let's get back to the table."

Their meals came, and the conversation between them was light. When the waiter brought the dessert menu, Monica declined.

"Oh, come on. Share something with me," Chase said.

"Well, nobody has to twist my arm," Cookie said. "I'll have the pistachio panna cotta."

"Okay," Monica said, giving in. "Let's do the cookie butter tiramisu."

"There's a secret room in this place." Cookie said. "They call it the Button Room. It's by invitation only."

"Yeah," Chase said. "I heard something about that."

The waiter brought their desserts. Monica stuck her fork into the sweet, creamy mascarpone filling and held it up to Chase. His eyes locked on hers, the desire in them sending a chill down her spine. He finished the bit of cake and then scooped up more and brought it over to her lips.

"How cute," a voice said. A voice Monica would recognize anywhere. She turned and raised her head. Eddie and Tony stood next to the table.

Unable to move or speak, she stared up at the two of them. Where did they come from? How could this be happening to her?

"Aren't you going to introduce me?" Eddie said, smiling at Chase.

"Go away, Eddie," Cookie blurted out. "Leave Monica alone."

"Boy, you're a feisty one," Tony said, eyeing Cookie.

Cookie pushed her chair back. "Stick around and I'll show you how feisty."

Tony smirked. "Am I supposed to be scared?"

Cookie went to stand up, but Damien leaned over and grabbed her arm. "Please, sit down. Ignore him. They're both drunk."

Chase set his fork down and looked at Monica. "Who are they?"

Monica took a breath. Several of the other customers were now focused on their table. She pushed her chair back and got up. "Chase, this is Eddie, Andrew's father." Pointing at a still wobbly Tony, she said. "And this is an acquaintance of his. Excuse us a moment."

Tony backed away and then bowed, an impish grin on his face. "Please continue eating."

Monica shoved Eddie forward, who called over his shoulder, "Nice meeting you, Chaz."

Turning, she pointed at Tony, "You, too. Let's go."

Tony glanced at Chase. "Oh, sorry," he blurted out. "It seems your date is stepping away. Not to worry, she'll return shortly."

Outside the restaurant, Tony smiled at Monica and then moved discreetly away from the two. Heat soaring through her body, she pushed Eddie up against the window of the restaurant.

"What the hell, Eddie?"

"I just wanted to say hello."

She drew back from the overwhelming odor of alcohol on his breath. "Bullshit!" Her fingers curled while blood rushed to her head. "How could you embarrass me like that?" She jerked her thumb toward Tony. "And then there's this clown."

"Clown?" Tony said. "Who me?"

"Yeah, you," Monica said. "You're both drunk." She turned back to Eddie, who swayed back and forth. "If you ever see me out with someone again, walk away, Eddie. Do you hear me? Walk away."

Eddie nodded. His hand cupped her face. "You look so beautiful. I remember when you used to dress like that for me."

Monica brushed his hand away. "Stop it." Before he could react, she reached into his pocket and grabbed his car keys. "Call an Uber and go home. Neither one of you is in any condition to drive."

Tony steadied himself and attempted to walk over to her. "If you see Kai, tell her I'm sorry. Tell her I can explain everything."

About to go back inside, Monica stopped cold. "What are you talking about?"

"Just tell her that for me, please." He looked over at Eddie and pulled out his cell phone. "Come on, let's go. I'll call an Uber."

Monica prepared to go inside. She stared at Eddie's car keys. She'd text him and let him know she would drop them into his mailbox.

It didn't feel good seeing first-hand how tight Eddie and Tony Morello were. But the bigger shock, besides Eddie being here, was Tony's remark about Kai.

Did Kai lie about not seeing him anymore? If so, how long had it been going on? Here she was about to go undercover, and Monica wasn't sure if she could trust her.

Straightening her dress, she stepped through the doors of the restaurant, her night ruined by Eddie Marconi once again.

Chapter 26 — Kai
The Interview

Kai zipped the beige skirt and then slipped into a pale pink silk blouse, leaving the top two buttons open at the neck. The skirt hit high above the knee, but not too high, and the blouse showed only a slight hint of cleavage. Her white pumps accentuated her shapely legs. Deciding to leave her long hair pulled back into a ponytail, she stepped in front of the mirror for one last look.

Her interview with Konstantin this afternoon couldn't come soon enough. Going undercover had come just in time to keep her from dwelling on Tony. Since they had only used burner phones, she suspected he got her cell number from Eddie. Refusing to respond to his numerous text messages and calls, she finally blocked his number and deleted any communication from him.

Yesterday, with Andrew scheduled for a follow-up visit at the doctor, Monica had briefed her over the phone on the story Nico set up. Kai caught an odd tone in her voice. She tried pressing her further, but Monica insisted nothing was wrong.

On the drive to the Acropolis diner, she rehearsed everything in her head. As she drew closer, the adrenaline rush of going undercover crested inside her. She squeezed into what looked like the last spot in the parking lot. Slowly inhaling and then letting out a long breath, she whispered, "Here we go." Hopefully, the job would be hers.

Inside, she took stock of the décor, which was just a fraction above the typical diner. Maroon booths hugging the walls, plus some square tables and chairs with colorful pendulum lights hanging above them. Various pictures depicting locales in Greece covered half the walls.

The long counter in front held oversized cakes and freshly baked cookies—the familiar smell of the sweets mixed with the odor of grilled meat. Servers soared around the room, taking orders and delivering food and beverages. A lone busboy was clearing a booth.

A young girl behind the counter smiled at her. "Can I help you?"

"Yes, I have an appointment with Mr. Konstantin Zervas."

"One moment. I'll go and get him."

There was no mistaking Konstantin as he came through the swinging kitchen doors. Tall, broad-shouldered, with thick silver hair and dark eyes exactly like the photographs in the FBI files. The stern expression on his face disappeared, and he stretched out his hand.

"You must be Kathleen, Nico's cousin."

Kai reached and shook his hand. "Yes, Kathleen Vasilios, but everyone calls me Kitty."

"Come. I have an office in the back. We can talk there."

Kai followed him through the kitchen, where mayhem prevailed. Cooks chopped and diced, pots boiled on the twelve-burner stove, and burgers sizzled on the grill. At the rear of the kitchen, he led Kai through another door and down a short hallway.

Konstantin's office held a small desk, too small, Kai thought, for a man his size. Stacks of folders, a mountain of papers, and a laptop computer covered the surface. Two chairs and two tall filing cabinets completed the room. The stark white walls were bare.

"Please sit," Konstantin said and pointed to the chair opposite his desk. He sat and rested his elbows on top, his hands clasped together.

"Thank you for taking the time to see me," Kai said.

"Nico is very special to me, so when he told me what happened, I immediately agreed to meet with you. Tell me, how are you doing now after…" He motioned with his hand.

Kai blinked several times, forcing tears. A trick she had mastered since childhood, when she was afraid of getting in trouble with her mother. She opened her purse and drew out a tissue.

Konstantin, visibly upset, shook his head. "No, no. We don't have to talk about it."

"It's okay. The accident happened a little over three years ago. My parents were driving to their hotel in Patras. It was their second time returning to the city. They fell in love with it one summer on vacation and vowed to go back again."

"Ah, yes," Konstantin said. "One of my favorite cities at the foot of Mount Panachaïkó.

"The man who hit them was drunk," Kai continued. "They were killed instantly," she said, dabbing at her eyes. As an only child, I inherited everything."

"Yes, Nico told me, you have enough money but would like something to occupy your time. I told him I needed a hostess. None of my current employees is suited for the job. I'm looking for someone who can make a great first impression and is customer-friendly. Do you have any experience?"

"I'm kind of ashamed to say my parents spoiled me. I have an accounting degree, but I never put it to good use. I traveled extensively and was able to do as I pleased. But I don't want you to think I didn't appreciate the life my parents afforded me."

"I see," Konstantin said. "Excuse me if I'm being too forward, but you don't have the features of a Greek woman. Usually, I can spot them right away."

"Yes, that's because my mother was not Greek. She was descended from the Navajo. It's a funny story. I mean … how they met."

"I would be interested to hear it. That is, if you don't mind."

"Not at all. I love telling the story." Kai settled back into the chair and crossed her legs, making sure her skirt revealed just a bit too much. "You see, my father traveled a lot for business, and he was scouting some real estate for his commercial company when he became ill. He ended up in the hospital where my mother worked as a nurse." Kai let her eyes mist again. "My father said, he took one look at her and knew this was the woman he was going to marry."

"Well, that is quite a story," Konstantin said. "So, the rest is history, as they say?"

"Well, yes and no. You see, my mother's people did not want her to marry outside the Navajo Tribe. They were afraid she would give up all her native traditions. But she persisted, and in the end, they married two years later."

"And did she give them up?" Konstantin asked. "I mean, her traditions."

"No. She taught me many things about her culture, even though her family never spoke to her again. I was never able to meet any of her people."

Konstantin frowned. "How sad."

"Yes," Kai said. "But she loved my father with all her heart." She fingered the ghost beads at her throat. "These belonged to her. They are important to the Navajo. I wear them to honor her memory."

"Do they have meaning?"

"Mainly ceremonial," Kai said. "Some believe they are used for protection."

"I see. But I don't believe in superstitions. Though it is nice that you wear them to remember your mother." His eyes swept over her.

Kai cringed inside but shifted in her chair, causing her skirt to hike up even more.

"And what about you? Is it too forward of me to ask if you're married?" he asked.

"No, not at all. I was married once. It only lasted eighteen months. He was unfaithful, and since then, I've found it hard to trust again." Tony's face flashed before her, and she forced it away.

Konstantin leaned back, the chair creaking in protest. "I think I would like to give you a chance, Kitty. If things work out, maybe you can help with bookkeeping." A chuckle escaped his lips as he spread out his arms. "As you can see, I am not very good at it."

Kai gave him her sweetest smile. "Thank you so much, Mr. Zervas. I won't disappoint you."

"Please, Kitty, call me Konstantin. There are no formalities here."

Kai nodded. "When would you like me to start?"

"Let's see, how about next week. Monday, if possible. The diner is open twenty-four hours a day. There may be times when you will have to work a weekend or an evening shift."

"That's fine. There is no one waiting at home for me."

Konstantin peered up at her. "That's surprising." He shuffled through the papers on his desk. "Ah," he said. "I found one." He handed her a job application with what looked like a ketchup stain at the bottom. "Take this home and fill it out. You can bring it back with you."

***

Kai left the diner feeling much lighter than when she first walked in. Having overcome the biggest hurdle of getting the job, the real work would now begin. She had thrown in the accounting degree on a whim, and it had worked to her advantage.

Her reverie was interrupted by the ringing of her cell phone. It was Monica.

"I was just about to call you," Kai said. "I got the job." She related the details of the interview.

"Accounting, huh? That was brilliant, Kai. Your backstory is all set if he should search the internet for the accident. Do you think you have time to drop by my place? I got home with Andrew a little while ago. But I'm not going into the office. I'll have lunch ready."

"Sure," Kai said. "Be there in thirty minutes if the traffic is reasonable." Kai's euphoric feeling slipped a bit. Why would Monica ask her to come all the way to Staten Island? Apparently, it wasn't something she wanted to discuss at the office.

With traffic lighter than usual, she arrived at Monica's, parked, and went up the steps. Before she could ring the bell, Monica opened the front door.

"I was watching for you. I just put Andrew down. That damn bell always wakes him up. Come on in."

Kai had been to Monica's before and still appreciated the fact she took her under her wing when New York was still a strange new city to her. But gone were the days of getting on the wrong train when she took public transportation. New York had become her home.

She sat at the kitchen table while Monica set out a variety of cold cuts, bread, condiments, plates, and glasses. "Fix whatever you like," Monica said. "Water, soda, or lemonade?"

"Water's fine. Thanks for the lunch. I didn't realize how hungry I was."

As they prepared their sandwiches, Monica said. "I guess you're wondering why I asked you to come out here instead of meeting in the office tomorrow."

"Yeah, the thought did occur to me." She took a bite of her sandwich and waited.

"There was an incident the other night."

Kai listened as Monica related the events of her date night and its aftermath. "They were at the same restaurant?"

"Yes. There's a private room by invitation only. They must have arrived before we did. But when I escorted them outside, Tony wanted me to tell you he was sorry and that he could explain everything. I need you to be honest with me. I have to be able to trust you, Kai. Are you still seeing Tony Morello?"

Kai set her sandwich down and stared at the plate. She breathed through the silence between them. If she told the truth, everything she worked for could be gone, but if she lied, and Monica found out, things would be even worse. She slowly raised her head. "Am I in trouble?"

"That depends," Monica said, her facial expression neutral.

"Yes. I was seeing him, but it's been over for a while." Tears threatened to spill out, and she pushed them back. She had done enough crying over Tony Morello.

"What's a while?" Monica asked.

"Over a month. We're done for good. I don't have any desire to have any contact with him ever again."

"So then, that's why you were hesitant about going undercover?"

"Yes. I had to be sure there was no chance of Tony finding out I worked at the diner."

"Does Tony know where you live?"

"No. We always met at his hotel. There are no photographs, and we used burner phones—nothing ties us together."

"Wow," Monica said. "You had everything figured out. Why would you jeopardize your career for him?"

Kai felt a rush of warmth throughout her body. "I think you know why. Just like when you made sure Eddie saw a picture of Andrew when he was in witness protection. We're both aware of how you were able to do that."

Monica slapped the tabletop with her hand. "Don't you dare compare the two. I have a son with Eddie."

Kai got up. "I think I should leave. If you decide to pull me off the case, I'll live with it. Just remember, Monica. We're a lot alike, you and me. When we fall in love, we fall hard. All in all, I don't think that's such a bad thing. The only problem is who we fell for."

Kai stormed out of the house, knowing she might have lost her position on the task force but not her job with the FBI. If Monica tried to get her fired, the information about Eddie and witness protection, hidden for so long, would definitely come out.

Chapter 27 — Cookie
Digging

Rain had been coming down in sheets all night long. Cookie laid strips of bacon on a foil-lined baking sheet and set it in the oven. Grabbing a mixing bowl, she cracked and beat four eggs. Twenty minutes later, Damien entered the kitchen still in pajama bottoms and a t-shirt. It was one of his rare days off, and Cookie relished spending time with him. She set the breakfast on the table and then held up the coffee pot.

"Coffee?" she asked. His quiet mood still lingering, she was determined to find out why.

"Definitely," Damien said, collapsing into one of the chairs at the table.

She filled two cups and brought them over. Before sitting down, she grabbed the cream and sugar, fixing each cup the way they liked it. "I love quiet mornings like this with just the two of us."

"We need to enjoy them before the baby comes."

Cookie sipped the hot coffee and let its warmth wash over her. "I guess it's time for us to tell your mother. I'll be showing soon."

His expression soured. "If you want to." He filled his plate and picked up his fork.

"Damien, you've been in a mood for days. Is it because I went to Allenwood with your mother?"

He stopped eating and looked up from his plate. "Could I have stopped you?"

"Truthfully, no," Cookie said. "It's over and done with, so I can't change it. Besides, your father got a chance to see Alex. I think that's a good thing."

"Sure, taking my nephew to visit a murderer is wonderful," he said coldly.

Cookie ignored the remark. "But there was something odd going on between your mother and father."

"What do you mean? More arguing over why I don't visit."

"No. Your name only came up near the end. He wanted you to know he is glad you're happy."

"Happy?" Damien pushed his plate away. "What? Happy he's a criminal, and my brother is dead because of him."

"Damien, listen to me. Your father will never get out of prison. He's paying for the crimes he committed."

"So, I should feel sorry for him?"

Cookie shook her head. "No. But I don't think you've had closure."

His amber eyes cut into hers. "I will never have closure. Not with Roman dead."

She had never seen him act this way. Almost feeling guilty for bringing up the subject, she said. "I understand how much you miss him. Why do you still blame yourself for not saving him? I wish I could do something to help you."

Damien settled back into the chair. "I'm sorry. I shouldn't get angry with you. None of it is your fault." He reached over and patted her hand. "I don't want you to get upset because of me. But tell me, you said there was something odd going on. What did you mean?"

"Well, it all started with the man who came into the store to buy flowers." She related everything she remembered about the man, including her visit with Darya, where she saw the flower arrangement again. "It was odd, the way your mother reacted when I described him to her."

"How come you never told me about this?" he asked.

"I meant to," Cookie said. "With the pregnancy, it kinda slipped my mind until I went to Allenwood. Then after I came home, you seemed mad, so I didn't want to bring it up."

"Did they talk about this man?"

"Your mother told him Dimitri Orlov is here in America. Your father said it was impossible, and then he said if he came into the store again to call your mother. Do you have any idea who they're talking about?"

Damien grew silent. He planted his elbows on the table and covered his face.

Alarmed, Cookie jumped up and went over to him. "What's wrong. Do you know something about this Dimitri person?"

He dropped his hands and looked up at her. "Maybe," he said. "I need to find out some more information before I'm sure."

"Is he dangerous? If he is, I need to know. He might show up again at the store."

"You don't have to worry. He only used the store to send the flowers."

"Who is he?" Cookie demanded.

"I need to talk to my mother. There are some things I discovered about her and Alexei before they left Russia. Please understand, I'm not trying to hide anything from you."

Confused, Cookie said, "Exactly what did you find out?"

"I think that man might be my father."

Chapter 28 — Brooke
Dreams

On Friday morning, Brooke woke up covered in sweat. She flung the comforter back and sat up. Ever since the day Austin had walked her home, a fearful restlessness refused to leave her. Seeing that figure standing outside in the pouring rain caused her to look over her shoulder when navigating the neighborhood streets near her apartment building.

She forced herself to shower and get ready for work. Staying focused on the task force needed to be the number one priority. The agents were doing a great job so far, and she needed to acknowledge them. Perhaps a little after-hours get-together would be in order.

Arriving at the office by cab, she assembled everyone in the conference room. Monica brought her up to speed on Kai's landing the job at the diner.

"Excellent," Brooke said. "Keep track of the comings and goings, Kai. But be careful. If you do get access to the accounts, it's unlikely Konstantin will keep any pertinent information on his illegal activities in full view, but you never know."

"Got it," Kai said. "I start on Monday."

"Nico should be in and out, so you two need to play up the cousin thing," Monica added.

"I'm well aware," Kai said.

Brooke caught the glaring look between them. Could something be going on regarding the two? She'd have to pay closer attention to their interaction. The last thing she needed was dissension within the task force.

"If everyone is available later this evening, say six thirty, I've reserved a table at Trinity Place, inside the vault. Dinner and drinks are on me as a way of saying thank you for all your continued hard work."

"Sounds great," Monica said. "I'll leave early and drop Andrew off with my parents and head back to the city."

"Everyone else in?" Brooke asked.

"Works for me," Austin said.

"Me, too," Kai said.

"It's too bad we can't have Nico there," Brooke said. "He's going above and beyond with his undercover work. I'll make it up to him after we have enough evidence to move forward with the indictments."

The meeting at an end, Brooke returned to her office. She settled down to tackle a small backlog of paperwork to keep her mind free of distractions. Closing in on an hour or more of completing several reports, her cell phone buzzed. An unknown number stared back at her. Her mouth went dry. She couldn't go on like this.

Grabbing her cell, she took the call. "Hello."

"Brookie. How are you, darling?"

"Charlie, I told you before this needs to stop. If you continue to harass me, I'm going to have to take things further."

"That's exciting. How far are we going?"

"We're not going anywhere, Charlie, but I'll make sure you are. I'm tired of this game you're playing. Because of you, an agent almost got killed. Don't you feel any responsibility at all for your actions?"

"No harm done. He's still alive, isn't he? Still undercover, and I know where."

A cold sweat enveloped her. "Are you threatening to blow his cover? Because if you are, after I get through, you'll be behind bars for a long, long time. How would that feel? No booze, no coke, just endless hours in a cell."

"No. I'm not threatening, just stating a fact. I stopped drinking and using cocaine after you left. Been sober for months now. How about you?"

"I'm fine, Charlie. You know it was only one time. If you're clean, then your head should be on straight," Brooke said. "Go on with your life and leave me alone."

"I've tried, Brookie. I really have, but I can't shake you, can't shake us being together. Don't you miss me even a little?"

Heart palpitations thrummed through her body. "Guess what I don't miss, Charlie?"

"What's that babydoll?"

"You knocking me around."

"That was the booze and the drugs talking. I told you I'm clean and sober now. I'm so straight now that I've moved to a new city."

"Good for you. So wherever you are, just stay there."

"But I'm here, Brookie. New York turned out to be my kind of town."

A cold wave erupted throughout her body. Charlie here? In New York. After everything she did to get away from him.

"Listen to me, Charlie," Brooke said through clenched teeth. "You stay away from me. If you call me again, I'll find out where you are, and you'll find an army of FBI agents outside your door." Brooke ended the call and slammed her cell phone down.

Her imagination hadn't played tricks on her. Charlie was here in New York. The eyes she saw peeking into the glass door were his. If he didn't go away, with what he knew, her career could be finished.

Seeing him in person and trying to persuade him to leave the city altogether wasn't an option. Besides, his determination showed itself in his move from Texas to here.

Brooke sank into the leather chair. She needed to find a way to rid herself of Charlie for good.

*****

The Trinity Place bar and restaurant at 115 Broadway, situated in a basement vault, had become a go-to watering hole. Walking through the massive doors, into its exposed five-inch steel walls gave patrons the sense of just how secure the old vault was. A gleaming full-service bar rested beneath elaborate coffered ceilings made from the original steel. At the far end, a former meeting room of the bank had been converted into a restaurant.

With everyone seated and holding cocktails in their hands, Brooke raised a glass to toast her team.

"Thank you for all your hard work and for accepting a lone gal from Texas."

"And, thank you," Monica said. "For always being willing to listen to our ideas about the current case and having our backs. We all know how hard it can be having to convince your boss, we're on the right track."

As they dined on dishes like Gorgonzola & Ricotta Ravioli, Duck Leg Confit Risotto, and Pan-Roasted Heritage Pork Chops, Brooke tried to shake off her phone call with Charlie. She glanced at Austin Faulkner sitting across from her in conversation with Kai.

There was a brief moment the other day, when she looked into his eyes and thought—maybe she could give someone a chance again. But what would he think if he knew her whole story with Charlie? Not to mention, she was Austin's superior.

During desserts of Sticky Toffee Pudding and slices of New York Cheesecake, Brooke noticed Monica and Kai had retreated to an empty table a distance away.

"Are you still with us?"

Roused from her thinking, she realized Austin was talking to her. "Oh, sorry."

"Is everything okay?" Austin asked.

"Yes, fine," Brooke said. "Long day. I really needed this."

Austin nodded. "I think we all did. How are you finding living in New York?"

"It's growing on me," Brooke said, tucking a loose strand of her perfectly cut bob behind one ear.

"Good. I'm glad to hear that."

"So, do you miss being in the Nevada field office?"

"Not much," Austin said. "I worked with some great agents out there, but being here is a whole different animal. It's a bit more complicated, and I like a challenge."

"Austin, do you know what's going on between those two?" She nodded toward Kai and Monica.

"No clue. Everything seemed fine until today. I noticed the tension between them right away."

Brooke made a mental note to talk to Monica tomorrow. They finished dessert, and everyone prepared to leave. Monica left first, followed by Kai. Austin walked to the door and held it open for Brooke.

Outside, he asked. "Need a lift?"

"I can grab a cab," Brooke said.

"Not necessary. We live so close to each other, let me drop you off."

"Alright." She surprised herself by how fast she agreed to his offer. On the ride uptown, she tried to relax, her conversation with Charlie popping in and out of her head.

"Have you worked organized crime before?" Austin asked.

"Yes, back in Texas. Before that, I worked on the National Cyber Investigative Joint Task Force and the Fugitive Task Force. But with Bob Acosta transferring, the opportunity to come here arose, and I wanted something different."

Austin laughed. "Different is putting it mildly. I worked in organized crime in Nevada, and it was mild compared to here. But I like sinking my teeth in."

"Yes. You did exceptionally well on your last case. I know you were forced to use your weapon at the seaport raid. Are you coping okay with it?"

"The first couple of weeks, it didn't feel real," Austin said. "But after the debriefing and a short stint with the Critical Incident Management Program, I've settled with it."

"Good," Brooke said. "It always helps to use every resource the Bureau has."

They pulled up to her building, and Austin got out and opened the door for her. Afraid of seeing Charlie lurking around, Brooke glanced up and down the block.

"Can I ask you something?" Austin said as he escorted her to the door.

Brooke stopped. "That depends."

"On what?"

"Whether it's too personal or not." As soon as the words left her mouth, she regretted them. The crestfallen look on his face made her wince inside.

"Never mind," Austin said. "Thanks for the conversation. I enjoyed it. See you at the office." He turned and strode to his car.

"Wait!" Brooke called, following after him. When they were standing toe to toe, she said, "I'm sorry. That didn't come out the right way. It's just that …"

Austin's gaze captured her own, his eyes soft and inviting, almost willing her to take a chance.

"We had a moment the other day when I dropped you off," Austin said, his voice tender and warm. "Tell me if I'm wrong and I'll walk away."

Brooke's nerves fired all at once, her pulse escalated, causing a rush through her body. "No," she said, her voice almost a whisper. "You're not wrong."

He cradled her face in his hands and kissed her lips. First softly, then with more urgency.

Brooke's tongue lashed his. She moaned deep inside her throat. Their lips parted, and she stepped back. "I need to go."

Austin caught her hand. "Don't," he said, his eyes pleading.

Without another word, she led him inside and up to her apartment. That night, Brooke forgot about Charlie, his threats, and all those awful things from her past. All she wanted was to bask in the newness of Austin and how he made her feel. There was always tomorrow to figure out what to do about Charlie.

Chapter 29 — Tony
Losing Hope

Tony waited in a sandwich shop across the street from the Trinity Bar and Restaurant. He had followed Kai and her little troop of FBI agents there. He checked his watch. Almost ninety minutes had gone by. The door opened and Monica jumped into a waiting car. He quickly paid for the check and stepped outside. Kai came out next, her eyes searching up and down the street, growing bigger when she spotted him. She turned and walked in the opposite direction, disappearing around the corner.

Tony ran to catch up with her, his breath coming in spurts not only from his pace, but seeing her again made his adrenaline soar. Several people on the street stared after him as he sprinted beneath the streetlights. He ignored the honk of a car screeching to a halt as he dashed in front of it. He slapped the hood and kept going. Rounding the corner, he caught up with her.

"Kai, please wait up."

She abruptly stopped and faced him. "Leave me alone, Tony. I have nothing to say to you."

Tony steadied his racing heart. "Give me five minutes. Just five minutes, so I can explain everything."

Her cold eyes swept over him. "There is nothing you can say that will change my mind about us."

"I won't walk away, Kai. Not after all we meant to each other. I love you, baby."

Arms folded, she stared him down. "Go on, talk."

Tony glanced around. "Can we go somewhere a little more private?"

"No. This is good enough," Kai said, retreating to a doorway of a closed clothing store. She looked at her watch. "Start talking. You have five minutes."

"The woman you saw me with … I brought her to Paulie's club just for show. He's been crying in Eddie's ear about how I never bring anyone around like the other guys. It looked suspicious, so I picked her up and took her to the club."

"So, I didn't see you at the hotel with her. It was all a mirage," Kai said. "I should just forget the whole thing."

Tony reached out and attempted to touch her cheek.

She slapped his hand away. "Don't, Tony."

"I never meant to hurt you, baby. Yes, I took her there, just in case Paulie had someone keeping an eye out. But nothing was gonna happen. I swear." He waited through the silence between them, the aching inside him growing bigger. If he didn't get her back, his life would never be the same.

Kai held up her wrist. "Three minutes left."

"Didn't you hear me? Nothing was gonna happen," he repeated. "It was all for Paulie. You can ask Eddie if you don't believe me."

"Oh, the same Eddie who came and pleaded with me to give you up. Do you mean that Eddie? Maybe he was doing me a favor after all."

Tony leaned back against the door of the shop. "He should never have done that. Our relationship is none of his business. When I found out, I told him so."

"That was nice of you," Kai said. "You have about a minute and a half left. Anything else you want to tell me?"

Tony turned and focused on her dark eyes, the same ones that once stared back at him with such love, were filled with a hate he grappled to understand. "I'll do anything, baby. Anything you want. Just tell me what I need to do for you to forgive me."

"I came to your hotel that day because I needed more than anything to be reassured about how much you loved me," Kai said. "But things were never going to end well between us. You won't give up the mob, and I won't give up the Bureau. I guess it's better things happened the way they did. I've finally stopped crying over you … over us and what we once had. So, there isn't anything, Tony. Nothing you can say or do to change my mind."

He shook his head. "You still love me. I know you do."

Kai pushed past him. "You're five minutes are up." She hurried to the corner and waved her hand. An empty cab pulled up, and she disappeared inside.

It drove away, the red taillights fading into the night—inside, the woman he would love for the rest of his life. He wouldn't give up, he'd keep trying until she was his again. He stepped out of the doorway. His determination returning, he strode up the block.

***

The following day, he sat in the private room of La Vita Vino waiting for Paulie to appear. After seeing Kai last night, he couldn't seem to get his mind straight. Kai's expression, so full of hate for him, was unbearable. He hung his head and studied the white tablecloth. The aroma of all the delicious dishes being prepared in the kitchen, once so enticing, now nauseated him.

"Hey, what's with the face?"

He raised his head. Paulie, dressed as usual in a suit and tie, slipped into a chair across from him. "Tired, I guess," he lied.

One of the servers immediately appeared from the kitchen. "Just a Negroni," Paulie said. He nodded at Tony. "Should I make it two?"

Tony never had the taste for the cocktail, made of equal parts gin, vermouth rosso, and Campari, and garnished with an orange slice. "No, I'm good."

"Okay, I'm not going to drag things out," Paulie said after the server brought his drink and left. "I need to know what happened at the meeting with Konstantin Zervas."

"The deal is done," Tony said. "We get the dice game."

Paulie's steel grey eyes swept over him. "That's not what I asked you. I heard you got bent out of shape over some guy he brought with him."

"Oh, that," Tony said, trying to sound light. "Yeah, we agreed no extras, and he brought a third man with him besides Nico."

"And now, I hear that man is missing." Paulie sipped his drink and set the glass down. "So, I'm only gonna ask you once, Tony. Did you have anything to do with it?"

Tony focused on Paulie's face. "No. I heard the same as you that the guy vanished. Do you think I'm stupid enough to have him clipped?"

"Are you?" Paulie asked. "Because starting a war between us and the Greeks is a major thing. No one clips somebody from an outside gang without permission from the families."

"Of course," Tony said. He kept his gaze steady, but deep down, he didn't care what Paulie or anyone else thought. No one was going to disrespect him.

"So, I don't need to worry?"

"Not at all," Tony said. "I wouldn't make a call like that, especially for something so trivial. We worked it out. Everything was fine when Konstantin and Nico left."

Paulie finished off his Negroni. "Good. I can relax because nothing is going to blow back on me or you." He got up and straightened his tie. "That's a good deal you and Eddie made. I'll take care of you two after the first drop comes in."

"Thanks, Paulie," Tony said. When he was gone, Tony pulled out his cell phone. "Stan, we need to meet. Come by the hotel in half an hour."

***

Tony opened the door to his suite and let Stan Amato in. He took note of his stooped posture and grim expression. He pointed to one of the chairs opposite the sofa. "Take a seat, Stan."

Stan lowered himself into the chair. "What's up?"

"Are you good?" Tony asked, sitting across from him.

"Yeah, sure."

"You don't look it, Stan. Anything going on?"

"Naw. Just dealing with stuff at home. You know the wife and kids. Two little ones and two teenagers can give you a run for your money."

Tony grinned. "Yeah. At least I don't have to think about those things yet."

"Lucky you," Stan said, his face relaxing a bit.

"Who was the button man on Konstantin's guy, Stavros?" Tony asked.

"I gave it to Ray." Stan leaned forward. "He took Pete with him. Is there a problem?"

"No. No problem. How did it go down?"

"Ray said they grabbed him a couple of blocks from his house. Two quick bullets at a warehouse outside of Queens."

"Where did they dump him?" Tony asked.

Stan shook his head. "I think they did a double-decker. Campanelli's Funeral Home. He's buried in Holy Name Cemetery in Jersey underneath some old man who died."

"You think, or you know? This is important, Stan. I got Paulie breathing down my neck on this. I don't want a body turning up."

"No, for sure, Tony. The guy's not gonna be found."

"Good," Tony said. He got up and went to the hotel safe in the bedroom. He removed three stacks of cash and then handed them to

Stan. "One is for you and the other two are for Ray and Pete. You tell them how grateful I am. But make sure they're not going to rat. Especially, not to Paulie or any of his guys."

Stan got up. "Sure thing. And thanks for the extra cash."

After he left, Tony paced the living room suite. If Paulie ever found out what he had done, his life would be over. As long as the body stayed where it should be, he'd be fine.

If there were no proof and nothing connecting him to the hit, he'd still be on the right side of Paulie 'The Shiv' Martello.

But could he count on Ray and Pete? If Paulie approached anyone in his crew and offered them something they couldn't refuse, they might squeal.

It left him only one other option. Get rid of Ray and Pete, two of his best earners. He didn't need permission to off a soldier in his own crew. It happened all the time. Or he could trust they'd stay loyal to him.

Unsure of what he wanted to do, he sent Eddie a text. *"We need to meet. It's important."*

His text was answered in less than thirty seconds. *"Come to Staten Island. Romano's. Early tomorrow morning, around 8:30."*

He needed to run this whole thing by someone with a clear head. And Eddie was that person.

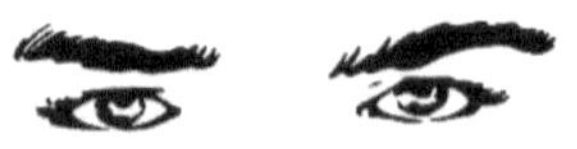

Chapter 30 — Austin
Double Bind

The Whistling Rail Coffeehouse and Cocktail Bar in Bronxville, a village in Westchester County, New York, served as the next meeting place for Stan and Austin. Both had agreed never to meet in the same place twice. Approximately 15 miles north of Midtown Manhattan and situated in an affluent neighborhood made it comfortable enough for the two to meet.

Austin took a seat next to Stan at the end of the Carrera marble-topped bar and ordered two Espresso's. He glanced around at the brick walls and arched windows. At 3:00 in the afternoon, only a handful of people were scattered about the room.

The space embodied a soothing atmosphere, one he hoped would ease Stan's trepidation. His constant fidgeting, hunched posture, and twitching eye told him something was off with his C.I..

"Are you okay?" Austin asked.

"Sure," Stan said, sipping his espresso.

"You don't look it. What's going on?"

Stan stared down into his cup. "Something happened. But I want you to know I had no choice in the matter."

Austin's radar went up. "What are you talking about, Stan?"

He swiveled around on his stool. "You gotta promise me that I won't get pinched for this."

"How can I promise you anything when I have no idea what you're talking about?" A slight rumble hit the pit of Austin's stomach. Whatever it was couldn't be good.

Stan held up a hand. "Okay, okay. You remember I told you about the meeting concerning the Greek card game. It got heated because Konstantin brought someone with him who wasn't supposed to be there."

"How heated?" Austin asked.

"Tony ordered me to have the man clipped."

Austin took a breath. This could only mean Stavros Papadakis was dead. Nico's intel was spot on. "Did you—"

"No, no. I didn't," Stan said. "But I had to pick the men who clipped him." His eyes pleading, he continued. "You have to understand, it was an order. I couldn't say no. Not to Tony Morello."

"Let me ask you this," Austin said. "Does Tony's boss know?"

Stan's eyes bulged. "Hell no. As a matter of fact, Tony gave me extra cash and some for the two button men. He's afraid what he did will get back to Paulie."

"So, he did it without permission."

"Yeah. If Paulie finds out, Tony's a dead man." Stan picked up his cup with trembling hands. "Where does all this leave me? I mean, with the Bureau."

Austin chose his next words carefully. "I can't guarantee anything, but they'll understand you had no choice. Right now, you're an accessory to murder and at the same time very valuable to the Bureau. When we negotiated your agreement, murder was off the table, Stan. You know that."

"But, what else could I have done?"

"You should have contacted me. Maybe we could have prevented this whole thing. Made it look like you made Stavros Papadakis disappear. We could have grabbed him and stashed him somewhere until this whole operation was finished."

Stan shook his head. "I guess you're right. Everything happened so quick. I'm used to following orders."

"Where's the body?"

"Holy Name Cemetery. Underneath someone else's body in a coffin."

"Geez, "Austin said. Stan was right. Stavros Papadakis would never be found without someone like Stan giving him the location. "Look, this goes on the back burner for now. We're close to getting indictments. I need you to promise me you're not gonna run, Stan. If you do, I can't protect you."

"There is no place to run to. I'll wait it out. The guilt I'm feeling over this whole thing is eating away at me. I'll face whatever comes as long as my family is safe."

"You need not worry, Stan. That part of your agreement is solid."

***

Later, as Austin drove to Manhattan, he contemplated Stan's dilemma. C.I.'s are granted some degree of immunity, but not for unauthorized illegal activity such as accessory to murder. Informing Monica meant she would need to report it to the Department of Justice. Complicating things further, there was no automatic right for a C.I.'s case to be reviewed by the Conviction Integrity Unit within the prosecutor's office.

Taking the matter straight to Brooke gave him second thoughts. He'd be jumping the chain of command, and Brooke might think he was asking for a favor. The night they spent together couldn't have gone any better. Their chemistry was off the charts, and Austin felt himself falling for her in a big way.

But there were moments when she seemed skittish, almost afraid of something. He didn't want to spoil things by trying to pin her down. Brooke appeared to be the type of woman who held things close to the vest.

Maybe one day, she would let him in. Until then, he'd tread carefully. The last thing he wanted to do was spoil things between them. Besides, he needed time to think this thing with Stan through before deciding what to do.

But how long could Stan hold on before Tony Morello noticed those telltale signs like he did today? Stan was a man on the edge. Austin hoped he wouldn't fall off a cliff.

Chapter 31 — Nico
Still Missing

It was 3:00 in the afternoon, right after the lunch rush and before dinner when Nico walked into the Acropolis Diner gripping a small black satchel. Hearing nothing since his discussion with Eddie regarding Stavros' disappearance only served to heighten his anxiety. About to take his usual seat in a private booth at the rear, he stopped cold.

"Hello, cousin. How are you?"

Her arms came around his neck. She pulled him close for a brief hug and then stepped back.

So, this was his undercover counterpart. Never could he have imagined this beauty standing before him. Her dark eyes, high cheekbones, and full lips were mesmerizing.

Quickly recovering from his surprise, he said, "Tell me, Kitty. How are things going?"

"Fine. I'm getting the hang of it. Mainly greeting and seating people. Making sure each waitress gets their fair share of customers."

"Good. I'm glad to hear it. Is Konstantin here?"

"Yes. I'll go and get him."

Nico took his usual seat in a booth way at the back of the diner. He looked up as Dina sauntered toward him, coffee pot and cup in her hand."

"The usual. Coffee black," she said, pouring a cup and setting it down before him. "Anything else?"

"I think I'll have an order of Moussaka."

"Coming right up," Dina said, smiling so wide it produced a dimple on her left cheek.

Nico sipped his coffee and glanced around. What was taking Konstantin so long?"

Dina returned and set two plates down. "Here you go. Enjoy." She turned and left to take care of a customer who Kai sat at her station near the other end of the diner, the ample sway of her hips on display just for him.

In spite of himself, Nico's mouth watered at the aroma of the sauteed eggplant, minced meat, spiced tomato, and bechamel sauce. A chunky tomato, cucumber, parsley, and mint salad sat on a dish beside it, along with slices of crusty bread.

"So, it's Moussaka today," Konstantin said, sliding into the booth across from him with a plate of his own. "You know we make the best."

Nico nodded. "Of course." He slid the satchel to Konstantin under the table and then dug into his meal, letting the rich flavors bathe his tongue. The two ate in silence for several minutes, and Nico could not have been more thankful.

Konstantin wiped his plate clean with the last slice of bread and pushed it away. "Did you speak to Kitty?" he asked.

"Yes. And I want to thank you for giving her a chance. She needs to stay busy and not get stuck in that apartment all the time. How is she working out?"

"Fine. I'm glad you suggested I hire her. No disrespect, but she is a beautiful woman. Good with the customers so far, too. The regulars are getting acquainted with her."

Aware of how handsy Konstantin could be with women, it made Nico a bit nervous. But from what Monica had told him, Kai Nez should be able to handle herself.

"Tell me, what did Eddie Marconi have to say?"

Nico swallowed and wiped his mouth. He needed to tread carefully. Although Konstantin appeared relaxed, his anger bubbled beneath the surface like a volcano waiting to erupt.

"He claims he doesn't know anything about Stavros' disappearance."

"And you believe him?"

"What I'm inclined to believe is he may not be involved, but Tony Morello is another story. Eddie said he'll talk to him."

Thunder in his eyes, Konstantin leaned forward, his palms pressed flat against the table. "Talk to him and then what? Tell me, Nico. Do you think if Morello is involved, Eddie will speak the truth? They are partners, after all."

"Look, what else can we do?" Nico asked. "Let's see what he comes back with. You still have your shipment at the seaport to consider."

"I spoke to their boss," Konstantin said. "He appeared to be very surprised by what I had to say. He claims no one on his side sanctioned anything against us."

"Then maybe, Stavros is missing for some other reason. We don't know everything about his private life, do we?"

"Stop talking nonsense, Nico. Are you trying to protect the Italians? Stavros disappeared because someone on their side put an end to him. I have always relied on your judgment. When my brother sent you here from Texas, he swore I could trust you with my life."

"And you can," Nico shot back. "I worked hard for your brother."

"Yes, but you need to understand, for me to sit here idle while poor Stavros lies dead somewhere is not in my nature."

Nico held up his hands. "Okay, okay. Let's say you're right. We need to wait until the shipment clears and we have it in our possession. To act now will jeopardize everything."

His posture relaxing, Konstantin let out a long breath. "I guess we must wait. But after we have our goods, someone is going to pay for Stavros and no more *barbouti* for the Italians."

"One thing at a time," Nico said, rising. He tossed two twenty-dollar bills on the table.

Konstantin shook his head. "No need to pay," he said.

"I'm not," Nico said, grinning. "That's for Dina. She works hard enough." Nico swore he caught a slight smile on Konstantin's face. "We'll talk soon. I'll go check on the games. See how things are going."

After Konstantin returned to the kitchen, Nico stopped at the register to talk to Kai. "Stay safe. If you need anything or have any questions, let me know."

She nodded and slipped him a piece of paper. "I do … have questions, that is. Here's my address. I get off at 7:00."

Outside, he tucked the paper inside his jacket pocket. He looked forward to learning more about Kai Nez later tonight.

***

On the way to his apartment, he stopped at a local grocery store to pick up some simple items. As he wound his way down an aisle, he tossed a can of ground coffee into his basket. Always alert, he glanced back as he made his way to the refrigerated section.

Nico froze as a figure ducked and turned down another aisle. He hurried toward the same aisle, only to find it empty. Were his eyes playing tricks on him? Continuing, he checked every aisle, with no luck. He strode to the front of the store, where he caught a glimpse of the person heading out the sliding doors.

Nico dropped his basket and made his way outside. His eyes scanned left, right, and then across the busy street with no luck. The person appeared to have vanished. How could this be happening again? He dug inside his pocket for the burner phone and punched in a number.

"Monica, we need to meet. Yes, tomorrow afternoon, I'll text you the time and place."

Chapter 32 — Damien
The Talk

Calling the number again on the note hadn't been easy. As soon as the man answered, Damien almost hung up. Fingers gripping his cell phone, he steadied himself while they decided on a meeting place.

Promptly at noon, Damien pulled up and parked in a public garage steps away from the entrance to Central Park. They had agreed to meet in the heart of the park, by Bethesda Terrace. He traveled down the long, tree-lined promenade known as the mall, which overlooked the lake.

A few minutes early and wanting to calm his nerves, when he reached the terrace, he stopped to admire the display of art and the incredible architecture with its intricate carvings. In the center stood the Bethesda Fountain, the Angel of the Waters.

He climbed up one of the staircases flanking the structure by the Arcade, similar to a bridge with tall arches, which were part of the park's circulation system. Standing on the bridge, his eyes scanned the crowd below. An array of people lazed by the fountain steps under a brilliant azure blue sky.

Not having any idea what this man looked like, he assumed this person would recognize him. A moment later, he jumped at the light tap on his shoulder.

Turning, he looked into the eyes of a slender man, the same height as himself, with deep-set light brown eyes. His lips formed into an uneven grin as he held out his hand.

"Dimitri Orlov," he said, his voice only a few decibels above a whisper.

Damien extended his hand. "Apparently, you already know who I am."

"Yes," Dimitri replied. "Come, let's walk a bit. Find a quiet spot to talk."

Immediately, Damien noticed the slight limp in his left leg as they moved down the path toward an empty bench away from the crowds.

Dimitri sat while Damien remained standing, suddenly unsure if he had made the right decision to come here.

"I won't bite." Dimitri patted the bench. "I only wanted to see you in person."

Damien eased down. Sitting beside this man, he felt raw, exposed, as if all the hidden secrets were about to be set free. "Why now, after all this time?"

"I've tried so hard to make this day come true. Back in Russia, I often wondered about you and how your life turned out—if you were happy. But most of all, if you were loved."

Damien fidgeted with the car fob in his pocket. "So, it's true then, isn't it?"

"Ah, what is truth? It is whatever someone believes, no?"

"I need to know," Damien demanded. "Are you my father?"

Dimitri turned toward him. His eyes filled with a deep sorrow Damien could literally feel. His body trembled as he asked again, "Are you my father?"

"Yes. I am."

"Why then did you abandon my mother and me all those years ago in Russia?"

Dimitri shook his head. "Leave you? No, my son. I would never have done that. I loved your mother. I wanted to build a life with her. But then he came along and destroyed everything."

At the word 'he' Damien, shuddered inside. Those letters and papers he discovered in his mother's apartment became even more real. "I found the letters," Damien said. "Please tell me what happened all those years ago. There are still some things I don't understand."

"Are you sure? Because nothing can be done to change it. And once you digest the truth, you will never be the same. I only hope you will forgive me for my part in things, and maybe even your mother."

Damien nodded for him to continue.

Dimitri squeezed his eyes shut. Looking almost as if he were in a trance, he began. "We were so young, your mother and I. But I believe we loved each other. How could we have known what was to befall us? When Darya became pregnant out of wedlock, her family warned me to stay away. Her people were upper class, while mine were considered working class, or as they say here in America, blue collar."

A deep sigh escaped Dimitri's lips, and he slowly opened his eyes. "Forgive me, but they wanted her to … terminate the pregnancy. Darya refused, and we decided to try to find a way to be together. This infuriated her family, and to put a stop to things, they reached out to Radimir Volkov."

"Radimir?" Damien said. "I don't ever remember hearing that name."

"Radimir was a member of the *Solntsevskaya Bratva,* Russia's most feared criminal gang. By this time, he was convicted of murder and incarcerated in the notorious Black Dolphin Prison. One of the worst in Russia."

"But if he was in prison, how could—"

"He still had many connections to the *Solntsevskaya Bratva,*" Dimitri continued. Which now included his son, your adoptive father, Alexei Volkov."

"Radimir was my grandfather?"

"Yes. I'm afraid so."

The knowledge Alexei's criminal activities started all the way back in Russia made Damien cringe inside. It wasn't America that had turned him into a monster.

"By this time, Darya and I were living together on the outskirts of Russia in a small town called *Kinerma* near my family's home. We thought we were safe. Things remained quiet for a few years after Darya gave birth. We had finally saved enough money and were planning a small wedding.

"But then, Alexei and his thugs started coming around. He demanded I let Darya go back to Moscow with him. I knew from the beginning he had eyes for her."

"And my mother?" Damien asked. "How did she react to all of this?"

"Oh, Alexei promised her a new life here in America. He began sending gifts. Things I could never afford to give her at that time. I could feel her pulling away from me." Dimitri slumped forward on the bench and stared at the ground. "If only she had waited … given me a chance, we could have been happy together.

"But Alexei was relentless in his pursuit of her until I could not stand it any longer."

He raised his head, and for the first time, Damien could see the fire smoldering inside his eyes. "What did you do?" he asked.

"I told him I would never give Darya up. He needed to leave my family alone. That if he ever came around again, I would kill him." Dimitri shook his head. "I was foolish enough to believe he would listen."

"Did you really mean it?"

"At the time, yes," Dimitri said. "But I did not realize the power he possessed even at such a young age. He returned one night with a bunch of his thugs. They dragged me from the house and took me into the woods. All I remember is fists coming at me, a bat slamming into my kneecap. I am not sure how long it continued. I barely escaped with my life. When I made it back home, you and Darya were gone.

"I lay in a hospital for over two months recovering from the beating. While I was there, a note came saying that if I ever showed my face around Moscow or tried to contact Darya, my life would end for sure."

"So, you never pursued things after that?"

"I could not because—"

"Because of what?" Damien snapped. "There is something you're not telling me. I read the letters you sent to my mother asking about me. Did she ever write back to you?"

"Never, but I kept on writing. I had hired someone in America to find out where she was living. The collusion between the gangs and the government ensured I would never be able to leave Russia. I can only imagine how much Alexei paid them for it."

"And all this time," Damien said, "almost every single day of my life, I wondered about you. I thought you never wanted me."

"Is that what your mother told you?" Dimitri asked, the rasp in his voice rising a few octaves.

"No. She refused to speak about you. She said I should be glad Alexei cared enough for me to adopt me legally, and I should only think of him as my father."

Dimitri turned toward him, his eyes focused on Damien. "I would have done anything to be with you, watch you grow and ..."

Damien felt his anger rising. What was he holding back? "So, then, you stayed in Russia. Just thinking about me?"

"No. Not just thinking about you." A visible shudder ran through his body. "I couldn't go to Moscow and possibly lose my life ... because I had a daughter to raise."

"A daughter? So, you married after my mother left?"

"No. I never married anyone. I couldn't, not after Darya. But most of all, I needed to stay alive to raise your sister."

"My ... my sister?" The air around Damien thinned. His pulse spiked. A gasp escaped his throat.

"Yes," Dimitri said. "My son, you have a twin sister."

Chapter 33 — Kai

Nico

Kai removed her makeup and showered off the smell of grease and sickly sweets from her body. She finished changing into jeans and a sweatshirt just as her buzzer rang. Cautious, she peered through the peephole before unlatching the door. Being undercover always meant staying alert.

"Come in," Kai said, her body relaxing.

Nico, casually dressed in a pale blue shirt open at the collar, dark denim jeans, and a black leather jacket, stepped inside and closed the door behind him. Kai tried to ignore his easy, good looks. Although she had seen his file, those pictures didn't do him justice.

She led him into the small, neat, carpeted living room. A sofa, two chairs, end tables, lamps, and a television completed the scene. One wall held a large photograph of Kai standing next to a man and a woman. Several more displayed, Nico, Kai, and a different man and woman.

"Ah," Nico said, pointing to the first one. "Your mother and father?"

"Yes. Aren't they lovely?" Kai said, laughing. "And the other two people are your parents."

"I thought they looked familiar," Nico chimed in. "They're in photographs at my apartment, too."

Kai went into the kitchen, where she opened a bottle of red wine, grabbed two glasses, and brought everything to the living room. They settled on the sofa.

"Long day," she said, pouring and then handing Nico a glass.

"Thanks. What did you want to see me about?" he asked.

"Bring me up to speed on Konstantin. You know him better than anyone else."

"Pleasant when he wants to be, but a temper that always simmers below the surface."

"Does he hold meetings at the diner with anyone else besides you?"

"Not too often. Sometimes in his office or at his house."

"Personal life?" Kai asked, sipping some wine. "I'm aware he lost his wife about seven years ago. Anyone since?"

Nico raised an eyebrow. "Of course. His flavor of the month right now is Dina."

"The pretty waitress?"

"Yeah. But who's to say how long it will last? He's gone through several since I've been with him. Konstantin gets bored fast, so you need to be careful."

"No worries. I can handle him," Kai said. She shook her head. "The things we do for the Bureau."

"But it's good work, Kai. Necessary work."

The slight shake in his hand when she gave him the glass of wine had not gone unnoticed. "You've been under a long time. Can I ask you something?"

"Anything," Nico said.

"How do you turn it off … I mean, you've dug yourself in so deep, there has to be times when you want to get out."

"Sure," Nico said. "But I force myself to refocus because I know what the end goal is." He shifted uncomfortably and drained the rest of his wine. "I heard you have accounting experience. Konstantin was impressed."

"Yeah, I kinda threw that one in there. I took some classes a long time ago. I can skate by." Kai lifted the bottle. "More wine?"

Nico held out his empty glass. "Just a little."

Kai poured him a bit more. She raised her head and met his eyes, flecks of gold in the green drawing her in. A flush swept through her body. How could she be feeling this way? It must be the wine getting to her head. She quickly averted her eyes.

"So, tell me a little about you," Nico said. "What made you join the Bureau?"

Kai spoke of growing up on the Navajo Reservation and how her mother worked for the Tribal Police. The importance of staying true to her traditions and wanting more out of life led her to choose a career that would make a difference. She left out the bad parts—the sexual abuse at the hands of her uncle. All that needed to stay buried with him.

"I admire your respect for your culture. I feel the same way about mine." Nico checked his watch and set his wine glass down. "Maybe one day we can compare notes, but for now, I have an early day tomorrow."

"One more question before you go," Kai said, rising. "Stavros Papadakis."

"What about him?"

"Do you think Tony Morello put out a hit on him?"

"If I were to make a bet," Nico said. "My money would be on Tony for the hit."

***

After Nico left, Kai rinsed the wine glasses, all the while her mind focused on Nico and her reaction to him tonight. It was way too soon to be attracted to another man after everything that happened with Tony.

Never seeing herself as naive, feelings of shame washed over her. All those times she lay with Tony, knowing who he was but loving him just the same, formed a sick feeling deep inside her. How many murders were on his hands? Frank Uzelli for sure, and now maybe Stavros Papadakis.

But Tony had been in the mob for a long time. First, as a soldier for Frank, then becoming a made man, and finally a Capo. She believed what Austin said at their last briefing. Tony was power hungry. Power hungry enough to do a lot of damage. Perhaps, it could even spark a war between the Greeks and Italians, leaving Nico caught in the middle.

She picked up her cell phone and punched in a number. "Monica, it's me, Kai. We need to talk."

Chapter 34 — Monica
Sticky Wickets

The day matched Monica's mood. Waiting for Kai in her office, she stared out the floor-to-ceiling windows behind her desk. Thick drops of heavy rain poured from a gunmetal grey sky. Pedestrians below dodged the onslaught while a wicked wind threatened to turn their umbrellas inside out. Cars, cabs, and buses sped up and down the street, their tires lapping up mud puddles and then spitting them out onto the black top.

A gentle tap on the door broke into her thoughts, and she called out, "Come in," before dropping down into her leather chair.

Kai entered, her tan raincoat displayed numerous wet patches, and droplets glistened in her dark hair.

"Geez, the rain is good for the spring flowers, but this is ridiculous," she complained. Shrugging out of her wet coat, she hung it on a hook by the door and sat in one of the two chairs across from Monica.

"I got caught in it getting off the ferry with Andrew," Monica said. And you can imagine just how slow a four-year-old walks." An awkward silence fell between the two. They hadn't spoken much since Kai stormed out of her house.

"Listen," Kai said. "I owe you an apology for the way I acted."

"I appreciate that. You put me in a bad spot. You're lying about not being with Tony is a clear violation."

"Yes. There is no excuse for what I did. Nico's undercover work and his comments about Tony have opened my eyes. I'm ashamed of not wanting to face the truth about who he is and what he is capable of."

Monica acknowledged the sincerity in her voice—finally, a breakthrough. A very painful one, she knew firsthand.

"So, you spoke with Nico?" Monica asked.

"Yes, and about Konstantin, so I could gauge him better. Nico is convinced Tony had Stavros Papadakis killed. Plus, Austin's C.I. claiming the disappearance of Frank Uzelli points to Tony makes sense."

"Yes. It certainly looks that way."

Kai moved to the edge of the chair. "Listen, Monica. The last time Tony and I were together, he mentioned wanting to move up and be an Under Boss one day. He's definitely power hungry."

"True. But if he ordered a hit without permission, it wouldn't sit well with Paulie Martello. Listen, Kai. I'm obligated to make Brooke aware of you continuing your relationship with Tony while he's under investigation."

"If you need to report it, then go ahead. I'll face whatever consequences I have to."

Monica sighed and leaned back in her chair. Understanding what was right and doing it were two different things. If Brooke pulled Kai off the task force at this juncture, it could ruin the progress they were making. "Listen, I'll hold off informing Brooke, but I need to have your word that you and Tony are done for good."

"We are done," Kai said. "But I don't want you compromising your position for something I did."

"There's no harm done at this point. Stay clean, Kai. I'm going way out on a limb here in trusting you again."

"You won't regret it," Kai said. "I want this investigation to move forward, and if it means prosecuting Tony, I'll help see it through to the end."

"I'm glad to hear that. Have you noticed anything meaningful at the diner so far?"

"No. But I'm going to try to worm my way into doing some accounting for Konstantin. You know, cozy up to him a bit. Nico indicated he's got an eye for women, and I already felt it when he interviewed me."

"Be careful," Monica said. "Don't get caught up in something you can't get out of."

"Don't worry, I can handle him." Kai got up. "Thanks again, Monica." She grabbed her coat and left.

Monica wrestled with the decision she made not to report Kai. If anything blew back, it would land all over her. About to go and get a cup of coffee from the break room, she stopped when a frazzled-looking Austin appeared outside her office door. Drenched from the onslaught continuing outside, he swiped his hand through his wet hair. His face seemed drawn, with puffiness under his eyes indicating a lack of sleep.

"What's going on? You look awful," Monica said, following him inside and closing the door.

He collapsed onto a chair. "We need to talk."

Monica sat next to him. "What's this all about?"

Austin shook his head. Hands folded in his lap, he began. "I met with Stan Amato again. He assured me that Konstantin's man is dead."

"And he knows this how?"

"Tony Morello ordered him to get two of his men to handle it."

"Oh, crap!" Monica rose and began to pace. "I'm assuming he followed orders."

"Yes," Austin said. "He's now an accessory to murder."

"Did you inform the deal he signed with us is off the table?"

"Yes … but."

Monica stopped pacing. Her eyes focused on Austin. "There are no buts. I'm supposed to report this to the DOJ and inform Brooke."

"The thing is, even though he denied it, Stan is showing all the signs of someone who's gonna run," Austin said. "If he does, Tony Morello will figure something is up. It might even lead to breaking Nico's cover."

"That can't happen, Austin. Listen, for now, you need to reassure him the Bureau understands that, under the circumstances, he had no choice. Make him believe we are open to honoring his agreement."

Austin got up and faced her. "There is one caveat he can offer. He knows where the body is buried. Underneath another one at Holy Name Cemetery."

"It figures. That's an old trick the mob's been using for a long time. That may help him a little bit."

"Are you going to hold back this information from the Department of Justice?"

"For right now," Monica said. "Even though it goes against regulations. If I report it, they'll shut us down, pull Stan in, and all our hard work will go down the drain, including Nico's undercover work. We would have to try to prosecute with what we have. Sure, we would get Tony Morello, but that leaves Paulie, his boss, Konstantin, and maybe others, off the hook."

"So, what's the plan, then?" Austin asked.

"We wait until after that drug shipment comes in. They all have their fingers in that pie."

"And Brooke?"

"Let me handle Brooke. I think I might be able to persuade her to go along with this. I'll meet with her."

"What if you can't?"

Monica hesitated. "Then I guess we stick to regulations and let things take their course."

"I'm not comfortable with this, but I also don't want everything we did to build a case to account for nothing."

"Me, either," Monica said. "If it blows back, I'll take full responsibility."

***

After Austin left, Monica checked the time. She put on her trench coat and snatched her umbrella from the door. Downstairs, she grabbed a cab and instructed the driver to take her to the Roosevelt Island Tramway on the Upper East Side of Manhattan.

The rain had let up just a bit as she made her way to a waiting aerial car. Traveling across the East River at 11:00 in the morning enabled her to grab a seat on one of the two benches inside the only commuter tram in New York. Surrounded by the large windows, Monica peered out at the mist hanging over the Manhattan skyline and Queensboro Bridge as the tram glided along the cables.

She reached Roosevelt Island and made her way to Granny Annie's Bar and Kitchen. The hostess led her to a table by the window overlooking the main street. The restaurant appeared to be the typical place with a long bar on one side of the room and numerous tables and chairs stationed about. Quiet, except for some soft music playing in the background and a limited number of patrons, it had a soothing atmosphere. Glancing at her watch, she noted for the first time Nico was late. She'd give him another ten minutes before using her burner phone to call him. Having nothing but coffee early this morning, she ordered a house salad and the French Onion Soup. To her relief, Nico walked in while she was ordering.

He nodded, surveyed the menu, and ordered the Turkey Jack Burger. They both opted for water as their drinks.

"How are you, Nico?" Monica asked, slipping her straw into her glass.

"Konstantin is getting impatient. This thing with Stavros has him on edge."

"Well, I can confirm that Austin's C.I. told him Tony Morello ordered the hit on Konstantin's man."

"Exactly what I thought," Nico said. "I never heard back from Eddie Marconi. But I will reach out and see how he spins this thing."

For the second time, Monica observed the slight shake in his hand as he lifted his glass.

"You never answered me. How are you doing, Nico?"

"I'm fine. The drug shipment arrives in a couple of weeks. I'm trying to keep Konstantin focused on that."

"Good. It might distract him for a while."

The waitress set their plates down, and after she left, Nico sat staring at his food.

Monica started on her soup and then stopped. "Is there something else going on?"

"Remember when you asked me about my last handler?"

"Yes. But so far you haven't told me anything."

"My last handler was Brooke Adams."

Monica set her soup spoon aside. This was the last thing she expected to hear. "I'm confused. Brooke worked in the Dallas Division."

"Yes," Nico said. "And so did I. When I first went under, I worked for Konstantin's brother, Demetrius, in Texas. But the case wasn't moving as fast as the Bureau wanted it to. He called me one day and said his brother in New York could use someone like me, so that's how I ended up here. The Bureau felt I could do more good working for Konstantin."

"Wait," Monica said. "There is nothing in your file about Texas."

"I'm not surprised," Nico said. "Brooke probably eliminated some of that."

Monica's jaw tightened. Brooke tampering with a file? "That's illegal, Nico. Why would she do such a thing?"

"Brooke almost got me killed back in Texas. Let me explain from the beginning. I went under and worked in Demetrius' bar. Things were moving along okay. Then one day, this guy comes in, takes a seat at the bar, and strikes up a conversation with me. He starts talking about the woman he's seeing—that she's an FBI agent." Nico leaned forward and lowered his voice. "This woman also does cocaine with him in her off hours. Wanting more information, I continue to pour him drinks, and he continues to talk. But I couldn't get a name out of him."

"So how did you find out who it was?" Monica asked.

"He comes back into the bar one night. Drinks himself silly. Just as I was about to close up, I asked him to leave, and he became angry. Then he says he knows who I really am—that he followed Brooke to a meeting with me. I must be in the FBI, too. Now, Demetrius is at the other end of the bar, and his ears perk up immediately."

"Oh my God, Nico. I can't imagine how you felt."

"Yeah. So, now I start yelling at the guy. I tell him he's out of his mind. Then I asked, "Who is this woman he's talking about? Where did I meet her? What was I wearing?" I go on and on trying to confuse him because he's so drunk. Finally, he comes out with Brooke's name, and then he says he thought it was me, but he must be wrong.

"Then Demetrius comes over to me, asking what this is all about. Did he hear the word FBI? So, I don't lie. I say yes, this guy says he is dating an FBI agent, and that they do drugs together.

"Demetrius asks him if he has ever brought her around to his bar. The guy says no, then Demetrius grabs him and takes him out to the back alley. He comes in a few minutes later and tells me the guy won't be coming around here anymore. I believe he must have beaten him. I never saw him again after that."

"Did you confront Brooke?"

"Of course. She swore up and down she had no idea who this guy was, and she never used drugs in her life. I accused her of lying and threatened to go to the Bureau. She became hysterical and begged me not to."

"Did she tell you the truth?"

"Yeah, finally. She still denied using drugs, but she said he was an old boyfriend of hers who wouldn't leave her alone."

"So, you didn't report her?"

"No. Only because I knew I was going to transfer here to New York. But I had no idea she would end up here almost a year later."

Monica shook her head. "Now I understand why she would never tell me who your previous handler was."

"If Demetrius had believed this guy. I could have ended up dead for sure."

"Why then are you telling me all this now, Nico?"

"Because I never thought I'd ever see the guy again—that is, until today."

"Where did you see him?" Monica listened as he related the grocery store incident.

"I'm positive it was him. His name is Charlie Blevins. He's a former detective."

"Former?"

"He worked for the Dallas P.D.. Was thrown off the force for misconduct. I didn't mean to put all this on you, Monica. But you need to find out if Brooke knows he's here. I can't afford to have this guy threatening to blow my cover again."

"Believe me," Monica said. "I'll take care of it."

***

At home in the evening, Monica contemplated what had landed in her lap from Kai being with Tony and Stan, an accessory to murder, plus Brooke's ex, Charlie. The first two meant risking her job for the sake of this case. Was it right to put the task force before the integrity of the Bureau?

The last thing was to make sure Nico remained safe. Did this Charlie lie about Brooke using drugs with him? There were no signs of any kind she was doing drugs now. But she clearly violated regulations by giving her an incomplete file on Nico. Tomorrow, she needed to confront Brooke. No way would she jeopardize Nico's life. The rest … she needed to think about.

Chapter 35 — Eddie
Chaos

Hours before opening time, Romano's Restaurant sat silently waiting. Eddie checked his watch. Two hours until the first employees came and started preparing for the lunch crowd. The driving rain outside only served to raise his anxiety. He glanced at the empty tables covered in white linen. By noon, they would all be full. A tap on the door made him look up. Tony Morello peered through the glass and waved.

"Coming," Eddie called, going to the door and snapping the lock. He swung it open and let Tony inside before locking it again. He pointed to one of the tables where a bottle of whiskey and two glasses waited.

"Kinda early," Tony said, brushing away the droplets of rain from his leather jacket before taking a seat.

"It's just in case," Eddie said. "I have the feeling it will be warranted after we talk."

Tony rocked back, his chair lifting up on two legs for a moment before he planted all four down again. "I need your advice about something. I was still pissed after the meeting with Konstantin, so I asked—"

"Stop," Eddie said. "Don't say it. I vouched for you with Paulie because I had to and because I didn't want to believe you did something so stupid. But I won't be an accessory."

Tony's face flushed. "But you didn't do anything."

"Exactly," Eddie said. "And I want to keep it that way. Giving me knowledge of a hit makes me just as culpable as you."

"I can't believe you just said that. We've always had each other's backs. Why now, Eddie? Why are you doing me like this?"

He took in the hurt in his friend's eyes. Though it pained him to not be able to ease it, he held firm. "I warned you more than once about putting your pride before business. Things like that get people killed. I attend a meeting to get things done. You go to show how much power you have in the game."

"Power is necessary," Tony shot back. "People have to respect who's in charge and what the consequences are if they don't follow orders. What the hell is the matter with you? It's how things have always worked, even when we were soldiers."

"Maybe so. But we're not soldiers anymore, and we shouldn't act like one. They're at the bottom. They do the dirty work. It's the Caporegime, like us, who have to keep a level head—not lash out unless it threatens our business or our Boss. Konstantin's man being there posed no threat to anyone."

"It was a matter of respect," Tony said through clenched teeth. "We agreed, and Konstantin broke the agreement."

Eddie poured some whiskey into a shot glass and downed it. "Who are you kidding? You had Stan Amato there, didn't you?"

"I make the rules. It doesn't matter who I bring."

Eddie shook his head. "Listen to yourself. Are you starving for attention?"

Tony poured himself a drink. He lifted the glass and swallowed. His eyes swept over Eddie. "Don't you want more?"

"No. I'm content where I am."

"Just stop and think a minute. You and me as Under Bosses."

Eddie's pulse skipped. This couldn't be happening. He had always known Tony was ambitious, but this was way too much. Becoming an Under Boss meant the current one had to be replaced. Things like that didn't happen too often unless—unless permission was granted because the person had fallen out of favor with the five families."

"Do you have a death wish?" Eddie asked.

"Just thinking ahead."

"No, thinking without your head," Eddie said. "You need to pump the brakes and fast. First of all, Paulie isn't going anywhere. He's solid."

Tony grinned. "Come on, Staten Island. It's a slippery slope and you know it."

Eddie's hands clenched into fists underneath the table. This was like talking to a madman. "Why exactly did you come here today, Tony? There must be some other reason besides plotting a coup." The expression on Tony's face changed. Was it fear Eddie detected in his eyes?

Fingers fidgeting with his shot glass, Tony said. "I want to make sure three of my men remain tight-lipped. I'm not positive I can trust them. I guess, I'm asking, what would you do to ensure their loyalty besides throwing some extra cash their way?"

Eddie's hands relaxed. So it *was* fear he caught in Tony's eyes. He thought about his crew and how he knew they would do anything for him. Always careful to never mistreat anyone, he had earned their respect and loyalty.

"Where's this distrust coming from?" Eddie asked. "You groom a crew, you make sure they want for nothing—see to it that they feel special so there is no jealousy brewing among them."

"Is that what you do?" Tony asked.

"Sure. It's not that hard. Think back to when we were soldiers. All we ever wanted was to be recognized and respected. You need to give them a personal touch. Go a little bit out of your way for them. I do it all the time."

Tony nodded in agreement. He rested his chin in his hand as if deep in thought. "Yeah, you're right. I remember all I ever felt working for Frank Uzelli was fear. That was his way of keeping everyone in line."

"And look where it got him," Eddie said.

Tony finished off another shot of whiskey and got up. "Thanks for listening. Forget what I said earlier about Paulie. It's just me running my mouth." He extended his hand.

They shook, and Eddie walked him to the door. How easily lies rolled off his tongue. He had no doubt Tony meant every word he said.

Tony turned to him before going out the door. "We good?" he asked.

"Sure," Eddie said. The two bear-hugged, and Tony left. Eddie lingered at the door, watching as Tony got into his car. An uneasiness engulfed him. His friend had made the wrong move. It was only a matter of time before Paulie found out the truth. Soldiers talk—especially ones who fear their boss and want him out of the way.

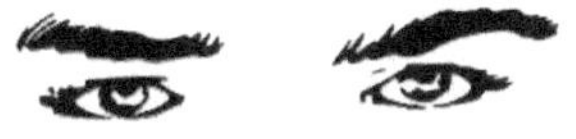

Chapter 36 — Damien
The Sister

Barely able to breathe, Damien tried to absorb what his father had revealed to him a few days ago. That same afternoon, he told Cookie everything. There need be no secrets between them. Cookie urged him to meet with his father again and find out more about his sister. With unsteady hands, he dialed Dimitri's number.

"Damien? I was not sure I would hear from you."

"I needed time to think about everything," Damien said. "I want to move forward."

"Wonderful," Dimitri said. "Let's meet at the same place, say 2:00 this afternoon. The rain has finally gone away. Those gloomy skies started to remind me of Russia too much."

Damien completed his early morning surgeries, then had his office administrator reschedule his afternoon appointments at his private practice.

Arriving fifteen minutes early, he sat on the same bench where he had first talked to his father. It was hard to think of Dimitri that way. The only father he had ever known was Alexei. But wanting this man to be in his life filled a hole inside Damien he never realized existed until now.

Down the path leading to the bench, he saw Dimitri approaching. A woman walked beside him, her arm looped around his. Tall, with blonde hair the color of butterscotch … like his own, her lips parted in an engaging smile when she spotted him. Damien rose, feeling the smile on his face even bigger than hers.

She stretched out her arms. "My brother," she said, her Russian accent stirring something profound inside him. They embraced, and she kissed him on both cheeks. He reciprocated. "I have waited all my life for this moment. I'm Anastasia." Her amber eyes were a perfect match to his own.

"I hardly know what to say. I never even knew you existed," Damien said, a hard lump forming in his throat.

They seated themselves on the bench, Damien in the middle of Anastasia and Dimitri.

"Did you not feel me?" Anastasia asked. "They say twins can experience certain things between them."

Damien felt himself blushing. "So, you were aware of me all this time?"

"Yes. Our father hid nothing from me."

"All this time I was feeling … out of place, like something was missing."

"Father tells me you are a doctor."

"Yes. An orthopedic trauma surgeon. And what about you?"

"I attended Lomonosov Moscow University. Father insisted I go to the best. I have a law degree, where my concentration is in Family Law."

"Impressive," Damien said.

Dimitri chuckled. "A son who is a doctor and a daughter who is a lawyer. Could a father ask for more?"

"How did you manage to get out of Russia?" Damien asked. "I mean … are you here to stay?"

"Let's just say, I became wealthy enough to be able to bribe the government on my own. It took many years to start and grow my diamond business. Exports to Hong Kong, India, and the United Arab Emirates proved to be very successful. Today, I can run my business from anywhere in the world, but I still have holdings in Russia as part of the deal."

A sense of relief washed over Damien. His father was a legitimate businessman and not aligned with the criminal element in Russia or here in the United States.

"So," Dimitri continued. "To answer your question. We are staying here. I have purchased a house not far from where you live. Yes, son. I did my research. Anastasia and I are residing in South Beach."

"So, you're single then, Anastasia?" Damien asked.

"*Da,*" she said, a slight catch in her voice. "My practice in Russia kept me quite busy, and now I have to establish myself here in America."

Damien laughed. "I completely understand. I was single for a very long time. But when I met Carlotta or Cookie, as she prefers to be called, my entire life changed." Damien pulled out his cell phone. "Here, this is the two of us on our wedding day."

Dimitri studied the picture. "So, that is how she knew so much about the flower arrangement I sent your mother."

"You gave her a bit of a fright," Damien said.

Dimitri nodded. "I can understand. I hope I will be forgiven."

"Of course," Damien said. "She wants nothing more than to meet with you and Anastasia."

"She is lovely," Anastasia said.

"Well, she doesn't look the same now. We are expecting a baby soon."

Dimitri's eyes lit up. "*Da blagoslovit vas Bog!*"

"Yes," Anastasia chimed in. "May God bless you both."

As he looked from his father to his sister, Damien's heart filled with insurmountable joy. All these years, he had a father who never stopped loving him and a sister he could start to build a relationship with.

Anastasia's face grew serious. "What about our mother, Damien?"

"Yes," Dimitri said. "How is Darya since Alexei has been imprisoned. I heard she also lost a son."

Damien felt the old familiar longing surge up. "Yes. My younger brother, Roman. I blame my father … I mean Alexei for his death. He was young and immature. His trying to emulate Alexei contributed to his demise. I will never forgive him for that." He hung his head and stared at the ground for a moment. "I wish I could have saved him."

Dimitri's arm wrapped around his shoulders. "I understand, but some things we cannot bear responsibility for. Otherwise, it takes away the happiness we truly deserve."

At his father's comforting words, Damien finally understood how Roman's death killed a part of him that should never have died. He looked into Dimitri's eyes. "Thank you for never giving up." He turned to Anastasia. "I will speak to Mother. There is a much-needed conversation to have before you meet her."

"I understand," Anastasia said.

As he sat content with his father and sister, he wondered how he could ever begin to forgive his mother. It was time to face her and decide if the hurt she caused had any possibility of healing.

***

Six the same evening, Damien rang the bell, his finger steady on the small round buzzer while he held the expandable file folder in his other hand. Coming here after today was not an easy thing to do. He needed answers, but most of all, he wanted the truth. Footsteps shuffled, and then the door swung open. His mother's face lit up.

"My *Pcholka*," she cried. "How nice it is to see you. Why have you stayed away so long?"

"Hello," Damien said tersely, tolerating the kiss planted on both his cheeks, which he did not return. He slipped off his shoes. Ignoring the pairs of slippers by the door, he remained in his stocking feet.

"Is something wrong?" Darya asked. "Is Carlotta okay?" She looked down and stared at the folder in his hand. She pointed at it. "What is it you have there?"

"Never mind this right now," Damien said. "Carlotta is fine, Mother. But we need to talk." He made his way into the living room and dropped onto a chair. He pointed at the sofa. "Please sit."

Worry lines creasing her face, Darya nodded and eased down. "Damien, what is the matter with you? Why are you acting this way with me?"

"First of all," Damien began. "I found out some things concerning your time in Russia." The hurt he was about to cause her unsettled him. But the damage she had done to him could not be ignored. "I want to know about my father. You've never spoken to me regarding him."

Her face pinched, the sudden furrows in her brow prominent. "There is nothing to tell. He left me when I became pregnant with you and—"

"Stop!" Damien shouted. "Stop lying and tell me the truth. After all these years, you owe me at least that much." He undid the clasp on the envelope, turned it upside down, and let the letters fall onto the coffee table."

Darya shrieked, her mouth fell open. "Where did you get those?"

"Where you thought I would never find them. I read every one of them from beginning to end." He pointed at the table. "My father's letters to you. Begging you for answers about me, about my life here in America. Letters you never even bothered to answer. Plus, my original birth certificate with the official Russian Seal. I guess Alexei was able to have a phony one made without my father's name on it!"

Darya's eyes filled. "Damien, please. You need to understand. We were so young, and my family did not want us together. I met Alexei and then—"

"More lies!" Damien grabbed a handful of letters. "Shall I begin reading these to you?"

Tears slid down her cheeks. She covered her face with both hands and rocked back and forth. "Okay, okay. Let me explain."

"Only the truth this time, otherwise you will never see me and Carlotta ever again … or meet your grandchild." Damien declared.

Darya stopped rocking. Her hands fell to her lap. "Grandchild?"

"Yes. Carlotta is pregnant. But I will not have our child around a grandmother who lies."

Darya wiped her eyes and let out a long breath. "You're father and I—"

"Please have the courtesy to use his name. Dimitri, isn't it?"

She shook her head. "Yes, yes, Dimitri Orlov. We were so young when I became pregnant with you. The part about my family is true. I eventually left home, and Dimitri and I tried to start a life together. We didn't have much money, and Dimitri came from a poor family. His prospects were not good."

"What happened then?" Damien asked.

"Alexei started coming around. My family sent him to break us up."

"Apparently, he succeeded," Damien spat. "Go on."

"He threatened Dimitri, and he was no match for Alexei. I was afraid for him, so I started accepting the gifts he sent, thinking it would appease him and he might leave Dimitri alone."

"Did you ask him to go away, Mother? Tell him you wanted to be with my father?"

"You do not understand, Damien. Alexei had power. Power he inherited from his father."

"And he used that power to beat *my* father half to death." Damien pointed his finger at her. "You knew, and still you left with a known criminal and came to America, where he continued the same life he left behind in Russia."

"I had no other choice," Darya said. "I didn't want Dimitri to die."

"But you enjoyed all those things Alexei gave you. Things bought with blood money. How easy it was for you to look the other way while enjoying your wonderful life here in America … while he murdered and tortured people."

"I was unaware of such things. He promised me he would not do anything illegal here. I was afraid, so I decided to start over with my life. Besides, Alexei would have never let me go."

"Tell me the truth. Carlotta said you still love him, even today."

Darya's shoulders slumped. "After I left Russia, I grew to love him. I cannot explain it any other way."

"Let's not forget he made a criminal out of Roman, who wanted nothing more than to emulate him. My little brother would have done anything for his approval," Damien said.

"Please do not speak of Roman. It is like a knife through my heart," Darya begged. "I blame myself. I should have paid more attention to him."

"It wouldn't have mattered, because instead of helping him, Alexei covered up all of Roman's misdeeds."

"But Alexei gave us a good life," Darya said. "He put you through medical school, something Dimitri and I could never have done in Russia."

"Oh," Damien said. "You would be surprised by what my father has accomplished."

Darya brushed at the tears still cascading down her cheeks. "What do you mean?"

"He is a well-respected diamond merchant. He even put my twin sister through law school."

Darya's face turned ashen. Her bottom lip trembled uncontrollably. "You know about her?"

"Who? Anastasia? That is her name, isn't it? Can you explain why you left my sister behind?"

She shook her head. "I couldn't take her with me. Alexei didn't want her. He only wanted you, a boy, a son to raise. So, I left her with Dimitri. I thought at least he would have his daughter."

"How kind of you, Mother." Damien got up.

"Wait," Darya cried. "Is Anastasia here?"

"Yes. So is Dimitri, but from what Carlotta told me, you already knew he was here. You abandoned him and my sister, yet he still sent you flowers. He is more of a man than Alexei ever was." Damien left the folder on the coffee table and strode out of the living room to the front door.

Darya hurried after him. "Please stay. I am sorry. I made some bad decisions back then when I did not know any better."

Damien moved closer until they stood face to face, his body inches from hers. "You'd better take the time to reflect on what you did. As a mother, you did know better, but you chose the easy way out. You left my father barely clinging to life with a daughter to raise, and then you lied to me about him." Damien slipped on his shoes.

"Wait, please, Damien. Can you ever forgive me?"

"Not now. Maybe never," he said, walking out and slamming the door behind him.

Chapter 37 — Brooke
Charlie

Brooke perched on a stool in a corner bar called Stella's on the Lower East Side of Manhattan. The dim interior reeked of stale whiskey with an undercurrent of marijuana. The few empty tables and chairs had seen better days. Long slits in several black clad leather booths exposed the white stuffing underneath. A slow, bassy, jazz tune oozed from an old jukebox in the far corner.

A man with a prominent scar across his cheek sat with a woman whose deep facial wrinkles reminded Brooke of a Shar-Pei dog. Two older men perched at the other end of the bar, one with his head planted face down, the other speaking at him as if he were still upright. The bartender, ignoring it all, stared at an overhead television set displaying a baseball game.

Brooke sipped a glass of plain seltzer water, hoping it had arrived minus any bacteria. Her mind and body vigilant, she waited for Charlie to arrive, her only comfort the firearm concealed underneath her coat. Agreeing to meet with him might be a grave mistake. But the circumstances gave her little choice. She needed him out of her life for good.

The door opened, and she swiveled on her stool. Charlie came toward her, grinning like a Cheshire Cat, dimples appearing on either side of his square jawline. Still as handsome as she remembered, his full head of jet-black hair and hazel eyes evoked memories of better times.

But she drew back as he leaned in to kiss her cheek. "Not a wise move, Charlie," Brooke said.

"Not even a hello?" he asked. He plopped down on the stool next to her, a hurt expression on his face.

"Nice meeting place you picked. I hope we make it out unscathed," Brooke quipped. "Funny how you claimed to be sober, yet you wanted to meet in a bar."

Charlie raised an eyebrow. "Sorry, I can't afford a fancy place uptown like you. Given that my employment has been terminated, I don't have the luxury of being too choosy about where I live. This place was convenient. That's all."

"Your current situation is not my fault," Brooke said, hoping to escape and head back to the office as soon as possible. "I warned you about the drugs—about your erratic behavior."

"As if you didn't partake."

"It was one time. You act as if I became a full-blown cocaine addict."

He signaled the bartender. "Just a tonic water, please."

"What do I have here?" the bartender said. "Two on the wagon?"

Brooke motioned to herself and Charlie. "We're just trying hard to remain civil. It's best we stay away from the booze."

The bartender chuckled and set a glass of tonic water in front of Charlie and resumed watching the ball game.

"Look," Brooke said. "Whether you believe me or not, I really am sorry about you losing your job. I wish …" She lowered her head.

"What? What do you wish?" Charlie gulped down his tonic water and then set the glass aside.

"That things had turned out differently for us." She raised her head, her gaze fixated on his hazel eyes, the ones she believed she couldn't ever live without. "You need to let go of me, Charlie. There is no 'us' and there never will be again."

"But I've told you I've changed. Come on, Brookie. Just give me a chance. I'll prove you can trust me again."

She cringed at him calling her Brookie. A once-endearing term, it had soured long ago.

"No. You need to move on."

"Is it because of what I did to you … I mean …?"

"Oh, are you talking about the split lip, or the bloody nose, or maybe the black eye I had to lie to my colleagues about?"

A flush crept up his face, and he looked away. "That was the drugs and the booze. I told you, I'm done with all that."

Brooke tossed a few bills on the bar and slid off her stool. "If you ever loved me at all, Charlie, you'll do the right thing." She moved toward the door, but he grabbed her arm.

"Please. Don't leave yet. I haven't finished talking to you."

Brooke looked down at his fingers curled around her forearm. "Let go, Charlie," she hissed. "Let go right now." She reached inside her coat with her other arm.

"What are you gonna do? Shoot me," he shot back.

Brooke yanked herself away. The softness on his face had evaporated and sparks of anger flashed in his eyes. In them, she saw all the hurt and pain he had caused her.

"Go ahead and try me, Charlie. This is your last warning. Go back to Texas or wherever else you like, but leave me alone. No more phone calls, no more lurking around my building. If I ever see or hear from you again, I'll make sure you're put away for a long time."

An eerie laugh escaped his lips. "Who are you kidding? All I have to do is inform the Bureau about our past activities. I ain't going anywhere without you."

His voice had the familiar finality she remembered so well. He wasn't going to stop. Unless she took matters into her own hands, this nightmare would continue until one of them was dead.

"If I were you, I'd be really careful from now on, Charlie. You never know who, besides me, might be waiting to put you down." Turning away, she strode to the door.

"Oh, you mean the guy you're sleeping with? The one who works at the Bureau?"

Brooke stopped. A shudder ran through her body. He even knew about her and Austin. The last thing she wanted was for Austin to be entangled in the issues between her and Charlie.

Without answering, she opened the door and stepped out of the bar. Hurrying up the street and around the corner to the safety of her car, she slammed the door and locked it.

Checking the rearview, she saw no sign of him. Quickly pulling away, she drove to the Federal Building, thoughts of Charlie and how to get rid of him once and for all foremost in her mind.

Chapter 38 — Austin
Falling

Austin woke to the aroma of freshly brewed coffee. He reached, feeling the warmth on the sheet next to him where Brooke had lain. They had been seeing one another for a few weeks now. Keeping a low profile when he was around her at work was becoming increasingly difficult. Unsure of how she felt about him, his feelings for her were growing. The chemistry between them couldn't be denied, and he hoped it would never end. There wasn't any mention of his issue with Stan Amato, so he assumed Monica had smoothed things over.

Brooke entered the bedroom in a pink lace robe, her blonde bob tousled by a night of fierce lovemaking. She brought two cups of coffee over and handed one to Austin.

"Good morning," she said warmly, her lips edging up into a smile.

"It sure is," Austin said, easing up against the pillows. "Thanks for the coffee." He sipped the hot liquid, feeling it go down easily. "I was thinking since we're both off today, why not do something special?"

Brooke set her cup on the end table and slipped down beside him. She rested her head against his bare chest. "What do you have in mind?"

"Maybe a stroll through the Metropolitan. They house a collection of over seventy-five thousand works from the invention of photography to the present."

"I didn't know you were interested in photography," Brooke said, her fingers trailing along his chest.

"My father was a photographer. A pretty good one. Of course, he never achieved international fame, but he did have some exhibitions at several galleries back home in Southern California." At his last words, it dawned on him how little they knew about one another.

"Is Texas home for you?" he asked.

She glanced up and then rested her head again. "Seattle, Washington. My parents still live there. What about yours?"

"After my dad retired, my parents left California and settled in Hawaii. They dreamed of doing that for years. It was all they ever talked about. But I have two sisters," Austin said. "One's a nurse at Cedars Sinai, and the other is a professor at USC."

Brooke giggled and snuggled against him.

"What's so funny?" Austin asked.

"You. Growing up with only sisters as siblings. I bet that was a lot of fun."

"Yeah, we were pretty rambunctious. I teased the heck out of them. My poor parents were at their wits' end at times. What about you? Any brothers or sisters?" Her deep sigh reverberated through his chest.

"I had an older brother. His name was Quentin. He was killed in a car crash when he was seventeen."

Austin swept his hand through her hair. "I'm so sorry, Brooke. That must have been awful."

"Yes, it was. My parents have never gotten over his death. Maybe it's the reason I make it a point to go home for the holidays. I'm the only one left, and I feel they need me to be there."

"Okay," Austin said. "Enough talk for now. How about we go out, grab breakfast, and head to the Met?"

She rolled away from him and got up. "Better yet. You shower while I make us some breakfast."

"You don't need to do that," Austin said.

She grinned down at him. "I know. But I want to."

After she left the bedroom, Austin rose and got in the shower. A funny feeling hit the pit of his stomach. Why did she never want to go out much? It was becoming a struggle just to eat dinner at a restaurant. Most of the time, she insisted on ordering in or cooking up something.

He toweled off, dressed in jeans and a sweatshirt, the smell of bacon beckoning him to the kitchen. Brooke placed a platter of scrambled eggs, toast, and strips of Maplewood bacon in the center of the kitchen table. She poured two fresh cups of coffee and set them down.

"Looks great," Austin said, taking a seat across from her and filling his plate.

"I see you're dressed already," she said.

He caught the look of disappointment on her face and almost caved. "Yes. Because after this fabulous breakfast, I'm taking you to the Met."

"Oh. I thought maybe we could stay in today."

Austin set his fork down. "How come you never want to go out? Are you afraid we'll run into someone from the Bureau?"

Brooke shook her head. "No, not at all. I like being alone with you."

"I think it's more than that. I'm not sure what it is, but it almost seems as if, at times, you're bothered by something. Whatever it is, you can tell me. I won't judge you, Brooke."

"Don't be silly. Everything is fine."

Austin noticed the slight tremor in her hand as she picked up her fork. Something spooked her, and he could feel it. But not wanting to push her away, he caved.

"I guess we'll stay in then."

Her eyes locked on him. "No. You're right. We should go out. You finish eating while I shower and dress." She got up and kissed the top of his head. "The Met it is."

***

They traversed the halls of the Metropolitan Museum of Art, its rounded marble arches holding so many treasures. Dozens of people wandered through each area, all pointing and commenting on what they saw.

The Chinoiserie exhibit, with its beautiful porcelain pottery, held Brooke's attention more so than Austin's. Glad she agreed to go, he remained patient when they lingered there a bit longer than he would have liked. Moving on, they marveled at the African Art in the Rockefeller Wing, along with Ancient American Art, Egyptian Art, and European Sculpture and Decorative Arts.

Brooke insisted they see the Costume Institute with its displays of famous designer clothes and a history of the evolution of fashion. Their last stop was the Photography Exhibits. Austin felt he could have spent a lifetime there and still not have seen everything. Memories of his father's work kept popping into his head.

"Thank you," Austin said, kissing Brooke lightly on the lips. "I really needed this. It brings me close to my father even though he's so far away. I can't wait to tell him about some of the things we've seen."

Hand in hand, they continued their stroll when suddenly Brooke's hand drifted away from his. She had stopped a few feet behind him, her eyes searching the gallery.

Austin stood beside her. "What is it?"

"Nothing," she responded, her smile forced, somewhat artificial, and her eyes a bit wild.

"Did you see someone you know?" Austin asked.

"No. It's nothing. Let's continue." She grasped his hand again as they took in the following exhibit. Austin checked his watch and couldn't believe they had spent almost three hours at the museum.

"Enough for today?" he asked.

"I think so," Brooke said, glancing behind her.

"How about dinner somewhere nice?"

"I'm kinda tired," Brooke said. "Let's order in."

It was then that Austin knew for sure, something scared her. He stopped at the bottom of the entrance steps. "You need to tell me what's wrong. And don't say nothing. At times, you acted like you were being hunted back there."

Grabbing his hand, she tugged him forward. "Don't be silly. Everything's fine."

As they made their way back to her apartment, Austin vowed not to leave her until she came clean. He was falling hard for her. Tonight, he would find out just what was wrong with Brooke Adams."

Chapter 39 — Cookie Revelation

Cookie opened the door to the Vintage Tea House. Darya's frantic calls to meet her here had gone unanswered until today. Damien's revelations about her mother-in-law angered her. To think she kept Dimitri and Damien's twin sister a secret all these years altered her opinion of Darya.

Surrounded by elegant floral settees and wingback chairs, she was led to a corner table at the far end where Darya waited. She passed by groups of women drinking from ornate porcelain teacups. Tall tiers of small sandwiches made of cucumber, egg salad, smoked salmon, and pimento cheese were piled high on the laced clothed tables in front of them. Another tray held petit fours consisting of dark chocolate dipped maraschino cherries, lemon tarts, and French Macarons.

Darya rose as she approached. "Carlotta, I am so glad you agreed to meet with me." Her eyes filled with tears at the sight of Cookie's well-rounded stomach underneath her simple beige dress.

Cookie stiffened as she kissed each of her cheeks. She reciprocated and eased into a chair across from her. "I want you to understand Damien has no idea I'm here. But since you've been so good to me these past few years, I felt I owed it to you to hear what you have to say."

"Thank you," Darya said. She picked up a teapot adorned with colorful butterflies and poured them each a cup. She pointed to the tray of sandwiches. "Please eat, Carlotta. I remember how it is when you are carrying a baby."

Cookie plucked one of the sandwiches from the tray and set it down on her plate.

"I do not know what Damien told you."

"Everything," Cookie said. "You broke his heart, Darya. As his mother, how could you do that to him?"

"I have done a terrible thing." A tear splashed down her cheek, and she dabbed at it with her napkin. "I never meant to hurt him. I only wanted to protect him."

"From what?" Cookie snapped, unmoved by her tears. "He had a right to know his father didn't forget about him and that he had a twin sister. Help me understand Darya, or I'm afraid this thing between the two of you will never be repaired."

Darya's hand shook as she brought her teacup to her lips and sipped. "Dimitri is lying to Damien. He is not the man he portrays himself to be."

"What do you mean?"

"I understand he told Damien that he is in the diamond business."

"Yes. Dimitri and Anastasia even came to our apartment to have dinner with us. He seems very sincere." Unable to deny her hunger, Cookie bit into her sandwich. The taste of the cucumber and herbed cream cheese a bit unsettling in her mouth, she set the rest aside.

"I am sure he presented himself well, but…"

"Darya, if you have more information about Dimitri, then you need to tell me."

"I could not disappoint Damien. He had just found his father. His anger towards me was almost more than I could bear. I did not want to fuel it further."

"Disappoint him how?"

Darya leaned forward and clasped her shaking hands. "Back in Russia, Dimitri was part of Alexei's gang. As a matter of fact, the two were close. Almost like brothers."

Cookie couldn't believe what she was hearing. Was Darya making it all up?

"But Alexei had eyes for me," she continued. "Even knowing I was pregnant with Dimitri's child, he still pursued me. It continued after I gave birth to Damien and Anastasia. He and Dimitri came to blows. But even that didn't stop Alexei. He rounded up some of his other men, and they beat Dimitri half to death.

"Then, Alexei told me if I did not go with him to America, he would kill Dimitri. I could not let that happen, so I agreed."

"What about Anastasia?" Cookie asked. "Why didn't you take her with you?"

"I told Damien the truth. Alexei only wanted him, a son he could raise." Her eyes glistened, and she looked away for a moment. "I did not want Dimitri to have lost everything, so I left her with him. As a mother, you can imagine the pain it caused me. I have thought of her every single day since I left Russia."

"Are you telling me Dimitri is a criminal?" Cookie asked, her head spinning at what Darya had told her.

"Yes. He was well known and feared in Russia. But you need to understand, Carlotta. I was so young when I met him. I did not find out until it was too late. My family disowned me because of my pregnancy. I had no one and nowhere to go."

"Is that why the flowers upset you so much?"

"Yes. I could not believe he came to America. Maybe he deals with diamonds, but I am sure it is not a legal business."

"What about Anastasia? Do you think she's aware of his background?"

"Growing up in Russia, there is no way he could hide this from her. Dimitri is most likely well-known. Over the years, rumors circulated about Dimitri. Alexei believed they were true."

After listening to Darya, Cookie understood the conversation between her and Alexei at the prison. It all made sense. But telling Damien the truth was another story. She almost wished she hadn't agreed to meet her mother-in-law. On the other hand, if Dimitri was lying, Damien needed to know.

"Carlotta, listen to me. Before you say anything to Damien, you must find out about Dimitri. If he did change his life, then no harm is done, but if not, he has brought his life of crime here to America."

"Tell me something," Cookie said. "What you said about loving Alexei, were you being honest?"

"As I told Damien. I learned to love him. Maybe it was wrong, but it is my truth."

Cookie nodded. "If I tell Damien about all this, he'll want proof. I have someone who can look into it." Cookie got up. "I need to go."

"Wait, please, before you leave. When is my grandchild coming?"

Cookie patted her baby bump. "Three more months. We didn't want to know the sex."

For the first time, Darya smiled. "Thank you again for coming. May I ask one other thing?"

"Yes. What is it?"

"Tell me about Anastasia. Does she seem happy?"

"As far as I can tell, yes," Cookie said. "She graduated from Law School in Russia. She and Damien look so much alike. You can tell in an instant they're brother and sister."

"Well, I pray Damien will forgive me one day … and I hope Anastasia can, too. Tell them both how sorry I am. Maybe you could ask if my daughter will see me?"

Cookie shook her head. "No, not unless she brings it up. I won't be put in the middle, Darya. Now, I have to go."

Outside the tearoom, Cookie immediately dialed Monica's number. "I need your help."

"What's up?" Monica asked. "Are you and the baby okay?"

"We're fine. Remember I told you about Damien meeting his father and sister for the first time?"

"Sure. You said the dinner with everyone went fine. I still can't imagine how Damien feels, not knowing his father and having a twin sister he never met."

"Well, it seems there's more to the story." She filled Monica in on Darya's information about Dimitri.

"Sure. I can look into it. Dimitri Orlov, right?"

"Yes. How long will it take?"

"Not long. I'll run his name through our system. If we're lucky, maybe he turned legit, and there's nothing to worry about."

"I hope so. Thanks, Monica. I won't say anything to Damien until I hear from you."

***

Unable to sleep, Cookie tossed and turned while Damien slept soundly beside her. How much more heartache could her husband stand if Dimitri turned out to be a criminal?

Chapter 40 — Eddie
A Conversation

Eddie grumbled at the thought of meeting with Nico again. What was he supposed to tell the guy regarding Tony? Even though he refused to let Tony speak out loud about eliminating Stavros Papadakis, he knew the truth. Being forced to lie to Paulie and now to Nico didn't make him feel good.

As he meandered down the sidewalk on busy Victory Boulevard, the late spring air hummed with the possibility of a warm summer. Passing Monica and Cookie's florist shop, he stopped and went inside.

"Oh no," Cookie said from behind the counter, where she was in the middle of arranging flowers. She set down the pink rose in her hand and picked up a glass vase. "You have some nerve coming in here after that stunt you and your idiot friend pulled a while back." She aimed and let the vase fly.

Eddie held up his hands and caught it in midair. "Geez, Cookie! Why do you have to get violent? You could have cracked my head open."

Her hands cinched what was left of her waist, the growing baby inside of her having claimed most of it. "I wish," she shot back. Coming out from behind the counter, she stomped over to him, her eyes blazing. "I am so sick and tired of you ruining things for Monica."

"Come on," Eddie said, taking a step back. "It wasn't so bad. We were a little drunk, that's all."

"Your whole life has been one big excuse. First, when you cheated, and then going back into the mob—"

"Enough, Cookie," Eddie said. "We're both familiar with my history, let's not rehash it. I didn't come here to upset you. I came to apologize for my behavior."

"Really. What about that asshole friend of yours?"

Eddie blinked. "What about him?"

"He should be standing right here with you doing the same thing."

Eddie couldn't help but smirk. "I'm afraid that's not going to happen. Besides, you'll never see Tony again."

"Lucky for him," Cookie said, raising her fist. "Calling me feisty. I'll give him feisty right between his—"

"Yeah, okay," Eddie cut in. "I get the picture. I'm truly sorry for what happened, and I hope Monica will forgive me. I didn't mean to ruin her night."

Cookie's eyes swept over him. "Yes, you did. You're lying as usual. You couldn't stand to see her with some other guy."

Fearing his face would tell the tale, Eddie looked away. He walked to the door. "Just please tell her for me. And by the way, congratulations on the baby. I'm happy for you, Cookie." He slipped out of the shop before she could say anything else.

He checked his watch and headed up the street to the West Shore Inn and Steakhouse to meet Nico. Once inside the dark interior, he ordered a gin and tonic from the gleaming oak bar and sat on one of the high-back tufted red leather stools. Gino, the bartender, someone Eddie knew from the neighborhood, set his drink down.

"On the house, Eddie," Gino said.

Eddie winked. "Thanks." Glancing around, he picked up his drink and slid into one of the remaining empty booths across from the bar. The chatter from others around him was soft and low. The aroma of steak sizzling filled the air. Two menus lay on the table. A few minutes later, Nico came in and sat across from him.

"Drink?" Eddie asked and signaled Gino.

"Sure," Nico said. "Scotch neat." He retrieved his drink from the bar and joined Eddie again. "I guess you already know why I wanted to meet with you again."

"Yes. You're becoming a bit of a thorn in my side, Nico."

"You said you would find out if Tony had anything to do with Stavros disappearing."

"Look," Eddie said. "I met with Tony. He didn't say anything about Stavros. Maybe you're looking in the wrong direction."

Nico's eyes narrowed. His hand clenched into a fist on top of the table. "What direction do you suppose I look in, Eddie?"

"All I'm saying is, maybe Stavros going missing has nothing to do with our side. You're assuming it does, and that's not fair. How well do you know Stavros and what he was into?"

Before Nico could answer, a waitress appeared, her eyes devouring the two handsome men. Her long blonde hair was pulled back into a ponytail. "What can I get you fellas?"

Eddie nodded toward Nico. "Let me order. I come here all the time." Her flawless complexion and full lips beckoned to him. She must be new. He smiled at her, knowing she wanted more than to take his order. "We'll both have the Volcanic Steak Tips, with garlic mashed potatoes, gravy, and fried onions, medium well."

"Great choice," she said. "I'll put the order right in."

"Are you trying to distract me?" Nico asked. "There is no other explanation for his going missing. But I can tell you this. Konstantin is adamant it points to Tony. He is not a patient man, Eddie. I can only hold him off for so long."

Eddie sipped his gin and tonic. Throwing the Greeks off Tony's trail wasn't working. He didn't blame them one bit. If he were in their shoes, he'd believe the same thing. "Are we talking retaliation, Nico? Because if so, we all lose."

The waitress set down their plates. "Is there anything else you need?"

"No," Eddie said. "This looks great."

"All I'm saying is I don't know how long I can keep Konstantin from doing something crazy."

Eddie cut into one of the strips of steak and dipped it into the mashed potatoes. He chewed, relishing the taste of the tender meat. He observed Nico taking his first bite. "Good, isn't it?" he remarked.

"Nice choice," Nico said. "But make no mistake. A pleasant meal with you isn't going to change the current circumstances."

Eddie grinned. "Maybe. But it might encourage you to convince Konstantin to move on. We do a lot of business together. I would hate for all that to end. I'm sure your boss realizes how much he stands to lose if we walk away."

"There would be loss on both sides," Nico said, gulping the last of his scotch.

"More on yours than ours. Don't forget the seaport." Eddie clenched his fork in one hand and his knife in the other. The conversation began to bore him. "I'm gonna be frank with you, Nico. Get Konstantin to focus on something else. Word is he has a shipment coming in soon. I don't think he would want anything to happen to it."

"Is that a threat?" Nico said, his face like iron.

"Look, I'm not involved in the seaport stuff, but if you rub Tony the wrong way, I can almost guarantee Konstantin will be on the losing end of things."

Both men grew silent as they finished their food. Eddie cursed inside, knowing the mess Tony had almost certainly created. Nico's anxiety wasn't a good sign. His gut told him something was going to jump off sooner or later. "Go back to Konstantin," Eddie said. "Tell him there is no proof Tony did anything to Stavros Papadakis. This way, we can all move on."

Nico got up. "I can't make any promises. Thanks for the meal." He turned and left the restaurant.

Eddie seethed inside, the food unsettling his stomach. Tony had put him in the middle between the Greeks and Paulie. How long before retaliation turned into an all-out war? He needed a diversion. The waitress came to the table, and he glanced at her nametag.

"Frankie?" he said. "That's unusual for a girl."

She bit her bottom lip as her cheeks flushed a pale pink. "It's really Francine—Frankie's just a nickname.

"What time do you get off, Frankie?" Eddie asked. She might be just the thing to settle his mind.

"Half-hour from now."

"There's a white BMW parked out front. I'll be waiting inside." He got up, tossed a hundred-dollar bill on the table, and left.

***

After some small talk, Eddie secured a hotel room. He never took any women to his apartment. If they didn't understand his no attachments rule, there could be trouble down the line.

He pulled Frankie close and undid the clasp on her ponytail. His hands swept through her long hair. Their lips met, and she let out a moan. Eddie made the kiss go deeper, then, breaking away, he led her to the bed. They undressed and lay down, hands and tongues exploring new territory. Eddie closed his eyes. All he could see was Monica and how much he hungered for her. Would the rest of his life be like this? No matter who he took to bed, he imagined the woman was Monica.

After he and Frankie finished, he made an excuse about a meeting he needed to attend and drove her home. He thanked God she didn't live anywhere near him.

"Will I see you again, Eddie?"

"Sure, I'll be around."

"Don't you want my number?" she asked.

"I know where to find you," Eddie said and winked. Glad when she got out of the car, he pulled away, satisfied with the short distraction. Unable to stop himself, he drove to Monica's street and parked on the opposite side a few cars away. He cut the ignition and waited.

It was early evening, but the lights were off in her apartment. He wondered about Andrew and where they could be. About to drive away, he stopped when a silver Lexus LS slid into a parking spot in front of Monica's. A man got out. Eddie recognized him right away. It was the same man from Violetta's. So, Andrew must be at her parents' house.

He opened the car door for Monica. His arms caught her waist, and he pulled her close. They kissed, then climbed the steps and went inside.

Eddie's pulse spiked. He slapped his hand against the steering wheel. Had he lost Monica for good? Seeing her with another man became unbearable. He wanted to run up the steps and pound on her door—tell her how much he still loved her.

Instead, he turned on the ignition and sped away, his heart aching, his mind exploding. There had to be a way to repair what they once had. He'd give up everything, no matter what the consequences.

Tomorrow, he told himself. Tomorrow, he would tell her all the things he was feeling. He loved her deeply and missed being together. That they could leave Staten Island, be a family, just the three of them. A tear trailed down his cheek, and he wiped it away with the back of his hand.

He reached his apartment and parked. The urgency for tomorrow to come failed to leave him. He showered and tried to sleep, but thoughts of Monica wouldn't subside. She couldn't refuse him anymore.

The next morning, sunlight breached his bedroom. As he came awake, reality settled itself all around him. He sat up against the pillows, the constant ache in his heart so strong he felt his chest might burst open. Monica would never be his again.

Chapter 41 — Kai
The Diner

After grabbing a booster seat, Kai seated the family of four and set the menus down on the table. She found her job as a hostess over the past few weeks to be an easy one. The staff were likable enough and welcomed her warmly, with one exception. Dina. From the first day, she made her feelings known to Kai. She saw her as a threat to her relationship with Konstantin. Everyone knew the two were real cozy. Dina made it a point of showing off the jewelry he had given her. If she only knew how little interest Kai had in a man like Konstantin.

"Your server will be right with you," Kai said, returning to the front of the diner.

Konstantin came through the swinging kitchen doors and planted himself in front of her—just a bit too close, Kai noticed.

"I see things are going well."

"Yes. I'm enjoying it," Kai said. "Most of the customers are very nice. I haven't had any trouble so far."

"Speaking of trouble, I am almost afraid to ask if you might be able to organize my desk. I cannot seem to get it in order. You could look at the payroll account. I have been making a few errors and would appreciate any help."

'Sure," Kai said. "I'll be glad to take a look. When would you want me to start?"

He shoved his hands into the side pockets of his pants and rocked back on his heels as if deep in thought. "Would tonight after your shift be okay?"

"Certainly."

"I need to go out for a bit later, so I will leave you the key." With a nod and a wink, he returned to the kitchen.

Her adrenaline pumping, Kai couldn't wait for her shift to end. This was what she had been waiting for. A chance to see the books and maybe find some other interesting details that could help when it came time for indictments."

Nico came through the door and stopped. As per their usual routine, he bent and kissed her on each cheek, and she did the same to him.

"How are you, Kitty?" he asked.

"Fine. Konstantin asked me to stay and organize his accounts tonight, so I'm sorry we can't have dinner." She spoke loudly so that some of the others could hear. First, so Nico would know precisely where she was, and second, to cement their relationship as cousins.

"No worries," Nico said. "We can do it some other time."

Konstantin hurried toward them. "Here is the key, Kitty." He placed it in her hand, his own lingering there for a fraction of a second. "The password for the computer is Acropolis. You will find the payroll file there." He nodded at Nico. "Come. The others are waiting."

Shocked that he had given her his computer password, Kai checked her watch. Ten more minutes until the end of her shift. She led two more people to a booth before telling Connie, the cashier, she was done for the day. Winding her way through the kitchen, she stopped at her locker and grabbed her purse. About to insert the key into the office door, she felt someone come up behind her.

"What are you doing back here?"

Kai swung around and came face-to-face with Dina. Her face a mask of defiance, she folded her arms and stood stock still.

"Konstantin asked me to organize his desk," Kai said, stepping toe to toe with her. "Is that a problem?" Kai held up the key.

"I guess not," Dina said, inching backwards.

"Good," Kai said. She inserted the key and then opened the door. Dina remained, with her lips pursed together, her eyes flashing Kai a hateful look.

Kai stepped inside. She turned and smiled before slamming the door in Dina's face and locking it. "*Bitch*," she hissed under her breath.

Plopping down on the chair behind Konstantin's desk, she surveyed the mountain of papers in front of her and dug in. Most were invoices and receipts from orders for the diner. She separated them by category and date and stacked them neatly together.

She stared at his computer, turned it on, and entered the password. Only one file appeared on the desktop. She clicked and found it was the payroll. Doing a search from the start menu turned up nothing. Why would he have a computer with only payroll on it?

Perplexed, she turned her attention to the two tall file cabinets. She got up and tried the drawers. To her surprise, they opened. Starting from the top, she checked each one only to find more old invoices and receipts. Disappointed, she returned to the desk. There were three drawers down one side. She tugged on each one. All opened freely. None of it made sense unless he kept other records at home.

She got up and wandered around the room, her heels clicking on the wood floor until she heard a hollow sound emanating from the floorboards beside one of the cabinets. She tapped her heels again and hurried over to the desk. She pulled the top drawer open and grabbed a silver letter opener. Kneeling over the hollow spot, she pried a floorboard loose. It lifted easily, and she set it aside. Her hand dipped inside, pulling out a red leather-bound ledger.

Her adrenaline soared as she brought it over to the desk and began flipping through the pages. At first, she wasn't sure what she was looking at. The first column listed names like The Mary Jane, Emmett Lee, Serenity, and Freedom. The second column listed dates, and the third column listed monetary amounts.

Kai looked at the last column. Her breath caught when she read numbers with kilos listed beside them. Her whole body thrummed with excitement. The first column must be the names of ships. This was a log of drug shipments. She pulled out her cell phone, intending to snap a few pictures when she heard Konstantin's voice coming from the kitchen.

She slammed the ledger shut, jumped up, and placed it back underneath the floorboard.

The doorknob twisted and then jiggled. "Kitty! Konstantin called. "Open the door."

Grabbing the key off the desk, she quickly opened it. "Sorry," she said.

"Why was the door locked?" he said gruffly. "You are safe. There is no reason to lock it."

"Dina gave me a bit of trouble earlier."

He scowled at her and shook his head. "No. Dina would not do that."

"But she did," Kai protested. "She wanted to know what I was doing in here, and she kept standing by the door, so I closed it and turned the lock."

His body visibly relaxed. "Oh, I see. Dina is very protective of me. I am sure she did not mean anything by it. In the future, you will keep the door wide open and unlocked. As I said, you are safe here."

"Of course," Kai said.

His eyes surveyed the desk. "This is so much better."

"I'll need to get some folders. I didn't have time to look at the payroll yet."

"Sure, sure," he said, finally breaking into a smile. "Whatever you need."

Kai grabbed her purse and went to the door. "Guess I'll be heading home."

"Wait," Konstantin said.

Barely able to breathe, a cold wave swept through her body as she turned around to face him.

"You forgot this." He held up her cell phone and brought it over to her.

"Thanks," Kai said. "See you in the morning."

"Goodnight," Konstantin called after her.

***

When she reached her apartment, Nico was waiting outside.

"What are you doing here?"

"I wanted to make sure you made it home. I couldn't go back to the diner because Konstantin sent me to check on one of the gambling houses."

"Well, here I am safe and sound. Come with me. I have some news."

He followed her inside and dropped down onto the living room sofa. "What is it?"

She paced back and forth as she related what she had found in Konstantin's office. "I couldn't get any photos because Konstantin came back. I almost got caught."

Nico got up and went over to her. "You hit the jackpot when you found that ledger, but you need to be more careful. Leave the ledger alone. There will be time enough to get it when all this is finished."

"Not if he moves it somewhere else."

"If he had come back sooner," Nico said. "We wouldn't be standing here having this conversation, and my cover would have been blown. You're supposed to be my cousin after all ..."

His voice drifted off. Her eyes caught his and held them. A funny feeling swept through her. They were still until Nico broke the silence between them. Shifting his gaze away from her, he said, "I should go." Before she could respond, he slipped out the door.

In the bedroom, Kai removed her heels and sat on the edge of the bed. Nico's face swam before her. What was this pull she felt toward him? Different from anything she experienced with Tony, it unnerved her. Tonight, when his eyes captured hers, she was certain he felt it, too.

But right now, their focus had to be on this case and nothing else, she cautioned herself. One false move could ruin everything. You never knew who might be watching. Luck was on her side earlier tonight, only to remind her to stay vigilant while undercover. She sent Monica a text about the ledger and then deleted it from her phone.

Slowly, she undressed and got into bed. She slept soundly through the night with dreams of Nico easing her mind.

Chapter 42 — Monica
Assembling A Case

Monica and Brooke sat in the conference room. A little at a time, things had fallen into place. She updated her on Kai's discovery of Konstantin's Ledger.

"That's a huge find," Brooke said. "Maybe we should issue a sneak and peek search warrant. I'd feel better if the Bureau got its hands on it."

"That type of warrant is iffy," Monica said. "They're known to be suppressed in court mostly because of the deliberate delayed notification of the suspect. Plus, if we do that," Monica continued. "We lose the other side of our investigation. There is not enough to charge Tony Morello and the others yet. We need the date and time of the next drug shipment. Hopefully, Nico will be able to pin that down soon."

"I'm not sure I agree. We should be able to throw in illegal gambling along with the trafficking charges. Plus, the Mafia has its crew of enforcers. It wouldn't be hard to throw in extortion and racketeering and indict some of their soldiers."

The amount of information Monica withheld from Brooke began to eat away at her. But she still couldn't bring herself to let her in on Austin's intel regarding the murder of Stavros Papadakis. If she knew that piece of the puzzle, she'd pull the plug on everything and hand it over to the DOJ.

"Nico has worked so hard," Monica said. "Let's give this a little more time. I wouldn't want him to feel we didn't value his undercover work."

Brooke sighed and rested her hands on the table. "That's just the thing, Monica. Nico's exceeded what we all thought would be a short-term undercover operation. You're his handler. How do you think he's doing mentally and physically?"

Monica paused. "I won't lie and say he's fine. I've seen signs of stress. But even he insists he wants to see this case to the end. Pulling him out now might hurt his psyche more than leaving him in."

"This is a tough decision for me, Monica. Let me mull it over. But make no mistake, if I say we are done, then we call Nico and Kai in and go with what we have so far."

Monica nodded. "I understand."

***

Riding the Staten Island Ferry home that evening with Andrew in tow, Monica hoped the decisions she had been making these past few weeks wouldn't end up getting her fired from the Bureau. They were so close to wrapping this case up tight—making the indictments stick. She prayed Nico would have some news soon regarding the drug shipment. Although relevant, the ledger only showed past shipments. Since she was interrupted, Kai wasn't able to take any pictures.

The ferry docked, and she joined the stream of commuters disembarking. Holding tight to Andrew's hand, she made her way to the public parking lot. She strapped Andrew into the car seat in the rear and got behind the wheel.

"Look, Mommy!" Andrew cried

Her eyes focused on the rearview mirror. "What is it?" Her son's face lit up into a huge grin.

"It's Daddy."

Before she could take another breath, the car door opened on the passenger side and Eddie got in. He turned and looked over his shoulder at Andrew, who squealed with delight.

"Hey, how's my buddy?" Eddie said. "I miss you."

"Miss you, too, Daddy."

Eddie reached into his pocket and pulled out a lollipop. He unwrapped it and handed it to Andrew.

Her teeth clenched so tight, Monica thought she might chip a tooth. Her eyes shot daggers at Eddie. "What do you think you're doing?"

"Saying hello," he said, a devilish grin on his face. "I had some business not far from here. I took a chance and came to the terminal. When I spotted your car in the lot, I—"

"Don't, Eddie. Don't make believe your being here is okay."

He rolled his eyes and frowned. "Why do you always have to make such a big deal over everything? Why can't I just see my son and say hello?"

Andrew's little voice echoed, "Hello." He sucked loudly on his lollipop and giggled.

"God!" Monica said. "He's getting more and more like you."

"Nothing wrong with that," Eddie remarked.

"You don't want to go there, do you?" Monica asked. "Please, just let me get Andrew home."

"Sure," Eddie said. "He climbed out of the car. "Meet you there."

Before she could answer, he hurried away.

"Daddy!" Andrew screamed. "Come back."

Monica turned to look at her son. "Hush. He's coming to the house. You'll see him in a few minutes."

Her head beginning to pound, she put the car in gear and drove out of the lot. By the time she reached her house, Eddie was sitting on the front steps.

"Daddy, Daddy!" Andrew chanted like Eddie was some kind of hero. She took him out of the car, and Eddie followed them inside.

Monica shrugged out of her light jacket and tossed it along with her purse on the sofa. She removed her service revolver and locked it in the metal box on the closet shelf.

Eddie moved toward her with a huge smile on his face.

She glanced down at her white silk blouse and quickly buttoned it all the way up to the collar.

"Really? Are you that scared of me?" Eddie mocked.

"Just being cautious," Monica quipped. "Come into the kitchen, Andrew. Mommy's going to make dinner."

Andrew stomped his foot. "No. I want to stay with Daddy."

"You go on," Eddie said. "I'll keep him occupied."

"Okay." Monica pointed at Andrew's foot. "But that's gotta go."

"Don't worry. I'll have a talk with him," Eddie said.

Monica whipped up a quick dinner of chicken breasts, mashed potatoes, and broccoli. By the time they sat down at the table, Andrew could hardly contain himself. It almost broke her heart to see him this happy all because the three of them were together.

When they finished, Eddie offered to bathe him while she cleaned up the kitchen. Later, he read Andrew a story, and they both tucked him in.

Back in the living room, Eddie made himself comfortable on the couch. "Admit it, Monica," he said. "Wasn't this nice for Andrew? I mean to see us together as a family."

Monica sat on the opposite end of the sofa and tucked her legs underneath her. "I love seeing our son so happy, but I don't want him getting the wrong idea in his head."

"What do you mean?"

"That this is going to be normal."

"What's wrong with normal?" Eddie asked, quirking a brow. "Every kid wants to see their parents together."

"But we're not together. He's used to our routine, and I don't want to confuse him."

Eddie got up and then kneeled in front of her. "I saw you the other night," he said softly.

Alarm bells rang in Monica's head. "What do you mean?"

"With that guy. The same one from the restaurant. Chaz, something or other."

"You better not be spying on me, Eddie. And by the way, his name is Chase."

"I wasn't. I rode past and—"

"Funny, how you seem to be riding past my house so much," Monica cut in. "It's creepy, Eddie. Only stalkers do that."

He got up and sat next to her. "I'm not a stalker, Monica. I'm the guy who's still in love with you. It hurts me to see you with someone else."

Those mesmerizing nautical blue eyes of his were pulling her into some place she didn't want to go. She quickly looked away. "Come on, Eddie. Like you haven't been with anyone else."

"I told you I would never lie to you again, and I'll keep that promise. Yes, I've been with other women, but you know what happens every single time. All I see is you. Your face, your body, the way we used to—"

Monica shoved him and jumped up from the sofa. "Stop, Eddie. Just stop. I don't want to hear anymore." Tears stung her eyes, and she turned her back on him, going to the window overlooking the park.

Eddie came up behind her. "Baby, please. Listen to me. I love you and Andrew more than anything else in this world."

She spun around. "But not enough to stay straight. That's all you had to do, Eddie. For me and Andrew. Did you ever stop to think that someday I might have to arrest you? What will our son think of me then? How will I ever explain things to him so he doesn't hate me?"

"You wouldn't do that, Monica. I know you. And I swear, it's only the gambling, I'm not involved in the drugs."

No longer able to hold back her tears, she let them rain down her face. "No. You don't know me, Eddie. I'm not even sure you ever did." She balled her fists and flung herself at him, pounding on his chest. "I would do it! I would do it!" she cried, collapsing into him.

Eddie took hold of her wrists and forced them down to her sides. His arms came around her, and he held her close. He bent and buried his face against her neck. "Hush," he soothed, his voice low, and his warm breath fanning her skin. "Let's not talk anymore. It's okay, baby. I've got you." Soft kisses trailed down her neck, and his lips found hers.

They kissed, Monica's sobs trapped inside her throat. In her heart, she wanted him as much as he wanted her. She clung to him, glad to drown in his kisses, feel his strong arms holding her. She pulled her head back and cupped his face with her hands.

"Eddie, we can't do this."

He placed his finger gently over her lips. "Yes, we can. Give me this night, Monica. That's all I'm asking for. Just this night."

She nodded slowly and led him into her bedroom. Without words, they undressed and came together. Her hunger for him almost unbearable, her hands explored the familiar territory she knew so well. She felt his hands travel down the length of her spine and back up again. A shiver ran through her as she urged him on, repeating his name over and over again.

They made love twice that night. Afterwards, she rested, content to lie with his arms wrapped around her, their legs entwined. God, how she had missed him. If only everything outside would go away and leave the two of them alone with Andrew.

No Bureau, no Mafia. Only a life they could share together. Her eyes closed, and she drifted off to sleep, refusing to accept what she had just done.

Chapter 43 — Cookie
The Truth About Dimitri

The temperature was unseasonably warm as Cookie set out to meet with Monica. An electric blue sky peeked out from behind cotton clouds. Humid air brought hints of the summer soon due to arrive.

Cookie waddled up the street. She opened the door of Brides and Blooms, the heady floral scent soothing her anxiety a bit. Her pink maternity blouse hung loosely over a pair of black stretch pants. She glanced down at the pair of ballerina flats. The swelling no longer allowed her beloved high heels to adorn her feet. "It's only temporary," she said aloud, while switching on the lights. She checked the glass refrigerated cabinets holding various bouquets and was satisfied nothing needed replacement.

The bell above the door jingled, and Monica came in. After a quick hug and a relocking of the door, they retreated to Monica's old office at the rear of the shop.

"I haven't been here in a while," Monica said. "Everything looks great." She took a seat across from Cookie, who eased down behind the desk.

"Thanks," Cookie said. She rubbed her protruding stomach. "I can't wait for this kid to vacate the premises. I'm peeing twenty times a day. Always trying to shove my swollen feet into shoes that don't fit. And, let me not forget the heartburn keeping me up at night."

Monica laughed. "It won't be much longer. Then instead of heartburn, you'll have some little person keeping you up at night."

Cookie's face grew serious. She edged forward, elbows on the desk. "So, what did you find out about Dimitri Orlov?"

"It's not good," Monica said. "The Bureau's been digging, trying to find out who took Alexei's place in the Russian Mob hierarchy."

"Please don't tell me it's Dimitri."

"I'm afraid so. He does deal in diamonds. That part is true, but he also deals in lots of illegal stuff just like Alexei."

Cookie blinked, her false eyelashes fluttering like crows' wings. "Murder, too?"

"Not here that we know of. Back in Russia, it might be another story. It's probably only a matter of time before he does. He's come to fill some big shoes."

"How in the heck am I going to tell Damien his biological father is a criminal just like his adoptive one?"

"I'm afraid there's more bad news," Monica said. "It seems Damien's sister is an integral part of his dealings."

"But she's a lawyer," Cookie pointed out.

"Exactly. A lawyer who works for the Russian Mob. She graduated with a degree in Criminal Justice. When there is a legal problem, they call Anastasia Romanoff."

Cookie shook her head. "No, you must have the wrong person. Anastasia never married.

Monica sighed. "Not only was Anastasia married, but her husband, Maksim Romanoff, mysteriously disappeared in Russia about five years ago."

Cookie gasped. "You've got to be kidding me. I feel like I'm trapped in some kind of Hollywood disaster movie."

"I'm sorry," Monica said. "For you and Damien especially. But it's better to tell him the truth before he gets too attached. There's another task force at the Bureau already tracking these two."

"It feels like the world is full of nothing but criminals?" Cookie said. "Speaking of which. One stopped by here not too long ago."

"What do you mean?"

"Yours truly. Eddie, of course. He said he wanted to apologize for the scene at the restaurant and … wait a minute. What's that look on your face?" Cookie sprang up from the chair, almost losing her balance. "Please, tell me you didn't, Monica."

"Unfortunately, I did."

"How can you be so nonchalant about it? And Chase?"

"I know," Monica said, staring down at the floor. "The last thing I wanted to do was hurt him. But I can't be dishonest either. I've already broken things off with Chase."

"Does this mean you and Eddie are back together?"

"No. It was one night."

Cookie crossed her arms and rested them on her protruding belly. "Why did you have to tell Chase? You could have continued seeing him, given him a fair chance." Cookie said.

"Come on, Cookie. That isn't right. If he did it to me with some old girlfriend, I would want him to tell me."

Cookie shook her fist. "That Eddie Marconi. If he were here right now, I'd kick him right in the—"

"Enough. You might want to kick me, too. It wasn't all his fault."

"Tell me the truth, Monica, even though I think I already know, and I told Damien as much. Are you still in love with him?" She saw her friend's eyes water and instantly regretted the question.

"The problem is," Monica said softly. "I'll always love Eddie. I don't think I could ever feel this strongly for anyone else. Yes, Chase makes me forget him for a while, but my love for Eddie is something I can't let go."

"Oh, Monica. I wish there were something I could do to help you. What if he breaks the law?"

"It's not a matter of if, but when," Monica said. "He knows it and I know it."

Cookie sat. "Just look at the two of us. I've got to deliver bad news to Damien, and you may have to arrest the man you love. Even though I can't stand him."

"Cookie, stop," Monica admonished. "What is this thing between you and Eddie. And don't say he cheated. That was ages ago. I got over it, and so should you."

"You're right. I'm sorry. I'll try not to speak ill of him."

Monica burst out laughing. "Who are you kidding? Oil and water will never blend."

Cookie joined in the laughter. "Which one of us is oil?"

****

After Monica left, Cookie tried to stay busy at the shop. She took care of several customers and arranged a bridal bouquet. Her mind kept drifting to Damien and how to tell him what she learned from Monica. Here, he believed this man was the father he had always wanted, plus a sibling he could form a relationship with. Finding out the truth would crush him.

That night during dinner, Cookie tried to keep the conversation light, but when she could stand it no longer, she blurted out, "Damien, we need to talk. Come, sit in the living room with me."

Alarmed, he asked. "Did I do something wrong? Is the baby okay? Are you—"

"I'm fine and the baby is fine. It's nothing like that."

He eased down beside her, his arm resting across her shoulders. "What is it?"

Slowly, she shared her visit with his mother and the information Monica had uncovered. With each sentence, she could feel him pulling away. His arm came from around her, and he sat straight up, staring down at the floor.

"I'm so sorry," Cookie said. "What can I do to help you?"

"Nothing." His voice was hollow and flat. He rose and hurried towards the apartment door.

"Damien, where are you going?" Cookie pushed up and followed him.

"I need to be alone."

The anguished look on his face broke her heart, but she understood. "Okay."

He grabbed his jacket off a hook and bolted out the door. Cookie headed for the terrace. A soft breeze caught the strands of her auburn hair, gently lifting them. She crossed over the cement floor, the hard surface cold beneath her feet.

At the railing, she studied the waves rippling across the water in the distance. The sturdy Verrazano Bridge, with its rigid steel cables standing firm, gripped something inside her. Damien would be okay. The love between them, like the bridge, remained strong enough to bring them through anything.

Not wanting to believe otherwise, Cookie quickly turned away and slipped through the slider.

Chapter 44 — Nico
An Eye for an Eye

Nico sat at a round table in a small room at the rear of the diner with Konstantin and two other men. The first, Theodore 'Theo,' Caras, ran most of the backroom gambling in the borough of Queens. A large, burly man with a coal black mustache, he ruled the games with an iron hand. He held an unlit cigar in his sausage-like fingers.

The second man, Elias Antonio, was the polar opposite of his counterpart—tall and muscular with a clean-shaven face and bald head. When he smiled, a gold tooth appeared on his right lateral incisor. Elias had become Stavros Papadakis' replacement as Konstantin's bodyguard.

"The container ship, *Calypso*, is docking the day after tomorrow," Konstantin said. "Tony Morello has assured me it will make it through customs at the Jersey Terminal."

"Will he be there?" Theo asked.

Konstantin nodded. "Of course. He will want his share of the drugs. Then we will strike. I want that man to pay for whatever he did to Stavros."

"You are going to give him his cut after what he has done?" Elias asked, a blue vein pulsing on the front of his forehead.

"I agree with Konstantin," Nico said. "We need to make things appear normal."

"What is the plan?" Theo asked, chopping down on his cigar.

Konstantin surveyed the men for a moment. "Elias, you and Nico will follow Tony. Then wait for the opportunity to grab him and bring him to me at the usual place."

"What about his man? Stan Amato?" Nico asked.

"You need to cause a distraction or wait until he is not close by."

Elias raised an eyebrow. "And if we can't shake him?"

"Then I'm afraid he becomes, as they say, collateral damage," Konstantin said. He eyed Nico. "Are you good with everything?"

"Of course. I have no love for Tony Morello. I'll do whatever needs to be done."

"Good, then everything is settled." Konstantin got up and went to a small liquor cabinet stationed in the corner of the room. He produced a bottle of Ouzo and four shot glasses. He poured each of them a drink.

"*Yia mas*," he said, raising his glass.

"Yes," Nico replied. "To our health."

***

Back in his apartment, Nico grabbed his laptop. His fingers flew over the keyboard. He inserted a thumb drive and downloaded what he had written before deleting everything. He called Monica on his burner phone.

"This is urgent," he said. "We need to meet right now. I'll see you at the Unisphere in Flushing Meadow park in an hour. I'm leaving now."

The trembling in Nico's hands worsened as he tried to steady the wheel. He inhaled a deep breath to calm himself. With the drugs arriving soon, everything he worked so hard for would finally pay off.

By the time he exited the Grand Central Parkway, the thrumming inside his chest remained constant, and his hands failed to obey. He pulled in and parked. There was no way he could let Monica see him in this state. He climbed out of his car and shoved his hands into the front pockets of his jeans. He ambled toward the Unisphere, the massive stainless steel globe, once a symbol of the 1964 World's Fair. On a weekday, the park was not as crowded as usual. A few people walked dogs, while a group of youngsters kicked a soccer ball on the grassy lawn behind him. He paced back and forth, checking his watch several times. Monica approached, and he quickly dug his hands back inside the pockets of his jeans. She pointed to the steps below, away from the globe, and sat.

Nico dropped down beside her. "I have the name of the ship that's coming into the Jersey Port the day after tomorrow. He pulled out the thumb drive and handed it to her. All the info is on there."

"Thank God," Monica said. "Brooke is threatening to pull the plug."

Nico scowled. "You can't let her do that, Monica. There's much more on the horizon."

"Like what?"

Nico brought her up to date on his earlier discussion and Konstantin's orders to kill Tony Morello."

"This is big, Nico," Monica said. "So, it's not going to happen at the seaport?"

"No. Elias and I are to grab him and bring him to a building Konstantin owns off of Queens Boulevard, not far from the Queensborough Bridge."

"You've been there before?"

"It's new. A few times, but only when it's used as his counting house for all the drug and gambling proceeds. The money is divided up and then distributed to several other legitimate businesses, where it is cleaned. The thing is, he doesn't always use the same place. He moves things around every few months."

"Does he store drugs there?"

"No, he's too clever for that. The drugs are taken from the seaport and then transported to the basement of a house he owns on five acres outside of Manhattan in the suburbs of Scarsdale."

"Wait a minute," Monica said. "I don't remember the Bureau having any knowledge of property in Scarsdale."

"No. It's under a different name. I only found out about it recently. He took me for a ride there. This is the first time he's trusted me with having any part of the drug side of things. Prior to the past few months, he would mention it but never give me any pertinent details. He always put me in charge of the gaming houses, the ones I gave you on the previous thumb drive. And of course, he used me as a go-between for negotiations with the Italians at times."

"For him to ask you to commit murder is big, Nico," Monica said. Appearing to be deep in thought, she grew silent for a few moments before speaking again.

"Here's what's going to happen. We'll have agents hiding at the seaport the day the ship arrives. Photographs will be taken, but no arrests will be made there. Agents will follow the drugs after they are divided up and the money exchanged. The house in Scarsdale will be a target, with additional agents stationed nearby. Arrests will begin there and continue later at all the gambling houses.

"When you and Elias grab Tony Morello and bring him to the warehouse where Konstantin will eventually be, we'll make our final arrests. It's going to be close, Nico. You have to make sure Tony Morello isn't killed before we have a chance to nab Elias and Konstantin."

"I'll do my best."

"By the way. Have you seen this Charlie Bevins character again?"

"No. I've been looking. Maybe I was wrong."

She pointed at his jeans. "You can take your hands out of your pockets now," she said. "I know why you're keeping them there, and the sooner we are done with all this, the better."

Nico complied and then held his arms straight out. A slight trembling still remained.

"Boy, you really are good at what you do," he said. "Funny, they don't shake around Konstantin."

"Yes," Monica said. "When you've dug yourself in so deep that you're comfortable around the criminals, it signals it's time to get out."

Nico nodded. "Yes. And just in case, I need to say something to you. Thank you, Monica. I couldn't have asked for a better handler."

"And I couldn't have asked for a better undercover agent. I'm sure there will be commendations coming your way from the Bureau. Stay safe, Nico. See you on the other side."

***

Nico headed back to his apartment, a million things buzzing inside his head. Monica's plan, although a good one, wasn't foolproof. He showered and, exhausted, fell into bed thinking he would fall asleep immediately. He closed his eyes, and instead, all he saw was Kai. If he hadn't left her apartment the other night, there was no doubt things would have progressed between them. She exuded beauty, intelligence, and was sexy all at the same time.

But first and foremost, he needed to ensure her safety. Kai took risks, and those risks could blow back on her. Big things were about to happen, and he needed to stay focused. For the first time in many weeks, Nico fell asleep, the image of Kai putting him at ease.

Chapter 45 — Austin
A Slip of the Tongue

Happy Brooke finally agreed to go somewhere nice for dinner. Austin ordered a bottle of red wine and relaxed in his seat at the Gramercy Tavern. Heavy wood beams traveled the length of the curved ceiling, and rounded arches with lattice work inserts atop the doorways gave the room a rustic old-world feel. Soft lighting reflected off the white gold rimmed bone china and silver place settings.

Austin studied Brooke's face. His eyes focused on her sensuous lips, the curve of her neck, and the hollow at the base of her throat. Her strapless black dress exposed the golden-toned skin across her shoulders.

"What?" Brooke asked, her sea green eyes catching his. "She looked down at her dress and then back up. "Is there something wrong?"

"Just the opposite," Austin said. "Everything about you is right."

A blush swept her cheeks. "Nobody's perfect. We all have flaws."

"I haven't found any in you yet," he said before taking a sip of wine.

The waiter appeared, and they ordered from the restaurant's seasonal menu. They started with golden beets with cucumbers, pine nuts, yuzu, and hay-smoked gnocchi. The main course consisted of Elysian Fields Lamb with farro, zucchini, and spigarello for her and Roasted Sirloin with cauliflower, dandelion greens, and pickled shallot for him.

"Austin, this is all too much," Brooke remarked. "We could have eaten on the tavern side instead of the main dining room."

Austin shook his head. "Not a chance. We rarely go out, so I wanted this to be special."

"True," Brooke said. "I just prefer staying in and cuddling with you." She cut into her lamb and took a bite. "Wow. I've had lamb before, but nothing that tasted this good."

"I'm glad you're enjoying it."

After finishing their main course and almost the whole bottle of wine, Austin insisted on ordering dessert. The waiter brought a chocolate meringue pie with blackberry, blackcurrant, and malt, which they shared over cups of coffee.

"This is divine," Brooke said. "But I'm stuffed."

"Ready to go?"

"Yes." Brooke reached and squeezed his hand. "And more than ready to show you my appreciation for a fabulous meal."

Austin paid the check, and they grabbed a cab for the ride to Brooke's place. Graced with an earlier misty light rain, the blacktop glistened in the moonlight as the cab made its way uptown, weaving in and out of traffic.

Brooke snuggled against him in the backseat, her head resting on his shoulder. He kissed the top of her head, the delicate scent of her shampoo filling his nose. Everything with Brooke felt right. A sense of contentment washed over him, something which had eluded him for so long. She was the missing piece that finally made his life whole.

They reached her apartment, stepped out of the cab, and hurried inside. As soon as the elevator doors closed, Brooke's arms wrapped around his neck, and she pulled him to her. A breathless whisper escaped her mouth as he teased and nibbled at her bottom lip.

The doors opened, and they ran down the hall together, giggling and laughing, frantic to get inside. Austin kicked the door closed behind them. Not bothering to turn on the lights, they stumbled to the bedroom, leaving a trail of clothing behind them.

***

Just before dawn, they lay naked together beneath the sheets, happy and spent after a night of fierce lovemaking.

Sunlight filtered in. Austin opened his eyes and squinted at the dust mites hovering in the air. As usual, Brooke was already up, the now familiar smell of fresh-brewed coffee filling the apartment. Collecting his watch from the nightstand, he checked the time. "Crap," he muttered. Only an hour until he was due at work.

He got up and searched for his pants. Finding them in the far corner of the room, he pulled them on and went into the kitchen. Brooke sat at the small table, her head buried behind the pages of the New York Times.

She lowered the newspaper and smiled. "Good morning, Agent Faulkner. Did you sleep well?"

He grinned down at her. "Hardly. Some crazy woman kept me up half the night. I think a cup of coffee will hit the spot." Grabbing a mug from inside a cabinet, he took the coffee pot and poured a decent amount into it, taking two quick gulps before he sat across from her.

"I'm a bit surprised," he said.

"About what?"

"Well, you haven't mentioned anything about my C.I., Stan Amato. Under the circumstances, I thought for sure you would be a little upset."

Brooke closed and folded the newspaper. "What about him? Please enlighten me, because I have no idea what you're talking about."

The minute she finished talking, Austin comprehended the monumental mistake he had just made. Apparently, Monica did not make Brooke aware of Stan being an accessory to murder. Why in the world would she make a decision that could lead to her dismissal from the Bureau?

Austin sank into a chair and rubbed the back of his neck. He informed Brooke about his conversation with Stan Amato.

"Did you report this to Monica?"

"Yes. She told me she was going to speak to you about it. Maybe she didn't get the chance to—"

"Don't you dare try to defend her. This speaks directly to the DOJ. It's our duty to inform them." Brooke flew up from the chair and slammed the newspaper down. "I can't believe both of you kept this from me. My position at the Bureau could be compromised, too."

"Not if you weren't made aware," Austin said weakly. "I honestly thought you were given the information from Monica. Can things be that bad now Stan Amato has revealed where Stavros' body is? I'm hoping once the DOJ gets all the details, they'll cut him some slack on the accessory charges.

"There is no telling which way they would lean since we have not informed them in a timely manner."

"Talk to Monica. Maybe there's a good reason why she held back the information," Austin said.

Brooke stomped past him and out of the room. "Get dressed," she called over her shoulder. "We're heading to the office right now."

"I need to go by my place first and get my laptop. I'll see you there." He sighed and then gulped down the rest of his coffee. The last thing he wanted was to be caught between Monica and Brooke.

He rose and headed for the bedroom to finish dressing. It was about to be an explosive day at work, for sure.

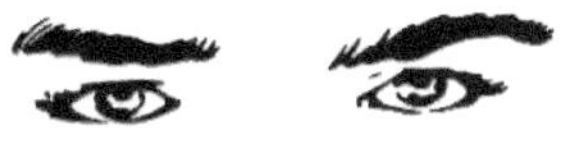

Chapter 46 — Brooke

Blackout

With Austin gone, Brooke, now fully dressed in a navy pantsuit with a pale pink blouse, grabbed her cell and called Monica. She paced the living room while waiting for her to answer. How could she not bring something this important to her immediately? When she heard Monica's voicemail, she wanted to scream. "You need to return my call as soon as you get this message."

Her adrenaline pumping, she tossed her cell into her purse along with her service revolver and picked up her briefcase. The buzzer rang, and she frowned. What did Austin forget now? Since they were seeing so much of each other, she had given him her extra key card so he could access her building.

Brooke opened the door and froze. "Charlie?" She tried to shove it closed but wasn't quick enough. He pushed back against it and barged in, slamming it shut behind him.

On instinct, she backed away, her hands trembling as her fingers fumbled with the clasp on her purse.

It took Charlie only two strides to reach her. He snatched the purse away and flung it to the other side of the living room.

"Oh, no, you don't," he hissed. "I'm well aware of what's inside."

"Charlie, stop all this right now," Booke cried. The odor of alcohol on his breath stung her nose. "You must be crazy coming here? How did you get into the building?"

"I have my ways," he said, pulling her by the arm and pushing her down onto the sofa. His once handsome face twisted into an ugly scowl. He swayed back and forth slightly before centering himself. "You think you're so clever, don't you?"

"I have no idea what you're talking about. You need to leave before—"

"Before what!" he shouted. "That lover of yours is long gone. He can't help you, Brookie."

She tried to slow her racing heart. The situation called for her to remain calm. Her FBI training had taught her not to antagonize an aggressor. "Okay, Charlie," she said, forcing her voice to remain level. "Let's talk about all of this. Tell me why you're so upset. I thought we agreed to part ways."

"Oh, did we now?" he snapped, his arm raised inches above her head.

Brooke's stomach clenched at the harsh tone of his voice. Memories of slaps and punches roared to the surface. She inched away, pushing herself back into the cushions. "Charlie, you need to calm down. We can't talk things out while you're in this state."

"And what state is that?" His eyes bore into her. "You mean the alcohol, don't you?"

"Yes. You promised me you weren't going to drink anymore, remember."

"Sure. And *you* promised me we would always be together. Whatever happened to that promise?"

Brooke eyed her purse lying on the floor across the room. Even if she tried, she couldn't make it before he grabbed her again. "That was a long time ago, Charlie."

"Why … why did you have to go and ruin everything between us? I still love you, and I know you must still have feelings for me."

"Of course I do," Brooke said softly. "I haven't forgotten everything we had together."

He dropped his arm. His shoulders slumped, and he eased down beside her. "I knew it," he said. "I knew you still cared for me. Can't we start over?"

"Sure, maybe we can do that, Charlie. But first, you need to let me leave. I'll call you after work, and we can sit and talk. I don't have the time right now. Okay?"

He fell silent and stared at her. The air around her grew thinner as she fought to maintain control of the situation. Her only escape was out the front door and down the stairwell. In his inebriated state, she was sure she could outrun him. She inched away and attempted to get up.

Charlie reached and dug his hand into her hair—his fingers twisting the strands. Needles and pins marched across her scalp. She screeched at the burning pain. He dragged her off the sofa and down onto the floor, flinging himself on top of her. One of his hands covered her mouth while the other held her arms over her head, his long fingers wrapping around her tiny wrists.

"You don't have time for me, but you have plenty of time for him. I've been watching the two of you—him coming and going. The fancy dinner you both had last night."

Brooke struggled beneath him. She shook her head from left to right. His hand loosened on her mouth. Opening wide, she bit down on his fingers.

Charlie howled and pulled his hand away. "You bitch! You shouldn't have done that." He drew back his fist—a crazed look in his eyes. It came down hard and fast, hitting her bottom lip and splitting it open.

Numbing pain pulsed through her. The taste of blood bathed her tongue. Tears stung the corners of her eyes. Muscles tightening, she prepared for another onslaught when he raised his arm again.

"Please, Charlie. Don't. Not if you love me," she pleaded.

His fist stopped inches from her cheek. Slowly, he lifted himself off of her and slumped against the bottom of the sofa.

Brooke rolled onto her side and then up into a sitting position. Her bottom lip ached, the swelling making itself known as she wiped her mouth with the back of her hand and winced. Blood dripped from her fingers. She looked over at Charlie.

"I … I'm s … sorry, Brookie," he stammered.

Brooke got to her feet. Her legs nearly collapsed beneath her. She steadied herself and stumbled toward her purse. An arm came around her neck from behind. She gasped and tried tugging it away. The pressure on her neck increased, and she struggled to take in air.

Charlie held on, dragging her back to the sofa, releasing his arm, and pushing her face down. He stumbled over to her purse. He dug inside and pulled out the revolver. "Is this what you want?"

Brooke turned onto her back. "No. Charlie, please put the gun down," she said, her voice just above a whisper.

He staggered toward her and, with a shaky hand, aimed the gun. "I really do love you," he said, tears streaming down his face.

The last thing Brooke heard was an audible click and a loud crack. The last thing she felt was something white hot hitting her chest before her world turned black.

Chapter 47 — Kai
Caught

With the door wide open, Kai sat at Konstantin's desk again. Her eyes focused on the floorboard where the ledger lay underneath. Noise from the kitchen echoed in the hallway. She ignored the banging of pots and pans, the clatter of silverware, the chef's yelling back and forth to one another, and servers calling out orders.

She understood Nico's warning and his concern for her, but her job as an FBI agent called for risks. If the ledger disappeared for some reason, they wouldn't have sufficient evidence of drug trafficking that had gone on for months, possibly years.

Konstantin had been in and out several times, pulling open filing cabinets and shuffling through them. Every time, she made sure to pretend to be working on his payroll accounts. Her stomach rumbled, and she realized the coffee and oatmeal she had for breakfast were long gone. About to get up and go to the kitchen, she heard Konstantin talking to someone out in the hall.

She hadn't seen Nico all morning, and this other man's voice was unfamiliar.

"I can take care of it," the man said.

"I will be leaving soon," Konstantin replied. "Everything has arrived. Nico and Elias are ready. You must not do anything before we finish at the seaport. I will join you after."

Monica had informed her about the agents stationed at the New Jersey Seaport who would get photographic evidence of the drug transfer. Thoughts of Tony briefly crossed her mind but quickly receded. He chose the life of a criminal and would suffer the consequences.

Konstantin and the man appeared in the doorway. She recoiled at the sight of the man with him. He had a heavy build and a thick black mustache on his upper lip. His dark, coal eyes swept over her.

"Kitty, I would like you to meet Theo."

"Hello," Kai said as a chill marched down her spine.

The two men stepped farther inside, and Konstantin closed and locked the door behind them. Something was terribly wrong. Trying to remain calm, she said, "Can I help you with anything?"

Theo rubbed his mustache. "We have come to ask you a few questions. First, we need to know who you really are."

Kai's pulse raced, but she tried to keep her composure. "What do you mean?" She looked at Konstantin. "That's a silly question. I'm Kitty, Nico's cousin."

"That is what you both told me, but I am not sure it is the truth." He leaned against the desk, and hovered over her.

"Of course it is," Kai said.

"Get up!" Konstantin shouted.

While judging the position of the two men, Kai slowly rose. With Theo blocking the door, her chances of escape were minimal. Her eyes scanned the room for a possible weapon, but she found none.

He grabbed her arm and pulled her out from behind the desk. "You will start talking, or I will have Theo here make you talk. It would be a shame to mess up such a pretty face."

Theo's eyes gleamed. Kai shuddered inside at the thought of this man anywhere near her. "I … I don't have anything to say," she stammered. "I'm going to call Nico. He won't be happy when he finds out how you're treating me."

"Never mind about Nico." Konstantin pointed to a floorboard. "I know you were snooping around, and I am sure you found what you were looking for."

Kai remained silent. Her mind still working to find a way out.

"You think you are so clever finding my ledger."

"What ledger?" Kai asked, her body trembling.

Theo crossed the room as Konstantin stepped aside. He was so quick, she almost didn't see it coming. He slapped her hard across the face. She cried out, her head jerking back from the stinging pain. On instinct, she raised her knee and aimed between his legs. But Theo caught her ankle and yanked her leg out from under her. She lost her balance and fell to the floor.

Konstantin looked down at her. "You see, I have a little trick when I hide something. You missed the slip of paper that fell out into the space when you lifted the ledger."

"I have no idea what you're talking about." Kai insisted. "Maybe it was someone else."

"Like who?" he growled.

"Dina," she spouted. "It could have been her or anyone else."

"I'm afraid not, Kitty, or whatever your name is. You see, you are the only one I gave the key to. The only person I let work at my desk. No one else comes in here without my permission."

Konstantin reached down, yanked her up off the floor, and pushed her against the desk. He unlocked the door and left, returning a few moments later with a large zip tie. He bound Kai's wrists together and then turned to Theo.

"I will bring the car around. Take her, and I will meet you there later. Nico will drive me. I need to know what he has to say about his so-called cousin."

Kai was about to scream when Theo pulled out a revolver. "Do not give me any trouble, or you will regret it." He shoved her through the doorway and out the rear door of the diner. Konstantin pulled up in a black sedan. The trunk popped open.

"Please don't put me in there," Kai pleaded. "I won't try anything."

Without a word, Theo shoved her inside and slammed the trunk shut.

Chapter 48 — Austin
The Admission

Austin reached the Federal Building and went straight to Monica's office, hoping he had arrived before Brooke. Her door was open, and she beckoned him in.

"Just the person I want to see," she said, without looking up from her computer screen. "Agents have arrived at the seaport. They are portraying dock workers, and the management has been made aware of our investigation. We should get some good photographs. You and I will be heading out to Konstantin's warehouse in Queens after the drug drop is finished. Stan Amato will be taken into protective custody. I've also called in more agents as back-up. The rest are following Konstantin and Tony's drug shipments."

Austin stood with his arms folded, his anger at Monica simmering below the surface.

"Why didn't you talk to Brooke about Stan Amato?"

Monica raised her eyes. "If you want to know the truth—"

"Yeah, good idea. Let's start with that," Austin snapped.

"Did something happen?" she asked.

"Oh, something happened, alright. I thought you told her, and when I mentioned it, she flew off the handle."

"That explains the voicemail," Monica said sheepishly. "I just needed to buy us a little more time. If Brooke shut us down, all our work and Nico's would be for nothing."

"I trusted you, Monica."

"I'm sorry. I should have reported it to her and let her make the final decision."

"Has she talked to you yet?"

"No. Just a voicemail, but I haven't seen her."

"You mean, she's not here?"

"Let me check." She picked up the desk phone and dialed Brooke's extension. "Alice, it's Monica. Is Brooke in yet?"

"Oh, I see. Buzz me when she arrives." Monica leaned back in her chair and frowned. "Alice hasn't heard from her. She's been trying to reach her."

Austin whipped out his cell phone and called Brooke's number.

Monica raised her eyebrows. "Oh, now I see," she said.

Austin ignored her remark. He paced while Brooke's phone rang and then went to voicemail. "Brooke, please call the office," he said. "People are worried about you." He ended the call and stopped pacing. "Something's wrong, Monica. When I left her place this morning, she was headed here. You and I both know, as Assistant Director, she would never be out of pocket."

"I'm going to her apartment," Austin said. "I need to find out if she's okay."

Monica checked the time. "I'm going with you."

***

They pulled out of the underground garage in a government vehicle. Austin placed the blue light on top of the dashboard and switched it on." They careened through traffic with the siren blaring until they reached Brooke's building.

When he saw two NYPD patrol cars and a Coroner's Mobile Unit outside, Austin's anxiety escalated. Both hung their badges around their necks, got out, and hurried inside. They showed their badges to an officer stationed at the elevator.

"What's going on?" Austin asked.

"I haven't been up to the apartment, but I heard murder, suicide. One of them is FBI," the officer said.

His words hit Austin like a punch to the gut. They rode the elevator in silence to Brooke's floor. Austin flew down the hall where another officer was waiting outside her door. They showed their badges again, and he let them pass.

A grisly scene awaited them. A man's body lay on the floor with an apparent gunshot wound to the head. Brooke lay on the sofa, blood oozing from her chest, while an officer kneeled beside her.

"Don't worry, ma'am," he said. "You hold on now. An ambulance is on the way."

A tall man with grey hair approached them. "Detective Albright." He stuck out his hand to each. "I see you two are FBI."

"That's right, Monica said. "Special Agents Cappelino and Faulkner."

"Neighbor called it in when she heard gunshots. The guy lying on the floor is Charlie Bevins," Albright said. "We ran his name. He was a detective back in Dallas. Kicked off the force over a year ago. Not sure what the connection between these two is. Looks like he tried to kill her and then shot himself in the head."

Austin made his way over to Brooke. Holding back tears, he said. "I got you. You're going to be okay." She nodded and gave him a weak smile.

The paramedics arrived and, after assessing her wound, they put Brooke on a stretcher and wheeled her out of the apartment.

"Thanks, Detective," Monica said, grabbing Austin's arm. "We're going to the hospital.

"But what about the warehouse?"

"There's still time. We need to make sure Brooke is going to be okay."

Forty-five minutes later, with Brooke in surgery, they remained in the waiting area for word on her condition.

Austin couldn't keep still. He sat for a few minutes and then got up and paced before sitting again. He repeated this scenario over and over until Monica said, "Austin, try to relax. I'm sure she is going to be okay."

He shook his head. "Do you know anything about this Bevins guy?"

Monica sighed. She related what Nico had told her. "But that's just one side of the story. You need to let Brooke speak for herself."

Austin rubbed the back of his neck and plopped down next to her. "It all makes sense now," he said. "Her wanting to stay in all the time and always looking over her shoulder. Why didn't she tell me about him?"

"Maybe she was embarrassed. Sometimes it isn't easy for people to reveal certain things."

"I guess so," Austin said. "But I would have understood."

Monica smiled. "You're in love with her, aren't you?"

"Hell, yes," he said. "And when she wakes up, it's the first thing I'm going to tell her."

A doctor in scrubs wearing a surgical mask entered the room. He let his mask down. "Are you here for Ms. Adams?"

"Yes," Austin said. "How is she?"

"She got lucky. The bullet missed her heart. It didn't do too much damage. The surgery went well, but she'll be in recovery for a while."

"Thanks," Monica said. She turned to Austin. "I'll understand if you want to stay here until she wakes up."

He shook his head. "Knowing Brooke, she'd want me to do my job. Let's go and tie up this case."

Monica's cell buzzed as they climbed into the car. "Got a text from Nico saying Tony Morello will soon be in the hands of Konstantin Zervas. I'm going to make sure our backup is in place near the warehouse." She removed her burner phone from her purse and tapped in a number. "I want Kai out of that diner now."

Austin caught the look on her face. "She's not answering?" he asked.

"No, and I don't like it."

"Maybe, she's busy working," Austin said.

"Yeah, you're probably right." Monica dropped her cell inside her purse. "When it comes to the agents on my task force, I tend to rattle easier these days. Let's grab a surveillance van from the Bureau and head over to the warehouse."

"Okay," Austin said. "The sooner we wrap things up, the better. I can hardly wait for Tony Morello to be behind bars."

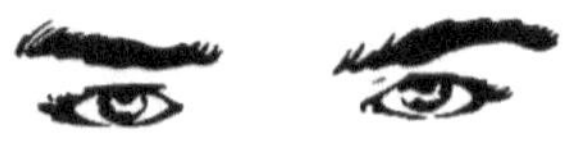

Chapter 49 — Tony
The Cut

With the front windows down, Tony sat in Stan Amato's car down by the docks at the New Jersey Seaport. A white van was parked several feet away. He lit a cigarette and took a deep drag …a new habit he acquired after his breakup with Kai. Always feeling out of sorts these days without her, he had tried and failed to forget her.

He peered up at the darkening sky and then out at the foamy white caps skipping across the water. A flash of lightning zigzagging across the horizon and the explosion of thunder broke the silence between them.

"How did it go with Ray and Pete?" Tony asked. "Will they keep their mouths shut?"

Heavy drops of rain beat against the windshield as Stan raised the windows. "They appreciated the extra cash," Stan said. "I think they'll remain loyal."

Tony shot him a look. "There you go again with that word I don't like."

"Okay," Stan muttered. "I *know* they'll remain loyal. The two understand where their bread is buttered."

"I can't stand having to deal with Konstantin, but since he has the overseas connection, I guess I have to live with it." Tony cracked the window and tossed his cigarette butt out. You scoped everything out earlier? No law enforcement hiding somewhere?"

"Came here before I picked you up. Just dock workers. Lou and Willy are parked nearby with the van."

"Good," Tony said. "We'll take our cut for rendering customs protection plus our share of the drugs and load up the van. I'll drive your car and you guys go to the usual place."

"You got it, Boss," Stan said.

Tony pointed out the window. "Do you see that cabin cruiser out there?"

Stan laughed. "Yeah, the one bobbing up and down over the waves. It's crazy taking a boat like that out in a storm."

"Eddie's Uncle Sal had a similar boat. Man, he was big time not too long ago. Word is many bodies took their last ride on it. You dump them in the ocean, and you never have to worry about evidence turning up. It belongs to Eddie now, but according to him, he hardly ever uses it. If it were mine, I could think of so many things to do with it besides joy rides or fishing."

"I wouldn't mind owning a boat like that," Stan said.

Tony yawned and stretched. He checked the time. "I hate waiting."

Stan nodded. "For sure."

"The ship docked two hours ago. I should have gotten the all clear by now."

The heavy rain turned into a drizzle and then a light mist. Tony's cell buzzed, and he viewed the text screen. "Okay, we're good. I'll send a message to Konstantin. He should be nearby."

Ten minutes later, a car and a black van pulled up beside them. The car window came down, and Konstantin nodded at Tony. "We're ready."

"Follow us," Tony said. They drove along the length of the dock to the far end. A massive container ship with the name *Calypso* written on its side sat in its berth. Tall Quay Cranes stationed along the port hovered over the boat. Their spreaders were hard at work clamping onto the ship's containers and depositing them onto the port.

Tony and Konstantin exited their cars. A man at the end of a gangway signaled to Tony. He approached and handed him a yellow slip of paper and then pointed to one of the red containers. The four men approached it, and Tony took out his cell phone.

"Let me check the numbers," Tony said. He made sure the four-letter prefix, six-digit serial number, and one-digit check number matched the information he had.

He nodded and said. "This is it."

A second van pulled up. Lou and Willy, two of Tony's men, jumped out. They reached the container and broke the customs seal. Willy lifted the latches on the locking bars and pulled the handles outward, opening the right door, and then did the same on the left one.

Konstantin and Tony stepped inside. Several large wooden crates lined the far end. Tony whistled and snapped his fingers. Lou hurried over with a crowbar and pried open a crate. To the novice eye, underneath the straw packing lay beautifully woven baskets with lids.

Konstantin lifted one out and removed the lid. He gestured to Tony. Bricks of cocaine lay stacked inside.

"Okay," Tony said. "Let's divide and conquer."

Between Tony and Konstantin's men, the exchange didn't take long. After the drugs were split and the vans loaded, Willy closed the container and put a fake customs seal on the outside.

Konstantin handed Tony an envelope. "You're cut for getting everything through customs."

"See, no worries," Tony said. "I told you everything would go smoothly."

Konstantin nodded and then drove away, followed by the black van.

Tony gestured to Stan. "Okay, it's a wrap. I'll take your car, and you go with the guys in the van. I need to make a stop."

Stan tossed him his car fob and got into the van. Glad everything had gone as planned, Tony let out a sigh of relief. He got into the car and lit a cigarette. Maybe he could keep doing business with Konstantin. The mountain of money he would make after his cut to Paulie was well worth the risk.

Driving along the New Jersey Turnpike, for the first time in a while, he felt a sense of euphoria. Whistling softly under his breath, he decided to stop at one of the bars he used to frequent when he worked for Frank Uzelli.

He exited the turnpike and drove to the Stingray Bar and parked. Inside, the odor of stale whiskey and beer brought back memories. Nothing in the place had changed. The same beat-up wooden tables and chairs were stationed about. It was here he first bonded with Eddie when he picked up an envelope of cash for his Uncle Sal. Surveying the room for a familiar face, to his disappointment, he found none. He stepped up to the bar, his finger trailing along one of the deep scratches across the top. Even the bartender was new. He ordered a whiskey neat and gulped it down.

He thought of his family still living nearby—all had disowned him years ago when he entered a life of crime. Still, he never longed to see any of them again. If they could turn their backs on him so easily, he didn't want them in his life.

Tony left the bar and made his way to Stan's car. He hit the fob and was about to get in when something jammed into his lower back. A hand reached underneath his leather jacket and removed his weapon.

"Let's take a walk," an unfamiliar voice said. The next thing he knew, a car pulled up and someone shoved him into the rear. A muscular, bald-headed man sat next to him with a gun. He stashed Tony's underneath the seat.

"Who the hell are you?" Tony asked.

"Elias. But I do not think we have ever met."

Tony looked away. It was then he noticed who was behind the wheel. "Nico?" Tony asked.

Nico glanced over his shoulder. "Yeah, it's me. We're going for a little ride."

A sinking feeling hit the pit of Tony's stomach. "What's this all about? Konstantin got his cut."

Elias chuckled. His eyes bore into Tony. "This has nothing to do with the cut. It has everything to do with Stavros Papadakis."

"I have no idea what you're talking about," Tony said, gruffly.

"Isn't it strange how he disappeared after our little meeting?" Nico chimed in.

"What does that have to do with me?" Tony snapped.

"You can hash things out with Konstantin," Nico said. "If you can prove you didn't have a hand in getting rid of Stavros, maybe he'll show you some mercy."

"Do you have any idea who you're dealing with?" Tony shouted. "Paulie is gonna be real upset if anything happens to me."

"Maybe," Nico said. "But he isn't our concern. No more talking. We'll be there soon."

Tony glanced over at Elias.

He grinned, his gold tooth catching the light. "Do not think about it," he said.

They reached Queens Boulevard, stopping short of entering the lane for the Queensborough Bridge. Nico made a sharp right and then parked behind a red brick building.

"Out," Elias said to Tony.

Tony got out, and Nico pointed to the entrance. "Inside."

With Elias' gun still shoved in the small of his back, Tony complied. Nico opened the door and pushed him. The large room had a dank, musty odor. The tall windows were covered in frosted glass. Several oil slicks stained the concrete floor. Stacks of cardboard boxes leaned against the far wall. Fluorescent bulbs hummed like swarms of bees in the dim light.

For the first time in his life, Tony felt fear. This couldn't be how he was going to die. Not in a place like this. What would they do with his body, he wondered?

"What now?" Tony asked.

"You wait," Nico said. He nodded at Elias and left.

Tony heard a car pull up outside and a trunk slam closed. The door opened, and a sliver of outside light seeped in before the door slammed shut again.

Tony's mouth dropped open. Kai stood in front of a big, heavyset man, with her hands tied in front of her. He pushed her toward Tony. He held out his hand. "Cell phones, please."

Tony reached inside his jacket and handed it to him. He tossed it down and stepped on it, crushing it beneath his shoe."

"What about you?" he asked Kai and held his hand out again.

"Sorry. If you recall, I left the diner in somewhat of a hurry. It's still there inside my purse.

"Very funny," Theo mocked. "Now, you two sit down against the wall."

Her eyes on the concrete floor, she slid down next to Tony. Theo stood several feet away, his weapon trained on them, while Elias sat on top of a cardboard box looking down at his cell phone screen.

"You were investigating me all this time," Tony said through clenched teeth. "Even while we were together?"

Kai cut her eyes at him. "I have nothing to say to you, Tony."

"Well, it appears you were found out. I guess we're going to die together then. What a relief. Now I don't have to picture you with another man."

"I don't plan on dying," Kai said. "Especially not with you."

"That's a knife to my heart, baby. No matter what, I'll always love you."

Elias got up. "They're here," he said to Theo as he stepped up to stand next to him. He pulled his weapon out. The door opened, and Nico and then Konstantin stepped inside.

Konstantin drew out a weapon. "Nico, drop your gun," he ordered.

Nico stared at Tony and Kai sitting on the floor. His face paled.

"Did you hear me, Nico!" Konstantin shouted, his words echoing through the building.

Slowly, Nico removed his revolver from his waistband and dropped it to the floor. Konstantin pushed him forward and then kicked his gun away. "Go and sit with the others."

"What is this?" Nico said, sitting beside Kai. "Why do you have my cousin here?"

"Are you sure she's your cousin?" Konstantin said. "Or maybe you would like to tell me who both of you are?"

"Wow," Tony said. "This is starting to get interesting."

"You know me," Nico said. "And she is my cousin. If you have some kind of beef with me, that's fine. But let Kitty go."

Tony started to open his mouth. Kai jabbed him in his ribs. "Don't you say a word."

"Now, I will get to the bottom of things," Konstantin said. He walked over to them, his heavy footsteps scraping the cement floor. "First, I will start with you, Tony. Where is Stavros Papadakis?"

"I told you," Tony said. "I have no idea."

Konstantin shook his head. "Wrong answer." He raised his gun and pulled the trigger.

Chapter 50 — Eddie

The Test

At 4.00 pm, the door to Romano's opened, and Paulie 'The Shiv' Martella walked in. Eddie got up from his usual table and went to greet him. They shook hands and bear hugged. His bodyguard nodded and took a seat at the bar, after which Eddie closed and locked the door. He led Paulie to his private table at the rear of the restaurant.

Empty before the dinner rush, they had the place to themselves. "What can I get you, Paulie?" Eddie asked. "My chef can whip up anything you want."

"No. Just a Campari Spritz."

Eddie called out to the bartender, who was getting things for the evening rush, and gave him the order to prepare two. Romano's bar produced a steady stream of regulars. He set down both drinks and returned to the bar.

Paulie opened the button of his grey suit jacket. "Salud," he said, raising his glass.

"Salud," Eddie repeated and then sipped the rich red liqueur.

"Very nice," Paulie said.

Eddie's insides thrummed. Why in the world had Paulie come all the way here to Romano's to see him? His earnings were far and above what was expected of him, and none of his crew had stepped out of line. "So, what can I do for you, Paulie?"

"It seems things are a little off balance?"

"What do you mean?"

"First, there's this thing with Tony. I'm positive he had that Stavros fella whacked."

Eddie tried to respond, but Paulie held up his hand. "Please, let me finish." He took another sip of Campari. "I'm not blaming you for any of it. I don't think you knew what Tony was going to do. At the same time, I can't have one of my Caporegime going rogue on me. It makes me look bad with the Commission."

"Of course," Eddie said.

"So, here's the deal. I need to fix this problem. Tony has to go."

"Go?"

"It's nothing for you to worry about. I took care of him already. You know the rules better than anyone else. If Tony doesn't go, the Greeks will start a war. I gave Konstantin Zervas permission to grab him, and he agreed it would be the end of things. We move forward, and business runs as usual."

Eddie's head throbbed. His hands broke out in a sweat. This couldn't be happening.

"Am I shocking you?" Paulie asked. "

"A little," Eddie said. "To have someone on the outside do it is unusual."

"True, but I thought everything was solved, and now another problem has come up."

"What problem?"

"I got a call from Konstantin a while ago. It seems Nico isn't who he said he is."

The hair on the back of Eddie's neck stood up. "I don't get it. What's the story with him?"

"Konstantin believes he's FBI. Even duped him into hiring some woman to work at the Acropolis Diner. She might be FBI, too."

Nerves buzzed throughout Eddie's body. Nico, FBI? How could this be?

"It's all gotten out of hand. Now we have a dilemma to fix. Nico knows way too much about the business between us and the Greeks."

"I imagine so," Eddie said, staring at the rich red color of the Campari in his glass.

"This kind of stuff can't go on," Paulie said. "And you can't continue to do business with the way things are, either. I understand your ex is an FBI agent."

Paulie's words crept over him like an icy chill. "Yes," Eddie said. "But she has nothing to do with any of this."

"No? Convince me otherwise, then."

"Look, we don't communicate much except when it comes to my son."

"The word is she is head of some Organized Crime Task Force," Paulie said. "I wouldn't be surprised if she's the one who put Nico undercover."

"I don't believe that," Eddie said. "It would mean possibly arresting me. Monica is very protective of my relationship with my son."

Paulie shook his head. "You've always been loyal, but I need to be sure your loyalty transcends everything else."

"Paulie, how much more can I do?"

"Get rid of her!" he snapped, his palm slapping the table. "Make her disappear. You'll get full custody of your son, and we can all move on knowing she's gone. Am I supposed to believe you're not trading information with her?"

The horror of what he said paralyzed Eddie with fear. Air refused to enter his lungs. For a moment, his mind shut down.

"Or," Paulie said, "do you want Andrew to grow up without a father?" He drank the rest of his Campari and got up. "Think about it. You can choose how … make it an easy death. Or else, I can get someone to do it. Who knows what kind of death it will be then? I'll wait to hear from you. But don't take too long. Do the right thing, Eddie."

He waved at his bodyguard and strode to the door. Eddie followed behind them.

"Paulie, is there any way you would reconsider?" Eddie asked, scrambling, hoping he would change his mind. "If I got her to leave the city. Go someplace else?"

He stopped and turned. "*Omerta*, Eddie. There can be no silence as long as you're connected to her. For now, this stays between you and me. Don't let me run out of patience."

His bodyguard unlocked the door and stepped out first. He surveyed the street and gestured for Paulie to come out. Eddie peered through the glass as they got into a car and drove away.

His whole body weakening, he trudged back to the table. Killing Monica was out of the question. But Paulie would never give him a pass. If he wanted something done, that was it, case closed. You didn't argue with the man.

He thought of Tony, the one person who was the cause of all this. It filled Eddie with rage. He didn't feel an ounce of remorse about what was going to happen to him. This man, whom he loved like a brother, had turned into a power-hungry monster. To think he tried to protect him from Paulie."

He pictured Monica and considered the love they still felt for each other. Just like Tony, Paulie had made a big mistake in coming here tonight. One he would soon regret. Eddie sat down, finished the rest of his drink, plans swirling in his head.

Chapter 51 — Damien
The Break

The cozy sofas and chairs in the living room always gave Cookie and Damien a sense of comfort. She had truly made the apartment a home. But today, as they sat waiting, a coffee mug in Damien's hand and a cup of tea in hers, it manifested only apprehension and a feeling of loss.

Damien had invited Dimitri and Anastasia here. Sitting opposite one another on chairs with a small table in between, they silently sipped their drinks.

A week of digesting the news about his newfound family left a constant bitter taste in Damien's mouth. His stomach refused to stop aching, and he spent many sleepless nights. Now, at Cookie's urging, he would confront them.

"You need to let them know how they hurt you," Cookie had said. "Otherwise, you'll never be able to heal."

Even so, he couldn't help wondering if this might be a mistake. Why not just pretend everything was okay and go forward with their lives? The criminal aspect of Dimitri's life would probably never touch them, just as Alexei kept his activities away from the family. But then, the image of his younger brother, Roman, came back to haunt him, and the price he paid being Alexei's son.

The doorbell buzzed. Damien got up and opened the door. Dimitri and Anastasia stepped inside, bringing with them a cold early morning breeze that sent a chill through the living room. Dimitri tried to hug Damien, but he moved away. Instead, he pointed toward the sofa.

"Please sit." The two sat across from Cookie and Damien.

"Good morning, my son," Dimitri said. "And my beautiful daughter-in-law, how is everything?"

"You tell me," Cookie responded.

A confused look on his face, he gestured toward Damien. "For you to invite us here again warms my heart."

Anastasia glanced at Cookie and then focused on Damien. "You do not look well. What is it? Talk to us, my brother."

Damien squeezed his eyes shut for a moment and took a breath. He opened them and addressed Dimitri. "Why did you lie to me about your time in Russia?"

"I have no idea what you are speaking of," Dimitri said.

"If I were you, I wouldn't start by telling lies," Cookie scoffed. "My husband asked you a question. The least you can do is give him an honest answer."

"I spoke to my mother," Damien said. "Is it true you worked with Alexei back in Russia? That you were … or are a criminal just like him?"

Anastasia pursed her lips and shook her head. "How could you ask our father such a question?"

"You better hold on, sister," Cookie said. "We haven't even gotten to you yet."

"Answer the question," Damien said, his voice rising. "Is it yes or no?"

Color rose up Dimitri's neck and swept across his face. He clasped his hands and leaned forward. "Those were difficult times. You would not understand the things I needed to do just to survive."

"Try me," Damien said. "Was it things like torture, beatings, maybe even murder?"

Dimitri's eyes flashed like lightning in a bottle. For the first time since meeting his father, Damien could see and feel the raw anger he had been hiding so well.

Dimitri held up his hand. "Stop. I do not know what Darya told you. All of it was a long time ago. I am a legitimate businessman now."

"So, you didn't come here to America to take Alexei's place?" Cookie asked.

"Such nonsense," Anastasia said. "My father deals in diamonds and nothing more."

"And your missing husband, Maksim Romanoff?" Cookie asked. "Whatever happened to him?"

An audible gasp escaped Anastasia's lips. She got up. "Father, I think we need to leave."

"Sit down," Dimitri ordered through clenched teeth. "We are not finished."

Anastasia dropped down onto the sofa, her face filled with fury.

"Well," Damien said. "What about your husband? You lied to me about being married."

"It was too painful to tell you," Anastasia said, her eyes misting. "He did not go missing. I was busy with my studies most of the time. It upset him. One day, I came home and he was gone."

"Likely story," Cookie said.

"Did you try to find him?" Damien asked.

"Of course," Dimitri answered. "But I do not think he wanted to be found."

"That aside," Damien said. "How can you prove to me you no longer deal with the Russian Mob and that Anastasia does not work on their behalf?" Damien noticed the surprised look on his face. "I know her degree is not in Family Law."

"Is Darya telling you all these things?" Dimitri asked.

"No," Cookie said. "The FBI is."

Dimitri flew up from the sofa. He glared at Damien. "You have been speaking to the FBI?"

"No. Cookie has a friend who is an FBI agent."

"So!" Dimitri shouted. "This is what you have been doing behind my back. First, you go running to Darya and then the FBI."

Damien got up. This was Alexei all over again. He looked Dimitri in the eye. "All I ever wanted was the truth."

"Is it not enough that I love you? I have loved you since the day you were born. It should be what matters most."

"You don't understand," Damien said. "Alexei loves me, too. But neither of you loves me enough to set an example by living a decent life and being a father I could be proud of instead of one I fear. And to top it all off, you thrust my sister into your world."

"Is that what you think?" Dimitri asked. "I want you to fear me."

"Growing up with Alexei, my whole life was filled with fear. But my brother and I were never allowed to show it. He ruled the house and instructed us never to ask questions about his business or the people he associated with."

"I would never treat you in such a way," Dimitri said.

"So, you'd tell me everything. Not keep any secrets from me?"

Dimitri hesitated. "That is a hard question. You do not need to know certain things if they do not involve you."

"Ah," Damien replied. "You are just the same as Alexei. I think we're done here."

"Please," Dimitri pleaded. "I am standing here right in front of you. Something I longed to do for many years. Do not turn me … us away."

"It's one of the hardest things I have ever had to do," Damien said, his voice breaking. "But my life with Cookie and our baby means more to me than anything else. I don't want to be associated with criminals, nor do I want my child to grow up with a grandfather and aunt who commit crimes." Damien went to the door and opened it.

Dimitri looked at Cookie. "I guess you are feeling the same?"

"Unfortunately, yes," she said. "I'll always stand by my husband."

Dimitri gestured to Anastasia. "Come. We will leave. There is nothing more to be done."

Anastasia stopped in the doorway while Dimitri continued down the hallway. "May I ask you something? It is about my mother."

"Yes," Damien said.

"Did she speak of me?"

"She has never forgiven herself for leaving you behind in Russia," Damien said quietly. "Wait here a moment." He scribbled Darya's number on a piece of paper and handed it to her. "I won't get between the two of you. But I think she would like to see you."

Anastasia raised up on tiptoes and kissed Damien's cheek. "Thank you. Goodbye, my brother." She hurried to catch up with Dimitri.

Damien closed the door and leaned against it. All his bodily strength had dissolved. Cookie came and wrapped her arms around him. She rested her head against his chest.

"I'm so proud of you, Damien. I know how difficult all this was for you."

A single tear splashed down his face and dripped off his chin. It glistened on top of Cookie's auburn hair. In his head, he knew he had done the right thing, but his heart was breaking into a million pieces. He stroked Cookie's hair and silently thanked God for her.

Their child couldn't come soon enough for him. He needed to forget. Forget about his father and sister. There was no way to convince them to live a different life, and he would never accept theirs.

"We are going to be fine," he whispered to Cookie. "Everything is going to be fine."

Chapter 52 — Nico
Getting Out

The sound of the gunshot reverberated throughout the warehouse along with Tony's anguished scream. The bullet had entered his lower leg, more than likely shattering a bone. He moaned, his hands grabbing his injured limb. Blood seeped through his fingers.

Nico sat silently next to Kai. He had felt her body flinch when the gun went off. This couldn't go on much longer. Konstantin was running out of patience, making Tony's death imminent. He hoped Monica and his fellow agents were nearby.

"Now!" Konstantin roared, his weapon aimed at Tony again. "I will ask you one more time. What happened to Stavros? Did you kill him or did someone else do it?"

Tony held onto his wounded leg. He rocked back and forth. "You son of a bitch!" he screamed. "When Paulie finds out what you did to me, you're a dead man."

"Paulie!" Konstantin shouted. "He is the one who gave me permission to kill you."

Tony shook his head. "You're lying. Paulie wouldn't do that. Not to me."

Konstantin snickered. "I guess you do not know him as well as you think. He has always believed you put a hit on my man. This made him very unhappy. His loyalty to you is finished!"

He pointed his gun at Nico. "And you," he said. "I trusted you. My brother trusted you. You are an excellent actor. You played your part so well."

"I don't think you want to make things worse for yourself by killing an FBI agent," Nico said calmly.

"So, you admit it then?"

Nico nodded. "Yes. It's been a pleasure working with you, Konstantin. Sorry, we have to part ways. I was kind of enjoying it."

"You think this is a joke?" He lowered his gun and moved closer while Theo and Elias kept their aim on the three of them. He nodded his head toward Kai. "What about her? Is she FBI, too?"

"Yup," Nico said. "So, you can see you have a real dilemma here. Not one, but two agents. That's a capital murder charge for sure."

"First, they have to find your bodies, and then they must prove I did it. I am going to make sure neither one happens." He focused on Kai. "What a shame, such a pretty woman." He turned to Theo and Elias. "Maybe, I should kill her last. We can have some fun first."

Elias' smile stretched clear across his face, his gold tooth gleaming. "Sounds good to me."

"I like the idea," Theo chimed in.

"Try it," Kai said. "You'll wish you killed me first."

"That's my girl," Tony said under his breath.

"Former," Kai said. "I'm nobody's girl."

Nico couldn't believe what he was hearing. Were these two in a relationship? Maybe he had pegged Kai all wrong. The main thing he needed to concentrate on now was stalling Konstantin somehow.

"What do you gain by killing us?" Nico asked him. "You've made enough money just to leave and disappear."

"And be hunted for the rest of my life? That is no way to live."

"Do you really think you're going to kill us and then go on as before, like nothing happened. The FBI will be relentless in trying to prove you're a murderer. At least by letting us live, you have a chance."

Konstantin raised his gun again. "No more talk." He walked over to Tony. "Where is Stavros buried, or did you cut him up into little pieces like you Mafia are inclined to do?"

"You will never find him!" Tony shouted. "Because I don't know where he is."

"Okay, then. You have made your choice." Konstantin cocked the gun, pulled the trigger, and fired.

Chapter 53 — Monica
The Cavalry

Near dusk, Monica and Austin sat in a surveillance van down the block from the warehouse, blueprints of the building spread out in front of them. They had observed the arrival of Nico and Elias, as well as another car with Theo behind the wheel. A bit confused when Nico left, but relieved when he sent a text message saying he was returning with Konstantin.

Still unable to reach Kai, Monica prayed she was safe. Nico would have gotten rid of his burner phone after the last communication as was the norm. Something in the pit of her stomach was telling her Kai might be in trouble.

"I called the hospital," Austin said. "Brooke still isn't awake, but she's doing okay."

"Good. As soon as we wrap things up here, you need to go and be with her. Your debriefing can wait until tomorrow."

"Nico's coming back," Austin said, his eyes on the surveillance cameras.

They remained silent while the car pulled in and disappeared around the back. Monica picked up her handheld radio. "It's a go," she said. "Secure the perimeter and then surround the building but be careful of the rear entrance."

With bulletproof vests in place, she and Austin secured their revolvers and then grabbed two HK416 rifles.

"Let's not forget the Detex Pro," Monica said before they exited the van.

"Right." Austin picked up a compact black box and a folded tripod.

They moved carefully up the street. Two other agents ushered pedestrians away from the street. Several meandered along, and Monica shouted. "FBI! Please clear the area!" Frightened looks on their faces, they hurried along.

They reached the building, where a dozen other agents, their weapons drawn, proceeded to encircle it. Pressed up against the side, Austin and Monica slowly made their way to the rear. They stationed themselves to the far left of the metal door.

Everyone remained silent as Austin set his rifle down and mounted the black box on the tripod, facing the building's wall, and then turned it on. The compact, ultra-wideband radar system would show them how many people were inside behind the wall and their movements. Monica removed her cell phone from her back pocket and waited for the images to appear. Muffled voices could be heard from inside. Austin and Monica both jumped when a shot rang out. Austin pointed toward the door handle while two other agents ran over holding a battering ram.

Monica shook her head no. Austin dropped his hand. She held her cell phone steady as the images appeared on the screen. It showed three people against one wall close to the floor. One person moving around near that wall and two standing nearby.

Her pulse sped up as the reality hit her that Kai must be one of those three by the wall. It appeared both she and Nico had been compromised.

"We don't know how armed they are," Monica whispered. "If we open that door, they could come at us guns blazing or turn their weapons on the people they are holding. Two of them are agents. I can't risk losing any one of you today."

"What do you want to do?" Austin asked.

Monica checked her phone. "There's movement from all three by the wall. Maybe the gunshot was a threat and not a kill shot." Her mind buzzed with what to do. She kept picturing different scenarios in her head. Finally, she whispered. "I'm going in. I'll let them know the building is surrounded and there is no chance of escape."

She handed Austin her cell phone and put down her weapons.

"Wait." Austin held up her cell phone. "One of them is moving toward the three by the wall." A moment later, a second gunshot rang out.

Monica grabbed her rifle. "Now, we have no choice. Let's go!" She and Austin positioned themselves, weapons drawn on either side of the door. The two agents with the battering ram charged. It only took two hits to breach the flimsy metal. The door swung inward, barely hanging on its hinges. Monica, Austin, and the rest of the agents poured inside.

"FBI!" Monica shouted. "Drop your weapons."

Eyes wide, Elias and Theo immediately dropped their guns.

"Down on the floor, hands above your heads!" Austin ordered.

"Okay," Elias shouted. "Don't shoot." The two men dropped face down beside each other.

Two agents approached Tony, who lay still. Blood seeped from two bullet wounds on his body. They carried him outside.

Konstantin stood by the far wall. His arm around Kai's neck, his weapon pointed at her head. Everyone stopped and stood still.

"You don't want to do that," Nico said, moving slowly toward him. "Don't make things worse for yourself. You will never make it out of here alive."

"Maybe so," Konstantin snapped. "But neither will she."

Nico stepped even closer. "Let her go." He patted his chest. "I'm right here. Shoot me instead."

"Nico, no!" Kai shouted.

Surrounded by agents, Konstantin waved his gun at him. "Do not come any closer, Nico."

In that fraction of a second, Monica took her shot, hitting him dead center in the forehead. His arm fell away from Kai's neck, and he collapsed to the floor with the gun still in his hand.

Her whole body trembling, Kai slid down next to him.

Nico ran over and removed the gun from Konstantin's hand. "Are you okay?"

Kai nodded slowly. "I think so."

Nico helped Kai to her feet while the rest of the agents handcuffed Elias and Theo before leading them away.

Austin hurried to Monica's side. "Nice shot," he said.

"Thanks. Now let's get the hell out of here."

Chapter 54 — Austin
Healing

Brooke's eyes slowly opened. She blinked several times and then coughed. Austin reached for her hand, relief flooding his body. She had been out of it for almost two days. Significant loss of blood, the doctor said. It may take a bit longer for her to wake up.

"Hello, beautiful," Austin said. "You scared me half to death."

"What … happened?" Brooke asked with a pronounced rasp in her voice.

"You were shot. Do you remember anything at all?"

Her gaze drifted from him to her surroundings. He felt her pulse jump beneath his fingers.

"Charlie," she said. "It was Charlie. He came and—"

"It's okay, Brooke. Charlie is gone for good."

"What do you mean?"

"After he shot you, Charlie committed suicide."

He heard her sharp intake of breath. She moved her head from side to side. "No, no, no," she repeated. "It's all my fault."

"Listen to me," Austin said. "None of it is your fault. Charlie chose to do everything he did. I don't want you to think about him anymore. He's gone."

Brooke squeezed his hand. "I should have told you about my past with him. But I was afraid it would drive you away."

"I want you to feel you can tell me anything. No matter what it is. Honesty plays a big part in a relationship. So, right now, I'm going to be honest with you."

He leaned closer to her and looked into her eyes. "I love you, Brooke Adams. And I don't ever want to be without you."

A tear slid down her cheek. "I love you, too, Austin."

"Good," he said. "At least we agree on something. All I want right now is for you to get well."

"But the case," she said, clearly becoming agitated.

Austin filled her in on the events of the previous day. "I know you were angry with Monica, but she did a helluva job. She prioritized the task force and all of the other agents involved. I think that says a lot."

"I agree she is one of the best, but you can't just go around breaking rules because you want things your way. What about the DOJ and Stan Amato?"

"Monica informed them yesterday. It seems they may cut him some slack since he gave us so much intel—not to mention where Stavros was buried."

"I see," Brooke said.

"Is there anything you want? Anything I can do for you?" Austin asked.

Brooke smiled, color returning to her face. "Just you," she said softly. You're the only thing I want."

Chapter 55 — Kai
New Beginnings

Only moments away from death yesterday, the joy of having survived made Kai feel everything they had gone through on this case was worth it. But the news she gave Monica here in her office was unsettling at best.

"Are you sure about this?" Monica asked. "Maybe take a break for a while before making any decisions."

"No," Kai said. "I've never been surer of anything in my life. I loved my job with the Bureau, but the satisfaction I used to feel just isn't there anymore. Besides, almost losing my life changed everything."

"By the way, Konstantin's ledger was found at his house in Scarsdale."

"Good to know," Kai said

"What will you do?" Monica asked.

"I want to go home. Back to the Reservation and clear my head. It's the only way I'll ever be able to find out what I really want."

"I believe your mother is with the Tribal Police?"

"Yes. My mom is a real bad ass."

Monica chuckled. "I understand now where you get it from."

"Nothing would make her happier than for me to stay and join the Tribal Police, too."

"It's not a bad idea. With your experience and training, you have a lot to bring to the table."

"I can't picture it, but who knows. Maybe I'll feel different. I've made so many wrong decisions. Put Tony at the top of that list."

"But you loved him."

"I guess," Kai said. "Not a healthy kind of love. It was more like an obsession with each other. I don't regret it because it taught me a lot about myself and what I need from someone."

"I'm going to miss you, Kai."

"I'll miss you, too. There are no words to convey how grateful I am to you for the opportunities you gave me and for saving my life."

"I'm sure you would do the same for me."

Kai got up, and Monica came from around her desk. They hugged, and for a brief moment, Kai thought she might give in and stay.

"If you're ever in Arizona," Kai said. "I expect a visit."

"You got it."

Kai walked to the door, then turned and said, "Give Andrew a hug from me and tell Eddie I said hello." She gave a sly wink and left before Monica had a chance to respond.

***

With all her things packed and ready for the move, Kai had one more thing she wanted to do. She caught a cab to Queens General Hospital, took the elevator to the 6th floor, and went down the hall. An FBI agent sat outside the room.

"May I go in?" Kai asked.

"He's not supposed to have any visitors."

"I just left the Federal Building. I worked on the task force that got him arrested."

"Got any I.D.?"

"No. She reached into her purse and scrolled through her cell phone. "Here's a number you can call. My name is Kai Nez. Former Special Agent, Kai Nez."

"Give me a second."

Kai paced the hallway while he took out his phone and called.

"Okay," he said. "You can go in."

She pushed open the door to Tony's room. He lay in bed, his wrist handcuffed to the rail. His eyes were closed, and his breathing somewhat labored. Handsome as ever, although a bit pale, she stroked his cheek. Funny how this man broke her heart but made her even stronger in the end.

"Goodbye, Tony," she whispered. Kai turned and went to the door.

"Kai? Is that you?"

His voice was a hoarse whisper. She spun around. His eyes were open, the expression on his face one she would never forget.

She eased over to the bed. "Yes. I came to say goodbye."

"No. Stay with me for a while."

"I can't, Tony."

"Why not?"

"Because I gave it all up. I have a flight to catch. I'm going home."

"You mean the Bureau?"

She nodded. "Yes."

"But you always told me you wouldn't do it."

"I couldn't do it for you, Tony. I had to do it for me."

"I don't understand," he said.

"Maybe one day you will."

He nodded toward his cuffed wrist. "Guess I'll be doing some time."

"Looks like it," she said.

"My lawyer says I'll make bail. Besides, most of the judges are in my pocket."

"It figures," Kai said.

"Before you go, I want you to know something, Kai."

"What's that?"

"First of all, I'm glad you survived. But more than anything else, you need to believe I'll never feel about anyone else the way I do about you. I love you, Kai, and I always will."

Kai bent, brushed his cheek again, and then kissed his forehead. "Take care, Tony."

She left the hospital feeling lighter, happier, and more confident. Tony would always be a part of her past. But her future lay ahead, and she couldn't wait to start living it.

Chapter 56 — Eddie
The Solution

It was a little past 9:00 pm when Eddie called Paulie from a burner phone and asked to meet at Romano's. Clearly annoyed, he asked to put it off until tomorrow. But Eddie persisted until he finally agreed.

"It's important. You wanted something done, so I need to go over my plan with you."

Eddie tucked his revolver behind him in his waistband and slipped on his jacket. When he arrived at Romanos, he pulled his car around to the back entrance. He opened his trunk and pulled out a roll of heavy plastic, along with several lengths of rope. Bringing everything inside to the small office at the rear of the restaurant would keep things private. Unrolling the plastic, he covered half the width of the room. He switched off the light, went into the dining room, and waited.

At 10:00 pm, headlights beamed outside as a black Cadillac SUV pulled up and parked. Eddie unlocked the door, let Paulie inside, and then locked it again behind him.

"This better be good," he said. "I had to drive all the way from Manhattan. Jackie is feeling ill. You know I don't like going out alone."

"Yeah, sorry about that," Eddie said.

The minute Eddie heard from one of his bagmen who dropped off a load of cash to Paulie earlier that day, Paulie's bodyguard called in sick, he knew the timing was right. Now he only had to deal with one body instead of two.

His adrenaline running at a fever pitch, Eddie tried to rein himself in. He led Paulie to the back of the dining room to his usual table.

"Want a drink?" Eddie asked. "I can pour us a couple of shots."

"Sure," Paulie said. "Since your kitchen is closed, it's the least you can do for me."

At the bar, he poured two shots of Johnny Walker Blue and set them down on the table along with the bottle.

"Salud," Paulie said and downed the shot. He reached for the bottle and refilled his glass. He nodded toward the other one. "Aren't you gonna drink with me?"

"Sure," Eddie said and finished off his shot.

Paulie let out a chuckle. "I'd better not get caught drinking and driving in this neighborhood. I don't own any of these cops."

"No worries," Eddie said. "I do."

"I didn't recognize your number. You're lucky I answered."

"Andrew was playing around with my phone," Eddie said. "Next thing I know, he can't find it. It's in my apartment somewhere. Now, I gotta turn the place upside down. One of the staff here lent me their phone."

"Okay, kid, what's the deal?" Paulie said. "You mentioned a plan."

"Look, you do realize what you're asking me to do is hard. Even harder because of who Monica is. I mean, getting rid of her has to be airtight. The FBI is going to go crazy."

"It's simple," Paulie said. "There can be no trace of a body and no evidence left behind. You need to do it in a neutral place away from here."

Eddie pretended to think. "Yeah. I plan to ask her to go upstate with me to look at a cabin I'm considering buying for us. A place we could take turns vacationing with Andrew."

"Sounds feasible," Paulie said. "But will she bite?"

"Anything I do that includes Andrew, she'll go for."

"So, you take this ride and what?" Paulie asked. "What happens next?"

"Well, of course, there is no cabin, but there's plenty of woods along the way. I do her and then bury her someplace nobody will find the body." Eddie couldn't stand the sound of his own voice. He was actually making up a plan to kill Monica. But Paulie needed to believe he would carry it out.

"Your plan is good up to a point," Paulie said.

"What do you mean?"

"The first person the authorities are gonna look at is you. There are several things you need to make sure of. Number one, she doesn't tell anyone else about going with you. It has to be an abrupt surprise. It comes out of nowhere when you're with her, and you both leave right away."

Eddie rubbed his chin. "I didn't think of that."

"And no cell phone. They can be tracked. Leave it somewhere else. Maybe home even. It can act like an alibi. Plus, don't use your own car. Get a rental. Tell her yours is in the shop."

"See," Eddie said. "That's why I called you. I never even thought about some of these things."

"Look," Paulie said. "You're important to me. I don't want to see you going away like our friend, Tony. The bum should have been whacked. But there'll be people waiting inside for him. I'm gonna make sure of it."

Eddie could see now how easily you can fall out of favor. You think it can never happen to you, but all it takes is one wrong move. His life couldn't go on like this. Paulie's asking the unthinkable of him had severed his loyalty to the mob.

Paulie filled his glass for the third time. He swallowed the shot and said, "You know what I'm gonna do for you, kid? After she's dead. You bring the body to Fanucci's Funeral Home in Manhattan. Tell Mike, the owner, that I sent you. Cremation is the best answer to your problem. Then, for sure, there's no trace."

His words made Eddie's skin crawl. How many bodies had ended up at Fanucci's? Too many probably. He couldn't stand to listen to Paulie any longer. "I'll do that. It takes too much time to dig a grave."

Eddie got up. "Come to my office. I need to show you something."

Paulie's brow furrowed. "I'm tired. I was about to head home."

"It will only take a minute. I got some nice goods from a guy. You might want to send Jackie with a van."

Eddie picked up the two shot glasses and the bottle. He went over to the bar and deposited everything in a trash bag below. He nodded at Paulie, "My office is right down the hall. Last door on the right."

Paulie pushed himself up. A bit unsteady on his feet, he made his way toward the office with Eddie right behind him, his gun now in his hand.

Paulie opened the door. The light from the hallway illuminated the plastic on the floor.

"Hey, what is this?" He tried to back away, but Eddie pushed him inside, the plastic rustling underneath their feet. Turning around, his face flushed with anger, he pointed at the gun.

"Is this the real reason you called me here?"

"Looks like it," Eddie said.

"You'll never get away with this. You'd better change your mind quick, and maybe I'll forgive you."

"Forgive me?" Eddie asked. "This from a man who asked me to kill the mother of my son. You should be begging *me* for forgiveness."

"I was only trying to protect you!" Paulie shouted.

"The only person I need protection from is you," Eddie growled. "Now, get on your knees, Paulie."

His face filled with rage, he charged at Eddie, knocking the gun from his hand. Eddie's back slammed against the wall, pain shooting up his spine. He tried to push Paulie away, but he reached for Eddie's neck, jabbing his thumb into his windpipe.

Gasping for air, Eddie raised his fist and slammed it into Paulie's jaw. Blood spurting from his mouth, he released his thumb and fell onto the floor. Eddie got down and hovered over him and continued beating his fists against his face and the side of his skull. With each blow, Paulie's head rolled from side to side, his nose bloodied and swollen.

Rage overtook Eddie. His knuckles screaming with pain, the skin red and raw, still failed to stop him. All he saw was Monica's face and how this man wanted to destroy the one person in the world who meant everything to him. With one last blow, Paulie lay still.

His breathing uncontrolled, heart battering against his chest, Eddie finally stopped. He moved away and sat with his back against the wall, staring at the now unrecognizable face lying on the floor in front of him.

His breathing slowed, and he eased up against the wall. He looked down, the knuckles on his hands were split open, and his fingers had swollen to twice their normal size.

Later, when he thought back to this night, he couldn't remember how long the beating continued—how long it took for Paulie to die. Only a deep-seated bitterness remained inside of him.

Eddie searched for his gun and stuck it back inside his waistband. He removed Paulie's car fob and cell phone from his pocket, placing them inside his. Slowly, he wrapped the plastic around Paulie's body before securing it with rope. Grabbing one end, he dragged it out into the hallway.

He scanned his office before turning out the light. A black mark stained one wall where Eddie had slammed into it—an easy fix. Otherwise, no one would be able to discern a murder had taken place inside.

Eddie checked the back alley, opened the trunk of his car, and stuffed Paulie's body inside. Pausing to catch his breath, he went back inside and retrieved the trash bag from behind the bar and tossed that inside the trunk, too.

Trying to decide what to do next. He reached into his pocket and removed Paulie's car fob. The car needed to go before someone saw it and might identify it. He pulled out his cell phone and made a quick call.

Eddie left the alley and got in Paulie's car. A destination in mind, he pulled away and then onto the Staten Island Expressway. He crossed the Verrazano Narrows Bridge and parked near it on the Brooklyn side.

He got out, making sure no one was around, and tossed his burner phone into the water along with Paulie's. His body a bundle of nerves, he repeatedly checked his watch. Thirty minutes later, a car drove up.

Eddie walked over to it. "Hey, Fred. I was afraid you wouldn't show."

"Eddie, my man," Fred said. He extended his hand.

"Sorry," Eddie said, holding out his swollen one.

"Wow, that looks painful. I hope you won."

"I'll be fine. I'm thankful you came."

"A promise is a promise," Fred said. "After everything you've done for me and my family. With all those medical bills piling up, if it weren't for you, we would have lost everything."

"Of course. How is your little one?" Eddie asked.

"Doing well." Fred walked over to Paulie's car. "Is this it?"

"Yeah"

"She's a beauty. It's a shame to crush her."

"Fred," Eddie said. "I need this car to completely disappear. I mean, like the thing never existed."

"Not a problem."

He opened the driver's side and slipped a tool beneath the dash, pulling part of the cover off. Removing a small flashlight from his pocket, he turned it on and inserted it into his mouth. Fred ducked his head under the dash, his hands searching.

A few moments later, he raised his head and removed the flashlight. "Yep, here it is." He held up a small black square with wires dangling from it. "GPS tracker gone," he said, giving Eddie a wink. "I'll crush the vehicle tonight, and tomorrow she'll be on her way to the shredder. Last known location ends right here."

"Thanks," Eddie said. "I'll take care of you in a few days."

"No. This one is on the house." Fred glanced around. "Need a ride?"

"Can I use your phone?" Eddie asked.

"Sure." He gave Eddie his cell and then went back over to the Cadillac.

It was nearing midnight, and Eddie hoped she would answer. After several rings, a groggy Monica said, "Who is this?"

"It's me, babe," Eddie said. "I need a favor. Can you come and pick me up?"

"Car breakdown?" she asked.

"No. I need you, Monica." Without warning, his hands shook uncontrollably, and he almost dropped Fred's cell phone.

"Do you realize what time it is?"

"Yes, I'm … I … I'm sorry."

"Eddie, you don't sound right. What's wrong?"

He forced his mouth to say the words. "Monica, I just killed somebody. Please, hurry."

Chapter 57 — Monica
An Accessory

Monica wanted to believe she hadn't heard Eddie right when he called. It must be a mistake. If it was true, did he kill someone by accident, or was it in self-defense? Different scenarios kept playing in her head. In all the years she had known him, Eddie murdering someone never entered her mind.

Dropping Andrew off at Cookie's in practically the middle of the night didn't endear her to Damien for sure. But she wasn't about to call her mother or take Andrew with her. She crossed the Verrazano Bridge and drove to the spot where Eddie waited.

He stood by the railing overlooking the water, his back to her. She cut the ignition and hurried over to him. He spun around and pulled her into his arms, squeezing her so tight she could hardly breathe. "It's okay, Eddie," she soothed. "I'm here."

His body shook, and sobs escaped his throat. "I had no choice, Monica. You gotta believe me."

Untangling herself, she cradled his face in her hands. Tears streamed from his eyes, and, as if ashamed, he looked away.

Monica stepped back. "You need to tell me what happened." She led him to a bench a few feet away. "Who did you kill?" she asked.

Eddie's whole body visibly shuddered. "Paulie. I killed Paulie Martello."

This was the last thing she expected to hear. "Why?" she asked.

Over the next fifteen minutes, he told her about Paulie coming to him and what he asked him to do. How he invited Paulie to

Romano's and what happened there in his office. Then what he did with the car and the cell phones."

"Eddie, you could have come to me with this. The Bureau would have handled it."

"No. You don't understand. I couldn't keep walking around thinking any minute someone would try to kill you. He said if I didn't do it, someone else would."

"Do you realize that by telling me, if I don't report it, I'm an accessory?"

"I need to get rid of the body," he said quietly. "It can never be found."

"Eddie, I can't help you. You need to turn yourself in."

"No, Monica. That can't happen. If you still love me and, for Andrew's sake, you'll help me. And you won't report it." He turned to her and placed his bruised hands on top of hers.

Monica gasped at the sight of them. "Oh, Eddie, please, you can't ask me to do that."

His eyes held hers. "But I am. It's time for you to decide whether we are going to be together. I'm tired of the life I've been living. You were right all along. I think deep down inside, I always knew it. I put the mob before you, and you put the Bureau before us. All it has done is tear us apart. I love you and Andrew, and I want us to make a life together."

"But how?" Monica said, pushing back against her true feelings. "Tonight, after what you've done, I …"

"If you tell me you don't love me anymore and there is no hope for a future together, then I'll walk away and let you do what you have to do."

What now? What was she supposed to do? Send Eddie to prison. Tell Andrew he wouldn't see his father for a long, long time, if ever. So many of the things he said were true. The Bureau came before anything else. Even her happiness. Was she going to spend the rest of her life regretting never being with the man she loved? Kai was right. The only way to find out was to let go of the Bureau and discover what she wanted.

She looked into Eddie's eyes. "Okay. Let's go."

"Where?" he asked, his face full of apprehension.

"I'll help you get rid of Paulie's body."

Chapter 58 — Eddie
Letting Go

Eddie Marconi trained his eyes on the body slipping below the surface of the Atlantic Ocean. A full moon cast just enough light over the water to illuminate the top of its head before it vanished, leaving no evidence behind. How many more lay asleep in the murky depths only to become bait for the sharks? With a good amount of weight attached, they could never emerge to tell the tale of their demise. The briny tang of the salty sea air filled Eddie's nostrils. He tasted bile in his throat, and for a moment, he thought he might be sick.

He pulled out a pack of cigarettes from inside his leather jacket and lit one. Dragging deep, he steadied himself against the rail of the rocking boat. Looking up toward the helm, he signaled Monica to head back to shore.

The engine caught, then roared. The boat lurched forward and sped away. Eddie sank onto a bench and took another drag of his cigarette. Whoever thought things would end this way? This hit had not been easy, but definitely necessary. He studied his hands—the knuckles bruised and red from pounding flesh.

What he remembered most was the wide eyes staring back at him in disbelief. They spoke of betrayal. The most heinous kind that made one want to rethink the decision they had made. When loyalty was everything, how could he justify what he had done? There was no coming back from this.

The decision to use the boat his Uncle Sal once owned came easily. He still remembered Little Frankie and how his life ended when Dominico shot him in a storage facility, his body cut up and thrown off this very same boat. Only tonight would be the last time the ocean gets to swallow his secrets.

Eddie rose from the bench and watched the shoreline lights twinkle in the distance. He stubbed out his cigarette and tossed it over the side. The engine slowed as they docked in Sheepshead Bay, Brooklyn. He and Monica jumped down onto the wooden planks. Grasping the heavy rope, they secured the boat. There were no words between them, no reason to speak. Trudging along the dock, they stepped off onto the sidewalk and disappeared into the night.

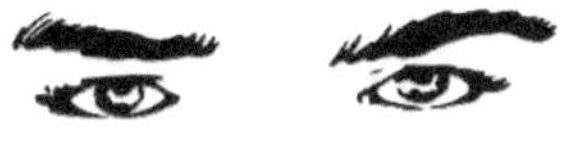

Chapter 59 — Cookie
Two Months Later
Making Things Whole

Cookie shook Damien awake and then switched on the light. Her nightgown and the bed sheet were soaking wet.

"We need to go to the hospital. My water just broke."

He squinted and rubbed his eyes. "Are you sure?"

"Unless we've been sleeping in a leaky waterbed, I'm positive." Cookie got up and went into the bathroom to change. She came out, hair and make-up done, including her false eyelashes.

Damien struggled to his feet. He stretched and let out a yawn.

"What are you doing?" Cookie shouted, waddling over to him. "We have to leave for the hospital now."

"Calm down. You probably have hours of labor ahead of you." He strolled into the bathroom.

"Oh, how delightful," Cookie said. "Great assessment, Dr. Volkov." She put on her shoes and grabbed the overnight bag already packed with what she would need. She heard the toilet flush and then Damien reappeared. He removed his pajama bottoms and then searched inside several drawers.

"Damien, really? What are you looking for?"

"A particular t-shirt I wanted to wear."

"It doesn't matter how you dress. You're not walking a runway at a fashion show."

"Okay, okay. I'll be ready in five minutes."

Cookie paced the living room and forced herself not to go after him. Ten minutes later, he came out fully dressed in jeans, sneakers, and a plaid shirt.

Cookie stopped. "Plaid? Where did you get that horrible thing? From some farmer?"

Damien sighed. "You just said it didn't matter what I wore."

"Yeah, but … there probably will be pictures."

"Pictures?" Damien looked at her dumbly.

"Yes. People always take pictures right after the baby is born."

His eyes swept over her. "You shouldn't have bothered with all that. I got news for you. In a few hours, you're going to be unrecognizable."

She patted the overnight bag. "I have a comb, brush, curling iron, and make-up, right here."

"I hope you included something to dress the baby in when we go home."

"I … I think I did." Cookie set the bag down and rummaged through it. She bit her lower lip and ran to the nursery, returning with a onesie and a little outfit in a neutral color.

"Let's go," Damien said. "It's going to be a long night. Maybe even a long tomorrow."

An hour later, with Cookie admitted and Damien sitting across from her in a chair, they both waited for her contractions to begin.

"Dr. Cynthia Rayburn, Cookie's OBGYN, came in to examine her. "No contractions yet?

Cookie shook her head. "I'm afraid not."

"Well, since you're already overdue, I think we'll induce. Have you thought about the epidural?"

"Yes. I don't think I'm going to need it."

"Once labor starts, there will come a point when we can't administer it."

"Cookie," Damien said. "I think you should get the epidural."

"Naw. I want a natural birth."

"Okay then, we'll get started inducing," Dr. Rayburn said. She nodded at Damien before leaving the room. "You've got a brave one there."

Six hours later, one false eyelash was missing. Her auburn hair was clamped to her head, wet with sweat, and obscenities flew out of her mouth like daggers aimed at Damien. Cookie was in full blown labor.

"How could you do this to me!" she shouted at him. "I think I'm going to die. I can't push anymore."

"I think you had a part in it, too," Damien said. He held her hand and pushed her hair away from her face.

"Come on," Dr. Rayburn said. "I can see the head. Just one more big push."

"If you can see the head, then please just grab it and pull," Cookie pleaded.

"It doesn't work like that. Come on, one last big push."

Cookie took a deep breath. Her body felt like it was being torn apart. She let out a yell and pushed with all her might.

"Perfect," Dr. Rayburn said, while a cry filled the room. "Here she is. You have a beautiful baby girl."

Cookie felt instant relief. She lay back on the pillows as they placed the baby in her arms and Damien cut the umbilical cord. Glad it was over, the pain almost a distant memory, she held her newborn daughter in disbelief. She looked up at Damien, tears running down his face.

"What are *you* crying for?" Cookie said. "I did all the hard work."

He wiped his face, leaned over, and kissed her forehead. "Yes, you did," he said softly.

They both studied this little human being who now belonged to them. Tufts of auburn hair dotted her little head, and her lips were an exact copy of Cookie's.

"Now that there are two of you, I don't stand a chance," Damien said.

"What shall we call her?" Cookie asked. "We never really talked about names."

"How about, Sofia?" Damien said. "It means wisdom."

"Sofia," Cookie repeated. "I like it. Sofia, Volkov."

Damien pulled out his cell phone.

"What are you doing?" Cookie asked.

"Well, first I'm going to call my mother and give her the news.

"I'm so glad you made amends," Cookie said. "And then we call my father, and Monica."

Damien nodded. "Of course. And then I'm going to snap a picture of the three of us."

"With me looking like this?" Cookie asked.

"Haven't you realized by now," Damien said. "You always look beautiful to me."

Cookie grinned, "Good answer. Snap away, Dr. Volkov."

Chapter 60 — Kai

Six Months Later

Peace

As the sun set, Kai marveled at the painted desert sky awash with colors. In the distance, red and orange rock formations jutted from the earth like flaming candles. Finally, she was living her life in *Hozho*—peace, balance, beauty, and harmony. All of the things she never found away from the Navajo Reservation were here. If only her grandmother had lived to see her so happy.

She gathered an armful of the desert lavender and inhaled its soothing scent, placing her treasure inside the cloth sack slung over her shoulder. Moving farther, she added bright yellow flowers from a brittle bush to her bundle. A cactus wren sang out its warbling cry from a thorny Palo Verde Tree.

Leaving the FBI proved to be a difficult decision but ultimately the right one for her.

The past months were filled with soul-searching, as she honored her cultural roots to find her true self. She spent endless days wandering the land, meditating, and reacquainting herself with the many things she had lost by leaving the Navajo Reservation.

Taking one last look at the horizon, she made her way home. The hogan, once belonging to her grandmother, had become hers. Kai paused in front of her mother's small ranch house, where her truck was parked next to a vehicle she didn't recognize. The soft light from inside penetrated the sheer window curtains and fanned out across the yard. She could barely make out two figures sitting at the kitchen table.

Kai set her sack on the steps. She tapped on the door and then proceeded inside, curious to see who the visitor was. Closing it behind her, she turned around, her eyes almost unable to process what she saw. There, sitting across from her mother, Secoya, was Nico Vasilios.

"There you are," Secoya said. "You were gone so long, I was about to send out a search party. Nico and I have been getting acquainted. He tells me you worked together at the FBI."

"Y ... yes," Kai stuttered, awkwardly.

"Well, don't just stand there, come and sit." Secoya got up. I'll brew some coffee." As she moved past Kai, she whispered, "I think I like this one."

A mixture of confusion, curiosity, and joy flooded through her.

"How have you been?" he asked. "I didn't get a chance to say goodbye when you left."

"You came all the way here to say goodbye?" Kai asked.

"I hope not," he said.

Secoya set two cups of coffee on the table. "I have some paperwork to do." She looked at Nico. "It was very nice meeting you."

"It was my pleasure," he said. "Have a good night."

Paperwork, my foot, Kai thought, but at the same time appreciating her mother exited the room.

"So, exactly why did you come?"

"I think we both know why," he said, an easy grin spreading across his face.

Kai peeked down the hallway. "I'm not exactly comfortable talking here. Do you mind if we go to my place?"

"Sure," Nico said. "What about the coffee your mother just made?"

"It's fine," Kai said. "She's got plenty more, unless you…"

"No," Nico said quickly. He got up and followed Kai out of the house.

They walked to her hogan, Kai conscious of the way his muscular body moved.

"Before we go inside," she said. "There are certain traditions I follow." She explained the ritual of entering and walking clockwise around the room, which symbolized honoring the sun.

Nico nodded. "Lead the way."

He said the words so naturally, as if eager to learn the ways of her culture. Kai stepped inside, her hand flipping the light switch by the door. Nico followed her every movement around the room.

Finished, she went to the small refrigerator. "Beer?" she asked.

"Yes. I could use one after the long drive."

She pulled out a bottle and handed him one.

"What about you?" he asked. "You're not going to make me drink alone, are you?"

"No. I have something special I want you to try." She reached inside a small cupboard above the stove and unwrapped the fry bread she had made earlier that day. Adjusting the oven's temperature, she set it inside to warm and then went to the wood-burning fireplace and lit a fire from the wood she had stacked there.

Within minutes, the hogan filled with a sweet aroma. Kai set a white porcelain jar of honey on the table and then returned to the oven. She shut it off and removed the fry bread.

"Now for the best part," she said to Nico, as she spread some honey across the top of each piece. She grabbed two plates and then beckoned him to a small table with two chairs in one corner of the room. When he was seated, she placed one slice on a plate for him and another on a plate for herself. Then, pulling another beer from the refrigerator, she sat across from him.

"Smells fantastic," Nico said.

Kai bit into the bread, delighting in the memories of her grandmother that the taste brought with it.

Nico nibbled on his. She could tell by his slow, deliberate chewing that he was savoring every bite.

"Fantastic," he said. "I could eat a dozen of these."

"I'm glad you like it."

Over the next few minutes, they sat eating the fry bread and sipping their beer. Kai found the silence between them comforting. When they finished, he helped her clear the table, and then they sat on the sofa, the back of which was draped with the red and black Navajo Chief's blanket. Kai explained that she had inherited it from her grandmother.

Nico ran his hand across the woolen fabric. "If this blanket could talk, I can only imagine what it would tell us."

"Yes," Kai said. "I've often wondered about its history." As they sat talking, she couldn't help but compare Tony's visit to the Rez with Nico's. Here sat a man who was genuinely interested in her traditions and culture. She in turn was filled with an urgency to hear everything about him—his family, their history, his likes and dislikes.

"I know so little about your background," Kai said.

Nico moved closer. "We have plenty of time for that."

"Are you still with the Bureau?" she asked.

"Not for right now. You could say I'm taking a break. I haven't decided if I want to continue."

"Understandable," Kai said. "You were undercover for a long time."

"What about you?"

"I'm inching my way toward joining the Tribal Police. I think it will be a nice change."

"So, I guess you'll be staying here then?"

She nodded. "I finally found the peace I've been looking for. I'm afraid I'll lose it if I leave."

"You can find peace anywhere, Kai. If you look in the right place."

"I guess," she said.

Nico got up and held out his hand. She took it and rose off the sofa. In the firelight, flecks of gold danced in his green eyes just as she remembered.

Nico drew her close, cradling her in his arms. "I've thought about you every day since you left. I need to know how you feel about me, Kai."

"I've dreamt about you, about us, many, many times, but I never thought I'd ever see you again. Now that you're here, I don't want to let you go."

"If you let me," he said softly. "I promise to make sure, no matter where we are, you'll never have to look for peace again."

He lifted her chin with his fingertip. His lips met hers, and he kissed her softly at first, then with more urgency.

Kai responded, and when he broke the kiss, she said. "I'm going to hold you to that promise, Nico Vasilios."

Chapter 61 — Monica

Three Years Later

At Last

Just before dawn, Monica padded across the wide-beam oak floors and into the kitchen. The frame and timber house in Flagstaff, Arizona, had been her and Eddie's home for the past two years. She made a cup of coffee and stoked last night's fire before settling in front of the living room window. In the distance, white mist hovered like a blanket over Humphrey's Peak. The aspen trees showed off brilliant shades of gold in contrast to the dark green of the ponderosa pines. Fall would be arriving soon, one of Monica's favorite times of the year.

It seemed almost impossible to believe this new life they created belonged to them. Their ghosts from the past had severed themselves, giving them a chance to fix what was once broken.

Her exit from the Bureau occurred six months after Eddie murdered Paulie Martello. But it wasn't only his death forcing her hand. Looking back, she had made decisions and broke rules, regardless of the regulations she had taken an oath to follow.

Ultimately, the task force's successes became her undoing—but the final break came while helping Eddie dispose of a body. She couldn't explain it and would never again deny the deep love she felt for him. The choice she made became relatively simple. Stay with a constantly changing FBI Bureau or live with the man she loved.

Eddie's untangling from the Mob proved to be not as difficult as they first believed it would be. Paulie Martello's disappearance pointed a finger directly at Tony. Those around him revealed his power-hungry ambitions to the commission.

Tony was released on bail for six months before his trial. Found guilty on all charges, he was sent to prison. Tony's life abruptly ended eight months later when an inmate stabbed him to death. It was found out later, the inmate had ties to the mob, and the order given by the Commission was payback not only for Paulie but also for the killing of Stavros Papadakis, which they did not sanction.

Eddie went before the Commission and relinquished his territory in Staten Island. Because of his loyalty to Paulie and his previous saving him from a hit, they struck a deal. He was never to divulge any information regarding the mechanisms of how they operated. If it was found out he broke the agreement, a contract would be made on his life.

Both of them had found their niche in Flagstaff. Eddie as the manager at one of the exclusive ski resorts. He was full of ideas about building one of their own one day. Monica worked as a consultant and security advisor to the Arizona Department of Public Safety.

She picked up her cell phone lying on the coffee table. She scrolled through the current pictures Cookie sent of her godchild, Sofia. Looking forward to her and Damien's visit in the coming weeks made her smile. Eddie and Cookie had finally made peace with each other, although they still wisecracked back and forth, neither one took it seriously.

Leaving everything behind in Staten Island had been hard, but necessary. She sold her house and gave Cookie full ownership of the shop. Of course, her mother and father couldn't stand to be separated from her, so they now resided in a house in Flagstaff, not far from her.

As for Darya and little Alex, they stayed on Staten Island, where Darya formed a new relationship with Anastasia, the daughter she left behind all those years ago in Russia. But Dimitri remained out of the picture. Darya refused to have anything to do with him.

Monica continued scrolling through her pictures until she came to the one of Kai and Nico standing outside Kai's hogan, a vivid desert sunset sky behind them. It made her glad to know Kai found happiness and much more by going home.

"Hey, what are you doing up so early?" Eddie said, sitting beside her.

"Looking at pictures," Monica said, snuggling against him. "I can't wait to see Cookie and Damien, but most of all, Sofia. She's already trying on Cookie's stilettos. Poor Damien has a miniature Cookie on his hands."

"Are Kai and Nico coming?" Eddie asked.

"Yes. Everyone will be here for Thanksgiving." She found it odd at times that Nico and Eddie had formed a friendship. But he told Monica he respected him for getting out of the mob.

"I guess that means your parents, too."

She gave him a quick jab on his side. "You and my mother are a hot mess," Monica said. "If you would just ignore those little remarks she makes. One day, she'll get over my marrying you."

Eddie slid his arm around her shoulders, pulling her closer. "You are more than I ever deserved," he said softly.

"I know," she teased. "But how lucky are we to have made it through everything?"

Their peaceful moment was interrupted by the patter of feet.

"Mommy! Andy's poking me."

"No, I'm not," Andrew said.

Monica held out her arms. "Come here, Catherine." She scooped up her daughter and then brushed back her dark curls. Also, the spitting image of her father, with the same nautical blue eyes, Monica sometimes felt slighted knowing Eddie possessed the stronger genes.

It brought tears to Eddie's eyes when Monica insisted they name their daughter after his mother.

"What are you doing to your sister?" Eddie asked, as Andrew wiggled between him and Monica on the sofa.

"Nothing," he said, looking up at the two of them, the same sly look on his face so reminiscent of Eddie's.

"You need to be nice to each other," Eddie said, kissing the top of Andrew's head. "Now you two go play for a while. Later, we'll go for a walk outside."

The children scampered off, and he looked over at Monica. "What were we thinking when we decided Andrew needed a sibling?"

Monica closed the distance between them and snuggled against him, a contentment she never thought she'd ever feel engulfed her. "Get ready," she said, "Because we are about to have another one."

Without even flinching, Eddie's fingers slipped under her chin. He raised her head, met her eyes, and then kissed her softly on the lips. "Baby, I wouldn't have things any other way."

Nominated for Georgia Author of the Year for her novel Redemption, Stephanie is dedicated to giving her readers fast-paced, high-stakes, page-turning stories that keep you on the edge of your seat and are full of surprising twists! Stephanie's second novel in her trilogy, Retribution, the thrilling sequel to Redemption, was released in 2019, followed by Reckoning in 2022. The collection makes up the Sicario Files Trilogy. The first novel in her second trilogy, Mobbed Up, was released in February 2023, followed by Mobbed Up II: Return to New York in September 2024. The final novel, Mobbed Up Endgame, is slated for release in February 2026.

You can find her online at **www.stephaniebaldi2.com** or follow her on Facebook, Instagram, and TikTok.

Other Titles by Stephanie Baldi

The Sicario Files
REDEMPTION

Murder is the catalyst pushing Carrie Overton headlong into the arms of the hitman sent to kill her.

Determined to escape her alcoholic and drug-addicted mother and distance herself from the memory of the son she lost, Carrie leaves home with Travis Montgomery, a man twenty years her senior who harbors shocking secrets connected to her past.

After Travis forces her to help him steal two million dollars from a drug lord, leaving two people dead, Carrie decides to add a third victim to her list, and Travis is left lying on the floor.

Eager to start over, she takes the stolen money and travels to the small mountain town of Laurel, Pennsylvania. Carrie lies about her past and relaxes into her new life. Before long, Carrie's lies are piling up, and her crimes are about to catch up to her.

Nicholas D'Angelo is known as a ghost, a contract killer for one of the biggest drug lords in Miami. His assignment is simple. Find the people, who stole the two million dollars, recover the money and eliminate them.

With a hitman on her trail, Carrie is forced to make a choice. Trust the hitman who vows to disobey his orders and protect her. Or stay in Laurel and face the drug lord determined to end her life. Either one might kill her.

RETRIBUTION

Almost six long years have passed since Carmela Santiago witnessed the hitman she loved assassinate her father. Now she is ready to exact her plan of revenge against him and the people he loves. Carmela will stop at nothing to tear his family apart. Running her father's drug smuggling empire, she will use every resource at her disposal, including money, sex, the men in her life, and her very own cold-blooded sicario, to help her carry out her deeds.

Nicholas D'Angelo, the contract killer, once employed by Carmela's father has his family safely tucked away in a compound in Tuscany, Italy. Many times, he has regretted his decision to let Carmela live. Forced by the government to return to the United States and resume the life of a killer, Nick knows will put his family in jeopardy.

Carmela Santiago has the means to destroy him and all those he holds dear. Carmela moves forward with her plan of revenge, but her closest allies are fast becoming her enemies. As she pushes things to the limit, Carmela gets caught in her own web of lies, murder, and deceit. With the stakes rising higher, she is determined to win. Nick will use everything at his disposal to stop her.

RECKONING

One terrible night in Tahoe left Carmela Santiago dead and a visible scar on Miguel Medina's face. After three long years, a still open wound lies hidden inside his cold heart.

Once Carmela's trusted Sicario and lover, he is determined to exact vengeance on the man responsible for her death. Miguel knows going up against such a man as Nicholas D'Angelo, will not be easy.

Both ghosts, hitmen at the top of their game, their past confrontation in Tahoe has proven they possess the skills to eliminate one another. Only Miguel's plans run much deeper.

Vowing to reclaim Carmela's daughter, Natalia, and raise her as his own, Miguel has struck at the heart of Nick's family by stealing away something they love.

With pressure mounting and time running out, Nick must find a way to take back what rightfully belongs to him and destroy Miguel Medina once and for all.

Available in paperback and eBook
And on Audible